The Chronicles of Elantra
by
New York Times bestselling author

Michelle Sagara

CAST IN SHADOW
CAST IN COURTLIGHT
CAST IN SECRET
CAST IN FURY
CAST IN SILENCE
CAST IN CHAOS
CAST IN RUIN
CAST IN PERIL
CAST IN SORROW
CAST IN FLAME
CAST IN HONOR
CAST IN FLIGHT
CAST IN DECEPTION
CAST IN OBLIVION

And

"Cast in Moonlight"
found in
HARVEST MOON,
an anthology with Mercedes Lackey and Cameron Haley

Look for the next story in
The Chronicles of Elantra,
coming soon from MIRA.

MICHELLE SAGARA

CAST IN WISDOM

mira

ISBN-13: 978-0-7783-0938-3

Cast in Wisdom

Mira
22 Adelaide St. West, 40th Floor
Toronto, Ontario M5H 4E3, Canada
BookClubbish.com

This is for Kari Sperring, who is not ancient, not male, not curmudgeonly and never condescending, but would nonetheless be my choice for Imperial Librarian if I were a Dragon emperor.

My library and its knowledge would be utterly safe in her hands.

CAST IN WISDOM

CHAPTER
1

The major disadvantage of being host to over a dozen people who had no need for something as trivial as sleep was that there was no real private time in the house. There was often silence, but it was full of people. The majority of Kaylin's current guests could speak among themselves without ever opening their mouths. But they did so while taking up space, their eyes flashing blue or green as words Kaylin couldn't hear were exchanged.

It wasn't the quiet that was lacking; it was the alone time. The privacy. It said something about her current life that she felt she had more of it in the *office*. Case in point: when she headed for breakfast before fleeing to the Halls of Law, the cohort were arguing.

They weren't arguing silently, which meant they either intended to involve Kaylin, who wasn't even in the room yet, or Bellusdeo, who was.

Kaylin knew it was going to be bad when discussion banked the minute she entered the dining room. All eyes turned toward her. A chair—located conveniently nearest the door by which she could make her escape—appeared in front of a plate that had food on it. Given the looks she was getting, her appetite dwindled to almost zero. She could, however, eat regardless, and proceeded to take the empty chair to do exactly that.

"Chew," Teela said, "before you swallow."

Teela's voice appeared to be a signal for discussion to resume. Discussion, however, did not.

"You're heading into the office today?" Kaylin asked the Barrani Hawk. It was her first day reporting since the battle in the High Halls.

"I am."

Oh. She thought she understood what the cohort had been arguing about. Kaylin exhaled. "Bellusdeo has Imperial permission to attend me when I work as a Hawk. No one else does."

"I've gone," Mandoran immediately said.

"You have, but that wasn't the result of Imperial permission."

"Then permission doesn't matter, right?"

Helen coughed.

"Permission in this case simply means Imperial Command, dear. The Emperor has essentially ordered the Hawks to accept that Bellusdeo will accompany Kaylin on her duties."

"The Leontine doesn't seem all that fond of her," Mandoran admitted.

"Marcus isn't fond of Dragons," Kaylin replied.

"He's not fond of anything."

"Nothing in the office. He's fond of his children. And his wives. But he's grown to appreciate Bellusdeo. And there's no force on earth that will get the Emperor to issue an Imperial Command that Barrani civilians be allowed to accompany Imperial Hawks anywhere they happen to go."

"So we just have to get the sergeant's permission, right?"

"There are eleven of you. There is no place where eleven extra Barrani on patrol aren't going to be a traffic hazard."

"We don't have to be seen—"

Kaylin turned to look at Teela, whose lips were compressed enough that they appeared to be almost white. The only small silver lining on this particular cloud was that it wasn't Bellusdeo who was angry.

Hope coughed. So did Helen.

It was Sedarias who broke the silence that had followed Mandoran's cut-off sentence. "We have been invited to attend the High Halls as Lords of the High Court," she said in a voice that was both regal and simultaneously disgruntled. "We are the guests of honor."

"I don't envy you," Kaylin replied.

At this, Sedarias's expression shifted into a sly smile. "You shouldn't. But on the off chance—that's correct, yes?" At Kaylin's nod, she continued. "On the off chance that you do, you'll be delighted to know that you are *also* invited to attend."

"What?"

"Apparently, the High Lord has summoned the High Court. Every High Lord will be present."

"Every High Lord?"

"Every single one. This would, of course, include you and Lord Severn."

Kaylin muttered a few choice Leontine words. Mandoran laughed. Even Annarion chuckled.

"We've been asked," Sedarias continued, "if there are any significant allies—those are the exact words—that we would like to honor with an invitation. Invitations of that nature are, of course, free to be declined."

Unlike Kaylin's, which was not an invitation so much as a royal command.

As one, all eyes—even Teela's—turned toward Bellusdeo.

"You can't be serious," Kaylin snapped.

"It will take time for the Lords to gather," Sedarias replied. Terrano, at the same time, said, "Of course we're serious."

The collision of words appeared to stop neither of them.

"The gathering will not, therefore, occur for some months."

"Without her, we wouldn't have made it out of the West March."

"You weren't trapped," Sedarias then said—to Terrano. "We were."

Terrano snorted and rolled his eyes—which were a shade of blue that only the cohort could achieve.

Kaylin dared a glance at Bellusdeo. Her eyes were orange. The mortal Hawk shoved food into her mouth at record speed before escaping the breakfast table.

"You are such a coward," Bellusdeo said when they'd reached the relative safety of the street. The roads in and around Helen were sparsely populated at the busiest of times, which this wasn't. They would soon join roads that were crowded at the slowest of times, but Kaylin was dressed for the office. The Hawk emblazoned on her tabard encouraged people to make space.

Had Bellusdeo hit the streets in her Draconic form, she'd have cleared far more of it—but some of that space would be created by panic, and panic could cause both accidents and the type of traffic congestion that caused the Swords to investigate. Also, it was illegal.

"It's not cowardice," Kaylin replied, scanning the windows of the buildings above ground level.

"What would you call it?"

"Wisdom."

"Oh, please."

"There's no point in arguing with them now. Sedarias thinks it'll be months before this ridiculous command performance occurs. We have months to attempt to talk her out of—"

"Out of expressing any appreciation or gratitude?"

Ugh. "You know they're grateful. This isn't about gratitude. It's about rubbing that gratitude in the faces of the Barrani who attempted to brand you a—an army. An attacking army."

"I believe the term you want is Flight." Bellusdeo's eyes were orange.

Hope squawked at the Dragon. Kaylin didn't understand what he was saying. Bellusdeo did, but her eyes didn't get any lighter.

"You know as well as I do," Kaylin said, emboldened by Hope's entry into the discussion, "that this is not the time to visit the High Halls. I'm not sure the Emperor has ever been a guest there."

"We visited the Halls—more or less—when they came under attack, and the Barrani needed our help."

"From the *outside*. No one invited the Dragon Court *in*."

The chorus of Barrani voices that sometimes offered entirely unasked for opinions on the inside of her head maintained their silence for half a beat. The first person to break that silence was the fieflord. His words were tinged with amusement.

You cannot expect that the cohort would suddenly cease to cause any difficulty, surely?

I'm almost certain that the cohort understands why inviting a Dragon—any Dragon—to attend the High Halls would be a disaster.

For the Dragons?

For everyone.

I believe some of the more conservative High Lords might be surprisingly supportive of such an invitation.

Of course they would. It would be their best shot at killing Bellusdeo. If Bellusdeo died, there would be no new Dragons. No hatchlings.

There's no way the Emperor would give her permission to attend.

Nightshade concurred. *In his position, I would not. But I would be prepared, should I refuse to grant that permission, for all-out war. My brother has grown inordinately fond of her; living with you has made him reckless.*

He's not—

He has known Bellusdeo for even less time than you. He is willing to trust her in a fashion no one older would. And do not cite the Consort, please.

Kaylin hadn't intended to. *The Consort seems to like her.*

Kaylin, the Consort "likes" me. But she does not trust me.

She does.

"Stop making that face, or it will freeze that way."

Kaylin reddened.

I understand that you are attempting to avoid the Emperor's ire. I consider this wise on your part. It is not, however, the ire of the Emperor that will be your most significant problem; he will do nothing to harm Bellusdeo.

I know that.

It is the ire of the High Lords. Sedarias is, I believe, genuinely grateful for Bellusdeo's intervention. She does wish to honor her. But gratitude can be expressed privately—and in most cases, it is. Only rulers feel obliged to make that expression public because the public expression elevates those to whom one feels gratitude. It makes clear to witnesses that the aid tendered—in whatever fashion—is important and significant. The Emperor has codified such significance in public ceremonies and public titles, has he not?

Kaylin shrugged.

For Sedarias, however, genuine gratitude is not an impediment to political displays. She can be genuinely grateful and simultaneously, extremely political. She wishes to highlight Bellusdeo's aid and import to Mellarionne. Why do you think this is?

Kaylin thought about this. After a long pause, she said, *She wants to thumb her nose at the rest of the High Lords, many of whom weren't helpful at all?*

Nightshade's silence was one of encouragement.

Bellusdeo's a Dragon. So...her presence means that even Dragons—with whom you've had a war or two—

Three.

Fine, a war or three, were more helpful, or at least more of a genuine ally, than any of the Barrani.

Yes. I believe that is some part of Sedarias's intent.

That's not going to help Mellarionne any.

Perhaps, perhaps not. She will do so as An'Mellarionne. It would be considered a very bold move—but there are those who would assume that Sedarias is confident in her own power, and they would hesitate to challenge her.

"If you are speaking about me," Bellusdeo said, her voice almost a whisper of sound, "I must insist that you include me."

Hope squawked.

"Well, yes, that could cause some difficulty," the Dragon replied. "But I dislike Kaylin's worry. She is mortal." Squawk. "The marks of the Chosen don't matter. She's mortal. I may be a displaced person in these lands; I may no longer have a home or lands of my own. But I am a Dragon."

"I'm not exactly worried about you," Kaylin said. When one golden brow rose in response, she added, "Not about you specifically. But—there's no way for Dragon and High Halls to combine that isn't political. Explosively political. On your own, you can survive more than any of the rest of the cohort—or me. But you won't be on your own. The cohort won't abandon you."

It was the Dragon's turn to snort.

Kaylin reconsidered her words and chose better ones. "Most of the cohort wouldn't abandon you. Annarion wouldn't. Mandoran wouldn't. I don't believe Allaron would either, from what I've seen. And you know what the cohort is like. The minute one of them enters combat to save you, they're all going to rush in. It doesn't matter if they're there for your sake or their friends'; they'll be there. But this is political, and anything political is far above my pay grade."

"You don't seem to find this insulting."

"I consider it one of the biggest advantages of my rank. Which is the lowest rank I could be given and still be called a Hawk."

"One of? What's another one?"

"I'm not in command. I don't need to make decisions that might cost the lives of other Hawks. No matter what happens in an action, large or small, I won't have their deaths on my hands."

"But you don't like being a private."

"Well, I could be a corporal, and it would still be mostly true. And the pay is higher."

"It's not much higher," a familiar voice said. It was Mandoran's. Of course it was. Kaylin didn't miss a step.

"I don't suggest you try to enter the Halls of Law looking like that."

"Like what?"

"Like thin air."

"Oh. That." Mandoran caused other people some consternation as he materialized to the side of Kaylin that Bellusdeo wasn't occupying. To be fair, most of the street didn't notice; people always had their own problems and their own schedules. "I was going to follow Teela into the office, but Teela's not heading there directly."

"So you followed us?"

"Not most of the way, no. I decided to head straight here to wait, but I caught up because you're doing the Hawk-walk." He glanced at Bellusdeo. "For what it's worth, I think insisting on your presence on the inside of the High Halls is suicidal."

"Oh?" The Dragon's voice was cool. "For who?"

Mandoran grinned. "Mostly Kaylin."

Kaylin watched as flecks of gold appeared in Bellusdeo's eyes. Mandoran had, once again, managed to set Bellusdeo at ease. Kaylin wondered if that was why he'd chosen to speak when he had. He never treated the Dragon with respect; had the Emperor been present for most of their spats, she wasn't certain Mandoran wouldn't be a pile of bleeding ash. Well, ash, because ash didn't bleed, but still.

"You left the rest of the cohort behind?" Kaylin asked.

"We had a vote, and Helen decided it was safest to send me."

"She was the tie-breaker?"

"Ah, no. She didn't consider the first choice viable. But— we can all see what I see anyway, so unless there's an attack, having more than one person here is superfluous. If Teela had been coming directly to the office, someone would have followed Teela."

"Not you?" Bellusdeo asked.

"I had to live with Tain for a few years. Compressed into a few weeks, I might add. He's stuffy and remarkably straightforward. Also, he hates fun."

"He hates *mess*," Kaylin said, as they approached the stairs that led into the Halls of Law.

"Define *mess*. No, wait, don't. The problem with Tain—at least for me—is that Teela might actually kill us if we're indirectly responsible for his death. He's not like the rest of us; we can't speak to him without shouting, and even if we can, he doesn't listen half the time. So...it's a lot less safe to tail Tain."

"I imagine it's safer to tail Tain than it is to tail Kaylin if you're worried about Teela's reaction," Bellusdeo said, frowning slightly.

"You need a better imagination."

It felt like it had been so long since Kaylin had seen Marcus's furry face she wanted to run up and hug him. She wanted to keep her job more, but it was surprisingly close. His eyes were a blend of orange and gold, but they shaded mostly to gold as Kaylin approached the desk. Bellusdeo had stopped at Caitlin's desk. Mandoran had wandered over to Teela's.

"I'm happy to see you remember you still have a job, Corporal," the Leontine sergeant growled. He pointed to the duty board.

Kaylin made it halfway there and then suddenly wheeled. "Did you say corporal?" She glanced at the roster. She and Severn were expected to resume their Elani beat. She then almost raced across the room to stand in front of Marcus's desk. His eyes were pure gold now. He smiled.

To people unfamiliar with Leontines, smiles looked a lot like bared fangs, never a good sign. Kaylin was familiar with Leontines. "Do I make mistakes when it comes to rank?"

She tried not to bounce on the spot.

"He just wants to be able to bust you down a rank when you screw up," someone farther into the office shouted. Joey, she thought.

"You've handled yourself well in a fraught situation for some time. You have been, by necessity, an ambassador for the Hawks." Although Marcus spoke, Kaylin highly doubted the words were his. "Your reaction upon hearing this news has lost a few people some money."

"What were they betting? Less dignity on my part, or more?"

"Less." The smile deepened. Clearly Marcus had not lost money if he'd bet at all. "The Hawklord, however, wishes to speak with you before you leave for Elani."

At this very moment, the Emperor himself could demand to speak with her, and it wouldn't put a dent in her mood.

Severn was already in the Hawklord's tower when Kaylin arrived. Her breathlessness had nothing to do with the climb up the stairs, but she was breathless as she entered the office. She struggled to find the appropriate rigidity and failed.

He doesn't look happy, Hope said.

She was still startled to hear her familiar speak actual syllables. He did sound kind of like a bird, though. Hope's eyes were clearly better than hers; at this distance, she couldn't quite make out the color of the Hawklord's eyes. But he couldn't be entirely unhappy; his wings were in the rest position.

Severn was standing at ease and turned to face Kaylin as she made her entrance.

"Visit the quartermaster before you leave for Elani," the Hawklord said.

This dimmed her enthusiasm somewhat. But of course, she needed to visit said quartermaster, who still held a grudge about a damaged dress. She was a corporal now. She needed to bear the insignia of that rank.

She saluted smartly, standing at attention in front of the Aerian who ruled the Hawks.

The Hawklord nodded to acknowledge this, and she lowered her arm. "It is my hope," he said, "that you will be able to pursue your normal duties for some time." Something about his tone implied that he doubted this would be possible. It wasn't the weary not-this-again tone, either.

"At the moment, you have Lord Bellusdeo by your side."

She nodded.

"The Emperor has made clear to me that Lord Bellusdeo will continue to—what was his word?—observe. He was not best pleased when that observation led you to the West March. The Arkon has requested some use of your time, as well. The Emperor wishes to prioritize this."

The Hawklord didn't. His eyes were gray. Not ash gray, just gray. It was the equivalent of orange in the Leontine gaze. "You are the only two Hawks currently on the roster who have extensive experience in the fiefs."

Kaylin glanced at Severn. Severn nodded. He seemed calm, but it was always hard to tell whether or not he was surprised.

"I know that your experience is centered around the fiefs of Nightshade and what is now Tiamaris. Corporal Handred, have you ever entered Candallar?"

"Yes."

"Have you encountered the fieflord?"

Severn nodded. "Never within the boundaries of his fief."

"He has been spending some time in the warrens, according to your report. Kaylin's written report has failed to reach the sergeant's desk. I expect this to be remedied."

The Hawklord did not dismiss them, which Kaylin half expected. He walked to the tall oval mirror that stood to his left. "Records."

The surface of the mirror rippled as if the silver were liquid. The ripple extended from the center of the mirror and spread, changing silver into a multitude of colors as it traveled. "The Emperor does not require a written report of your activities in the High Halls."

That was something.

"I believe, however, that the Arkon does and will. You are not required to obey his request, by law."

Theoretical law vs. angry Dragon. Not much of a choice.

She kept her eyes on the mirror that had become a Records conduit. The whole of Elantra, the city she protected and policed, appeared. The edges were gold. The center was red. Where river passed around that center, it was blue; the walls that served as a dividing line when the river deviated were also blue.

One of the red fiefs became a bright purple. Candallar.

"We have received some assurance that Candallar, and his crimes, fall within the laws of exemption."

"Meaning we've been told to leave it alone?"

"As we do not serve the Barrani Court, no, not in so many words."

"The Emperor?"

"Understands the use of the laws of exemption."

"They won't apply to Candallar, though."

"Oh?"

"He's outcaste. If they want to smack us with the exemption, they're going to have to repatriate him. Even if they did," she continued, frowning, "I doubt he'd allow himself to be culled behind the screen of those laws. He understands Elantran laws. If he's dead, it's going to be impossible for us to investigate that death if it occurs on this side. The Barrani are going to call in the laws of exemption, and as he won't be able to speak for himself—being dead and all—we're going to knuckle under.

"But if he's injured, I think he might come directly here."

"To the Halls of Law."

She nodded.

"I dislike any attempt to wield the Halls as a political tool." His eyes shaded to blue—the same blue as angry Barrani eyes. "We are aware that some of the political difficulties of the very recent past might have involved either the fieflord of Candallar or the fief he rules. The Emperor will not allow the laws of exemption to stand if his actions have endangered the city or any member of any race that calls it home.

"In my opinion, they've indirectly endangered the entire city." Even speaking, she hesitated.

"But?"

"But if it weren't for his intervention, I'm not sure we'd have a city. What he allowed to be brought out of the heart of the fiefs—we're pretty sure it was transported through Candallar—was necessary to communicate with the High Halls."

"Ah. You are perhaps aware of the changes in those halls?"

Kaylin glanced at the mirror. She wanted to know, of course, but the Hawklord hadn't yet moved the mirror's image from the fief of Candallar. She nodded because she was aware of some of those changes, and she was pretty certain she could easily fill in the rest—or at least the parts the Halls of Law knew—on her own time.

"Very well. The Emperor was concerned, but his advisors were less so." The Hawklord frowned, and the mirror image shifted instantly, as if it were a card that could be flipped.

A building Kaylin did not recognize filled the mirror.

CHAPTER
2

"As of two days ago," the Hawklord said, when Kaylin failed to speak, "this is the High Halls."

The only things she recognized were the statues that had once girded the exterior. They remained untouched. In size, the building seemed to occupy roughly the same plot of land, but the similarity ended there.

"…two days ago."

"Yes. I am assured that the building as it is now will be very, very difficult to infiltrate in any way."

"It's like a Hallionne."

"That is the supposition of the Imperial advisors."

Kaylin assumed that the Imperial advisors were the Arkon.

"It is the Emperor's desire that you have little to do with the physical High Halls in the near future."

"How near is that future?" she asked with what she hoped was a perfectly neutral expression.

The Hawklord raised his face. He exhaled as he lowered it. "Inasmuch as your activities outside of the Halls of Law are private, personal and legal, we do not have the right of command. If we assume the right of that command—"

"You have to pay me."

"—your actions in those activities are the work of a Hawk. It is therefore not a command; it is Imperial preference." The Hawklord's glance flicked to the side, but Severn's expression gave nothing away. "At this remove, we have a Barrani Hawk who can enter the High Halls and stand shoulder to shoulder with the High Lords who linger there. It is not your job.

"Your job, however—" and here, the mirror once again flipped, returning to the prior image of a slightly purple Candallar "—will be the fiefs. We wish to know what Candallar wants, what his connections are and what other decisions he's made with regard to the heart of the fiefs and what it contains. We have little information to offer. Our knowledge is secondhand, at best. Your knowledge is not."

"I've never been to Candallar."

"No. Corporal Handred has."

For the first time in the history of ever, Kaylin was excited to talk to the quartermaster. This excitement was not without anxiety, given the quartermaster's long memory and his ability to hold grudges, but she had a good reason to be here. She had the *best* reason to be here.

To her surprise, the quartermaster was almost friendly. He was actively friendly to Severn, possibly to emphasize the difference between grudging respect and genuine respect. At this point, however, Kaylin was willing to take the grudging with both hands and hold it fast. Since respect was, in the immediate present, intangible, she transferred that to the kit he handed across the counter.

He stared at her, his lips twitching. "You're going to have to let go of it to put it on. And you are not changing here. You've got a locker room for that. Get out." He paused and then added, "Congratulations."

★ ★ ★

It became clear to Kaylin that the world outside of the Halls of Law couldn't tell the difference between a corporal and a private. In any practical sense, the change in rank didn't saddle her with new duties, although in an emergency she had more pull than a private, in theory. None of that appeared to be evident to the Elani street regulars. Kaylin glanced at Margot's ever-present sandwich board. She had the strong urge to borrow one side of it to announce her promotion to the street—but she had no chalk.

Severn said, "Don't even think it. Marcus will be up to his armpits in paperwork from Margot's complaints—he'll probably have to bust you down a rank to mollify her."

Given how Marcus felt about paperwork, losing the newly gained rank would not be the worst of her worries. Hope hissed laughter.

Bellusdeo, however, paused in front of the sandwich board. While burning a message into the board would satisfy Kaylin—briefly—it was likely to destroy the board, which would be a crime. A petty crime, but a crime.

"Severn's right about the paperwork," Kaylin told their companion.

"I don't have to look at the paperwork," the Dragon replied, her eyes all gold. "And he can't demote me or fire me." She shrugged and stepped away from Margot's storefront. "But it's true that he has been more polite of late than he was when I initially entered the office."

"I told you why he doesn't like Dragons."

"Yes. I happen to agree with his assessment."

It was Kaylin's turn to shrug. "I didn't know about it at the time, and in hindsight, I understand why the Emperor considered me a risk." She lifted her arm and the bracer that kept her magic under control—or under complete wraps, as she had to remove it to do anything magically useful—caught sunlight. "The only important point—to me, the person who was at risk of execution—was that he listened to people who actually knew me."

"They no doubt downplayed your penchant for wandering into inconceivably dangerous trouble."

"Probably. You can check."

"Oh?"

"Well, the Arkon was there. The Emperor was there. It wasn't an actual trial, but I've heard it was pretty formal, so there are probably accessible Records—but palace Records, not Halls of Law. Or maybe not," she added, catching Severn's brief shake of head. "It's old news now."

Bellusdeo's eyes gathered a hint of orange.

Sorry, Kaylin told Severn. *I wasn't thinking. I mean, if I'm not mad about it, and it was my fate being discussed, I don't get why other people would be mad. I don't think Teela's mad about it, and she was there.*

The orange deepened.

"So, we won't be on Elani for the next couple of weeks," Kaylin said in an attempt to divert the Dragon's focus.

"You're going back to the warrens?"

"In a manner of speaking." The orange faded. It would. The warrens were considered a ground beat designed for Barrani; mortal Hawks without wings didn't fare well there. The Barrani always did, and any injuries that were inflicted were taken entirely by their attackers—none of whom then wandered into the Halls of Law to make a formal complaint.

Kaylin had only patrolled there at the side of Teela and Tain—or Bellusdeo. Bellusdeo had absolutely nothing to fear from the street gangs that ruled the warrens.

"Does this involve Candallar?"

"It does."

"When does this start?"

"Tomorrow. We'll probably start in Tiamaris, though. It's one of the two fiefs that border Candallar, and he's bound to have more accurate information than the Halls of Law."

"Maggaron will be excited."

Although Kaylin hated the fiefs that had been her childhood home, she made an exception for the fief of Tiamaris. Ruled by Lord Tiamaris of the Dragon Court, its interior laws mirrored the Emperor's laws. That had not always been the case, and it made Kaylin aware of how much a fief changed under different rulers.

She understood the necessity of the fiefs: each existed around a central Tower, and the Towers were created to stand sentinel against the fief of *Ravellon*—the only fief that had neither Tower nor lord that she knew of.

Ravellon was the home of the most dangerous of the Shadows, the one-offs that had unique abilities. She wasn't certain if they were spawned in the heart of *Ravellon*, or if they, like Spike, were prisoners enslaved and in service to…something.

But she knew that *Ravellon*—unlike the rest of the fiefs— appeared to exist in all worlds. One of those worlds had been Bellusdeo's home. It had been her kingdom, her empire. It was gone now. The Shadows had devoured it. They had taken control of Maggaron, Bellusdeo's Ascendant, and Bellusdeo had become some part of him—his weapon, to be exact.

Maggaron and Bellusdeo had escaped *Ravellon*, but the Dragon's hatred of Shadow, and of the outcaste Dragon who appeared to make *Ravellon* his home, would end only when *Ravellon* did. Being a Dragon, Bellusdeo had perfect memory. There was nothing she had experienced that she couldn't recall.

Kaylin and Severn, Bellusdeo in tow, crossed the Ablayne

by the bridge that led into the fief of Tiamaris. Under the rule of Tiamaris, the fief itself had changed; even the bridge, while sparsely crowded, seemed to be a natural part of the city. As fieflord, he had applied the laws of the Empire—with a few notable exceptions—to the citizens of the fief, and he had started to hire tradesmen to repair the damages the fief had undergone when Barren's dubious control had finally allowed Shadows to enter the fief.

Since Dragons in their more or less human forms weren't recognized by most of Elantra's citizens at a distance, Bellusdeo didn't cause concern. Maggaron, however, did. His presence on the walk to the bridge meant there was a lot of room in the streets; at almost eight feet in height, he garnered apprehensive attention. He was walking with two Hawks, which might have lessened the fear, but Kaylin was willing to bet her own money that the Swords would be fielding reports.

There was no one across the bridge who would report him; it was in Tiamaris that the remainder of his surviving people lived. They lived near the border between *Ravellon* and Tiamaris, and they stood guard against the Shadows that had already destroyed their homeland. In Tiamaris, this was known. Yes, the size of the *Norannir* was intimidating—but they looked like very large people, not Shadow.

Nor did the tabard of the Hawk cause either resentment or fear, although here and there it caused curiosity, followed by lectures—some loud, some hissed whispers—from the parents or grandparents of those brave enough to express it.

Kaylin often answered the young-child questions, not because Severn was terrible with children—he wasn't—but because she was smaller; size and gender made her look like much less of a threat. To the children asking, neither she nor Severn was dangerous; to the parents or grandparents, however, it was different.

This was the biggest change in Tiamaris, to Kaylin's eye.

Children who felt safe expressed curiosity this way.

In Nightshade, curiosity had been death.

And maybe she was judging the entirety of the fief from her personal experience with it. Same way she'd judged Barren. But Barren was now Tiamaris, and its Tower was now Tara's; she'd been given free rein to express herself and her own desires, and now had vegetable gardens practically in the streets surrounding the looming white edifice.

"Do you want to inspect the border?" Kaylin asked Bellusdeo.

"Not really." The Dragon smiled and glanced at Maggaron, who had somehow managed *not* to terrify children into invisibility. "You might want to look in the other direction, though."

"Which other direction— Oh."

Bellusdeo carefully removed her clothing. Maggaron held out both hands, and she dumped its various layers into them. He could do this and avert his gaze, which he did. He didn't seem embarrassed, though. That took more effort, not that Bellusdeo was against that.

It was not illegal for Dragons to *be* Draconic in Tiamaris. And it was not illegal for Dragons to take to the sky in their second form. Bellusdeo, mindful of the damage done to clothing—or perhaps the cost of replacing it—didn't seem to care all that much if she stood in the streets exposed and stark naked—but even in that form, there was little in the streets that could harm her. Plus, she had Maggaron. And Severn. And Kaylin.

Kaylin was grateful that she'd waited until there were no small children close at hand. The Dragon pushed off the ground with her wings bunched close to her back; she spread them as she gained height. Her shadow shrank as she gained distance.

"I wish," Kaylin said softly, "that the Emperor would nix the law about Dragons in flight above the city."

"She doesn't understand it, either. But the city is the Emperor's, and she accepts that."

"I think she'd be happier if she could do this more often."

Maggaron said nothing.

"You don't?"

"I don't know. She is...not what she was, when she ruled." He glanced at Kaylin. "I am grateful for you. The problems you face are new to her. They are no less dangerous, and they require some attention. She is allowed to face most of them by your side, and given the nature of some of your enemies, she doesn't have the time to think about..." He trailed off.

"What will she do?" Kaylin asked as Bellusdeo circled the boundaries of Tiamaris from above.

"She will do what she must. She has always done what she must."

"And after?"

"And after, I think it would almost be better for her if she found—if she took—a fief Tower for herself."

Kaylin shook her head. "It's too close to *Ravellon*."

"Perhaps. But that, Chosen, is the war she was trained— and raised—to fight. She knows no other."

Tara was in her gardening clothing when the Tower's base came into view. This would be because she was in her garden. Morse was standing guard, but Morse was decorative. This close to the Tower, there was little that could harm Tara. Tara, like Helen, was an Avatar, a way of interacting with the people of Tiamaris.

There were residents in similar gardening clothing who

were at work; some were too young to be truly helpful, and some old enough they required more rest. None seemed afraid to see the Hawks or the *Norannir*.

Morse came to greet them. "Things have been pretty quiet."

"And you're bored?"

"Not bored, exactly." Morse shrugged. "I don't trust the quiet." Her grin was brief. Dark. It was also hard to maintain when Tara was near. "It never stays quiet around you, you know?"

"I'm not bringing trouble with me."

"Why're you here, then?"

"To speak with Tiamaris."

"Emperor sent you?"

"The Hawklord. We're only here to learn what Tiamaris knows."

Morse snorted. "You've got a year or ten?"

"About the fiefs. Not his," Kaylin added. "But a neighbor's. Did you know Tiamaris spent some time entering various fiefs—as research?"

"I'd heard."

"He told you?"

Morse shook her head. "Tara did. She likes to talk. Sometimes she likes to talk a lot." Kaylin winced. Morse had never been even remotely chatty. "She's giving lessons; she'll be done soon."

"Do you know where Tiamaris is?"

Morse shaded her eyes and looked up. "I know where he will be, soon."

Tara took a break after a quarter of an hour, by which time there were two Dragons in the air. One was gold. One was, hmmm, bronze? It was harder to pinpoint the color. Kaylin was pretty certain she'd seen red scales on at least one of them.

"Yes," Tara said as she approached. "The colors can shift when the Dragon is under duress. As the Dragons age, that shift is less likely—although I am told the colors deepen or change with age. Tiamaris is considered young by his kin."

"But Bellusdeo has always been gold."

"Bellusdeo is female." Before Kaylin could speak, she added, "I believe the female of any species is somewhat mysterious to the nonfemales of the same species."

"Meaning you don't know?"

"I know what my Lord knows."

"Well…" She watched the Dragons cross paths. It was almost playful.

"They are conversing," Tara said, her voice softer. "My Lord worries about Bellusdeo."

"About her decision?"

"No. He trusts that she will accept the responsibility of being, of becoming—however temporarily—the mother of her race. But…he does not think it will make her happy."

"You think he's right."

"I don't know for certain," Tara replied. "I don't know what makes people happy or unhappy. I don't know why some children can be happy in my garden, and some resent being forced to be here—it is the same activity for both. I understand that there are variances in personality, but I don't understand what creates those variances.

"And no, Kaylin," she added, although Kaylin hadn't spoken a word, "I don't think Dragons are more complicated than humans, *Norannir* or Barrani. They have different concerns."

"And can hold longer grudges."

Tara shook her head. "I think very few can hold a grudge as intensely as Morse can."

"Yes, but that's decades—that's all we have."

"Is that how you see it?"

"That's not how you do?"

"No. I think Morse can hold a grudge for the entirety of her life."

"Which is shorter—"

"I'm not sure it feels different from the inside, but I admit that I know far fewer Immortals."

Morse cleared her throat. "I'm standing right here," she told them both; the sharp edge of her glare was aimed at Kaylin.

"We know," Tara said.

Morse snorted. "She forgets a lot, doesn't she?"

"You're going to criticize her manners?"

Morse chuckled. "Not hers, no."

Right. "Do you understand what Bellusdeo needs?"

"I have been trying," Tara confessed. She didn't look up to the sky, but it wasn't necessary; she could see what was happening. If Helen was Kaylin's House, Tara was, in some fashion, the fief itself.

"My powers at the edge of my borders are very weak," Tara then said. "If Bellusdeo were a Hallionne or a Tower, I would have far better guesses. But even the Towers and Hallionne differ. We have one imperative; that imperative produces necessary rules. But beyond those? Happiness is just as elusive as it is for you. Or Morse.

"And sometimes, in our attempts to find that happiness, we make mistakes; we confuse *want* with happiness. We discover that they are not the same, often at our peril."

"She wants to be here."

"She wants to be fighting Shadow. She wants to be part of the council of war that is concerned with Shadow, yes. But she wants that, I think, because she is confident that she has much to offer in that regard. The only other thing about which she can be certain is the continuation of her race.

"She is lonely."

Kaylin opened her mouth and shut it again.

Tara nodded anyway. "Hatchlings might make her life busier, but I am not at all certain they would make it less lonely."

"What would?"

Tara hesitated, which was unusual for the Tower. "Come," she finally said. "Your stomach is making noise, and Morse has to eat, as well." She then turned to Severn and said, "Good morning, Corporal."

Tiamaris returned to join them in the small dining hall. Bellusdeo was not with him.

"She has gone to the border to visit her people," Tara said in response to Kaylin's wordless observation. To Kaylin, this was much like being at home.

"Tara says you've come to ask questions about my early years investigating the fiefs." He spoke to both Severn and Kaylin as he joined them at the table. Morse had eaten and vacated her chair; she took up a position by the door. Her posture was casual—she was leaning against the wall with folded arms—but she was, in theory, a guard here.

Kaylin nodded. "We have experience in the fiefs because we were born in them. But Nightshade is not the fief we've been sent to investigate."

"I assume it is not Tiamaris, either."

"No. Inasmuch as a fieflord is trusted—by the Halls of Law—Tiamaris is trusted." She wanted to add that if all fieflords were Dragons, maybe all of the fiefs would feel like part of the city proper. It was a nice thought, but even if that had been Imperial intent, there weren't enough Dragons. The

Arkon would never be pried from the library, and the Emperor would never be beholden to a Tower.

"We want to know what you learned of Candallar—or what you know now. He borders Tiamaris."

"Finish eating your meal; we will retire to the mirror room before I attempt to answer any questions you have."

"Candallar's been hanging out in the warrens," Kaylin said as they walked down the long, wide halls that led to the pool of water Tara called a mirror. Although Elantra proper was full of mirrors in various sizes, Tara—like Helen—considered their presence an unacceptable security risk. Understanding that Kaylin and Tiamaris considered them a necessity, the two buildings had created single rooms in which they reluctantly allowed mirror messages to both enter and leave their domain.

Tiamaris exhaled a thin stream of smoke, but said nothing. His eyes were orange, but orange was the standard Dragon color when discussing the fiefs.

"He's not like Nightshade."

"You've met him."

"We have." She nodded in Severn's direction.

"It is my understanding that the mortal Hawks are not responsible for the warrens."

"We had the cohort; Teela was off duty. And we had Bellusdeo."

This did cause a shift in eye color, and not in the good direction.

"Have you ever tried to say no to her when she wants something the Emperor has specifically already said she can have?"

He grimaced, his eye color lightening. "What was Candallar doing in the warrens?"

"On hearsay, he was waiting to meet with a Barrani High Lord or two."

"Would this meeting have occurred around the same time as the reconfiguration of the High Halls?"

"Yes. How much have you heard?"

"Not much. Tara was not concerned with the change in the building's state. She considered it an unexpectedly good sign. If Candallar was involved—"

"Any good that came out of his involvement was accidental." Kaylin then detailed what she could remember about Candallar, his Barrani connections, and Spike, a Shadow who'd worked with them to preserve the High Halls. Hope was dangling across both shoulders looking bored when Tara interrupted her.

"You are saying that the fieflord of Candallar allowed a Lord of the High Court to enter *Ravellon* through his domain?"

"Yes."

"And that Lord then found Spike and carried him across the border?"

Kaylin nodded.

"And Spike remained in the High Halls."

"I think he'd be willing to talk to us if we visited. He knows a lot about *Ravellon*. But he said…" She trailed off, uncertain of how to proceed. Tara was militant about Shadow in the same way Bellusdeo was—but there was less flexibility in Tara's response because Tara's purpose as a Tower was the defense against, and destruction of, Shadow.

"That is true." The doors to the mirror room faded. Standing beside the rounded lip of the pool's circumference was the Avatar of the Tower. She was not wearing gardening clothing; her robes were a long, loose drape of pale ivory and green. Her eyes, as she turned them toward her lord and his approaching guests, were obsidian.

"Bellusdeo was controlled by Shadow for—actually, I don't

know how long it was, objectively speaking. Maggaron was controlled in a similar fashion. They're not controlled now. And Spike seemed happy not to be enslaved."

"And you now believe that we could somehow free all of Shadow?" Tara's tone did not encourage optimism.

"I just think—"

"You can barely survive one of the individual Shadows when it crosses the inner boundary," Tiamaris cut in. "If what you believe is true—and I am willing to lend it credence—it is functionally irrelevant. To get to the enslaver, you would have to fight through the slaves—and the slaves are more dangerous than you could ever hope to be."

"That is not entirely true," Tara then said, her voice gentling. "She is Chosen."

"You have never explained what that means, in a practical sense."

"We do not fully understand it ourselves, my Lord." She then looked at the still surface of clear water. Her eyes lost the look and texture of black stone as the water began to move. "But it is true that the Barrani—the High Court, the High Lords, and perhaps Candallar himself—don't understand the Shadows, either."

"They expected Spike to be of use. And he probably was, at least briefly. He's like a portable memory crystal and portable Records rolled into one, but he…" Kaylin hesitated, trying to choose the right words, or any words at all, to describe what had occurred when the cohort had fled into the outlands.

Spike had not been small, portable or harmless there.

She didn't need to find the right words in Tiamaris. Tara could see what she was attempting to squeeze into Elantran with so much difficulty. The mirror responded to Tara, and the image of that giant Spike—with a Kaylin-size Barrani, probably Sedarias, by his side—appeared.

"In the High Halls, as well?"

"In the Tower of testing, yes. He looked different in the Tower, but he was about the same size."

"He is dangerous."

"He didn't—"

"He could meld with you so completely he could not be detected by the Tower of Candallar. And he could become this, as well. Doing so in the outlands is impressive, but it is not dangerous in the same fashion, for reasons I'm sure you understand."

Kaylin didn't.

Tara, gaze focused on Spike, continued. "Candallar's Tower allowed the Lord into *Ravellon*. The Lord returned bearing Spike. He then released Spike, who flew—at speed—to where you were, in the West March, across the continent. What did you do to free Spike?"

"I think—nothing? I think Terrano did that."

"I believe we would like to speak with Terrano."

Kaylin thought the chances of that pretty low, given the fieflord was a Dragon. They weren't zero, because Terrano still lived with her, but it wasn't to speak of Spike or Terrano that she'd come to Tiamaris.

"Candallar first."

Tara looked to Tiamaris for permission. It wasn't particularly subtle. Tiamaris didn't appear to notice.

"I have encountered Candallar twice since I made the fief my home."

Kaylin nodded. The water of the mirror remained water, the surface so still it reflected the light perfectly.

"I have encountered Nightshade more often, but he was one of the few who was willing—on occasion—to speak with the Halls of Law."

"Candallar hasn't."

"Actually, he has," Tiamaris replied.

"I checked Records."

"You checked Records relevant to your duties as a Hawk."

"No, I— Oh."

"Indeed. The Imperial Records—to which you had no access—are more complete. I believe you will find that some loose permissions have been granted for the duration of your current investigation. Those permissions would be irrelevant in the Halls of Law, but you have access to the palace. I suggest you avail yourself of it.

"In the meanwhile, is this the man you encountered in the warrens?" As he spoke, the surface of the water in the large basin began to move. Waves broke its stillness. This time, however, the water didn't remain flat. The center of the pool began to rise. The water moved as if it were elemental. As if it were *the* water.

Tara shook her head. "It is not. In the Tower—and in similar buildings and environs—the elements require some rudimentary permissions to form fully, unless the elemental gateway is large. But the Towers can take control, if such control is required. Do you require it?" The last was said a little doubtfully. "If so, this is not the room you wish to be in."

"I don't need to talk to the water," Kaylin said with some haste. "If I need to do that, I'll go bother Evanton." As she finished the sentence, the water finished its slow climb; it then dribbled down as if it were wax.

What was left in the wake of this accretion of liquid was the height, the shape, of a man. As the water's movement slowed to a crawl, a face emerged, followed by arms, legs, clothing.

"Yes," Kaylin said, replying to Tara's first question. "This is the man I'd identify as Candallar. His clothing was different, but that's his face."

The water sculpture of Candallar remained standing.

"You've been to Candallar," Kaylin said.

Tiamaris nodded.

"Did you see its Tower?"

"Not as closely as Nightshade's, or perhaps not as extensively. I have entered the periphery of the Tower in Candallar."

"When Candallar was present?"

"No. The fieflord of Candallar leaves his home more frequently than other fieflords. I was aware of the purpose of the Towers, but desired to understand them better. I merely waited until he stepped out."

"Is Candallar's Tower like Castle Nightshade?"

"Not exactly, no. It is less obviously martial."

"Given what happened to Barren—"

"I am pleased with the outcome," he said, his voice lower. Kaylin discarded that line of questioning.

"We think Candallar wants to be repatriated."

"And he attempted to support a faction within the High Court that offered him what he wanted?"

"That's our best guess. It's only a guess," she added. "You'd know if his borders became dangerously insecure, wouldn't you?"

"Candallar stands guard against the largest of the fief borders to face *Ravellon*. I believe we would know."

Tara, eyes obsidian, said, "We would not know unless that breach threatened our fief. If Shadow came in through any of our borders, we would be aware of it."

"Could you allow someone to enter *Ravellon*?"

Tara exhaled. "Yes. But Kaylin, the *Norannir* could enter *Ravellon* if they chose to do so. We could stop them, but it would require physical intervention."

"Meaning Tiamaris would have to fly there?"

"Yes."

"From what you've said, this wasn't accidental. Spike was told to meet someone at the border. The Lord was there. Either Candallar's Tower didn't notice Spike, or Candallar *could* give permission."

"It seems that way. The Barrani who emerged from *Ravellon* carrying Spike did not carry other Shadows. He was allowed to leave. Towers cannot prevent people from entering *Ravellon* without the aid of their lords. What we prevent is the escape of Shadow. Had the Barrani Lord not entered *Ravellon*, it is highly doubtful that Spike could have left."

Kaylin nodded.

"Something directed Spike toward the Barrani Lord. Something knew that the Barrani Lord was coming."

Kaylin nodded again.

"I doubt that Candallar himself is on speaking terms—for want of a better word—with *Ravellon*. Were he, he would no longer be fieflord. There is a creature that calls *Ravellon* home, but he is capable of leaving it at his discretion."

"The outcaste Dragon."

"The outcaste Dragon," Tara agreed. "It would be trivial for the outcaste himself to approach members of the High Court. Or even Candallar. The outcaste is not of Shadow."

CHAPTER 3

"I don't understand what the outcaste wants," Kaylin said, breaking an awkward silence. "I don't think it's revenge—from all I've heard of his history as a Dragon, the revenge motive would fit better in the other direction. He's done damage to the Dragons. They might want to hunt him down. Bellusdeo certainly does.

"But from here it looks like he wanted the Shadow beneath the High Halls freed. Giving Spike to a member of the previous Mellarionne faction would be part of that. Spike was not happy with whatever it was Sedarias's brother was doing before he died." At Severn's expression, she added, "By not happy, I mean afraid. He was afraid of both the ritual and the trapped creature."

"But he remained with that creature when it was freed," Tiamaris said with a slight rise at the end of the sentence.

"Yes. I think Towers get lonely—it just takes them longer. But no. You're right. We could unlock the chains binding that Shadow to *Ravellon*—because it had those chains. So did Spike. Some essential part of their beings was also part of *Ravellon*—like a continuous mirror connection, without the need for actual mirrors, but with the compulsion to obey every order, every whim." Kaylin turned thoughtful. "I don't think the Shadows are evil. But whatever lies at the heart of *Ravellon* might be."

"Might?" The single word was heated.

Kaylin shrugged. "It's going to try to escape its prison. If it manages, we'll all die in the process—but I'm not sure that it cares about our deaths, one way or the other. We're collateral damage. And I care more about us and our lives than I care about its freedom. I don't think that makes me a monster, either."

"Why do you think this?"

"Which part?"

"That our destruction is not its intent?"

"I don't know," she replied, after puzzling it through. "I've talked with Shadows we would have once destroyed on sight. Gilbert. Spike. The being beneath the High Halls, although admittedly that wasn't a lot of talk. They're afraid of *Ravellon*. They don't want to go back. They don't like being slaves. I think they'd be happy if *Ravellon*'s Lord was dead and gone.

"But they've never implied that they were sent to destroy everything. Or us. We didn't figure at all. The Barrani might. The Dragons might. They're immortal, and they wield a power that the Shadows understand on some level."

"The breach of Barren's defenses killed a significant number of people," Tiamaris said.

"Yes—but I'm not certain that that wasn't the intent of whatever it was that controls them. Attract attention. Divert attention. Killing the people achieves both of those. I don't get the sense that the heart of *Ravellon* derives power from those deaths."

Silence.

"If whatever dwells at the heart of *Ravellon* could derive power from deaths—and I know there are schools of *totally forbidden* magic that can—don't you think it would be free by now? It's eaten worlds—at least one that we know of for certain. The life of a world? It's got to be worth more than my life or your life or the lives of a single fief.

"So…that's why I don't think sacrifice gives *Ravellon* power."

Tiamaris nodded. Tara's nod was reluctant and stiff, but any discussion about Shadow had that effect on a building that would rather be an outdoor gardener. A vegetable gardener.

"The Dragon outcaste was certainly driving the Aerians." Kaylin hesitated, and then added, "He was driving the Aerians from within the Aerie *as* an Aerian. The Aerians couldn't tell the difference. Neither could the rest of us."

Tiamaris exhaled smoke, and not a small amount.

"If we understood what the outcaste wants, we'd have a better chance of blocking him. Right now, we don't know. We only know that he's interested in Bellusdeo; that he wants her to join him."

More Draconic silence, but this time, it was accompanied by an orange that was shading to red as Kaylin watched.

"And that doesn't change the concerns about Candallar."

"Are you certain that Lord Nightshade has not been approached by similar agents of *Ravellon*?"

"No."

"Then I suggest you ask him." He exhaled less smoke; this time, when he gestured, the image of Candallar melted, the water that formed it flowing back into the basin. "This is what I know of what Candallar is. Records, fiefs." The fiefs appeared instantly.

The fief of Tiamaris was gold, as was the fief of Nightshade. The rest of the fiefs existed in outline. "We know enough about the fief of Nightshade to be certain that these are its boundaries.

"The thick white lines between the fiefs represent the border zones. The lines vary in width by the subjective difficulty in penetrating them. My subjective difficulty," Tiamaris added. "The borders are not entirely fixed. Lord Nightshade has crossed the borders between Tiamaris and Nightshade, as have you. I do not believe his crossing was as difficult. It is in the borders that some of the rules of magic as we currently understand them seem to break down.

"The Tower locations marked on the map are accurate. Tara does not believe that the Towers themselves can move or be moved. The street names in the border zone, however, are meaningless for the current investigation."

"Why are they there, then?"

"They are taken from archival records. The Arkon's," he added before Kaylin could ask why those archives had not found their way into the Halls of Law. "We have rough maps and some odd biographical information from before the fall. Where those streets align with the shape of streets in the fiefs as they are now, I have chosen to identify them by the ancient names.

"Those names will mean nothing to the occupants of the fiefs themselves. Even the streets in my fief have been renamed in places. You will see streets in relation to the Tower and in relation to the fief boundaries. Unfortunately for you, the two fiefs that are bordered by wall and the Ablayne cannot be as easily crossed if you cannot fly. There are gates, but the gates do not, as you can imagine, see much use."

"Not none."

"No, not none. The fiefs are not entirely self-sustaining. But in my experience, the gates into Farlonne and Liatt require some permission to use. As the fiefs are not part of the Empire, that permission cannot be demanded."

"You flew."

"I did."

"Farlonne and Liatt aren't our problem."

After a longer than necessary pause, Tiamaris said, "Not at present."

Tiamaris's map did have a marked route from the external border of each fief to their Towers. Those routes did not cross borders. "You spoke of the difficulty of the border zone. If you didn't cross the border—"

"I did not say I did not cross the borders, but the border crossings—here and here, as an example—were attempted after the initial foray into each of the six fiefs. I wished to see where the borders were in relation to each other; it was an attempt to map the fiefs correctly. I do not suggest this as an investigative approach—but the Towers do not control the borders." He glanced at Tara.

She took over. "We are aware of the borders of our own domains, or rather, we are aware of where they begin. My Lord is correct, however. Beyond the borders that were transcribed for us at our creation, we have no control. Nor can we see what occurs within them."

"Are you more aware or less aware of which border is crossed?"

Tara considered this. "The border that would cause immediate alarm is the *Ravellon* border. Am I aware of other crossings? Yes, but not immediately, and not in the same way."

"So if I came here via Nightshade, instead of the much safer bridge, you wouldn't be alarmed?"

"Those borders are not the borders we consider dangerous. The crossing might be noted, but the borders are not entirely fixed, and there are occupied buildings that are at the limit. People at the edge flicker in and out from time to time, entirely due to the location of their living quarters."

Kaylin nodded.

"If your supposition about Candallar is correct, two borders were crossed. The border that is formed by the Ablayne river, and the border adjacent to *Ravellon*. Candallar's Tower may be aware of areas on the *Ravellon*-facing border that are weaker or more easily breached. I highly doubt that the Tower would allow anyone to both cross that border and return in secret, with the single exception of the fieflord.

"If, however, the fieflord commanded the Tower to accept passage into and out of *Ravellon*, the Tower would be on high alert; the chance of carrying Shadow and its contaminant into the fief itself would be considered a high probability. Or it would, if I were the Tower. We may therefore assume that either Spike is unusual or the Tower itself has been compromised."

"Spike is pretty unusual," Kaylin offered.

"I would advise you to investigate the man who entered and left *Ravellon*."

"I think he's dead. Things were a little messy in the High Halls at the end. Also, Teela is investigating that angle, and she's made pretty clear that she doesn't want my help." Teela's exact words had been much more unkindly emphatic.

Tara frowned. "I feel that *bumbling* is harsh."

"I thought so, too, but she had that look on her face, so I didn't argue. If our investigation leads into Teela's, she'll have to accept us, but she won't be happy."

"I often feel that Teela is never happy."

"She's Barrani."

"I think we should cross at the internal border," Kaylin said as the Hawks left the Tower. "If Candallar knows that he's under suspicion, he'll know that we're coming if we cross the bridge."

"He'll know that we're coming regardless," Severn said. He had fallen in beside her in a patrol-speed walk.

"He'll have to be looking. Tara said that the people who live in the buildings directly adjacent to the borders sometimes flicker in her awareness. If that's the case, the border is our best bet of not being detected."

"That's clearly the case for Tara. It might not be the case for Candallar's Tower."

"She seemed pretty certain that the Towers share the same imperatives."

"So were we until we met Tara."

This was a fair point. Hope apparently agreed; he pushed himself into the sitting position on her shoulder and gave Severn a brief but regal nod.

"There are few people who try to sneak into the fiefs, and most of those are fleeing to a place where Imperial Law doesn't apply." Severn glanced at her. "My forays into the fiefs were done at the command of the Wolflord."

"Candallar probably didn't notice. The inhabitants of the fiefs are mostly mortals."

Severn's nod wasn't quite agreement.

"You think he knows too much about mortals and Imperial Laws."

"I think he knows enough not to make the assumption we're harmless, but Barrani arrogance is fairly pervasive." He looked up as a large shadow crossed their path.

Bellusdeo, Maggaron on her back, descended into an empty patch of road. Maggaron immediately dismounted and returned the Dragon's clothing to her; she took a bloody long time putting it on.

"Where are we going next?"

Kaylin wanted to tell Bellusdeo that she was going home. Her compromise was to ask Bellusdeo to return Maggaron to

Helen. If she and Severn intended to cross the border without immediately alerting the Tower of Candallar, having an eight-foot-tall companion was going to make it impossible.

Maggaron didn't seem happy with this compromise. Bellusdeo couldn't fly him to Helen and fly back without breaking the law. It was, in the gold Dragon's opinion, a very stupid law, and it wouldn't be the first time she had chosen to break it—but at this point in her tenure in Elantra, flight was not the hill to die on.

Maggaron, understanding this, offered to walk home alone. Bellusdeo growled—literally—but accepted his offer. Even Kaylin felt slightly guilty. It wasn't his fault that he was so damn tall, and if this had been a city of *Norannir*, his presence wouldn't have mattered. But Tiamaris was the only home of the *Norannir* who had survived the destruction of their world, and they seldom crossed the Ablayne into Elantra proper.

It was unlikely that anyone would be stupid enough to attempt to mug or steal from him. Not impossible, but at this time of day, most people wouldn't be drunk enough that stupid became the new normal.

Kaylin chose a section of the border midway between safety—Elantra—and death, being *Ravellon*. A street, with buildings on either side, was bisected by the border. Like any neighborhood border, it was invisible; a thing for laws and papers, a claim that made no material difference to the lay of the land. But invisible in the fiefs had a different weight, a different meaning.

Here, the borders weren't a matter of bureaucracy and maps. The Towers that existed in each fief were the reason the fiefs existed at all: they were meant to guard against the intrusion of Shadow in a specific area known to the Towers and their creators. The fieflords could sense the borders of the fiefs whose Towers they ruled.

Bellusdeo let Severn take the lead, but her eyes shaded to orange when Hope lifted a translucent wing and smacked it across Kaylin's eyes.

Kaylin called a silent halt; Severn stopped. If True Names had done nothing else for their partnership, they'd allowed communication across distances that raised voices wouldn't penetrate.

For the first time, Kaylin could see the border boundary. It wasn't a line on the ground, but a transparent wall. Perhaps double her height, it extended in either direction. Her gaze followed the line of that wall, first to the city that was her home, and second, to the heart of the fiefs themselves: *Ravellon*. There, the wall was not wall, but dome.

Hope didn't lower his wing.

Sorry, Kaylin told Severn. *There's nothing dangerous that I can see—but I've never looked at the border like this before.*

He nodded and continued to move. When he sent an all-clear, Kaylin followed, Bellusdeo by her side.

Dragons weren't naturally stealthy creatures. Although Bellusdeo didn't make any noise, she radiated an almost aggressive self-confidence. Kaylin was fairly certain she could walk on her own and go unmolested in Nightshade—or Candallar. The tabard of the Hawk couldn't grant Kaylin that aura of certainty or confidence.

Crossing the border of Tiamaris didn't feel different. It looked different because of Hope's wing, but she could step through it without the pain and nausea caused by portals or other forms of protective magic. The world rippled as she did, but it was the same ripple a stone might cause if dropped into a still pond.

Reality reasserted itself, but in doing so, seemed to have lost some of its color. This she'd experienced before. The street beneath her feet felt the same, but it seemed to her eyes like a faded replica—as if someone had taken white and blended it with everything present to soften the vibrancy of distinguishing color. This was, on the other hand, what the border zone always looked like, even without Hope's wing.

Kaylin looked to the right as she crossed the weed-strewn lawn of the building directly to their left. From this vantage, she could see a two-story building opposite a three-story one. It looked unlike any of the other buildings on this street; for one, it seemed new. It also lacked windows and doors. She frowned as Severn turned toward it.

"Roof?"

"Flat, at least from this angle."

The Dragon glanced at Severn. "Investigate?"

"Leave it," Kaylin said, regretting Bellusdeo's presence. It was harder to take calculated risks while in the company of the future of an entire race.

Hope squawked.

"...or not." Kaylin turned back to the windowless, doorless building.

"Have you seen something like the border zone before?" Kaylin asked the Dragon as they approached a street-facing solid wall.

The Dragon shook her head. "There were no Towers, no protective ring of fiefs around the *Ravellon* that existed in my world." She stretched out a hand to touch what appeared to be a stone wall. "This feels solid to me. It smells solid. It would not surprise me if people were living in the buildings here. If they can enter them."

It had never occurred to Kaylin to live in the border zone.

It is not safe, Hope said, the squawks that formed syllables far quieter than they usually were this close to her ear. *It is not a land that was meant to be inhabited by your kind.*

"Why does it exist at all?"

I do not know. But it is possible that the Towers and their responsibilities cannot overlap without danger to those responsibilities. Each Tower knows its own lands; each Tower must. Here, between those defining borders, they are absent.

"And the Shadows can't come through the border territories?"

Look to Ravellon.

She did. *Ravellon*, enclosed in a translucent, faintly shining barrier, could no longer be seen. She moved, then, to attempt to see past the squat, featureless building; *Ravellon* didn't exist. She then turned in the direction they'd come. The street was clear, and it continued—pale and faded—into Tiamaris.

"Can either of you see *Ravellon*?"

Severn shook his head. Bellusdeo said, "No."

"Neither can I. Hope, what *is* this place?"

I have already said I do not know, the familiar replied. *But I see what you see. And I fail to see what you fail to see. These lands are not malleable in the fashion of the outlands and the portal paths of the Hallionne. They do not take commands or suggestions with regard to their shape. I believe they are as you see them now.*

I do not believe they are always as you see them now. There is something that tastes wrong in the air.

"How wrong?"

She didn't understand Hope's answer. It was squawking but seemed deliberate, and the tone trailed into disgust. Probably at mortals, definitely at Kaylin's lack of comprehension.

"Would you sense Shadow here if you saw it?"

It was Bellusdeo who answered. "I would."

There was no arguing with that. Even if Kaylin was skeptical, there was still no arguing. She examined the squat cube of a building. There was no obvious door facing the street, and no obvious windows, either. The lack of both was probably what made the building seem wrong to her. That, and the color. It had some. The rest of the street was leeched of color as if by a fog that was otherwise invisible. Her hand fell to her dagger; Bellusdeo cleared her throat.

Right. Right, she had a Dragon, and Bellusdeo could breathe fire quite comfortably in an otherwise human body.

"Magic?" Severn asked.

"Not yet. My skin is fine."

He headed around the corner of the building. *No doors here.*

Back of the building?

Heading there now.

Hope suddenly stiffened on her shoulder; she felt the claws of his tiny feet pressing into her collarbone as he pushed himself off her shoulder, taking to air at speed. He headed directly toward Severn.

Bellusdeo's eyes shaded to a darker orange. "There is never a moment's peace when you're around, is there?"

Kaylin shrugged. "For the record, none of this stuff is started by me. In case you hadn't noticed."

"I'm not complaining," the Dragon replied, her smile showing decidedly sharp canines. "It's never boring."

"Have you seen a building like this before?"

"In this exact shape? No. But if Severn hasn't found an entrance on any of the outward facing sides, I've seen something similar."

"What?"

"A very large coffin, in essence."

"A...coffin. Like, the kind you put dead bodies in."

"Yes."

"Because dead bodies need more room."

"Don't ask me. It's not the way we honor our dead—but you'd find that disturbing."

"I don't think we're going to be worried about coffins. Unless it's our own." She clenched her jaw.

"Magic?"

"My arms are beginning to ache."

Whatever you find, pay attention to Hope. He flew off in your direction. Bellusdeo and I will come around the other side; I'll let you know if it has a door, and we'll regroup at the back of the building.

Severn didn't reply. She could feel his presence; they hadn't been cut off by any of the bizarre dislocations that could happen within Hallionne and other sentient buildings.

There were no doors on the right side of the building. There were no doors on the back of it, either. There was, however, something in the middle of an otherwise feature-less stone wall: an eye. At first glance, the eye appeared to be carved in relief. But that first glance became a second one when the stone lid blinked, and the curve of lashes both closed and opened.

"Magic," Kaylin said.

"You think?" Bellusdeo took a step toward that eye, and Hope got in her face. Literally.

Severn was nowhere to be seen.

"He's not on the other side of the building, is he?"

No.

"Is this eye some sort of warped portal?"

Yes.

"Do you know where it goes?"

Silence.

"Come back and lend me your wing." Hope checked to make certain that Bellusdeo didn't approach the eye a sec-ond time. He then alighted on Kaylin's shoulder, but he was ramrod straight and tense. She could feel a slight tremor in the wing that now rested against her upper face.

She examined the eye at a safe distance, which would be the same distance that Hope had demanded Bellusdeo keep.

Beneath Hope's wing, the eye didn't look like carved stone. It looked and moved the way a normal eye did—if a normal eye were the size of her head. It had an eyelid, lashes; she couldn't tell, at this vantage, if it had the normal pupil, iris and white bits. She moved, taking a step back to widen her field of vision.

The movement caught the eye's attention, and it shifted toward her.

Yes, it had the pupil, iris and white bits a normal eye contained. But as it caught sight of Kaylin, it strained to face her. The angle was wrong; the side-glance was the most that single eye could attain. Or it would have been the most Kaylin could have done if she couldn't physically move her face.

As if it could hear this observation, the wall shifted. The stone didn't magically develop facial features, but the wall moved as if it were a face, until the eye was fully facing both Kaylin and Bellusdeo.

Hope inhaled.

Kaylin, meeting the gaze of that single eye, saw light begin to spread across her field of vision, moving as if it were white fire. And then, before she could cover her eyes with more than her eyelids, the light went out. With it went the earth beneath her feet.

CHAPTER 4

"Really, really never boring," Bellusdeo said.

Kaylin opened her eyes, which made no effective difference. They were standing—Kaylin knelt briefly to place a tentative hand down—on stone. Hope was with her; the membrane of his wing remained pressed against her eyes.

"We don't have time for this," Kaylin said to no one in particular.

"Unless it's relevant to the Candallar problem," Bellusdeo pointed out. "And it may well be. Or perhaps it's a different Candallar problem."

"There's no Shadow here."

"No," the Dragon replied after a pause.

"Can you see anything?"

"Yes, but not well. It's dark here, but it's a normal darkness." The Dragon then spoke three sharp words, a thunder of syllables emphasizing each one. "It's not a magical darkness. How are your arms?"

"Sore, given the spell you just cast."

"Better or worse?"

"I'd like you not to use me as your hotter-colder tool, if it's all the same to you."

"Why not? It's practical. You generally appreciate the practical."

"I'd suggest," a familiar voice said, "that we keep discussion to a minimum." It was Severn.

"You looked at the eye?"

It looked at me.

How new did the stone of this building look to you?

In comparison to the rest of the buildings in the border zone, very new.

Thought so. It seems to be in remarkably good shape for a...block of stone. With a moving eye in the wall. Bellusdeo thinks it's a coffin. Or she thought it might be, on account of no windows or doors. I don't suppose you've found any corpses?

No. I've done little scouting here. I haven't explored the whole of the building, but there doesn't seem to be an exit so far.

Great. Just great. To Hope she said, "Can you breathe on a wall and melt us a way out of here?"

"I don't think melting that wall," Bellusdeo said, her voice lower, "will necessarily get us back to where we were."

"It didn't feel like a portal to me."

"No?"

"Am I on my hands and knees struggling not to throw up?"

"No. I would be willing to make a bet, though."

"Stakes?"

Bellusdeo snorted. Fire followed smoke; it was a slender stream of flame that didn't appear to be directed at anything but air. "Do you consider illumination safe?"

"I'd take the risk," Severn replied before Kaylin could. Bellusdeo spoke again, and a light appeared, suspended at shoulder height. Unlike the flame, it was bright, its color steady. "You should be the one doing this," she added to Kaylin.

"That's not what Sanabalis has been teaching me. Not that I've had time for his lessons for a little while now."

"I fail to see why you cannot miss Lord Diarmat's so-called lessons instead; Lord Sanabalis's lessons seem to be far more practical."

"I believe the Hawklord and the Emperor consider not causing offense to the rich and powerful to be more practical than creating lights. The lights can be bought or commandeered; an attempt to placate the aforementioned powerful—" Severn began.

"—can also be bought."

"For far more money or other less desirable concessions. We're still suffering the repercussions of your unexpected visit to the West March."

"That wasn't my fault!" Kaylin snapped.

"No. It wasn't Bellusdeo's, either. But the fact of her presence could be—and has been—used as a justification for political unrest among the Barrani."

"Etiquette lessons wouldn't have prevented that!" She wanted to shout; she hissed instead.

"No, probably not. I'm not the Hawklord or the Emperor; I don't get to make that decision. What do you see here?"

She turned in the direction of Severn's back, which wasn't transparent. Moving to his left, she squinted through Hope's raised wing.

"A statue, or a series of statues. Or reliefs. There's a wall there, right?"

"I see only an unbroken wall."

"I see what the corporal sees," Bellusdeo added.

"Hey—I'm a corporal now, too."

"Fine. I see what Severn sees."

"Let me take point," Kaylin told her partner.

Severn nodded. It was Bellusdeo who spoke. "Don't touch anything without giving the rest of us some warning."

★ ★ ★

The ground was, and remained, stone beneath her feet. The wall, which had seemed attached to the ceiling and the floor in the usual way, was farther from where Kaylin had been standing than it had first appeared; either that or the ground was enchanted in a particularly annoying way. It wouldn't be the first time this had happened, although the first time had been during training with the Hawks. Magic was often a criminal tool, and a subtle use of magic involved running in place. Or rather, making your pursuers run in place.

That magic, on the other hand, Kaylin could generally detect. Standing above it would be painful. At the moment, there was enough background use of magic that she couldn't separate spells in any useful fashion, but she had a strong suspicion that the floor itself was not a clever way of keeping her at a distance.

No. The wall was simply farther away than she had realized. She gestured, and Severn followed, Bellusdeo by his side.

"You still see the wall?" Kaylin asked.

"Stone block wall. The stone is smooth; there are no marks on it at all."

"I see reliefs carved across its surface." She hesitated, and then said, "But not by anyone with any artistic sensibility."

Bellusdeo snorted. "By that you mean your sensibilities?"

"Not exactly." She lifted a hand. Hope smacked her face with the wing she was looking through, and she lowered her hand again. "I...don't think this is actually carved." To Hope she said, "Can you let Severn look?"

No.

"You've done it before."

No.

"You have—"

What I did there was not what can be done here with any safety.

We are not near the portal paths. We are not near the outlands. He holds your name. *He has other ways of seeing what you see.* This last was accompanied by a second smack.

"He doesn't like to do that."

Hope tightened his grip on her shoulder.

Hope says—

I guessed, Severn replied, speaking internally. He asked permission without using the actual words, and she gave it. In his position, she wasn't certain she'd ask.

I think you're right.

"You think these used to be people."

He nodded.

"Do you recognize any of them?"

She expected the answer to be no. Or perhaps she hoped that it would be. He directed her gaze to the wall. "Bellus-deo?"

The Dragon nodded.

"When I was being grilled by Ironjaw one afternoon, you wandered off to Missing Persons."

"I did."

"Did you look through our current Records of unsolved cases?"

"I did."

Hope sighed. Loudly. In Kaylin's ear. She lost sight of the reliefs that might not be the work of an artist as the familiar pushed himself off her shoulder.

"What is he doing?" the Dragon asked, voice sharper.

"I'm not entirely sure—but I'd guess he's about to breathe on part of the wall."

"I don't consider that wise."

Kaylin shrugged. "He's annoyed and frustrated, but he's not worried."

Hope squawked loudly before he stopped in front of one

section of that wall. Hovering there, he inhaled. When he exhaled, it was the silver stream of smoke that seemed to terrify Barrani when it was aimed in their direction.

The smoke touched the wall as if the familiar was exhaling liquid; the liquid splashed against the stone and then dripped toward the floor, melting stone as it did—but not all of the stone. Some solid parts remained, and they formed a recognizable shape; Kaylin had seen it through Hope's wing. Severn had seen it through Kaylin's eyes. It was the figure that Severn thought he recognized.

Bellusdeo's breath was slower but sharper. "Yes," she finally said. "This could be one of two or three missing children reported to Missing Persons. I'm sorry, but the Hawk's artist's rendition is not as precise as this statue."

"This boy was reported missing at the Halls of Law?"

It was Severn who said, "I believe so. Robin Perse. Twelve years of age."

"Missing from where?"

"Outside of the west warrens. Assumed missing in the warrens. The Barrani Hawks searched, but he couldn't be found, dead or alive."

"What is he doing *here*?"

"That would be the question."

Bellusdeo frowned. "There are others like this boy in the wall?"

Kaylin could no longer see anything. "There were."

"How many?"

"I didn't count. At least a dozen. Probably more."

"Probably?"

"They weren't completely distinct. It was like looking at a crowd made of stone."

"Were they all human?"

"I'm not sure."

"All, or almost all," Severn said at about the same time. "There may have been Barrani, but they were at the back of the crowd, not the forefront."

The familiar returned to Kaylin's shoulder, where he wrapped himself around her neck like a limp shawl. When she poked him, he swiveled one eye balefully in her direction. "Sorry, buddy, but—the wing would be helpful."

He pushed himself into his relaxed seated position and lifted his wing. He didn't even hit her with it first.

She then began a slower examination of the wall. "What do you think the wall is?"

Severn shrugged. "At the very least, a convenient way to get rid of people."

"If it's just that, it seems like a big outlay of magic and planning."

"Corpses breed questions. Questions get the Halls of Law involved. Enough deaths, enough questions, and the Imperial Mages might be called. There. Stop there."

She did. She looked through Hope's wing.

"Barrani," she said. "I don't recognize him."

"No. You don't have to recognize him. I believe there's another—the farthest one back. The figure is small, but the features appear distinct, even given the size."

"How many of those missing persons reports involved people from the warrens?" Kaylin asked the Dragon, the closest thing to Records on hand.

"Not many people who live in the warrens visit the Halls of Law," the Dragon replied. "I begin to understand why Mandoran is so foolish in his desire to give his name—and the power that implies—to you. I find it intensely frustrating not to be able to see what you're seeing; you are clearly making decisions based on it."

"Do *not* give me the name I didn't take when it was clear to me. I like my head more or less where it is."

This annoyed Bellusdeo, which wasn't Kaylin's intent, but the subtext—that the Emperor would be angry and that Kaylin wished to avoid this—was clear. The Dragon exhaled smoke.

"People have been reported as missing from the warrens. If I can't see what you can see—and I don't suggest that your familiar attempt to breathe upon the entire wall—I can't tell you if any of them are here."

Kaylin nodded. "I think the two Barrani might be significant."

"More so than the mortals?"

"To Candallar, yes. And probably to the High Court, as well. We need to go back to the Halls."

Bellusdeo nodded. "One small problem, however."

"Yeah. Which way is out?"

That question became the only relevant question an hour later. It had edged past normal lunch hour, and while street duties could get in the way of timely meals, Kaylin's stomach didn't care much about duty. It made noise.

The building appeared to consist of one large room—the room with the wall—but it also had two rooms to either side of the major one. Kaylin assumed that they would be rectangles, roughly the length of the main room—a room that appeared to be featureless and empty without the visual aid provided by Hope.

Bellusdeo checked out the doors, assessing their possibly magical consequences before she allowed them to be touched or opened. Severn, accustomed to the Dragon, allowed this. Kaylin was almost certain that if he said *No*, Bellusdeo would step back, something she would never do for Kaylin.

"The marks on your arms aren't glowing," the Dragon said. "And your general whining hasn't increased. I think we're safe from magical difficulties for the moment."

She was right. The door—a small door better suited to a mudroom or a closet—opened into a long room. Unlike the first room, it appeared to be a study of some sort; two desks were flush against the far wall. There was no paper, no writing implements, nothing that implied that the desks had been used.

Kaylin exhaled and glanced at Hope. She attempted to open one of the drawers. It was locked. The knob felt oddly greasy, given the almost sterile room. "The other door?"

Severn nodded.

The second room was not a room; the door led to a hall with doorless walls that ended in stairs.

"Why do they always have to go down?"

Severn started into the hall. "There's no other door," he said. "And it's possible that the entrance and exit are underground."

"In Candallar?"

"If we're lucky."

This was not the first time they had entered an unexpected basement. Given her general luck, it probably wouldn't be the last, but the statue of a boy Bellusdeo thought had gone missing remained firmly fixed in mind. She couldn't be certain that people hadn't just been sucked into the wall when they touched it; couldn't be certain that they hadn't found their way into this place the same way she had. Giant eyeballs on the side of buildings would have been cause for gossip or worry—but not if no one who'd seen them made their way back.

And to be fair, if they had, they weren't likely to be believed by anyone who didn't live on the edge of the fiefs. Strange things happened in the border zone. It was both a whisper and a fear, and the only thing that could drive the desperate across the borders were the hunting Ferals. If the Ferals were on your heels, you knew what death awaited. The unknown was definitely worth the risk.

Hope squawked. "Hush. I'm counting steps."

"I don't suppose you've encountered giant eyeballs in your former career," Bellusdeo asked Severn.

"I've encountered worse. There are forty-eight," he added.

Kaylin turned to look back at the stairs. They remained solid, slightly worn stone. There were no magical runes, no sign of the sigils that implied that Arcanists or mages had been at work. There were no torches or other forms of light; if light came here, it was carried by the visitor—and most visitors, like, say, the missing boy, didn't carry light with them.

Hope lifted his head. He squawked.

"This is going to be trouble," Kaylin said out loud.

Bellusdeo didn't argue. She did push past Kaylin but allowed Severn to continue on point. Clearly, she hadn't fully absorbed the fact that Kaylin was also a corporal now.

"What trouble are you expecting?" Bellusdeo demanded.

"I think this might be a sentient building."

"What?"

"I think there's a chance that the building itself is sentient, like Helen or the Hallionne."

"Sentient buildings seldom eat people."

"I didn't say its personality was either Helen or Hallionne. I didn't know about Helen until I went to apply as a tenant. I did know the Towers existed, but I didn't understand how they worked."

Bellusdeo said nothing.

"This might be something like Helen."

"Your reasoning?"

"There's some magic here—but I think most of it is yours. The light, the scan you're doing to detect other magic. The eye on the external wall is the type of magic I'd associate with buildings that can play god within their own perimeters." She shrugged, uneasy. "Mostly, it's the portal."

"Pardon?"

"Portals make me ill most of the time." Literally. "I didn't feel any discomfort at the transition at all. And that happens mostly inside of sentient buildings."

"Can you sense any sentience?"

Hope squawked.

"Say that so I can understand it."

If you insist, although I am already fatigued. I do not dispute your logic, but I do not sense an overarching control. Helen is noticeable immediately, as are the Hallionne.

"You think I'm wrong."

No. I think you may be correct—but something is off in that case. He squawked again, this time in a short burst.

"How could there be a sentient building in the border zone?"

It was Severn who answered. "If it was built before the fall of *Ravellon*, its existence in the border zone would be poor luck on the part of the building. You can ask Helen; she might have more information. Or perhaps you can visit the High Halls and see if you can speak with Spike."

"Once we get out."

"Once we get out."

If this was a building that was, in some fashion, like Helen, it was sleeping. The hall that the stairs led to was dark, the ceilings short and distinctly basement-like. Nothing about the building except the wall of statues that could only be seen through Hope's wing implied that they were in a space defined—and rearranged at will—by any sentience other than a carpenter and stonemason.

If the eyeball on the external wall didn't count.

Bellusdeo's light brightened; the long corridor resolved itself into a wall with a door on each side, and a door at the end. These doors, like the side doors in the great room above, were better suited to closets. Or, to be fair, to Kaylin's first apartment.

The doors to the left and right, like the doors above, were locked. There were no door wards, nor was there Kaylin-detectable magic on either the knobs or the locks.

Severn continued past them to the door at the end of this basement hallway.

"It had better not be another set of stairs."

It wasn't. It was a hall like the one they were standing in. In fact, it appeared to be identical to the one they were standing in. There were doors to the left and right, both locked, and a door at the end.

The third such hall caused a small spate of Leontine. Kaylin drew a dagger and scored the right door; it was wood, but it was normal wood. Sadly, it was a harder grade of wood. Bellusdeo chose to end Kaylin's attempt to etch an X across the door's surface.

She breathed on it instead.

Given that they were half-afraid that the building was sentient, Kaylin didn't think this wise. But it was certainly faster, and the Dragon's flame was controlled enough that she didn't turn the door into ash. The mark was, of course, on the door in the next hall.

They were walking in a circle, an iterative loop. It was a defensive design; thieves or intruders couldn't leave should they somehow manage to get in. They couldn't return to the large room, either; the forty-eight steps that had brought them to this hall had vanished. Going back the way they'd come meant they were moving in the opposite direction through a series of connected halls that looked the same—because they were.

"Do you think it's the same hall behind the side doors?" Bellusdeo asked.

Hope squawked.

"That would be inconvenient." The Dragon was standing before the door she'd already blackened. "I am going to open this door."

"That's not a use of the word *open* that would pass legal muster."

"A pity that Imperial property laws do not apply in the fiefs." She exhaled flame in a cone that was large enough to catch the edge of stone walls around the frame. When she stopped, there was a large hole where the locked door had been standing.

She insisted on going through first. Given the color of the stone around the former door frame's edges, Kaylin didn't argue. Fire didn't hurt Dragons. It would do nothing good for their clothing, though.

The door didn't open into a hall. Kaylin allowed herself to feel a tiny bit of relief, but the room it did open into had a door on the opposite wall. There was a bed here, and a table that might serve as a desk if someone needed a flat surface; there was a single chair. There were books on a shelf that didn't look very stable; there was no dust. No cobwebs. The bed itself was made; it didn't look as if it had ever been slept in.

Kaylin exhaled and approached the door on the far wall.

This one wasn't locked, and it opened into a closet.

The same room existed on the opposite side of the hall. The same rooms, absent doors, existed in the long tunnel that they'd been walking for some time. There was no going back and no going forward. Even the door which Bellusdeo had destroyed remained destroyed as they reached the end of the hall, opened the door, and entered...the same hall.

The bookshelves of unsteadiness had now been thoroughly searched; the books themselves had been taken down and skimmed. Reading, at least for Kaylin, was impossible; the books weren't written in Barrani or Elantran. She didn't recognize the writing at all.

"I don't believe it's actual language," Bellusdeo finally said.

"You think it's random squiggles?"

"I think it's as real as the hall and the room in which we found the books, yes. But I doubt that the information we require to leave this place can be found on those pages."

There was nothing written on the ceilings; there were no magical sigils, either. The floor and walls were featureless; the floor was likewise mundane. Nothing felt like magic, although the door opening into the same hall was a dead giveaway. Kaylin cursed.

"I don't recall that phrase. It's Aerian, yes?"

"I'd appreciate it if you never repeated it where anyone Aerian can hear it. Or anyone who understands Aerian. The only magic I feel here is yours." Kaylin had tucked a book from either room under her arm; she had, in fact, taken them one at a time to see if taking a book through the door at the end of the hall would make any difference. It hadn't. No combination of books achieved different results, either.

"Remind me to put a dagger through that damn eyeball the next time we're here."

"It's stone; you'll ruin the knife."

"I'll feel better."

The Dragon snorted. "I would suggest that we not return if we manage to escape."

"As if we could ever be that lucky."

"The escape?"

"The not having to return." Kaylin paused, tucked the two volumes under one arm, took a step until she was standing in the door frame itself and closed her eyes. "I'm going to try something."

CHAPTER 5

The marks of the Chosen had remained invisible; they hadn't started to glow and hadn't pulled themselves up through the rest of her clothing to circle her arms or any other part of her.

Kaylin was accustomed to reacting to the marks. Experience had given her the ability to do so intelligently, mostly. But she'd waited for those marks to reveal themselves. She had always considered the glow or the separation from her skin to be their attempt to communicate with her.

Bellusdeo's attempt to use magic on the door through which they continually passed had gone nowhere. Kaylin's attempt to do the same would be even less successful. But she had the marks of the Chosen, and the marks of the Chosen didn't obey Sanabalis's rules of magic.

She didn't know how to use the marks. She didn't consciously invoke them when she healed people. She focused only on the patient and the connection between them; only on the desired result, not the mechanics of achieving it.

The doorway would never be considered a patient, which was beside the point.

Her use of the marks, the ink-black words that resided on the skin over half of her body, had always been reactive. She had no idea if, when healing, they glowed or rose from her arms; there was no one she could ask. People didn't see the marks the same way she did.

No, Chosen; they are yours. It was Hope.

Mine, and I don't know how to use them?

Even so.

She opened the cuff of her left sleeve and began to roll the cloth back from the skin it hid.

Hope snorted by her ear, but kept the words that snort implied to himself. It wasn't Hope that she heard, however. It was Sanabalis, in memory. *Words or gestures as part of invocation are crutches. They are irrelevant to the use of magic itself.*

Do they get in the way?

They hinder speed. If you require words or complicated gestures to enter the correct state of mind, you will find your abilities lend themselves only to the scholarly; you will never make use of magic—legal magic—in your duties as a Hawk. He exhaled. No smoke, though. *Mages learn how to grasp their power, how to recognize it, in entirely different ways. You are aware that those who can see the echoes of magic do not see them in the same way?*

She'd nodded. She nodded now, as she tilted her head up, lifting an arm—the exposed left arm—to touch the top of the door frame.

You see sigils. Words. Others see fabric, a weave—loose or tight. Colors. Some hear *the echoes. They hear the names of those who cast spells strong enough to leave those echoes. But all of magic, all of our ability to use it, to channel it, to bend it in the direction we wish it to take, is like that. You attempt to reach the source; how you reach it is not as important.*

Unless I'm wasting time with inefficient words or gestures? With a wand?

By the time that is a concern, you will understand how to arrive at your destination, and you may make adjustments, yes.

★ ★ ★

She touched the door.

The frame was wood. It wasn't alive. The normal healing paradigm was not going to work here. But elements of that paradigm *might*. The ability to heal had come with the marks. To heal, she had to bridge the gap caused by skin. Her skin. Her patient's. She had never considered the actual *how* of building that bridge.

The door was an inanimate object. But…she knew, in the moment she attempted to begin to heal it, that her understanding of the practical and pragmatic—some lucky people called this reality—had overlapped to form a tiny bridge that gave her confirmation of that information. Her arm fell away from the door as she lowered it.

She lifted a hand to touch her familiar and thought better of that. Instead, she called Severn over. She touched his cheek. Severn was alive. If she looked now, she could get lost in the internal details of his body. He suffered from no life-threatening injuries. She lifted her hand from his cheek, breaking that connection, and then gently touched him again. This time, she concentrated on the brief, brief second before she began to look at his physical health.

She exhaled, reclaimed her hand and tried the door again.

"Why are you reaching for the top of the frame? Why not the sides?" Bellusdeo asked.

"Keystones," Kaylin replied.

"There are no keystones here—this is not an arch."

"I know. But…humor me."

The Dragon fell silent, but the rustle of cloth at Kaylin's back implied that she'd folded her arms.

Kaylin touched the height of the door frame as if it were Severn's cheek, but with a lot more fingertip and less palm.

She felt a flicker of something that wasn't quite magic; a tremor.

"We're either going to be in real trouble soon," she told the Dragon grimly, "or there's something in the walls here, too."

"Like what?"

"Never mind. Can you take the entire door frame down?"

The Dragon snorted.

"I mean the way people who can't breathe fire would have to. I have to be able to touch the stone, and I can't if you heat it too much."

"There's a lot of exposed stone in this interminable hallway. You can't touch that instead?"

Kaylin shook her head. "It's the door. I'd be willing to bet on it."

"With your own money?"

"Yes. Lots of."

"Fine. I will remove the door the normal way, regardless of any inefficiency."

It took longer than reducing the door to ash, but she did destroy the central part of the door with fire, weakening its structural stability enough that she could then peel away the frame remaining and toss the wooden bits to the side.

Kaylin lifted her left arm and grimaced; without the frame, it was harder to keep her hand in contact with the building. She wondered if the need to touch was one of the crutches Sanabalis often talked about. Probably.

There. She slowed the point of contact to see it better. Felt the moment when she confirmed the fact that the doorway was not alive.

Felt the disconnect when she realized this was not entirely true. The wooden frame was gone; what she touched now was stone. No. It was like stone; it felt like stone beneath her fingertips. But there was something other about it.

"You know how I said I thought this might be a sentient building?"

No one answered.

"I'm about to test that."

When she tensed her arm again, she saw that the marks across her skin were glowing faintly. The glow was even; all of the visible marks were a pale blue now. No single word seemed to stand out. No mark rose that might accomplish her goal. The goal, however, was clear. She wanted this doorway—absent actual door—to take her to an exit, some way of leaving this endless iteration of the same damn hall.

The stone was alive. Not in the way that she, Severn or Bellusdeo were. Maybe in the same way Helen was. She had never tried to touch Helen in the way she now approached this empty frame.

No, Hope said. *But you have never had the need. Mark this well, Chosen.*

She spoke to the stone through the tips of her fingers. She wasn't certain if she was speaking the words aloud. Probably not. Her thoughts weren't easily poured into actual words, and it was the thought, the intent, the need to leave this space, that she kept at the forefront. But some small contaminant remained: she was trying to communicate with a nebulous something she wasn't even certain existed. She introduced herself, wordless, arm raised, marks glowing.

She listened. If listening took physical effort, she made it—and here, it did.

There was no answer.

"Keep doing what you're doing," Bellusdeo said.

No answer she could hear or grasp, no subvocal communication that flowed into her or through her. She realized she had closed her eyes, and opened them with effort; her eyelids felt as if they weighed as much, individually, as her arms.

What was left of a doorway opened into a hall, which was different. The doors on either side of this single hall—still made of stone, and still shorter in height—had increased in number. There were four doors. They were all closed. There was no door at the end of this hall; there were stairs. Stairs that ascended.

Severn slid past Kaylin and into this new hall; Bellusdeo, after a brief discussion, did the same.

Thank you, Kaylin said in the theory that manners never hurt when dealing with the equivalent of ancient, localized gods. *I'm sorry we broke your doors.*

Severn made no attempt to open the new closed doors, and Kaylin saw why instantly: at least two of those doors had seen use. The knobs retained tarnish and fingerprints. There was dust in this hall, in the corners; the center stretch of floor was clean.

Severn moved the way a cat moves; he was silent but swift. He headed directly for the stairs.

Bellusdeo could not move as quietly; her clothing, if nothing else, didn't allow for it. Her eyes were orange, but it was a gold-orange; she was not afraid of anything that might—just might—inhabit the rooms.

Only when she reached the stairs did Kaylin relax. Relax in this case meant allow different worries to take over. Severn was ahead of her in that regard. He didn't expect trouble, but he wasn't certain where this building was actually located. The eyeball was firmly in the border zone. But the building itself?

It can't be located in the fiefs. I don't think the Towers would accept it.

It could be located in the city beyond the fiefs. Say, in the warrens.

The warrens? No way.

Because?

Because there's a huge chunk of river between here and the warrens. And because a building's power tends to be centered in an actual space.

The jurisdictions of the Towers are the fiefs they stand in.

And Helen can't leave her boundaries. Look—if something has an area of effect that's larger than the Tower of the fief, there's no way it's in the warrens. It's a building.

Did it speak to you?

No.

But it responded to something you did.

Looks like it. She felt uneasy then.

Exactly. Severn picked up on everything. Always had. *Either we're wrong about the sentience, or the building itself was somehow broken in the creation of the fiefs. If we're wrong, and we're not in a sentient building...*

Then I just broke a magical spell of some kind.

Or you used one to force the trap to release us. You only think it's a building because you weren't sick when you passed through the portal, the eye's gaze.

She nodded. *I think it's a building, though. There was something there. Something that wasn't quite in reach—but something that felt like it might be sleeping. And no, I don't want to try to wake it up while we're inside its stomach, relatively speaking.*

The stairs opened up into another hall, which seemed identical to the hall they had just left. There was, however, one long streak, slanted between the two halls, that implied someone had charred the flooring.

"It wasn't me," Bellusdeo said as Kaylin knelt to examine the floor. "I only remove doors. If a floor gives way, it causes more problems than it usually solves."

"You know this from personal experience?"

"I occasionally lost my temper in inconvenient places, yes."

They spoke in low tones; Severn lifted a hand, and they fell silent. In silence, Kaylin could hear the creak of floors. It was a familiar sound, given her old apartment and the new rooms that Helen had created to make Kaylin feel more at home. The older, warped floors meant nothing larger than a rat could sneak up on her, or sneak into her room.

That wasn't going to be an issue, living with Helen—but old habits had kept her alive in places far less safe. She hadn't lost those bitter instincts yet. She wondered if she ever would. If she did, she wondered if she'd regret it. The creaking stopped, but Bellusdeo's tread, no matter how delicate her movements, was never going to be silent. Both Severn and Kaylin could manage it.

Hope, however, squawked. Loudly.

"Will you cut that out?" Kaylin whispered.

He squawked in response. Or rather, not in response. Ever since she had gone into the High Halls with the cohort, she could understand Hope when he was attempting to speak directly to her. His words to anyone else were just as angry—birdlike as they'd always been.

Kaylin glanced at Bellusdeo; the Dragon's eyes were a deep orange now, but her forehead had folded into a frown. It wasn't an expression of annoyance or anger; she was concentrating. Concentration often looked like ill temper to Kaylin.

Severn lifted a hand. Kaylin froze. Bellusdeo was not far behind, but her eyes weren't getting any lighter. She gestured, her brows furrowing; Kaylin's arms tingled. Having received whatever information she sought from the spell, Bellusdeo then moved past where Severn stood at the corner of a wall.

She reached for a weapon she wasn't carrying and exhaled a stream of smoke as she lowered her hand. The weapons that Hawks carried—daggers, sticks—were not, in the Dragon's opinion, weapons at all; Severn carried the weapon chain that the Halls of Law had granted dispensation for when he'd been a Wolf.

The Hawklord had never rescinded it. Neither had Marcus, but the latter was probably because it required paperwork. Kaylin thought if Bellusdeo accidentally sneezed a gout of flame on his paperwork, he might like her a lot more; no one would dress down a Dragon, or rather, no one in the Imperial Court would.

The Hawklord, however, might take a dimmer view.

Bellusdeo didn't slide around the corner; she stepped firmly past it and turned to her left. "Good afternoon," she said, raising her voice until the syllables were underscored by a Draconic rumble. "We appear to be lost."

"You do indeed," an unfamiliar voice replied. "I would consider this a poor choice of hiding place if you wish to remain hidden."

Kaylin stepped in immediately behind the Dragon, because Hope was on her shoulder and his protection against magical attack had a very small radius. She almost called Severn in when she saw the person who addressed Bellusdeo. He was Barrani.

Barrani had strikingly regular features unless they had retained a permanent injury. This man had. It wasn't something as subtle as a chipped tooth, either; he had lost an eye. He right eye socket sat, obviously empty, in the center of a network of scars. Kaylin wondered if that had been the result of Dragon flame. The single eye he possessed was Barrani blue—midnight blue. Bellusdeo's eyes could no longer be seen, because she kept Kaylin behind her.

The Dragon offered the Barrani a nod. He returned it, the

glimmer of a smile changing the shape of his closed mouth. It was brief.

"You are far from home," he said.

"Farther than you could imagine. And you?"

"For the nonce, I am at home. It is convenient. Your presence will likely make it less so."

"If you would care to show us the exit, we will apologize for encroaching—unintentionally—upon your home."

"Ah. And if I do not?"

"The floors are of wood, and this is not a Hallionne."

His brow—his left brow—rose at her use of the word. "How come you to know of the Hallionne?"

"We have always known of them. I have, however, had a recent opportunity to stay as the guest of Hallionne Alsanis."

"Truly?"

Bellusdeo nodded.

"You are well away from your lands, and to travel so—does that mean the war has at long last ended?"

"The wars between our people have ended, at cost to both."

Hope squawked loudly. Both the Barrani and the Dragon ignored him, and he pushed himself off Kaylin's shoulder to hover above them both at the height of the hall.

His squawking grew agitated—or angry. With Hope, it was sometimes hard to tell. The Barrani man did not seem to hear him. Bellusdeo did; she lifted a hand, flattening her palm at right angles to her arm, and Hope landed, still squawking up a storm.

The stranger wasn't deliberately ignoring Hope, as Bellusdeo and Severn had been. The Barrani man frowned as Bellusdeo lifted an arm, and his hands rose to chest height in response. Hope, however, seemed invisible to his remaining eye.

Agree, Severn said. This was probably more bond-talking

than he'd ever done. *Call Hope back. I want you to look at the Barrani through his wing.*

Hope usually slaps me in the face with the wing when he thinks I'm missing something, was Kaylin's doubtful reply.

You just don't want an earful of that squawking.

No kidding. But she was standing within arm's reach of the Dragon, and when she called Hope, he came, huffing in frustration. Kaylin didn't tell him what to do, given the Barrani stranger, but she pointedly indicated her eyes.

Hope landed and thwacked her in the face with his wing. To Kaylin's eyes—beneath Hope's wing—she was looking at a one-eyed Barrani man of average Barrani height. His hair was a drape of black sheen, and everything else about him seemed in the correct place. His clothing was a bit odd—but on some occasions, a bit odd was practically the new normal.

Hope snorted and lowered his wing.

"Have you," the Barrani man was saying to Bellusdeo, "paid the price of passage?"

"I seldom pay a price in ignorance. And even were I to do so in desperation, I am uncertain that the price would be yours."

He laughed, then. He had even, perfect teeth. "Very well, Dragon Queen. I will lead you to an exit while the possibility still exists for you. But you had best be away, and soon."

"Where does the exit lead?" Kaylin dared to ask, as the man turned away.

"Out."

Kaylin didn't expect a Barrani to be true to his word. Not if it weren't signed in blood, or signed in triplicate. But she trusted her ability to find a way out less than she trusted that single word, and even if she hadn't, Bellusdeo had started to follow. While Bellusdeo was tagging along, she was the most important person in any room; the most important in any meeting, and while patrolling any street.

"You live here, right?" Kaylin asked the Barrani man's back.

"Yes."

"Do you have any idea why your house is at least partly attached to the border zone?"

"The border zone? I am afraid I do not understand this term."

"The border zone is what we call the borders between the fiefs."

"Fiefs?"

"How old *are* you?"

Bellusdeo cleared her throat. It was a warning, and as the sound was largely Draconic, no words were necessary.

He ignored this. "How old are you, that you ask?"

"I'm twenty."

"Twenty?"

"Twenty years old."

He did stop, then, turning to look past the Dragon to the private. No, no, the *corporal*. She was corporal now. "Your world changes so swiftly, then. And perhaps that is why you guard your own name so poorly." He held up a hand as if forestalling further comment, but his gaze had moved to the Dragon as he did. "I intend no harm to your young charge."

"I am not her—" Kaylin stopped because Bellusdeo held up the same restraining hand.

"No? But she has the care of you, yes? She is your defense. And it is just and reasonable that it be so: you bear the marks of the Chosen."

The marks were not glowing in any way. But Kaylin had pulled her sleeve back in the reiterating hall below; there was some possibility that he had seen them when she'd done so.

It soured her opinion of him, not that she had much of one to begin with.

Severn joined Kaylin, walking by her side. The hall was too narrow for that to be a good fighting position, but Bellusdeo had chosen, for the moment, not to stand and fight. Probably a good thing, given what she'd said about fires and floors.

The halls themselves were wider than the halls beneath their feet—if that was where those halls even existed.

"It will be some small while yet," the stranger continued. "And perhaps while we walk, you might explain your fiefs and border zones. I understand the general use of all of these words, but you are using them specifically. I find language fascinating," he added.

Kaylin was nonplused.

Bellusdeo nodded, although she didn't bother to look back to see that Kaylin had seen the gesture of permission.

"There are six Towers near here. Or near where we accidentally entered your home."

He nodded. "The six." He then said six things that she assumed were words related to the Towers. She didn't understand them, and he spoke quickly as if he were murmuring to himself.

"The six were created—"

"To enclose *Ravellon*. To defend the rest of the world against what might seep out from within it."

"Okay, so you know that part. People were living in the areas in which the Towers were built. They still live around the Towers. We call those areas the fiefs."

"Why fief, exactly?"

"I don't know—that's what they've always been called." She bit back the frustration that almost pushed ruder words out of her mouth. Even if he was implying—heavily—that she was stupid, the stupid in this case wasn't her fault. The Lords of the High Court referred to them as fiefs. Hells, it was probably a translation of the original Barrani word.

"And the border zone?"

"The fiefs exist around each Tower. Each fief has boundaries or borders, one facing the city, one facing each of the fiefs it borders, and one facing *Ravellon*. The Towers have knowledge of, and power in, their own territories. They have no knowledge of, or power over, other territories.

"In the rest of the city—which is where I live and work—neighborhood borders are theoretical. The only people who care about them are men and women who love paperwork."

"Paperwork?"

Ugh. "Rules. Laws."

"Ah. Continue."

"The borders in the fiefs don't work like the borders anywhere else. When you step across a border you don't immediately enter the next fief. There's a stretch of gray, a band that seems to widen or constrict on its own, between all the fiefs. That zone doesn't seem to include *Ravellon*—at least not from intermittent reports. So...we were attempting to leave one fief—the fief of Tiamaris—to enter its neighbor, the fief of Candallar."

"And you therefore crossed the border."

"Yes."

"And entered the border zone of which you speak."

"Yes."

"And you entered my home from that border zone?"

"We didn't exactly *enter*, but yes. We were drawn into your home, or at least your version of jail, from the border zone between Tiamaris and Candallar."

He was silent, but continued to move, the Hawks and the Dragon in his wake. "I do have a question," she continued when no one else spoke. Hope squawked loudly, which robbed

Kaylin of hearing in one ear, but did not get the attention of the person he was shouting at.

"That wall of yours in the big room—"

"It is not my wall."

"Fine. The wall in the big room to the left of the stairs down. It appears to contain people of various races."

He froze. Severn's hands dropped to weapon hilts.

The man turned, his single eye a narrow slit of blue so dark it was black. "To what do you refer?"

"There's a very, very large stone room. Do you know that room?"

Silence.

"Look, it's either yes or no."

"This is my home, but I am not its master. The room of which you speak, I have not seen."

Hope had had enough, and once again attempted to leave Kaylin's shoulder. She reached up and caught his legs as he spread his wings and inhaled. The sound was very like the sound of Bellusdeo inhaling.

"No, not now!" Kaylin shouted.

Kaylin's shout, unlike Hope's, was perfectly audible. Their guide turned as Kaylin's arm was lifted by Hope. Even at his diminutive size, he had weight and momentum, and she was pulled up until she was balanced on her toes.

"Sorry," she said through clenched teeth, trying to offer what she hoped was a placating smile. "I'm having a minor disagreement with—stop it, Hope!"

The single eye was narrowed, the expression a series of graven lines that made the Barrani face look like chiseled stone.

Hope exhaled a cloud of silver with glinting colored bits contained in the stream. Bellusdeo side-stepped its mass; it was a much larger mass than Hope, at this size, usually emitted.

Kaylin was not in its path; Severn was not in its path.

Only the Barrani who had offered to show them the door—but politely, which was more than most intruders could expect—was. He didn't move. The cloud was part of Hope, and Hope remained invisible to him. Hope's effect on Kaylin was obvious; most people did not dangle on their toes the way she now did. But he couldn't see Hope, and as he stood there frowning, the cloud that was the familiar's version of Dragon breath hit his face and shoulders.

Hope then allowed himself to be returned to Kaylin's shoulders.

"What are you trying to do?" She demanded. "I mean it." It didn't matter if the Barrani thought she was hallucinating—or worse.

He cannot hear me, Hope replied. *What do you think I was trying to do?*

"We don't usually breathe on people's faces so they can *hear us.*"

"My apologies," the Barrani stranger said. From the direction of his gaze, he was now looking at Hope. His face had not melted; his eye had not changed shape, and the color had lightened to a normal Barrani blue.

"We're going to have words about this when we get home."

Hope squawked. Loudly.

"Yes," the man replied. "I apologize for the lack of introduction. I am called Killian when I am required to interact."

Squawk. Squawk.

"I cannot answer your question." His eye narrowed as Hope continued to squawk.

"Can you understand a word he's saying?" Kaylin asked Bellusdeo.

"No." Her eyes were a deeper orange now.

"I have no access to the room you describe. I will not lead

you there. I will show you the exit. I cannot guarantee that you will return to the same physical location you entered."

Everything about this conversation was strange. Given the circumstances, strange was expected, but it was strange on the wrong axis.

The man who had introduced himself as Killian then turned and once again resumed his graceful but unhurried walk.

The way out was six halls and one short flight of stairs away. Kaylin counted. The building was enormous, but oddly narrow. Geography was not her strong point; she navigated by landmarks when she could identify them, by instinctive memory when she couldn't.

But the last hall was wider, and looked like the entrance to an old, well-used building in which one expected guests, or if not guests, visitors. This was not so much a home, in Kaylin's opinion, but...maybe a boarding school? She'd had cause—once—to visit a school meant for adult students. She hadn't been comfortable there. This reminded her of that, except emptied. Although the floors and the carpet runners showed wear, all doors were closed; she could hear no sound of movement, no sound of discussion, outside of their own.

Hope squawked.

"I do not advise you to attempt to return. If you must, I advise you to avoid your previous method of entry. It is not well maintained, and could prove dangerous to your companions."

Kaylin had no desire to set foot in this building again. Killian reached two closed, but much larger, doors. She was surprised to see him move to physically open them. She stepped forward to help, but Hope bit her ear.

"This building was once—long ago—a school. The rooms

we passed were occupied by students; there are rooms you did not encounter that were occupied by teachers."

"Are you the building's sole occupant now?"

"No."

"And we've managed to avoid any of the other occupants?"

"Yes, it is best to avoid them. Some of them will not be pleased to encounter you or learn of your existence." The doors fully open, he stood to the side and offered them a bow.

The doors opened into the washed-out color of the streets of the border zone. The buildings were not the same buildings—there was far more street, for one thing, and fewer smaller buildings that might once have served as homes. She thought the shape of the street directly ahead of these doors could have served as a standing place in front of the Town Hall. Or the Imperial Palace.

She turned back to the door that Killian had not yet closed. "Do these streets always look like this?"

He nodded.

"Which Towers are closest to these doors?"

"Durandel, Aggarok and Karriamis." None were names she recognized. "Be wary. I must close the doors now." And so saying, he did.

The building didn't magically disappear when the doors had been closed. The streets didn't shift. They were in the border zone, between two Towers Kaylin had never heard of. She turned to Severn, raising a brow.

"We're in the border zone of Nightshade, closer to the *Ravellon* edge," Severn replied, although she hadn't actually asked the question.

"So, between Nightshade and Tiamaris?"

"Between Nightshade and Liatt."

"So this building somehow extends—under the ground—between two full fiefs."

"I do not believe it's that simple," Bellusdeo then said, in High Barrani.

"And we're nowhere near Candallar, where we're supposed to investigate."

"Looks like. I highly suggest that we return to the Halls of Law."

"And I," Bellusdeo said, pulling rank—even if she didn't have one, "suggest we repair to the Imperial Palace. We were supposed to consult with the Arkon anyway."

CHAPTER

6

Their exit from the border zone, orientation provided by Severn, took them into the fief of Nightshade in midafternoon. Nightshade was not where Kaylin wanted to be on the best of days. She didn't number the day so far to be among those.

This fief, unlike Tiamaris, radiated the grim despair of the desperate—a reminder of the life she'd had no choice but to lead, and never wanted to return to. But on the plus side, she knew Nightshade fairly well, and leaving it as a Hawk, with a Dragon as a companion, did not present problems, although it did somewhat clear the streets.

Most of the fief dwellers wouldn't recognize Dragons on sight—not unless they were in their scaled, Draconic forms. But they did recognize the Hawk, and Kaylin and Severn were both wearing tabards. It wasn't always safe to attract that kind of attention—but that happened outside of the fiefs, as well.

Given the day, she was almost surprised that Nightshade didn't just materialize on the streets as they made their way out.

I did not know that you would be in my fief until this moment, the fieflord replied.

You didn't know.

No. For some hours, you could not be reached at all. I am accustomed to this; Helen does not often allow communication unless you initiate it. You are not, he added, *with Helen.*

She hadn't noticed, but she hadn't attempted to contact any of the people whose thoughts could reach straight into the inside of her head while she'd been looking for a way out.

Do you recognize the names Durandel, Aggarok and Karriamis?

Had he been present, he would have blinked; she could feel his wordless surprise. *Durandel was the name of the Tower that is now called Castle Nightshade. It is a historical name. I am curious to see what the Arkon makes of it. For that reason, nothing will impede your passage across the Ablayne today. I would, however, appreciate it if Lord Bellusdeo refrained from transforming in my streets. Where there is panic in Nightshade, I prefer it to be orchestrated panic.*

Meaning he caused it.

Your brother would be a lot happier with you if—

My brother has only barely survived being himself. I have survived for centuries without his advice.

Kaylin shut down that line of thought, although it remained behind the words she struggled not to say. Which meant that Nightshade was aware of it anyway.

Candallar, she said, dragging different words and different worries to the forefront.

I understand your concern, given the events you have only recently survived. Nightshade's tone was less glacial. *You will find, however, that few of the fieflords spend the entirety of their existence within the fiefs that bear their names. Each have their own concerns.*

Have you met many of them?

Silence again.

Kaylin gave up.

The Arkon's library—or rather the Imperial Library—was open to the public. Public, in this case, involved a string of permissions that would discourage anyone who didn't like to sign papers in figurative blood—but there were a lot of people who were willing to do that.

During the day, during the hours in which people who were not Dragons were given judicious permission to look at the Imperial collection, the Arkon did not leave his rooms. His rooms were located in the depths of a collection that was never, to Kaylin's knowledge, open to the public.

Kaylin approached a desk so wide it served as a wall between the Imperial librarians and their visitors. Before she could speak, Bellusdeo stepped in front of her. "We are here," she said, "to speak with the Arkon."

The librarians were no more eager to face an irritated Dragon than Kaylin was. "Are you early for your appointment?" the standing librarian asked hopefully. Kaylin would have gotten something far less tentative. Like, *Go away if you don't have an appointment.*

Since the librarian at the desk was senior, he knew damn well that Bellusdeo had no appointment. He also knew that Bellusdeo was a Dragon. "Please wait a moment," he said. "The Arkon is occupied, but I am certain he will remember your appointment."

That said, he called a young woman over. After a short pause, she nodded and left the desk, heading in the direction of the Arkon's personal collection. Bellusdeo turned away from the librarian; she flashed Kaylin a toothy grin. Even in human form, Dragons had impressive canines.

"Are you in a betting mood?" the Dragon asked.

"Please don't ask that here."

"Oh? Why?"

"I don't want to be charged with corrupting public morals."

"I am hardly public."

"You know what I mean."

The grin deepened. "I do. Very well. I suggest that you marshal your curiosity and come up with the questions you wish Lannagaros to answer."

"He won't answer them if I ask."

"That's harsh. He'll answer, but he'll make it clear that you are wasting his time."

"He can make it clear without answering the questions, from prior experience."

"Ah. Well, perhaps it's best that I'm with you, after all."

The Arkon was, of course, available for Bellusdeo's nonexistent appointment. Kaylin wondered if any of the other Lords of the Dragon Court would have received the same treatment. She was pretty certain that the Emperor could march in at his own convenience—but just as certain that he would command the Arkon to attend him first.

The young page who had returned with the Arkon's message—that he was willing to meet with Bellusdeo earlier than the appointed time—led them to the Arkon. Or tried. Bellusdeo, somewhat impatient, said, "We know the way," and sent the young woman back to the desk.

She hesitated, but Bellusdeo was a Dragon. The young woman was a librarian, probably in training. Angering her boss was career-limiting. But breaking protocol, while frowned on, was acceptable if the Arkon was amenable. Kaylin hoped that the senior librarian in command of that long desk would make it clear to her.

Either way, it wasn't Kaylin's problem.

The Arkon was not in the room that had walls for doors. Those walls would open and close only at the Arkon's command. No, today he had either abandoned those rooms or was confronting paperwork that did not require heavy magical "precautions," as he called them.

He was at a normal, boring desk when Bellusdeo walked in. He stood immediately, his expression making clear that knocking should never be optional.

"What brings you to the library? I've taken the liberty of calling for refreshments if that is acceptable to you."

"It is not only acceptable; it is almost shocking. It makes me feel quite welcome here."

Kaylin wondered, glumly, if refreshments had also been arranged for the two Hawks.

"To answer your question, however, I have something of yours I wish to return." She then opened the flap of her satchel and removed a small cloth bag.

The Arkon's eyes narrowed, but even narrowed it was clear they were now a bright orange. He held out a hand, and Bellusdeo placed the bag in his palm. His fingers closed around it in a death grip that whitened his knuckles. "You carried them in your...pouch."

"It seemed the most convenient way to transport them, yes."

"In your unenchanted pouch."

"Yes."

"While you went on patrol with the private—"

"Corporal," Kaylin said.

He glanced at her as if seeing her for the first time. "Ah. I see that you have earned yourself a promotion. My apologies. Now *be quiet.*" When Kaylin's jaw snapped shut, he continued. "You went on patrol with the corporals while carrying these?"

Bellusdeo's eyes remained a solid, warm gold. "I did. Lannagaros, they were worn in the presence of the Barrani Consort to the High Lord. I fail to see how wandering about the mortal streets of this city could be more dangerous."

Kaylin began to study the tops of her boots as if they were the most fascinating thing she had ever seen.

"You are well aware that I am extremely fond of you," the Arkon replied. "But even my affection has limits. You went on patrol with Corporal Neya while carrying irreplaceable artifacts. Corporal Neya, who has managed—without intent—to cause more trouble than people who have planned trouble for decades."

"That is a tad harsh," Bellusdeo replied.

"Truth often is." His eyes remained orange, but moving toward the happy gold and not the dangerous red. "I am not comforted. If you are here on a normal day for the two Hawks, you are here because something untoward occurred. While you were carrying these."

"I was perfectly willing not to wear them at all," Bellusdeo replied, more edge in her tone.

"Indeed." The Arkon rose at a knock on the door—the open door. "Refreshments have arrived. We will not eat them in this room; it is already overcrowded."

"If you tended to your uninteresting responsibilities with more deliberate care, it wouldn't be. Your desk is almost as much of a disaster as Sergeant Kassan's."

The room in which refreshments were served reminded Kaylin of Helen's parlor, although everything about it was different. The chairs, the tables, the sideboard, the cabinets, had been chosen by someone who was not Helen, and it showed. Still, the chairs were comfortable.

Severn chose to stand.

Kaylin eyed the food and then eyed Bellusdeo's raised brow. She sat. The Arkon was willing to preserve the distance between him and Kaylin if it protected his precious private time; he was not willing to do it if it irritated Bellusdeo.

The Arkon drank tea but did not otherwise touch the food. Bellusdeo did, but delicately. Kaylin, however, was hungry. Hunger warred with dignity and won. It wasn't even a close contest.

"We encountered something interesting in the fiefs," Bellusdeo said while Kaylin's mouth was full.

"The fiefs."

"Indeed."

"You took these medallions to the fiefs."

"If you continue, Lannagaros, you will not hear about the interesting parts."

"I am not sure that this room—or its furnishings—will survive the interesting parts. Corporal Neya, were you aware of what she carried?"

Kaylin shook her head, swallowing to empty her mouth.

"Very well. The fiefs. Do continue."

"We went to Tiamaris at the behest of the Halls of Law. Indirectly. Kaylin has been tasked with investigating Candallar."

The Arkon nodded.

"I wished to see the border zone. To the eye, the borders in the fiefs are no more solid, no more real, than the borders between neighborhoods in the city, if one discounts legality. But the attempt to cross the borders that divide the fiefs is nowhere near as seamless."

"Tiamaris made a study of the fiefs, inasmuch as such a study has been made by our kin. He has continued his studies within the fief he now rules, but he has been encumbered with the responsibilities of ruling. The information we have about those borders is largely due to Tiamaris. You are aware that the streets within the border are not fixed in location?" The Arkon's voice was controlled.

"Are they not?" This was a weasel answer. She did know.

"I am certain that Tiamaris's Tower would be more than

willing to provide you with the relevant information. What did you find in the attempt to cross the border into Candallar?"

Bellusdeo leaned forward. "A building of interest. While the buildings within the border zone appear to be of similar make—and quality—as the rest of the fief, this one appeared to be in excellent repair."

The Arkon nodded, his eyes orange-gold. His left hand rested against his beard.

"It had no door, no windows; we assumed it was a two-story structure, given the height of the external walls."

"It was not? Don't make that face, Corporal. It's obvious that you somehow managed to gain entry into the building with no obvious entrances."

Bellusdeo chuckled. "The entrance was not planned. It was not intended. We gained entry because there was, for want of a better word, a stone eye—larger than your head—carved in relief on the side of the building opposite the street. When it moved its gaze to us, we were transported to the interior."

"A portal?"

"That appeared to be its function, yes. Kaylin is concerned, however."

The Arkon's expression became immediately less friendly. "Corporal?" In spite of the tone in which it was delivered, she felt immediately buoyed by her new rank. She tried not to let this show.

Impossible for you, Ynpharion said. He had been quiet enough lately Kaylin had managed to forget his annoying condescension.

"It was like a portal to Bellusdeo. She has no problems with normal portals." She grudged the use of the word *normal* in this context. "Portals from one place to another generally make me physically ill. This one…didn't. And the only place that's generally been true are in the sentient buildings. The Hallionne. Helen."

"You feel the difference is the location?"

"Portals within one part of a building to another are all in the same place. This one felt like that to me."

"You went from the outside to the inside in this fashion?" He glanced at Bellusdeo, whose nod was apparently worth far more than Kaylin's words. "You feel that you did not leave the outside."

"It would explain the state of the pristine building. If we had somehow stepped into territory or land that was part of a building's domain, I wouldn't feel the transition the same way I normally do."

"You came across this building in the border zone."

"Yes."

"Why are you certain it has sentience?"

She hesitated. Bellusdeo, however, did not. The Dragon proceeded to recount their adventures there. The Arkon's eyes shaded to orange when she spoke both of the wall that no one but Kaylin—with Hope's help—could see, and the overlap, or suspected overlap, with Missing Persons' reports. She skipped the parts in which she'd burned down doors.

If you wish to control the narrative, Ynpharion said, *you would do best to speak first.*

Says the man who isn't standing in front of two Dragons who breathe fire when they're cranky.

They would hardly breathe fire on you.

You know that I can be critical of myself without your help, right?

Yes. But you generally choose to fret about the wrong *things.*

"Corporal?"

"Uh, sorry. I was thinking."

"A change that we all welcome, I am certain."

"When I tried to change where the door led us, I touched the building. I tried to ask it to take us someplace else."

The Arkon pinched the bridge of his nose. "That is not specific."

"No. I didn't get an answer. The Hallionne and Helen would know what I wanted without the need to...reach out. But the door did lead to a different hall after I tried. And this hall looked occupied, or recently occupied, so someone heard me."

"You are certain that this change was in response to your attempt to communicate? You are certain you did not unintentionally utilize the powers granted the Chosen to move yourselves there?"

Was she? She frowned. "I shouldn't be, but...yes."

"I assume there is a reason for that."

Exhaling, she said, "The Barrani man who claimed not to be lord or master of the building—I think he said it used to be a school?—had only one eye; the other was an empty socket. It wouldn't fit an eye the size of the one on the back wall of the initial building we discovered—but. Eye.

"Second, the man did lead us to an exit, and while we were walking, he called me by name."

The silence in the room was sudden and glacial. The Arkon turned very orange eyes on Bellusdeo; she shrugged. "She doesn't have a name in any true sense."

"How, exactly, did a stranger who claims he is not in command of the space discover your name?"

"I may have introduced myself when I said thank you to what was left of the doorway. I don't think I said it out loud."

"You may have introduced yourself."

"I—wasn't certain that anything could hear me, but I figured it couldn't hurt to be polite. We'd already burned down a— Never mind."

"Do continue."

"It is irrelevant," Bellusdeo said.

"But either someone heard me and passed it on, or some part of the building's sentience still exists." She exhaled. "The wall—the wall that we first saw—might be composed of actual living people. There were Barrani there as well, but much farther back. We don't study esoteric magic or sorcery in practical classes—we leave that for the academics. But I've seen people who have been turned to stone before. In Castle Nightshade.

"I assumed that was Nightshade's power. But now I think it's the Tower's. And I think this building might have somehow trapped the people I could see, with Hope's help, in that stone wall. I mean, it could have been an Arcanist—but there's no appearance of sigils, no magical traces, left behind. Just a blank stone wall, unless you look through Hope's wing.

"Oh, and one other thing, but this isn't building related."

"Please continue."

"The Barrani man we interrupted—who called himself Killian—couldn't see or hear Hope."

"Killian?"

Bellusdeo frowned; there was an edge of disbelief in the Arkon's voice. "You are *certain*?"

"Pretty certain, but—"

"*I* am certain, Lannagaros."

He opened his mouth. Closed it again. "This Barrani couldn't see your familiar?"

"Hope was squawking his lungs out. Killian couldn't hear him at all. Not until Hope got fed up and breathed on him."

This caused a shift in the shape of the Arkon's eyes. "You let him breathe on someone. You *let him breathe* on another living being? One who was not attempting to kill you?"

"I did try to stop him. And in our defense, it didn't seem to harm Killian at all; it just allowed him to see Hope."

Without warning, the Arkon turned on Hope—which was very much like turning on Kaylin, given Hope's placement. He then let loose a volley of his native tongue.

Kaylin's teeth were chattering by the time he stopped.

"Lannagaros, I feel that is harsh."

"Perhaps. But the person who will pay the price for the familiar's misbehavior will not be you. It will be Kaylin."

Hope didn't seem to feel terribly chastised. Kaylin did. And hard of hearing until the aftershocks of the Arkon's lecture had passed. When she could be certain her voice wouldn't come out as a shout because she was overcompensating, she said, "This isn't even the reason why we came to talk to you. We're hoping to find out whether or not your archives contain information pertinent to our investigation."

A white brow disappeared into a silver hairline.

"Do you recognize the names *Durandel*, *Aggarok* or *Karriamis*?"

The Arkon did not immediately answer. Instead, he rose from his chair. "Come."

Bellusdeo frowned at his passing back, but fell in behind him; Severn and Kaylin took the rear.

"Touch nothing," the Arkon said, the words floating over his shoulder.

When Kaylin failed to respond, he did turn. "Recall what happened on a prior visit, Corporal. It is a command, not a request. I have had a trying day, and it does not appear to be nearing its end soon."

She nodded.

"You will either keep control of your familiar or have him wait outside. And by outside I mean outside of the library."

Hope squawked.

"I disagree. It is the consequence of your actions. Or perhaps a consequence of your Chosen." He turned again.

"Don't look at me like that," Kaylin told the familiar.

I knew what I was doing.

"You could have explained it so the rest of us understood."

It would take far too long.

The Arkon did not ask Kaylin to touch the door ward that led to his personal, private, touch-it-and-die collection. Normally, Kaylin would consider this a mercy or a kindness; his expression today made clear that he didn't trust her to touch even a door ward without causing problems.

The Arkon's warning aside, there was little—beside wall and doorway—that Kaylin could touch. Nothing seemed to catch Hope's eye. Although there were display cases and glass-fronted cabinets, all of which caused a ripple of magical discomfort across Kaylin's skin, nothing was within easy reach. This room, which was quite large, was a simple path to the next, as was the next room.

But even the room in which ancient scrolls, remnants of armor and weapons, and gods only knew what else, were housed was not the Arkon's destination.

She knew where he was going.

"Why did you ask about those names?"

"Because Killian mentioned them as Tower names. I don't think they've ever been called by those names—but I've only had access to Records in the Halls of Law for a few years. Nightshade has always been called Nightshade, in the living memory of anyone in the fief."

"The living memory of mortals is dim, and much history is lost to the narratives that supplant it, generation to generation."

"Not all of the fieflings are mortal."

"No. But I imagine there are very few who speak for long with the fieflords who are not."

The faint hope that her guess about the Arkon's destination was wrong was squashed when they arrived at a large wooden door. Three metal bands ran across it, and three locks waited for the Arkon's keys. On the positive side, there was no magic on this door; there were no wards. On the negative side, beyond this door was a narrow stone hall that descended toward a cavern.

The Arkon handed them lamps, which he lit by breathing on their wicks. Bellusdeo looked at them as if they were dead rats.

"You will not introduce magic into the hall beyond this door," the Arkon told her as he held the lamp out.

"Not even simple illumination?"

"Nothing at all. The wards that protect this area are easily provoked, but I consider them necessary."

Bellusdeo took the lantern but glared at the Arkon's back as he drew three keys in succession from the chain he wore around his neck. He opened the door.

Kaylin had had enough of caverns beneath fancy buildings to last at least two lifetimes. The Arkon didn't care what she'd had enough of, and at least this time, they weren't here to study—in person—the marks of the Chosen that adorned her body. She flinched, remembering that last time he'd ordered her to strip.

Then again, Dragons in their Draconic form were always naked; nudity didn't discomfit them in either form.

"I feel that these halls could do with excavation or modernization."

The Arkon exhaled smoke, with a tiny bit of fire at its heart.

"...I see," Bellusdeo replied. "But I find the height of these ceilings oppressive. The only person who can walk here with any ease is Kaylin."

"If I am content to walk with a stoop, I see no problem."

Bellusdeo glanced up at the ceiling, which was admittedly not far from her.

They reached the last door, which was not as impressive as the first one, and the Arkon opened it into, yes, darkness.

Bellusdeo was not more impressed with the cavern than she had been with the hall that led to it, but she understood, as her eyes hit the central piece it contained, why any other interior renovation suggestions would be met with the Arkon's lack of humor.

"An altar," the gold Dragon said. "It's...impressively large."

"It is. I will now ask you to go to the far wall—to your right—and retrieve the ladders there. We will need two unless you wish to see what lies at the top of the altar, in which case we will need three."

Bellusdeo wasn't often sent on strictly manual errands but obeyed. Kaylin could hear the ladders as they dragged across the stone of the floor. She'd never tried to move them herself; she suspected they weighed as much as she herself did.

"You could at least get ladders that are somewhat easier to move."

"I did not intend to have visitors."

To Kaylin's surprise, Bellusdeo didn't ask what was atop the altar. She assumed that the use of ladders would answer that question. "I don't suppose shedding clothing and this somewhat diminutive form would be acceptable?"

"Since you have already done so once today—yes, we were

aware of it—I fail to see why it would be necessary that you do so again." Which was no.

Given the color of Bellusdeo's eyes in this admittedly poorly lit space, it was clear that she'd expected the answer she received. She then positioned two of the ladders, leaving the Arkon to manage his own. The Arkon glanced briefly at a ceiling Kaylin's eyes couldn't see; it was a look that would have been at home on Marcus's face, in the office. And sadly, usually was.

The Arkon then reached the top of the altar, joining the Dragon and the Hawk; Severn neither asked for a ladder nor expressed an interest in seeing what the altar contained.

Bellusdeo, however, drew breath. "This is a mirror."

"It is an ancient mirror, yes."

"Tara's version of a mirror appears to be similar to this— and she doesn't require an ancient cavern and a hall that is meant for—"

"Me," Kaylin said quickly; the Arkon's eyes were a shade of orange that Bellusdeo didn't generally cause.

"Records," Bellusdeo said. She spoke in Elantran, and followed it with Barrani. Kaylin had enough time to cover her ears before she tried it a third time in her native tongue.

The Arkon waited until the echoes had died out—which, given they were in a cavern, took a while. "If you will allow me. The mirror is old. It requires a specific language."

"You might have warned me."

"You might have listened, but my experience has taught me better. I am too old to waste breath."

"You are wasting it now."

Kaylin thought it, but could not be paid enough to say it out loud.

The Arkon exhaled smoke. "Perhaps. I will need to concentrate. I am speaking in the old tongue."

Bellusdeo's eyes widened, but she fell silent and stayed that way.

Kaylin had come to understand that the old tongue and true words were almost the same. The Arkon found them difficult to speak—but he had an easier time than Kaylin, who spoke them only with prompting and coaching by others. Languages had been one of the few so-called academic subjects in which she'd been any good—but no basic classes of any kind taught true words.

The Arkon spoke, and as he uttered each syllable, Kaylin saw a golden rune begin to take shape in the air above the still, almost clear, water. She had seen it once, or something like it, the only other time she'd been brought to this cavern.

"We don't have the information in basic Records anywhere?" Bellusdeo nudged her gently. Kaylin, however, persisted. "This is about the Towers in the fiefs, right?"

The Arkon finished speaking, and the rune speech had produced, glowing brightly in the poor light, began to revolve in the air. Bellusdeo didn't seem to see the word the way Kaylin did, but she did see the marks on Kaylin's arms begin to glow, as if in sympathy. Or resonance. It didn't hurt, and the marks stayed where they were, beneath a layer of shirt.

"I will excuse you your infernal impatience," the older Dragon said as the word his speech had brought into being began its slow descent into the liquid the altar contained. "Because you have so little natural time. No, Corporal, this is not about the Towers in the fiefs. I'm certain you could just ask the Barrani."

"They don't generally answer."

"You are not offering them the right incentives."

"I can't fly, breathe fire or otherwise easily kill them, no."

The Arkon snorted. "The names you have mentioned are, I believe, the names the Towers were given when they were first created. But the name of Towers change. The Towers are not the Hallionne, although the Hallionne have similar function with regards to Shadow and its contaminant.

"Shadow is flexible. The form and shape it might take could not easily be predicted. Ah, no. The knowledge of future forms and shapes could not be predicted. The Hallionne have no masters. The Towers, however, do. The reason for that difference lies entirely in Shadow and its lack of predictability. The living lords are meant to inform and update the Towers so that knowledge is gained and understanding remains firmly wed to the present.

"But the lords of the Towers are not meant to exercise that control to the benefit of Shadow. There are, therefore, some lines that cannot be crossed; the base internal structure of the Tower will not permit it. You housed Gilbert."

"Not housed, exactly."

"The Towers could not, no matter the desire of their lords."

"Helen's not a Tower."

"No. But in my opinion, Helen is unique. She desired self-determination, had the will to destroy those parts of herself that prevented it, and did not manage to destroy the parts necessary for her to become the home that she now is. What she now provides for you—and by extension, your guests—was not what she was created to provide; it lacks ambition."

"I don't know, Lannagaros," Bellusdeo said. "I consider it beyond ambitious, given the difficulties Kaylin stumbles into on a constant basis. And in my experience, a happy, safe home *is* a daydream. It's an idle wish, an impossible yearning."

The Arkon's gaze had moved to Bellusdeo, and the gold of his eyes dimmed. The inner membrane rose, muting the color even further.

"If a Tower or a Hallionne could grant that wish, could maintain it in the face of the truth of the rest of the world, I would think it a grand design on the part of the Ancients. She could house my people. Maggaron is happy with his rooms—happy enough he almost never leaves them."

The Arkon bowed his head; his hand touched his beard. It was almost as if he were offering respect for the dead and the lost.

"That's unfair. He left them today," Kaylin said.

"Yes, true. But he is not what he was and I am not what I was; I think he feels at a loss. I should return him to the *Norannir.*"

"I don't think that's what he wants."

"Sometimes what we want isn't what we need." Bellusdeo shook herself. "My apologies. I did not mean to interrupt, and these ladders are not particularly comfortable."

"I should have my beard singed off for this," the Arkon replied—in Elantran. "You may, with my permission, forgo the ladder; try not to destroy the dress in the process; the Emperor is always uncomfortable with the armor in the open streets."

It took Kaylin a moment to fully understand that the Arkon was giving Bellusdeo permission to transform. There was certainly enough room for it, given that this was a cavern.

Bellusdeo hesitated for one long breath, and then leaped off the ladder, landing heavily enough to cause a tremor. She then disrobed; Kaylin turned away from her as she transformed. She'd seen it often enough that it shouldn't have been disturbing to watch, but it was; there was something about watching flesh melt that was always going to be a bit uncomfortable.

Bellusdeo returned to the altar. Or rather, the altar side. She could now look down on the surface of the mirror without effort.

Hope squawked at her.

She roared back.

The Arkon roared, as well.

Kaylin wished she were at her unambitious home, where Helen could mute conversational Dragons. "Records," she said. The surface of this gold-tinged mirror began to glitter. "If it's all right with you," she added to the Arkon, "the mirror will respond to me when I speak at the volume my ears were made for. You have to speak in your native tongue, and...I'd really, really appreciate it if you told me what you wanted to know and let me ask."

Bellusdeo chuckled. The Arkon did not. He did, however, nod. "We wish to know about the creation of the Towers."

Kaylin exhaled. To the mirror, to the swirling, moving water, she said, "Killian. Helen."

"Helen's name is not a name that should exist within these Records."

"No. I'm testing a theory."

CHAPTER 7

"Not smart," Bellusdeo rumbled.

Kaylin looked up and met the Arkon's eyes. "Sorry. I should have asked first."

"Continue."

"Groveling?"

"Explaining yourself."

The mirror, however, was now shimmering in place. The liquid was affected by a tremor that touched nothing else. As she watched, her attention split between annoyed Dragon and ancient Records, the liquid itself rose, as if it were elemental water.

A sculpture emerged as bits of the water fell; in the end, what was left was a building. No, Kaylin thought. Two buildings. Three. Four. One of these, she was certain, was Helen. No. It was what Helen had been on the eve of her creation. Kaylin couldn't tell which of the four was meant to be the building she now called home. Nor was she certain that one of the other three was the building that Killian called home.

The Arkon's eyes were a less deep orange; he lowered his inner membranes, his frown becoming one of concentration, rather than annoyance at the presumption of a lowly Hawk.

"Your theory, Corporal?"

"That the mirror responds not to the commands, but the person who is making them."

"You will not test your theories in the future without explaining them and receiving the requisite permission."

"The Towers were created after *Ravellon* fell, right? But there were buildings that were created before that fall. The Hallionne, for one. Helen. I want to see the buildings that existed in what eventually became Elantra, because buildings don't—in theory—have the ability to move."

The Arkon nodded.

"You've seen this before."

"Many, many times." The words were almost bitter.

"Do you know which one is Helen?"

"Ask the mirror to separate the buildings by geography. I can—with difficulty—command Imperial Records to overlay the boundaries of Elantra as it is currently constituted over it."

With difficulty meant a lot of spoken Dragon. Kaylin grimaced. "I'm not sure that's necessary," she said far too quickly.

He stared at her, unblinking.

"...but it could be helpful."

He then continued in his native tongue. There was a moment of serious dislocation; the water shuddered so violently in place, Kaylin wasn't certain it wouldn't explode outward—which would have been a career-limiting disaster of the worst kind given the Arkon, his hoard, and the fact that she would be tangentially related to the damage.

She exhaled only when the shaking stopped. The water sculptures then shrank, separating as a faint map of the city of Elantra came into view. It was, unlike the buildings, flat; it was difficult to read. If she hadn't been familiar with maps, and with this one in particular because it related to work, she wouldn't have been able to read it at all.

"Couldn't you do it in reverse?" When the Arkon failed to answer, she added, "Take the contents of this mirror and append them to Imperial Records?"

"Ask your Helen, when you return home, why I have made the decision not to do so." *And don't*, his curt tone implied, *bother the Arkon*. "This," he added, indicating one building, "is where your Helen now stands."

The building looked nothing at all like Helen. It looked far more like a Tower, and at that, an unfriendly one. It was situated in the center of a much larger patch of land than Helen currently occupied. Helen could—and did—change her appearance to better suit her inhabitants. But it was a pretty drastic change, in Kaylin's opinion. This building looked impressive and forbidding.

It was not Helen that she was interested in, or not immediately.

She looked across the city. There were three other buildings, distinct from Helen. Outside of the fiefs, Helen was, or had been, the only sentient building of which she'd been aware. Ah, no. There.

She recognized the old High Halls. It looked remarkably like the new High Halls; the period between creation and... repair...had been erased. That was two.

The Imperial Palace was not a sentient building. Kaylin sort of understood why. If a building like Helen existed, and the Imperial Palace could have been constructed around it, the Emperor was not the man to let anything else make decisions for him. Not when there were no effective remedies or consequences for the wrong ones.

There were two buildings left, but she focused on only one of them: it seemed to be in the center of the city. Near, if not in, *Ravellon*; the map itself was not large, and the building had not been created with scale in mind.

"This one," she said.

Three other buildings, including her own home, melted into liquid and vanished. The fourth remained.

Unlike Helen, this building didn't radiate doom on the surface. It appeared to be similar to what the High Halls had been prior to the repair of its central sentience. It was large—how large was hard to assess, given the lack of actual scale—and she remembered that Killian had said it had once been a school.

What kind of school would it have been? What would classes taught by something that could literally change the environment of its students on a whim have been like?

"Lannagaros?" Bellusdeo rumbled, concern in her voice.

"It is nothing. Continue, Corporal."

"I think this is the building we were in."

"You said that the building appeared to extend from the border zone between Tiamaris, to the one between Nightshade and Liatt." The Arkon's expression was now composed of chiseled lines.

Kaylin nodded.

"I do not believe that this building would cover that distance."

"Not outside of the border zone, no."

"The border zone itself is comprised of a space between the territories of each Tower. Those border areas do not, in theory, extend across fiefs in a fashion that renders the fiefs irrelevant, invisible."

"Fine. But this building—I think it was *in* the border zone when the Towers were created." As she spoke, the faint, flat map of the modern city faded into invisibility. The landscape changed abruptly, although some of the streets were old enough that she almost recognized the direction they traveled, the shape they retained, even now. The map that emerged from the heart of this mirror was foreign in most ways, a strong reminder that history was a different country, a different place.

The center of this map was not *Ravellon* as it existed now. The fiefs were not the fiefs. Those who had lived near the center of this foreign city lived in larger buildings; there was greenery here, and a sense of wealth. The smaller buildings existed, as well; it was almost as if the people who lived in this place before the fall of *Ravellon* had desired to be as close to *Ravellon* has possible, and had packed themselves into the various spaces accordingly.

In this context, the building was no longer its symbolic size; it was nestled in a large patch of otherwise unoccupied land.

"What happened?" she whispered.

"Pardon?"

"What happened in *Ravellon* that things changed so much?"

"I would not ask that question if you do not wish to stand on that ladder for the next eight hours."

"Give me the short version."

"The short version? We don't know. Some entity that made *Ravellon* its home fell, and *Ravellon* with it. There was no armed insurrection; no actual combat. Something changed. The change was slow and subtle at its beginning, and therefore hard to see; it was not so subtle at the end.

"But there was warning enough that the Towers could be built." As the Arkon spoke, the area that was now *Ravellon* darkened; the buildings and streets that led to it vanished from view. A visual barrier of dark shadow spread from a point in the center of the map to the edges of the lands it now occupied.

"I thought you couldn't speak to the mirror if you weren't speaking in your native tongue."

"I am not speaking to the mirror. You are."

"I didn't ask it for Towers. Or *Ravellon*."

"Not consciously, no. I find this both interesting and disturbing."

"Can we just stay on the interesting side of that equation?"

He snorted smoke.

Towers grew as the shadow spread. Kaylin had no sense of time passing; it was her private opinion that she, and people like her, would never have noticed the "fall" that was so catastrophic; they'd be born and they'd die before it finally became what it now was.

Either that, or the Towers had been constructed in a day. Given they were created by the Ancients, that was possible.

Yes.

Kaylin didn't recognize the voice. She shook her head, as if to dislodge all the other familiar voices that could intrude at any moment. She didn't hear it again.

The Towers grew; the buildings around them were abandoned by those who had either the desire or the ability to move. The land surrounding the six Towers took on a tinge of color; six different colors in all. There was no overlap.

She watched the sentient building that had once stood so close to *Ravellon*. It faded slowly from view. It wasn't, like the other buildings, abandoned. It was bisected by two of the Towers, its land absorbed on either side by what would now be Nightshade and Liatt, the latter a fief that Kaylin had never seen except on maps like these.

The building itself vanished, crumbling into mist and nothing as Kaylin watched.

"What are the border zones?"

No answer, no new image, no new words from an unfamiliar voice, came to answer that question.

The Arkon cleared his throat, which gave Kaylin enough time to cover her ears.

The map of the fiefs and the Towers sank, once again, into

liquid. The Arkon spoke, and spoke again; the mirror failed to respond. Or it responded in a fashion that she couldn't see; with this mirror that was possible.

The Arkon did not speak again until they had trudged back through the cavern, the doors, the narrow short hall, and the various private areas. They were surrounded by the office again when he at last spoke.

"The lands that surrounded *Ravellon* were contaminated by the will of the ruler of *Ravellon*; their existence as 'normal' lands had been heavily compromised. This would include the building nearest *Ravellon*. The Towers were created to anchor those lands, to return them to a base state that those who dwelled in them would recognize, and that Shadow could not as easily manipulate."

"Corporal Handred?"

Severn, who had said almost nothing since their arrival, nodded. "I concur. I have crossed the borders between many of the fiefs. They are not fixed; they appear so, from the outside, and when one emerges, the streets are very much the streets that would be expected between one step and the next. But the internals shift, sometimes dramatically, sometimes more subtly, when one has taken that step. If the Towers served as anchors for the lands that surrounded *Ravellon*, this would make some sense."

"And the building you discovered today?"

"The exit, and the building itself, seemed in keeping with the building Kaylin saw in her initial view of the pre-fief period."

The Arkon didn't ask Severn how he knew what Kaylin had seen, and Kaylin didn't bother to explain it. She was a bit surprised because Severn almost never acknowledged the actual connection.

"The placement of the exit was also in keeping with that vision. When I crossed that border, however, I did not see the building in question. I either crossed in a different place—"

"Given the size of the former building's lands, it would be difficult to miss," the Arkon countered.

Severn nodded. "Or other forces are at work within the border. I'm inclined to assume the latter."

"Do you also agree with Corporal Neya's conclusions?"

"It would not have been my initial guess, but...yes. If Kaylin believes that the Barrani man we met in the building was somehow the Avatar of the building itself, I would give that belief strong weight."

"Bellusdeo?"

She shrugged, the fief shrug that the rest of the cohort had taken up almost upon their arrival beneath Helen's roof. "I have far less experience with sentient buildings than any of you. But given their creators, I would guess that destroying them would be difficult if the creators themselves were not responsible for that destruction.

"The building clearly fell off the map that Kaylin's words invoked when the Towers rose. If it is indeed the same building, the permeability of the border zone might explain how we entered it at all."

"You don't believe that."

"No, sadly, I don't. I do, however, believe that Kaylin is materially correct. We were in that building. The building itself somehow survived the fall of *Ravellon* and the creation of the Towers; it surrendered its hold on the lands that it had once stewarded." She frowned.

So did Kaylin; the expressions were almost a mirror image. "If the lands, if the composition of the lands, changed— were changed—by Shadow or the fall of *Ravellon*, those lands wouldn't be the lands the Towers now hold, would they?"

"That, I believe, is an excellent question," the Arkon replied. Since Kaylin had asked it, he even nodded in her direction. "If it is necessary for you to return, make an appointment." He then turned his back and headed toward his desk.

It took Kaylin a moment to realize they were all being dismissed. Bellusdeo, however, snorted. "You have not changed at all, Lannagaros."

"You're worried about the Arkon," Kaylin said on the drive home, carriage provided by the palace.

Bellusdeo nodded, although she continued to stare out the open window, as if hoping something would distract her. "He was not himself."

"You said he never changes, and he seemed pretty normal to me."

"He failed to ask real questions," said the person who wasn't being grilled. "He seemed tense. I feel something is off, something is wrong."

Kaylin glanced at the Dragon and understood. The Arkon was the only remaining friend from a distant, distant childhood. "Given our luck, we'll find out what it is soon."

Helen was at the open doors when Kaylin entered the grounds. With her came Bellusdeo; Severn returned to the Halls of Law to make his report. Kaylin was grateful that he was willing to do it. Of all Hawk activities, the writing of reports was the one she still hated most. Especially given the joy with which their sergeant received them.

Keep an ear out, Kaylin told him.

I will. I want to pay a visit to Missing Persons. He was silent for one long moment and then said, *Yes, I saw what you saw.*

And you have a better memory for faces.

She felt his nod, but whatever she'd meant to say in response withered as she caught sight of Helen's face. The eyes of her home's Avatar were obsidian, and this was never a good sign.

Bellusdeo noticed, as well; the Dragon's eyes darkened to an orange that implied martial caution. At least Helen wasn't wearing armor. She looked like her usual gentle, maternal self if one didn't look at her eyes.

"Where," Helen said, dispensing with the usual *welcome home* that characterized her, "did you meet Killianas?"

Kaylin blinked. "You mean Killian?"

Helen stepped into the house to allow both Kaylin and Bellusdeo to enter. She then shut the door—a little more firmly than necessary—and exhaled sound. The sound had syllables in it, but also the roaring of ocean, the crash of lightning that followed the rumble of thunder, the crackle of fire as it devoured wood.

Bellusdeo waited, an almost bored expression transforming her features; the color of her eyes remained orange.

"What's happening?" Mandoran said from the height of the stairs that led to the foyer, and therefore, the door.

"I am trying," Helen said without looking up, "to find the right words to express a phrase."

"I don't think that's working out well for you." Mandoran descended the stairs.

"Did you understand it?" Bellusdeo asked.

"Not well, no. Serralyn thinks she might understand the gist of it."

"Pardon?"

"She was always good with language, in the old days." He reached the ground. Helen had fallen silent and seemed slightly pinker than usual. "Where did you guys go, anyway? Helen's not happy."

"You think?"

Bellusdeo snorted smoke. "We attempted to reach the fief of Candallar by crossing the border of Tiamaris. I believe it was meant to be a shortcut. It was not particularly short."

"What happened?"

Helen steered them to the dining room. Although the parlor existed, Kaylin was never entirely comfortable using it; that was a room meant for visitors who were above her pay grade and needed to be impressed somehow. The dining room could double as a mess hall, and given the cohort these days, it usually did. Although Helen tended to change the furniture when important guests visited, she didn't attempt to maintain it that way when they left.

The parlor, however, was always stuffy and fancy.

Helen could, and did, pick information from Kaylin's thoughts as she walked the stretch of hall that led to the comfortable common room. Hope was slumped across her shoulder, looking bored. Boredom apparently afflicted anything immortal.

They took their usual seats, although Teela came down to join them, her eyes a shade of midnight. Mandoran glanced at her, grimaced, and dropped his head to the tabletop. Repeatedly.

"If you don't want her to help you with that," Kaylin told him as she took her own chair, "I'd suggest you stop right now."

"Teela's in a foul mood."

Of course she was. Severn, Kaylin and Bellusdeo had gone to the fiefs *as* Hawks. Since Bellusdeo was a Dragon, Kaylin privately felt they had enough of a power escort that they didn't need to also take Barrani Hawks. Teela clearly disagreed.

"Remember when you said you'd make an effort to trust me more with my own survival?"

"I trust you to be yourself."

Mandoran grinned. "In Teela's defense—"

"Teela," Teela snapped, "will never be desperate enough to require your defense."

"—you manage to wander into more trouble than anyone we've ever met. Except Terrano." He laughed out loud. Terrano felt the same as Teela did. "Teela is now annoyed—"

"And Teela *will speak for herself.*"

"Fine. But you're taking too long, and Terrano wants us all to shut up so Kaylin and Bellusdeo can get to the interesting bits."

The cohort didn't need to be present to be part of any conversation—as long as one of its members was. Teela didn't count; she was so accustomed to keeping everything to herself, she had an excellent game face. She wouldn't ask questions or offer answers at the cohort's demand. Which was why Mandoran was here.

Kaylin glanced at Bellusdeo. "Do you want to continue, or do you want me to do it?"

"I'd prefer Severn, to be frank, but he managed to escape the debriefing by never passing through the front gate."

"Fine. We were taking a shortcut across the borders."

"You cannot possibly have considered that remotely sensible," Teela snapped.

"It's not the first time I've done it."

"The first time, you had no choice. You made it through. But the second time? You were attacked by someone wielding purple elemental fire."

"Probably Shadow fire, given what we now know."

"Fine, quibble. You took Bellusdeo into the border zone."

"Bellusdeo has been in far worse than your border zones." It was the Dragon's turn to snap.

Please don't mention the Emperor. Please don't mention the Em-

peror. Please. Since Kaylin wasn't part of the cohort, Teela couldn't hear her.

"Very well. Tell us what happened when you chose to save time." Teela folded her arms. She'd not yet taken a seat, and by the looks of it, wasn't about to start. Bending in half would have cracked something, given her mood.

"We found a building in the border zone, midway between the city and *Ravellon*. It had no doors, no windows, and seemed to be two stories in height. The one distinguishing feature it possessed, other than the pristine condition it was in, was a large, stone-appearing eye."

"Appearing?"

"Well, it moved. I mean, the lid opened, and the eyeball it contained moved. When it saw us—or when we stepped into its field of vision—we were instantly transported into a large stone room. It was one story; the ceiling was very high."

"To my eye," Bellusdeo added, "the walls were stone and featureless. It appeared to be of the same pristine manufacture as the exterior walls."

"In the border zone?" Teela asked. "That I know of, there has been no construction within that zone; the desperate might choose to take up residence within the dwellings, but the placement of those dwellings does not appear to be fixed or stable." She lifted a hand before anyone else could speak and added, "Some basic research has been done by scholars who make the High Halls their home."

Great. Another source of information that was likely to be more prickly and more difficult to navigate than the border zones themselves.

Helen's eyes were still the wrong color.

"Kaylin, however, did not see the room in the same way I did; she had her familiar's wing plastered to her face."

Teela raised one dark brow in Kaylin's direction; Kaylin

picked up the story. "I saw carved reliefs across one wall—the wall facing us when we arrived."

"Carved reliefs?"

Kaylin nodded. "Hope breathed on one of them, and when he did, Bellusdeo could see it. She believes—and Severn has gone to confirm—that that figure is a boy reported as missing.

"There were a lot of people, besides the possible missing person, engraved across the wall. It was like a sculptor's rendition of a crowd; the boy was one of the figures at the forefront. There were a couple of Barrani, but they were farther back, and therefore less visible to me."

"You didn't recognize them."

"No. We can assume," Kaylin continued, "that they're really old Barrani."

"Bellusdeo didn't see them."

"No—I thought it was risky enough to have Hope breathe on one section of the wall, and he breathed on a figure in the foreground. The Barrani were well back. It's because Bellusdeo could identify one of the figures—a missing person—that I thought Killian might be living in a sentient building." She didn't cringe but failed to mention Nightshade's intimidating audience chamber.

"But it's when he used my name that I thought he might *be* a building, somehow. He was missing an eye."

"And you think the eye that served as a portal was that missing eye?"

Did she? She considered the question with some care and then nodded. "If he's a building, the eye is figurative. But..."

Helen's eyes were obsidian, even if both remained firmly in her face. "He said he is not the master, and he does not seem to have control over the architecture?"

Kaylin nodded. She then turned to the Avatar of her house. "What is Killian, exactly? We know that there was a sentient building near the heart of the fiefs; it existed when the Towers were created."

Helen nodded.

Mandoran, however, demanded to know how Kaylin knew this—which was probably Sedarias speaking, given his tone and his expression.

Teela, however, said, "The Arkon?"

Which was more or less the truth. "Yes. He wasn't happy to see us, but he did confirm that before the creation of the Towers, there was a building near *Ravellon*. It existed between what's now Nightshade and Liatt. It appears to have vanished when the Towers—and their perimeters—were established." She now turned to Helen.

"You knew Killian." The last syllable tailed up slightly, but it wasn't really a question.

Helen nodded.

"How? As far as I can tell, buildings are entirely anchored in the lands they occupy. I mean, they *are* the lands they occupy."

Helen nodded again. "You use your mirrors to communicate with those who are not currently sharing the same space you share. The cohort," she continued, before Mandoran could speak—and he had opened his mouth, "use the bond of True Names. You have some experience with that."

It was Kaylin's turn to nod.

"We had something similar. Not as dire as True Names in the worst possible case, and not as flexible, in the best. But... I lost the ability to speak with others such as I when I made the choice to become as independent as I could.

"Some of the strictures that guided and enforced my behavior could not be changed—not safely. And yes, before you ask, every decision on my part was a calculated risk. But one of the things that could not be altered was the part of my function that required a lord, a master.

"I call them tenants," she added. "And I choose. But once chosen, that master cannot easily be displaced."

"It would be easy for you to kill them," Mandoran said.

"It would be impossible for me to kill them," Helen replied.

"Sedarias asks if that's why you choose mortal masters."

"No. It is not. Were I to meet a Barrani who was, in temperament and personality, identical to Kaylin, I would choose the Barrani as a tenant if I were otherwise empty."

"...Yeah, that's not likely."

"But you existed without a tenant before me," Kaylin pointed out.

"I did. There are things I could not do without a tenant. There are rooms and worlds I could not create; there are things I could not easily see. It is not all of one thing, or all of another. In order to make my own choices, I had to surrender the ability to obey a wider range of commands. I do not regret it, on most days."

"Now?"

"I am concerned, as you must know. Killianas and I were not friends; perhaps it is better to say we were kin. His function was not my function; the space he occupied was both larger and more flexible."

"So...he's like you were, when you had no tenant?" Mandoran asked.

"I do not know. I imagine, were he damaged in the fashion I damaged myself, he would operate under the last orders he received from his Lord."

"The Towers take different lords from time to time."

"Yes. But the Towers are not what we were or are. They were built for specific functions; all else is meant to serve those functions. The Towers accept lords for different reasons than we did. Perhaps.

"I am disturbed by two things. Killian's eye—and the eye that served as portal—and Killian's presence in the building itself, a building that does seem subject to some oversight. It is clear to me that he is operating by a very strict interpretation of the mandates of his construction."

"And the wall?"

"I am uncertain. People age, people die. If someone requires people of different ages, the wall—as you call it—might be the perfect containment. But you said or implied that Killian was not aware of the wall."

"That might not be what he considers it." Kaylin frowned. "When I attempted to contact the building itself, he didn't answer. But I think he heard me; he moved us out of the reiterating halls and into halls that would eventually lead to an actual exit. I'm not sure what his function was supposed to be, when he was created. The Arkon seemed to think he might have been a giant school. A university."

Helen nodded.

"So we might have been classed as lost students?"

"Very possible. But he did not lose the eye, or the ability to materialize it, on his own. It is quite possible he created the trap of endless hallways; it is almost certain that he created what you viewed as wall."

"If he *has* a lord, though, it's going to be hard for us to investigate at all."

"Perhaps. I find it interesting that the exit, as you call it, was within the border zone where he might otherwise have been standing after the tragedy. It is not easy to destroy a building; it is not trivial to command one."

"You had words. A name."

Helen grimaced. "I did. But it was not trivial to speak the

words in a fashion that could be heard. It has been attempted. People have come to me who understood the function of the name I was given; they knew the surface of the word itself. But the heart of command requires the ability *to* command, and that is something they lacked."

"I don't have that."

"Ah, no. But it is different. I desire to have you as a tenant; you desire to have me as a home. Where you lack the ability to forcefully compel—with no regard for my existence except as a tool—you have my desire to be your home. I cannot disobey you, should you now command me, however."

"Sedarias thinks that's not true," Mandoran said.

"Sedarias is wrong," Helen replied in a pleasant, even maternal tone.

Kaylin suspected that Sedarias was right, but was inclined to trust Helen's belief in herself. Either way, it wasn't the problem. "The fiefs are what happened when the Towers were created. Killian was in the lands on which they were situated. How did he survive?"

"That would be the question," Helen replied, in a much more neutral tone. Her black eyes were fixed on Kaylin's face; she didn't blink once.

"Helen?"

"Yes, dear."

"Do you think Killian created the border zone?"

CHAPTER
8

Helen didn't answer immediately. The cohort, who had seen little of the fiefs or the areas between them, had no immediate opinions to offer.

"Great," Mandoran said, for no obvious reason.

The reason came floating through the dining room doors: Terrano.

"What?" he asked as all eyes fell on him. "This is *way* more interesting than politics."

"You were talking politics?" Kaylin asked as he made his way to the table.

"I was in the same room as Sedarias." Terrano shrugged. "The question you posed is more interesting. I spent a lot of time in places almost entirely unlike this one. Meaning," he added, "not like the city. I spent a lot of my life inside a building, and I sort of understand buildings like the Hallionne. The Hallionne don't have the same core imperative that the Towers have.

"But Alsanis shut himself off from the outside world when we were his prisoners. And the Hallionne, unlike Helen, are entirely independent. They can respond to those who know how to speak with them, but they are not compelled to obey their commands."

"You're sure?"

He snorted. "What do you think?"

"You're sure." Kaylin turned to Helen. "Is he right?"

"He is correct about his assumptions in regard to Alsanis," Helen replied. "But Alsanis appears to have been particularly fond of Terrano, and of the cohort in general. I am not a Hallionne, but I believe my function was similar. Ah, no, I believe the intention was similar. A great deal of my power involves hospitality and security. Killian's function was not quite the same." A rare smile touched her lips, lingering in the corners. "There were some complaints about him in my youth."

"Complaints?"

"He did not believe in cozening students. Given his situation, his students were often considered among the elite of their people—there were very few mortals, for instance—but he had odd views on education in the eyes of those elites."

Terrano snorted. "Did all of his students survive?"

"That would be an excellent question. He oft said 'I've hardly misplaced any of them' in response to questions such as yours. He was said to have strict rules when applied to the students; the rules that governed his behavior were less clearly stated. I should add that he was the one who built the communication channels between us; he was, he said, quite bored."

"And he's been compromised."

"From the sounds of it, yes. And no. Had he a master or a lord, it would be more readily apparent."

"How?"

"Kaylin is my master—"

"Tenant."

"Tenant, if it makes you more comfortable. Tenant, then. Kaylin is my tenant, but even when she is not present within my walls, her desires and her rules hold sway. I could not simply dispose of one of you behind her back, no matter how tempting that might be. I could not hide the crime for long, if at all.

"What she wants from a home, I provide. That is true no matter where she is or how often she returns or leaves. If Killian says he has no master, it is best to take him at his word."

"And the wall full of people?" Kaylin asked.

"I am uncertain. You said he did not appear to be aware of the wall?"

"Or the room. Or he was lying." She hesitated and then said, "Buildings of my acquaintance don't seem to lie much."

"It is not beyond us," Helen replied. "But it takes both will and effort to utter words that have no meaning. I would imagine that if Killian was built to withstand the petty malice brought to bear by the young and the insecure, he might well have that function. He might also be able to choose not to offer information that he possessed, in the theory that that information had to be earned by more academic or observational endeavors."

"Do you think he has—or had—a master in the past?"

"Almost certainly."

"Do you think that master is gone?"

"Yes."

"So, getting back to border zones. Could *you* turn our front lawn into a border zone equivalent?" Terrano's eyes were practically sparkling as he leaned into his hands, his body angled entirely in Helen's direction.

"No, dear," she said to Terrano. "I highly doubt that that is a wise idea. I do not have an appreciable understanding of what, exactly, this border zone is. It is not like the outlands, but more than that I cannot ascertain. Kaylin, could you ask Severn to come over?"

"Why?"

"Because he has investigated the border, and I think it will cause less discomfort than attempting to have Lord Tiamaris as a guest."

"He'll come over after work tomorrow."

In the morning, Kaylin discovered that she had not only a Dragon in tow, but also one of the cohort; Mandoran had decided to tag along. He offered to do so incognito, by which he meant invisibly. Mandoran was nothing new.

Terrano, however, decided that he would come exploring as well, and that was now a crowd. Kaylin, like any other human being, didn't appreciate a crowd looking over her shoulder when she was trying to get work done. She wasn't an entertainer, after all.

"I think Terrano considers you very entertaining, dear," Helen said as Kaylin grumbled her way to the front doors.

"Not helpful, Helen."

Terrano snickered. Hope, the traitor, also snickered. Kaylin left the house with both Mandoran and Terrano, on top of the Dragon. Bellusdeo chose to find their company amusing, rather than insulting.

Clint and Tanner, on door duty, gave Mandoran and Terrano the side-eye as they entered the building. They had become completely accustomed to Bellusdeo and didn't blink when she entered the Halls of Law by Kaylin's side.

The group made their way down the hall, but Terrano got caught up in the aerial exercises of the Aerian trainees. Kaylin didn't blame him. She'd been part of the Halls for all of her adult life and a good chunk of her adolescence, and she still sometimes paused to watch them.

Today, however, she was a corporal, and she wanted that to have some meaning, so she struggled to remain responsible and reasonable. This involved dragging Terrano to the office by the shoulder so she wouldn't be late.

Marcus was at his desk. He, too, had become accustomed to the Dragon as an unofficial Hawk—which was nothing short of a miracle, given how the sergeant generally reacted to Dragons in his office. Marcus had a long memory and could hold a grudge forever. He was less sanguine about Mandoran and Terrano, but then again, so was Kaylin.

"This is not a tourist zone," he snapped, orange-eyed.

"That's a pretty impressive pile of paper," Terrano replied.

This didn't make the color of Marcus's eyes any happier. But at least his facial fur didn't rise.

"Lord Sanabalis has sent a missive," Marcus said, which wasn't what Kaylin expected.

She wilted. "About?"

"Magic lessons and your inability to make any of them. He is, what was the word he used? Concerned."

"We've been a bit busy."

"Indeed. I heard you had a bit of an adventure in the fiefs yesterday." He glared pointedly at a layer of paper near the top of one of his stacks. He also used the word *adventure* as if it were a cursed and despised thing.

Kaylin cringed. "Yes, sir."

"I see the Dragon returned unharmed."

"Yes, sir."

"Fine. Today, you are to take no shortcuts. Is that clear?"

"Yes, sir."

"Good. Why are these two with you?"

They were bored was not an acceptable answer, and Kaylin

prayed that Terrano wouldn't give it. Mandoran had done this drill before.

"The fieflord of Candallar is Barrani," Terrano said in a tone that was just this side of normal, for the office. "He's an old acquaintance of my family, although he's outcaste. We'd like to speak with him to ascertain just how invested he is—and was—in the events that transfigured the High Halls. I believe he'll speak with me. I'm new enough that I present no obvious threat. But I am a Lord of the High Court."

Marcus glared at Kaylin, his eyes unblinking.

Kaylin had *no idea* if anything that had fallen out of Terrano's mouth was actually true.

"And the other one?" Her Leontine sergeant finally said.

"I'm backup," was Mandoran's cheerful reply. "I'm also technically a Lord of the High Court, for what that's worth, but I'm Terrano's guard."

"And Candallar is going to accept you as guard, and your friend as diplomat while you're also accompanied by a Dragon?"

Mandoran winced. Terrano, notably, did not. Somewhere in the distance, Kaylin was almost certain she could hear Sedarias shrieking in frustration.

"This is the modern era," Terrano replied. "We're ruled by a Dragon; we have individually sworn personal oaths to serve his empire. Lord Bellusdeo is of the Dragon Court."

"I am not present as a Lord of that Court," Bellusdeo unhelpfully said.

"No. But if things go bad in Candallar, *we're* going to be happy to have you present. Given Candallar's possible involvement in the High Halls, and given the gray legality of some of those interactions—and his understanding of the Halls of Law and the rules of exemption—the Hawklord wants Kaylin and Severn to investigate.

"Having us there can only make that investigation safer for the mortals."

Marcus snorted. And growled. "I trust you understand all the ways what you've just said is inaccurate."

"It's aspirational, sir," Mandoran added.

Marcus snorted, but his eyes were a slightly paler orange. To Kaylin, he growled, "I expect a report of the day's activities to be on my desk by this evening." He had gouged a faint runnel in the surface of the desk. Hardwood was definitely better than soft. "But go to Candallar via the bridge, this time. No detours."

Terrano disappeared when they exited the Halls, and after a moment, so did Mandoran. Kaylin assumed they were somewhere above the crowded streets; Terrano didn't like crowds. If Kaylin had wings, she would have avoided them herself.

Bellusdeo didn't seem to mind, but she wouldn't. Crowds of mortals didn't hold much fear for her. Which was fair; no one who recognized a Dragon would be suicidal enough to attack them or attempt to pick their pockets.

They made their way to Candallar's bridge, skirting the warrens; the boardwalk was considered safe at this time of the day. Severn, however, was on alert; *safe* was always a relative term.

The bridge to Tiamaris was, by this point, well-traveled. People who had once avoided those bridges as if their lives depended on it now used them, as their livelihoods now did. Wagons, carts and the craftsmen who drove them could be seen lining up; there were no tolls to cross, but notice was taken by guards on either side of the bridge.

No other fief bridge saw similar use; during daylight hours, the bridges were entirely unoccupied. Candallar was no exception. There were no guards on either side of the Candallar bridge, but guards, in general, served little purpose. The warrens held no fear for the fief.

Kaylin wanted Bellusdeo to stay home.

Bellusdeo was not going to stay home. Kaylin had explained that rule of law, such as it was, didn't exist in the fiefs; the laws that governed the fiefs were the fieflord's. This meant, in theory, that there was no law preventing fieflings from attacking the Dragon, and if an attack on the Dragon were to occur, there was no safer place for the attackers.

"It won't be safe for them," the Dragon had countered. "I am not required to retain my human form, either. There is no prohibition against breathing on the foolish." Her smile had too many teeth in it.

Mandoran and Terrano chose to land—and reappear—when the Hawks reached the bridge; they crossed it on foot.

"You don't need to do that for my sake," Bellusdeo said.

"It's not for yours," Terrano replied. "Can't you see it?"

The Dragon's eyes narrowed.

"I'll take that as a no. Mandoran can't see it either, if that's helpful."

"It's not."

Terrano turned to Kaylin. "She's always like this, isn't she?"

Kaylin offered a universal fief shrug. "Can you dim your visibility here?"

"That? Yes. But the flying part isn't really safe for us when we're near the border."

"I have no issues flying over the borders."

"No, but you're a Dragon. You come by wings naturally. We have to fiddle a bit."

The Dragon's eyes were orange. "We are *definitely* saving this discussion for later. When we're surrounded by Helen."

"It doesn't matter whether you're visible or not. We're in Candallar. The fieflord will know. The Tower will know."

This fief looked far more like Nightshade than Tiamaris. The buildings were old and structurally questionable, but people occupied them, scurrying from window to window in the upper floors. Kaylin's gaze was drawn there; she felt almost as if she had never really left the fiefs.

It was a feeling she hated. The tabards she and Severn wore weren't exactly discouraging; the Barrani who accompanied them were more of a threat or a warning to anyone who might seek them out.

"You intend to go the direct route?" Terrano asked.

"Might as well. If he doesn't want to speak with us, we'll never find him."

"And if he does?"

"I don't suggest we do it on the inside of his Tower."

"No. If he insists, I will wait outside." Bellusdeo grinned. "I've half a mind to shift form and wait outside now. While the Tower does have control of elements of the fief, Towers wield absolute control only within their walls. Candallar will be aware of our presence and our location if the Tower alerts him or if he is looking. Or," she added with a sweeter smile, "if he is, in fact, in the fief at all."

Bellusdeo didn't go full Dragon. She walked, her escort mortal Hawks and theoretical Barrani. Neither Terrano nor Mandoran could stiffen their faces and postures into those suitable for Barrani guards, and neither were of a mind to try.

"He's here," Terrano said as Kaylin felt a twinge across her forearms.

"How close?"

"Not close. But he's aware of us now."

"I can't see him."

"No. Ask your familiar for help."

Hope lifted a wing before Kaylin could comply. Candallar

was standing in the center of the street, alone, some twenty yards from the formidable height of the Tower that bore his name. His eyes were firmly fixed on Bellusdeo.

The haze around his body shifted and lessened, dissipating as she watched. Hope once again withdrew his wing.

"Well met," Candallar said. "Well met, Lord Bellusdeo. Lords Kaylin, Severn, Terrano and Mandoran."

Kaylin stiffened.

"I had heard rumors that you might pay a visit to my humble abode. I am honored."

Mandoran stepped forward and stood one step to the left of Bellusdeo—but in front. Bellusdeo said nothing. Her eyes remained orange, not red; her expression implied a chilly lack of amusement. She did offer Candallar a nod. "Fieflord."

Mandoran, however, said, "Lord Candallar." He bowed.

"That is no longer what I am called by my kin."

"It is what you are called in the territory you rule. We have no quarrel with Candallar, although that was perhaps not always true."

The fieflord had an easy, friendly smile. It was almost charming, which put Kaylin further on guard, something she would have bet wasn't possible.

"You refer, perhaps, to your ascension in the High Court? I have heard only rumors; many of my sources of information have gone silent in the past few days."

"Indeed. It has long been true that choosing the wrong side has consequences."

"It has also been said that peaceful climes do not a warrior make."

"We were not raised in peaceful climes," Mandoran replied, Terrano stiff and almost lifeless at Kaylin's side. "We were not bred for it; we were not trained for it. If the wars that were responsible for our journey to the green have ended, and we are now at peace with the Dragons, the experiences that formed us remain."

This was *not* the discussion that Kaylin had come to Candallar to have. She had not, in fact, intended to have much in the way of discussion at all. That plan had changed because Bellusdeo was present. As mortals, no matter how they were dressed, they were not significant to the Tower. A Dragon would be. But everything about this discussion sounded exactly like Sedarias; this was a matter for the new An'Mellarionne.

"True. You are not, perhaps, aware of the experiences that drove me to take the reins of Candallar."

"No, indeed. We have been entrusted with an invitation; The An'Mellarionne wishes to better make your acquaintance in these troubled times."

His brows rose slightly, and the color of his eyes shifted. He was surprised. Surprised and delighted, judging by his laughter. Kaylin hated that the laughter itself was melodious and compelling because she disliked it intensely on principle.

"Lord Sedarias is indeed bold, as ancient rumors have suggested. I did not myself have experience of her before her sojourn in the West March, and I have not yet had the privilege of making her acquaintance since her ascension at Court. I have, however, been apprised of the astonishing changes that have occurred in the High Halls in very recent days. She is aware of my current status?"

"She is aware that you are outcaste, yes. Given your activities, or your implied activities, before we were invited to take the Test of Name, she believes that you were made outcaste for political reasons. And also that you have some interest in a return to legitimacy."

Kaylin bent to Terrano's ear—or as close as she could come

given their differences in height. *"This is not what we're supposed to be doing here,"* she whispered.

It is far more effective at present than bumbling across the fief searching for information that might somehow incriminate Candallar in an Imperial crime. It was Nightshade who now spoke. Kaylin could feel the sudden weight of his presence behind her eyes. *She is, indeed, bold, but she was always feared. She is ruthless, Kaylin. She is not to be trusted.*

She's living with me.

Yes. And while she is resident within Helen's domain, you will come to no harm. But Helen herself was not certain that she could contain the cohort should they decide to cause harm to either her or you. They are not what we are.

Do you think she means harm?

Almost certainly. But not to Helen, not to you, and not to Annarion. The last was his only real concern.

"And does she believe—she who was only barely able to take the Test of Name—that she might have something of value to offer a man in pursuit of that legitimacy?" There was a distinct edge in the words; the eyes were the color of suspicion, one barely touched by hope.

Mandoran's smile was pleasant and chilly. Kaylin found it enormously unsettling, because it was Sedarias's smile on the wrong face. "Have you seen the High Halls since the Test was taken?"

"I have seen them, as you must be aware, at a distance."

"That occurred, not coincidentally, after we had taken the Test and confronted what lies beneath. You have seen it yourself; you were once Lord of the High Court."

Silence, then. Sharp, cold; the colors of Candallar's eyes shifted in the ice of his face. He spoke a word that Kaylin did not understand.

"We do not know what aid was promised, what power offered; nor do we know what you offered in return for possible future favor. But we will ask you to consider your future—and your future alliances—with care. You have allies of a sort in the High Court; we are aware of a few. You will, of course, ascertain the truth of our words from those sources. But should you choose to ally yourself more wisely in future, there are discussions that must be had."

"You will not find reinstatement a simple affair," Candallar then said. "We are all aware that your happy return is a polite fiction, and etiquette hides many things."

Terrano was becoming impatient. Kaylin dropped a hand on his shoulder; he stiffened, but didn't move away.

"You are here because you believe I have an advantage to offer in what is likely to be a war fought on many, many fronts."

"No, actually," Kaylin said before Mandoran—or Sedarias, using Mandoran as a conduit—could reply. "They're here because we were asked to speak with you. As Imperial Hawks."

Both of his brows rose at the Elantran interruption; the rest of the words had been delivered in formal High Barrani. "You do not have jurisdiction in the fiefs."

"No." Kaylin folded her arms.

"Imperial Law," Bellusdeo said in the same Elantran, "doesn't rule the fiefs. None of those laws need be enforced."

Damn it.

Kaylin turned at the sound of tearing seams. Bellusdeo, standing in the streets of Candallar, which were now empty of anyone who wasn't a participant in this conversation, began to shift into her Draconic form.

In a much deeper voice, the Dragon continued. "Laws of exemption mean nothing in the fiefs. You have laws, yes?" The ground beneath their feet seemed to tremble in time with her syllables.

Candallar's expression did not shift. "You will not get far in the old Court with a Dragon as a...companion." He spoke to Mandoran.

Bellusdeo roared.

Kaylin considered the ignore-the-Dragon option to be a brave social choice.

"You stand accused," the Dragon continued, "of aiding and abetting those who seek to consort with Shadow. The only court you face now is a court of your peers. And to the High Court—as it is currently constituted—that is treason."

A brave social choice on Kaylin's part would have been to correct Bellusdeo. She was clearly a coward in comparison to the fieflord.

If she ate him, Ynpharion said, *it would solve a number of problems for the High Court.*

We want information. We want to know who his contacts were.

Some information is, we believe, forthcoming. The Barrani Lord Spike identified is not currently at Court or within reach; he evaded us. It is possible that he is to be found in Candallar. The Halls of Law have no concern—and no jurisdiction—over the High Court in matters that involve only the Barrani.

We want to know who his human *contacts were. The people who might know among us didn't consider them all that relevant at the time. And those are not the province of Barrani High Court bloody laws of exemption.*

As you say. But if the Dragon torches the fief, the Tower will react.

Kaylin knew. She wasn't certain that the Tower could *do* anything this far outside of its physical shape—but the power of the Towers was subtle, and it extended to all borders. She just hoped that Bellusdeo wouldn't casually torch one of the buildings as a show of force, because even if the buildings looked run-down and barely habitable—and these didn't—people like Kaylin still lived in them, or retreated to them;

falling apart was still better than open streets and hunting Ferals.

"Even in the High Court," Candallar replied with a touch less equanimity, "such accusations require proof."

"Speak," Bellusdeo said, "to your allies—if indeed they still exist."

Mandoran cleared his throat; Bellusdeo snorted. There was fire in it, not just the usual smoke. "Sedarias An'Mellarionne considers your desire to return to your kin to be commendable. She understands that the fiefs themselves are necessary, and you have long and voluntarily served in a position that none would gainsay. But if you wish to traverse the streets of the Imperial city in the future, she asks that you consider your current available choices with care.

"The mortals can be of little concern to a man of your former stature. If Lord Kaylin—" and here, there was emphasis on the title that Kaylin found so awkward "—requires some aid in identifying those mortals, would you keep their names and positions to yourself? We are beholden to Lord Kaylin, and would consider it a disservice."

"And will Sedarias An'Mellarionne pay a visit? She will find me at home."

Mandoran did chuckle them. "She invites you instead, with Lord Kaylin's acquiescence, to pay, as you call it, a visit; you will find her at home."

"If she wishes to resume her rightful place—"

"Resume? She is An'Mellarionne. There is nothing to resume or assume. There are none who would now dare to touch or take the seat she has finally claimed as her own."

"You're certain I can't eat him?" the Dragon asked.

"You wouldn't enjoy it," Kaylin replied.

Severn had begun to unwind his weapon chain, and given the absence of obvious aggression, Kaylin found this disturbing.

Candallar is a mage, Nightshade said. *Do not, however, watch Severn. Watch your familiar.*

He's not doing anything.

Then do likewise. I admit that even I underestimated Sedarias. It is…refreshing.

Barrani ideas of refreshing were *so* not Kaylin's.

You are annoyed that she did not discuss this with you?

Yes, actually, because this interferes with my *job.*

It does not. In case your High Barrani is inadequate, one of her conditions is that the information that you…somehow…thought you might receive should you come to Candallar be delivered to her.

We didn't come here expecting to be handed information.

Ah. And you came here in person for what reason?

To investigate Candallar. She exhaled. *And to take a look at the Ravellon border.*

Silence.

I do not believe that those were your orders.

Not specifically, no. But I'll bet you anything you want that's why Bellusdeo is here. The Tower let a High Lord cross the border and return bearing Spike. How that happened—how that could *happen—when the fieflord is present… You don't think he's like Barren, do you?*

No. Candallar is his. You can hear his name across the border; you can see it, if you look for it. Or rather, the fieflords and their Towers can.

Do you think he's like the fieflord before Barren?

That I cannot tell you. But I will say this: it is no small effort and requires no small will to captain one of the six Towers. You think of the animus of the Tower as Tara. It is with Tara that you have the broadest breadth of experience. But you are aware that my Tower is entirely unlike Tara; the living heart of Castle Nightshade is, or was, one of our Ancestors.

I have not likewise made the acquaintance of other Towers. I can no more tell you whether they are like Tara or like Castle Night-shade. I can tell you nothing of Candallar's Tower, and to glean any information, you would have to visit. I do not suggest you do so with the Dragon.

Or the cohort?

Or the cohort. You might recall what happened when Annarion visited me.

She did. The echoes of the loss of the Hawks and Swords still haunted the Halls of Law.

He did extend an invitation to Sedarias.

And she would never—as you heard—be fool enough to accept it. Not yet, and perhaps not ever. I am not at all certain that the Barrani who passed through the border to Ravellon ever spent time within Candallar's Tower, either. It is far too risky to place one's safety in the hands of such a building. They are not Hallionne.

Hope squawked.

Castle Nightshade is not always safe for those I accept as guests. If I accept a guest, I as host wish them no immediate harm. But the Castle does not always respect that; it is, as I said, a matter of will.

Hope squawked again.

I wish to know, however, when you plan to return to the border zone.

Why?

I wish to accompany you.

CHAPTER 9

Kaylin wasn't entirely certain how the full Dragon confrontation was going to go; Bellusdeo's eyes were a deep orange. She looked at Candallar as if he were a cockroach. Kaylin understood why. The act of treason of which he was accused was so profoundly personal to the Dragon, the echoes of rage and loss informed the way she viewed it.

She, therefore, stepped on the Dragon's foot. Her foot was insignificant in comparison—but so was a full, all-out body-check, and the former preserved some small shreds of Hawkly dignity.

Bellusdeo's head swiveled in Kaylin's direction; the Dragon's scaled neck was, in spite of natural armor, very flexible. "Yes?"

"We should head south. We can check the border for possible infestation while we're there."

Candallar said nothing.

Bellusdeo turned an eye on Candallar. "What have you done to your Tower?"

The question didn't surprise him. He didn't answer it, though.

"Sedarias An'Mellarionne has extended an offer," Mandoran said, as soon as he was certain that fiery death was not forthcoming. He hadn't said a word to interrupt Bellusdeo, no doubt at Sedarias's request.

An angry Dragon who is somewhat allied is nevertheless not under anyone's control. Sedarias understands this, but believes that Candallar would not die so easily. The threat, however, underpins her position as someone of considerable power. Not many of our kin could claim a Dragon as an ally.

Any?

Not many, Nightshade replied with more emphasis. *Candallar is not as old as Teela or the cohort, in theoretical terms. He is vastly more experienced than the cohort, but Teela's experience will weigh heavily with them.*

Have you ever met Sedarias?

She felt the ghost of a brief grin.

"If I accept your offer of...hospitality," Candallar then said, "I would request that you treat my fief as if it is, in fact, mine."

"What would that entail?" Mandoran asked, but his response was slower; to Kaylin, it implied dissent within the cohort.

"You will leave off inspecting my borders as if I am some part of your Imperial domain."

Bellusdeo turned on him then, eyes almost red. "We are aware that a Lord of the High Court entered—and left—*Ravellon* through Candallar. He carried Shadow *with him*."

Candallar said nothing.

Bellusdeo stepped toward him; the ground shook with the intensity of her rage. And her weight. She wasn't stepping lightly.

"You play games with forces you do not understand," the Dragon said, her lips pulled over the length of her jaw, her teeth glinting as if they were jeweled. "I have seen a world lost to what lies in wait in *Ravellon*. Not a court and not a useless title—a world. And it was lost in part *because of people like you.*"

He stepped back.

"You play at little territories, fieflord. If it pleases you, you may continue while you breathe. But Shadow is not an entity that respects borders or boundaries. Corporals," she added, her voice a growl.

Kaylin understood that this meant they were to join her. It wasn't the first time Kaylin had flown on Dragon back. She clambered up. Severn followed with greater ease, and she tried not to resent it. When they were both seated more or less as securely as they could be, Bellusdeo roared. There were syllables in it. Rage.

"I really think that's a terrible idea this close to *Ravellon!*" Kaylin shouted.

Bellusdeo's reply was also a roar. Kaylin had no need to understand Dragon to know that this was one of the "useful" words she might otherwise have picked up. The Dragon then pushed herself up off the streets of Candallar, leaving Mandoran and Terrano behind.

It wasn't Candallar that concerned Kaylin; it was the outcaste Dragon. *Ravellon* was his home and he had somehow survived it.

She's flown to the border in Tiamaris, Severn pointed out. It was audible; shouting in her ear while Bellusdeo trumpeted her rage might not have been.

That's different.

It's not. If she didn't catch the outcaste's attention in Tiamaris, she won't catch it here; if she did, he didn't rise to take that bait.

The borders are far more protected in Tiamaris than they are in Candallar.

Kaylin—you returned from the outlands by Tiamaris. The borders are susceptible in every fief.

We're not Shadow.

No.

Spike is.

Is he?

Kaylin settled in to think. The distance Bellusdeo covered was not strenuous, even by foot; the ground beneath Kaylin's feet rushed past. People under the Dragon's shadow scattered, which showed some sense. How had Spike passed through that barrier? Was the Tower compromised?

Tara had almost been compromised by the Shadows she was created to suppress. That she hadn't been was due to Tiamaris. And Kaylin herself. What Tara now built, she *wanted*. And she wanted to protect it. It was part of her now in a way that was neither trap nor cage.

Kaylin couldn't imagine that Candallar could give a Tower what Tiamaris could. She knew that Nightshade didn't—but knew, as well, that Nightshade's Tower, at base, would probably destroy itself, brick by brick, if it ever needed what Tara needed.

There was only one way to check, and that involved entering the heart of Candallar's power.

I consider that exceedingly unwise, Nightshade said, his interior voice soft.

Bellusdeo, the aforementioned groundhawks in tow, did land about ten yards from the border. She remained Draconic, shedding her passengers. When the Hawks had both feet on the ground, she folded wings that had remained high and ready to strike.

Kaylin approached the border slowly. Hope yawned and sat up on her shoulder. His wings remained folded. If invisible Shadow was approaching them, he didn't consider them consequential.

There are none, he said, squawks adorning the syllables like the background melody offered by street musicians. *What she seeks, she will not find.*

"Could you maybe tell her that?"

No. It is her own opinion she trusts, and at that, poorly. She is much unsettled by the news that one of the Barrani carried Spike from Ravellon.

"She accepted Spike."

She did. It is why I have some hope for her. But she is distraught about the High Halls. Mandoran explained what happened—using "small words"—and she is not at all certain that an extremely dangerous enemy has not been loosed in the middle of the city.

Kaylin exhaled. "Neither am I."

No. What will you do, Chosen?

"Talk to Spike."

Bellusdeo spoke, a rumble of sound that was almost an expression of movement. The hair on Kaylin's arms stood instantly on end; she winced. Bellusdeo didn't appear to notice. Given the color of her eyes this close to the border, Kaylin kept any complaints to herself.

It wasn't hard. The question of a Tower's compromise now occupied most of her thoughts. While she liked and trusted Tara, her first encounter with the Tower that Tiamaris now called home had not been good, and the odds that she would survive it, not high.

Castle Nightshade was a different beast. She trusted it only because Nightshade was its Lord, and even then the trust was mired in echoes of her childhood and the specters those raised. But she couldn't imagine that Nightshade's Tower could *be* compromised the way Tara had almost been compromised.

She didn't understand how Towers chose their lords. She knew that Barren could not be Lord of the fief that had nonetheless taken his name. She didn't understand the mechanics well.

And would you take Candallar, if you could? Nightshade asked.

No. Helen is my home. She exhaled. *I was just thinking that Dragon fieflords would work out better.*

There was genuine amusement in Nightshade's internal struggle. *Yes, you were. But Kaylin, that is only true for you because you have seen so few of Dragonkind. Were you to have the breadth of experience that those who fought in the wars possess, you would understand why I find the concept amusing. Those Dragons you have met, those Dragons about whom you have knowledge, were those who could accept the Eternal Emperor.*

She nodded as Bellusdeo breathed a plume of fire across the stones nearest the *Ravellon* border. The Dragon barked a single, curt word in Elantran, and Kaylin obeyed; she followed in the Dragon's wake. Severn, weapons in either hand, did the same. He wasn't tense or angry in the way Bellusdeo was, but he was on high alert.

Hope, Kaylin reflected, made her sloppy.

I hardly think it fair to blame that on the familiar, Nightshade observed. *Are you familiar with the method of investigation Lord Bellusdeo is now employing?*

Not really. I'm not sure it's something that she can teach the rest of us. The Norannir *have their own way of guarding against Shadow. Tiamaris trusts them.*

Yes. But his is the position of strength in that fief; he can afford to trust.

The Candallar border was judged secure by Bellusdeo, although her eyes remained a dark red as she gazed past the barrier and into the Shadow lands that had destroyed the home she had built. Kaylin's immediate fear was not of Shadow; she

watched the skies for any sign of dark wings, black body—
any hint of the rising of the Dragon outcaste.

Bellusdeo's angry roars had not summoned him. The
Dragon had nothing to fight, and Kaylin thought a fight
would be viscerally welcome—if incredibly dangerous—to
Bellusdeo. Kaylin kept an eye on the buildings that were closest to the border. Those closest were unoccupied by anything
that was larger than a rat; some were missing roofs, and the
walls were slanted.

Not even the desperate sought shelter here, so close to
where the Ferals started, and ended, their evening hunts. No
one would have done so in Nightshade, either. But in Tiamaris, the *Norannir* had peopled the border, and buildings very
unlike these were in the process of being erected. They feared
the Shadow, yes—but they hated it, as Bellusdeo hated it.

If they had lost their home and their world, they were grim
guardians against the possibility of a similar fate in this one.

"Where are you going?"

Kaylin looked away from the buildings and the hints of
scuttling mice.

Bellusdeo, golden scales muted as clouds rolled across the
sun's face, said, "The border zone."

Given Bellusdeo's mood, questioning her was a bit of a
gamble, and not the kind in which a stroke of good fortune
enriched the questioner. Kaylin had always been silent in the
presence of those with superior power, in the hope that she
wouldn't draw their attention or their ire. She knew Bellusdeo wouldn't hurt her, but old habits were hard to shake.

Instead, she thought about why Bellusdeo wanted to enter
the border zone here. "This leads to Durant."

"Indeed. We have visited the border zone between Tiamaris and Candallar, and I would like to see how it shifts—if it does—between other fiefs."

"Why?"

"Because Lannagaros's reaction implied information that he did not choose to share with me."

"Maybe he didn't think it relevant?"

"Unlikely."

"Maybe he was afraid if he did you'd do something reckless on your own. Like, say, fly across all the fiefs and enter the bloody border zones!"

A large Dragon could shrug in a very fief-like way. "It is all information he would find useful, and I will share it with him."

"After he coughs up the rest?"

Apparently enormous, heavily toothy Dragon jaws could imply a smug grin. "You understand."

Try to talk her out of it, Kaylin told her partner. *She's way more likely to listen to you.*

There's a trick to that, he replied in a resigned tone.

What is it?

Give her advice she'd be likely to follow anyway. She's going to do this—but I've been across the border zones before. It's not the border zones that are the problem. She can walk into the zone from Candallar; he knows she's here, and for the moment, he's willing— barely—to let her be.

And Durant won't be?

I don't know.

The border zone between Candallar and the fief of Durant was similar, in the end, to the zone between Tiamaris and Candallar, or between Nightshade and Tiamaris. That was Kaylin's first impression. Her second impression was slightly different. Although the same washed-out hues of gray were the predominant colors in the zone, and the buildings appeared to continue from the border itself, the length of passage felt shorter.

It's not just you, Severn told her. *The zone here is, like the zones between Nightshade and Tiamaris, amorphous; it shifts. But the elasticity of the space seems to have harder bounds. It did when I traversed them the first time.*

Can I ask why you did it?

You can ask. I can't answer.

Sometimes Kaylin resented the Wolves, which was petty. She struggled to set resentment aside, and managed to keep the actual words to herself. Harder, when they were on the inside of her head.

Severn's hands tightened on his weapons, but the three emerged into the fief of Durant without conflict or difficulty. Then again, Bellusdeo was traversing the zone closest to the *Ravellon* border all fiefs shared. Kaylin considered this risky; it was, in theory, here that the Towers' attention was focused.

But it did mean that no civilians, and no fieflord thugs, were in easy reach of a disgruntled gold Dragon, and Kaylin considered the risk worth the avoidance. Not that she had much love for fieflord thugs, but any situation in which she could avoid random killing, even in self-defense, was always the better one.

Bellusdeo, annoyance aside, had probably made the same decision. Or perhaps not. It was not just the border zones that she wanted to inspect; it was the border that each fief held with the shadow at the center of these separate lands.

The course of the day was about that border, and it wasn't exactly short. While Bellusdeo inspected the Durant border, Kaylin looked at the buildings. Durant was a walled fief; it wasn't the river that separated the fief from the rest of the city, for the most part. There was a bridge, but the wall itself occupied most of the city-facing border.

The buildings here were in better repair, which surprised Kaylin. If they were occupied, the occupants had chosen to stay away from open windows, and for the most part, those were rare; shutters ruled here, not glass, but the shutters were firmly closed. Or as firmly as warped wood could be.

Above the buildings—all of them, near or far—a Tower rose. It was unadorned, and it certainly wasn't white, as the Tower of Tiamaris had become; it was a very workmanlike stone, a Tower that, on the exterior, could have been built by mortal hands, and not the hands of a resident almost-deity.

"What the hell is that?" Kaylin murmured, her eyes narrowing.

Severn glanced in the direction of the Tower. "Durant's decor is a bit unusual."

"A bit? Is that supposed to be a word? Two dots and a curve?"

"No, I don't believe so."

"What *is* it?"

"I believe it's supposed to be a rudimentary representation of a smile."

"A smile." She turned to catch Severn's expression. "You're serious. Have you ever met Durant?"

"No. I've entered the fief before, but nothing I've been searching for has ended up in Durant."

She looked at the smile again. "I can't imagine why."

Bellusdeo snorted. "You are discomfited because you feel that a smile is somehow welcoming." She smiled. Given the size of her jaws, it was not in any way friendly.

"Durant's doesn't have any teeth in it."

★ ★ ★

The *Ravellon* border in the fief of Durant showed no cause for alarm, or at least no sign Bellusdeo was willing to share. The occupants of the buildings that faced the dangerous border were, like the occupants in every other zone the Dragon had strolled across, entirely absent. Evidence suggested that they existed, but this was not the time of day to find anyone who had much choice in the matter at home.

Kaylin almost regretted it. She could well imagine that a giant...smile...could come under some fairly harsh mockery, and she almost wanted to ask a Durant fiefling what their fieflord was like.

Bellusdeo's concern was more immediate. She cared about fieflords only as it pertained to the responsibilities of their Towers. She didn't have Kaylin's visceral and instinctive animosity because she didn't have Kaylin's experience. She couldn't have had it; Dragons couldn't be hunted by Ferals unless they wanted to be, and in the end, it was the Ferals who would suffer.

Dragons had wings; they could leave the fief anytime they wanted to. Even now, Bellusdeo couldn't put herself in danger here unless she ambled into the Tower.

Kaylin pulled her thoughts up short. While they were all true, they were irrelevant. Bellusdeo had not had Kaylin's life—but the life she'd had, the life she'd lost, was in some ways worse. Part of the reason Kaylin hated the fiefs was that they made it so easy to slide back into patterns of thought that she hated. Envy was the worst of it.

That life had led to this one. This one, she wanted. What other people had—or did not have—was irrelevant.

Bellusdeo didn't take to the skies again. Although she retained her more martial form, she now walked from one end of the *Ravellon* border to the other. "We cross the border zone here," she told her companions.

The border between Durant and Farlonne was, as zones went, similar to the zones they had already crossed. Shades of gray leeched color out of buildings that otherwise seemed a continuous stretch of low-rent dwellings. Bellusdeo had, in her other forays into that zone, moved away from *Ravellon*; this was the first time she had entered the border zone that skirted its edge.

Kaylin wasn't certain this was smart.

"I want to prove something to myself," the Dragon replied.

"And that is?"

"You're intelligent; you figure it out." When uttered by Dragon throat, with its rumble and its accompanying visual signals—mostly orange verging on red—this sounded far more condescending than it should have.

Kaylin bit back any knee-jerk reply and grudgingly did as asked because she did have questions that the Arkon hadn't answered. She'd assumed he was incapable of answering them. Bellusdeo was vastly more suspicious. Suspicion had once been a way of life. Practically the only way of life.

When they reached the nearest gap between buildings that faced *Ravellon*, she turned toward the fief that had defined Bellusdeo's adult life. She saw gray. Gray buildings. A gray street. That street continued into the heart of the last of the fiefs—the one that mandated the existence of the other six.

From this vantage, if she closed her eyes and spun in place, she couldn't tell that the heart of all Shadow—anchored to every world in existence in some fashion—was *Ravellon* at all. It might have been the way to Farlonne. She turned to look over her shoulder; the Tower of Durant rose above the gray buildings. In the border zone, it was unaltered, except for color.

There was no similar Tower in the heart of the fiefs. The buildings that led there, in theory, were like the Durant buildings. Or the buildings that characterized the other fiefs.

"What do you think would happen if we tried to walk those streets?"

"You catch fire."

"Did I forget I was with you?"

"Clearly."

"Okay. What do you think would happen to someone who didn't have you as a guard if they tried to walk down that street?"

"I imagine they'd walk down the street and when they passed it, they'd be food for Shadows. In the best-case scenario."

"Yes, but—"

"Yes?"

"But it doesn't seem like Shadows have much purchase here."

"No, it doesn't, does it?"

"I am not certain that Shadows can travel through the border zone," Severn said. "I haven't tested the supposition extensively."

"Or at all?" the Dragon asked.

"Or at all."

Kaylin frowned her way through the rest of the border zone, and the expression remained fixed to her face when she entered Farlonne.

Farlonne was, on the edge of *Ravellon*, quite different than any of the fiefs they'd seen so far. Where the border in the other fiefs was characterized by mostly deserted, flimsy buildings—with the exception of Tiamaris, and the lack of desertion there was new—Farlonne was occupied by a bristling array of fortified stone. These buildings were occupied, and the occupants did not seem to be terrified of either the Hawk, which was expected, or the Dragon, which was not.

Most of the people who therefore came out of these stone buildings, all too large to be simple dwellings unless their owners were monied, were alert, armed and human. They were, however, accompanied by Barrani. Armored Barrani.

Although Bellusdeo was alert as she all but ordered Kaylin and Severn to stand back, it was the first time since she'd landed that her eyes had lightened; they remained orange, but with a lot less red in them.

"Climb," she told the Hawks. "We may be forced to leave these streets and this border quickly."

There was a command structure that the three dozen men seemed to follow. To no one's surprise, the Barrani were at the top of it, but the men who were beneath them in the hierarchy didn't seem to resent it. The Barrani were blue-eyed; the blue was the midnight variety that could easily be mistaken for black at a distance.

"You have entered the lands of Farlonne," the Barrani who appeared to be in command said.

"Indeed," Bellusdeo rumbled back. "We came to inspect the Candallar border."

"You are not in Candallar now."

"No. We offer our apologies for our trespass. We come with no ill intent."

His expression said that he would be the judge of that, but it was a Barrani expression. Turning to another Barrani man, he said something that Kaylin's hearing couldn't pick up. The second Barrani then departed, heading back toward a building.

Hope squawked. The Barrani man frowned at the sound—angry birds obviously generally being an indicator of something in the background—and froze. His eyes couldn't get any darker, and his sword was already drawn. He tensed nonetheless, his expression shifting with the narrowing of his eyes.

"I really think," Kaylin said, "we should leave. I think the second man is probably informing the fieflord that we're here."

"I assume the fieflord is well aware of that. You don't want to speak with Farlonne?"

"I never want to speak with a fieflord unless I have a very specific purpose. Or an angry sergeant."

Bellusdeo pushed herself off the ground. "Please convey our apologies to Lord Farlonne," the Dragon said in a voice that could probably be heard *by* the absent Lord, although the syllables were High Barrani, "for our trespass. Lord Candallar allowed a man to enter *Ravellon* from his fief, and his Tower allowed that man, subsequently infested by Shadow, to leave *Ravellon*.

"We wished to ascertain, in a rudimentary fashion, that the other borders of *Ravellon* were not likewise compromised."

"The border of Farlonne," a new voice replied, "is not compromised."

A woman in full armor walked out of the building into which the Barrani soldier had walked. The men, gathered in a rough formation around the position Bellusdeo had held on the ground, stiffened. At a single word from the woman who was obviously their commander, they parted, a living wave.

"I would ask," she said as Bellusdeo had not yet gained height, "that you join me. I accept you at your word."

"That is not something that many of your kind would do."

"Many Barrani, or many fieflords?"

Bellusdeo chuckled. "The former. My experience with the latter is limited."

"I would hear more of your accusations against Candallar, if it pleases you to discuss it." She lifted an arm and gestured, fist becoming open hand at the end of that arm. Weapons found their sheaths instantly, the movement so precise and so synchronized it might have been performed by soldiers who had been trained to do nothing but drill.

Is Farlonne outcaste? Kaylin asked Ynpharion.

It astonishes me that you failed to even think of asking that question before now.

I didn't exactly plan *on meeting her.*

Given your plans to date—and I accept I have seen but a fraction of your life—your reliance on "planning" seems highly suspect. Were I you, I would abandon all hope of what passes for normal in your life and assume that everything will, as you colloquially put it, be on fire in the worst conceivable way possible.

She wondered briefly why it was Ynpharion she'd asked. Clearly, he was wondering the same thing.

Lord Farlonne, unlike Nightshade or Candallar, is not outcaste. She has passed the Test of Name; she is a Lord of the High Court. She has always, according to those who are acquainted with her, been a bit unusual. There has been no motion to have her stripped of her title; there is unlikely ever to be that motion. She has rarely played political games with any finesse.

Or at all?

Or at all.

Bellusdeo considered the fieflord's request from the air; her response was to land.

"Don't dismount," she said in as quiet a voice as a Dragon could use.

"It's going to be difficult to greet her properly from your back."

"I believe we'll survive it."

"She's not an outcaste." Although Kaylin was seated on the Dragon's back, she knew her well enough by now that she could practically see the grimace.

Hope squawked.

"Fine." Bellusdeo then transformed, shedding wings, weight, length and most of her scales. The scales that remained were what Kaylin considered Dragon armor. When the transformation was complete, Bellusdeo looked every inch the warrior queen she had once been in a different world.

CHAPTER 10

"Lord Farlonne." Plate armor wasn't known for its flexibility. Or at least not the regular kind that was worn on dress parades and pretty much nowhere else in the city. Unless you counted the palace guard—but Kaylin considered them dress guards or status symbols. Or condescending jerks.

"Lord Bellusdeo." Farlonne's armor was not plate; she bowed.

"I apologize for my concern and my interference in your territory. My companions are Imperial Hawks, but they were asked to accompany me."

"To the fiefs?"

"To the destination of my choice. I will admit," she added, her lips curving in an odd smile, "that that destination is seldom the fiefs."

"I would not imagine it would be. Very few people enter Farlonne without my consent—or my knowledge. You are a recent arrival in the fair city of Elantra, and perhaps events surrounding that arrival have been…hectic. Farlonne is walled. To pass into my territory, one either requires my permission or one sneaks in through the borders of either Durant or Liatt. Our borders are therefore watched.

"But I have heard only rumors. It has been long indeed since I have seen a Dragon in the flesh."

"The Eternal Emperor would no doubt remember you."

"And I, him." Her smile was twin to Bellusdeo's. For some reason, both women reminded Kaylin of Sedarias, which was not a terribly comforting thought. "You are welcome in Farlonne, should you desire to visit again. I would ask, as a courtesy, that you inform the guards at the gate of your arrival." She lifted a hand again, and the guards—except for the Barrani—dispersed.

"You are gracious, Lord Farlonne."

"That is not something of which I am often accused." The hard smile slid off her face. "Now, you offer information about Candallar, and I would be...grateful...to hear it. I have heard idle gossip at Court—but it is surprisingly scant. Candallar is outcaste; the outcaste are not oft discussed unless they pose too great a threat.

"Were you, as claimed at Court, in the West March?"

"Not as an attacking Dragon Flight of one, but yes."

"And you encountered the fieflord there?"

"No, of course not. I first encountered the fieflord in the area I am informed, by the corporals, is called the east warrens."

"If you had not previously encountered Candallar, how can you be certain that the Shadow was carried across his Tower's border, as has been claimed?"

Bellusdeo let the question settle before she punted. "Tell me, have you visited the High Halls in the past week?"

"No. I have heard that there have been some changes."

"There have. All of the answers to the questions you ask can be found there—if you have the permission required to hear them. The subject is considered, politically, a matter for the Barrani caste Court, and I am notably not Barrani. I will therefore allow those with knowledge to dispense it as they see fit.

"But I have seen—personally—the damage that *Ravellon* can do. I have seen a world lost. Not a city, but the whole of the world, enveloped in the end by the Shadows your Towers cage here."

"The Towers have never fallen."

"No. Not all worlds possessed such Towers. But Lord Farlonne, your cages have bars, and it is not beyond belief that the Shadows within can extend an arm between them."

"That is what you experienced?"

"That," Bellusdeo said, with a slight nod, "is what happened to me."

"Your people," Lord Farlonne continued, surprising at least Kaylin, "are rumored to live on the border, in the fief of Tiamaris."

"They are. They have been building dwellings capable of housing them; the *Norannir* are taller than your humans. They have the magic and the knowledge that they used to defend their homes, however imperfectly, from Shadow. It is not the same as the magic found in Elantra."

"That, too, I have heard. But I heard it at Court, a place I am seldom found, and I cannot attest to its veracity. Or could not. I believe, however, that you can."

"I can. In matters of Shadow, in matters of *Ravellon*, there is no help I, or my people, would not extend."

"And in return for this consideration?"

"Perhaps, in the near future, you might visit Tiamaris. It is where what remains of my people are currently situated. I would be gratified to entertain the specifics of your questions there, but I believe some permission would be required to enter the fief."

"No doubt similar to the permissions I myself require?"

Bellusdeo's smile deepened; it was still sharp, but nonetheless looked genuine. "And perhaps for the same reasons."

"You have my permission to continue your inspection of the border within Farlonne."

"Your permission, yes. But I feel that the effort would be largely wasted. It is clear to me that you take the duties imposed by the captaincy of a Tower very seriously."

"It was long considered a besetting sin and a sign of inflexibility in my character." Farlonne offered Bellusdeo another bow.

This time, Bellusdeo returned it. She then resumed her Draconic form, and once Kaylin and Severn were seated, flew to the border zone between Farlonne and Liatt. "I liked her," she said, the words almost guaranteed to carry to at least the fieflord.

"She seemed to like you, inasmuch as any Barrani likes anyone else."

I concur, Ynpharion said, sounding vaguely displeased. *You might—might, given your general squeamishness—find much you would admire in her.* His tone was grudging.

You don't care for her?

What does that even mean? He was now annoyed. *She is a Lord of the High Court. She is not of an age with the Lady, An'Teela, or Lord Annarion's brother.* Kaylin failed to see what her age had to do with anything, given the way age graced the Barrani. *She has less knowledge of things that occurred during the first two wars.*

That wasn't why she annoyed Ynpharion.

No. I found her lack of flexibility and her demands that others adopt her standards to be condescending.

Since most of the Barrani were locked in a struggle to corner the market on condescension, Kaylin shrugged.

But she accepts the responsibilities she chooses to carry, and she carries them almost to the exclusion of all else. She is not the head of her line; she lacks ambition in that regard. It is because of her lack of ambition that she is fieflord here. She knows what occurred, historically, in the distant past; she understands why the Towers were created. She also understands that the Towers require a captain, a Lord, to fulfill duties she sees as critically essential.

If Kaylin had been walking, she'd have stopped; she moved because Bellusdeo was currently responsible for her forward momentum.

Does she take all responsibilities as seriously?

As I said, she dedicates herself to the duties she undertakes.

Yes, that's what you said. What I'm asking—what I think I'm asking—is why did she dedicate herself to this one?

Ynpharion was silent, which meant he didn't know. Probably. *Why*, he finally said, *does your Dragon dedicate herself to it?*

Because she lost her home, her world, and her family to Ravellon.

You are unkind to Lord Ynpharion, Nightshade said. He was amused.

I'm as kind to him as he is to me.

You even believe that to be true. Ynpharion does not know. I myself do not know. I have, as Farlonne has, some rudimentary knowledge; those at Court enjoy discussions about the foibles and follies of their less fortunate peers. It is a trait that is common among all those who live. You might ask the Consort. All others will answer in a way that suits their political purposes, to their advantage, and your knowledge of the Court would not allow you to glean fact from their answers.

I'm not sure it's necessary.

Nor am I. It would not, given Sedarias's current plan, harm Lord Bellusdeo to make a tentative connection with a Lord of the High Court. Lord Farlonne is considered the equivalent of an overearnest country bumpkin by much of the High Court; such a liaison would not immediately indicate a threatening shift of alliances.

Sedarias and her relationship with the Dragon, however, will. I would suggest that Bellusdeo remove herself from your home, but I understand that this is not a suggestion she would welcome.

I wouldn't welcome it, either.

Yes. But you are not, in the Elantran phrasing, the boss of her. It is why she values you so highly.

It's safer for her to be with Helen than to be anywhere else. The only place that would be safer would be Tara.

Yes. Tara is Tower of Tiamaris, and that is where what remains of Bellusdeo's people live. If the Dragon intends to interact with the fiefs in any consistent fashion, Tara would be the home I would suggest.

I'm not even sure Tara would... Kaylin trailed off. She couldn't even bring herself to think it. *I'll ask. But not now.*

No. But Sedarias started to strategize before she left the West March. I believe she is capable of living outside of Helen's boundaries, but not all of the cohort can—not without causing unforeseen damage to the rest of the city. The cohort is the greater threat to the city.

She wasn't thinking about the city. She was thinking about Bellusdeo.

The border between Liatt and Farlonne was visually similar to the border between Durant and Farlonne. Farlonne's Tower looked like the peak of a citadel, and Kaylin was almost certain that the lower end of the building would match what would be seen above the skyline.

Liatt's Tower was different. If Durant's was workmanlike to its height, Liatt's was not. There was, about it, something that implied dreams. Or nightmares. Kaylin wasn't certain what. It was certainly ostentatious; where Tara was white, Liatt was hues of silver and gold, but the gold did not reflect sunlight in a way that made it painful to look at.

Ah, no.

It was gold and silver *in* the border zone. She could see its colors clearly. None of the other buildings had real color, just the hint of what their former color might have been when they'd been a natural part of the city. The Towers did not control the border zone. They were aware of the demarcations of their boundaries; they did not reach beyond them.

But they could still be seen here.

Kaylin frowned.

"What are you doing?" Bellusdeo asked as she slid off the Dragon's back.

"I can see the Tower of Liatt," Kaylin replied. "But we're between Farlonne and Liatt; I should at least be able to see the Tower of Farlonne just as well. Severn?"

He dismounted, as well. His vision was better than Kaylin's; always had been.

"Can you see them?" she asked as she turned toward what she assumed was Durant.

Severn was silent for a long beat as he narrowed his eyes.

"I can't see Farlonne," she continued, when he failed to answer. "I can only see Liatt. Or what I assume is Liatt—I've never been there in person."

"I can't see Farlonne. I can see Liatt."

"But this is a zone between the two fiefs, right?"

It was Bellusdeo who nodded.

"Do you think the Tower we can see shifts when we enter the border zone from the other side?"

"There is a way to determine that without the endless theorizing." The Dragon's voice was a rumble, but it was mostly amused.

Entering from the Liatt side of the border, Kaylin could see the Farlonne citadel. She could no longer perceive the Liatt Tower.

"How much exploration did you do?"

"Probably less than Tiamaris; we had different goals."

"He was trying to study ancient, mostly lost things, right?"

Severn shrugged. It wasn't precisely a fief shrug. "I would say that it wasn't entirely academic. He did want that information."

"Lannagaros wanted that information," Bellusdeo said. "I would bet on it."

"Tiamaris was interested in it, but...the Arkon, for whatever reason, doesn't seem to move much. I wouldn't be surprised if the interest overlapped; Tiamaris wanted to explore, and the Arkon wanted the information Tiamaris could dig up."

"Fair enough."

Kaylin looked at Bellusdeo. "You're worried," she finally said, voice flat.

"What gives it away? The eye color?"

"Your eyes are always that color when you're anywhere near the fiefs. They're probably mostly that color when you're sleeping."

Hope squawked; Bellusdeo snorted. "Let's take a look at the Liatt border." By which she meant the *Ravellon* border in Liatt.

The fief of Liatt's border into *Ravellon* resembled what Kaylin had come to expect: the buildings were run-down, the streets deserted. Only the truly desperate would choose to live here, and Kaylin doubted that they'd stay for long. Ferals could come into buildings, but buildings weren't their first choice—only if their prey fled through a door did they follow.

It was scant protection, but it was better than none.

Maybe. Kaylin had never had the entirety of a building collapse on her, and she guessed that that would do as much damage, but in different ways.

Bellusdeo was not impressed by the border itself, although it appeared to be similar to Nightshade's to Kaylin's eye. Perhaps the foray into Farlonne had given her hope that the other fieflords were not as neglectful. She could find nothing—aside from a total lack of early warning system—that indicated that there had been a breach. Kaylin wasn't certain how she determined this, and any attempt to get answers resulted in more confusion. Later, when they had time, she would try again.

None of the citizens of Liatt attempted to impede Bellusdeo's progress, and the gold Dragon followed the *Ravellon* border, heading toward Nightshade in silence.

Kaylin could see Castle Nightshade clearly as they entered the border zone; it was not as fanciful as Liatt's Tower, but nowhere near as mundane as Durant's. She had more experience with Nightshade's Tower, and very, very little of it had been positive. It was from Nightshade's Tower that the Barrani Ancestors had emerged, to wreak so much havoc in Elantra.

She didn't like the Tower; the Tower did not like her.

But it was in the Tower, or in the basement of the Tower, that she had first been called Chosen by the Ancients, or the ghosts of Ancients.

Nightshade—the Lord, not the fief—was waiting for them when they emerged. He offered Bellusdeo a deep and respectful bow.

"Lord Nightshade," the Dragon said, returning that bow with more reserve.

"My brother feels he owes you a great debt."

The Dragon's shrug was uncomfortable. "I do not consider him—or the rest of his cohort—to be in my debt." She began to walk, and Nightshade fell in beside her, aware—because of his bond with Kaylin—exactly what she intended. He made no move to dissuade her.

"I have seldom crossed the border zone in the fashion you chose to cross it today. Ah, that is inaccurate. I have not chosen to visit all of the border zones in sequence in that fashion. It has been enlightening."

"Oh?"

"Kaylin's observations about the visibility of the Towers, for one. I was aware that the border zone appears to extend to *Ravellon* in the same fashion it does into the rest of the fiefs. It is possible that Candallar's ally entered through the border zone itself. His exit might have been more difficult; the border zone from the other side is…not the same. If that were somehow the case, he might exit across the fief-*Ravellon* border."

"That doesn't explain how he could move, carrying Spike, across that border."

"No. But I feel that possible answers to that very question—which seems the heart of Lord Bellusdeo's concern—might be obtained if you visit the High Halls. It is not an avenue of research open to one such as me." He waited until Bellusdeo had finished her inspection, which was cursory at best. Although the buildings that faced *Ravellon* were, as remembered, in very questionable condition, the gold Dragon did not fear that Nightshade was Candallar.

Only when that inspection was complete did he stop. "You will cross over to Tiamaris," he said. "But I wish to return to the area you investigated yesterday."

"You want to see the building."

"I want to see if it is at all fixed in place. It is not—as the rest of the buildings contained within that space—a simple continuation of what the eye sees before one crosses the border; I had some sense of what Kaylin was seeing, but the connection was not perfect and it required active concentration to fully see what she was seeing." His tone implied that he had failed.

"There was some chance that the situation in which you found yourself was both unstable and unsafe. It was not the correct time to attempt to view what you viewed. Since you are now here, I wish to know whether or not you can find that building again."

Kaylin glanced at Bellusdeo. The gold Dragon considered this for a moment, and then nodded. "Why not?"

Kaylin could have answered: *lunch*. She didn't; she knew better. Her stomach argued. But she fell in beside Severn and began to walk as if Nightshade were her beat. Bellusdeo was therefore in the lead. It was a politeness extended by Nightshade; Kaylin was fairly certain that he knew the exact geographic location from which they'd exited the border zone.

I do. But you have been in the border zone before; it is often elastic. You believe that you see streets when you peer into it; those streets conform to what you expect to see; they seem a continuation of the actual street.

Kaylin nodded, although he didn't have eyes in the back of his head.

That has not been my experience. When I gaze into the border zone, I do not see what you see.

What do you see, then?

Sometimes I see the continuation you see. Sometimes I see nothing but a thick fog. Sometimes I see the vague outline of the road on which I stand as it continues into that fog. I believe that my view is influenced by the Tower and the Tower's awareness of the boundaries of its duties. I find it interesting that you thought to look for Towers; I found it interesting that you could, depending on the direction from which you entered, see only one.

Interesting was bad.

Interesting is interesting, he said with minor annoyance; for a moment, his tone reminded her of the Arkon. No, not the Arkon, Sanabalis.

This amused the fieflord. *I do suggest that you avoid inform-ing him of that.*

Which him?

Lord Sanabalis. *I believe nothing you could say or observe would offend the Arkon.*

So wrong.

I have often wished that I could—as you do—simply walk into the Imperial Library and introduce myself to the Arkon there.

She thought he probably could.

Sedarias is right to be concerned about you. Yes. I could. Outcaste is not a blanket legal definition unless one is a Dragon. But being acknowledged as a citizen with a right to a life lived within the con-fines of Imperial Law—the law you yourself protect—would cause a wealth of difficulties with the High Court and the High Halls. Not all difficulties are legal difficulties.

I could test the Emperor's tolerance or his taste for political unrest. I imagine that I would, in fact, be allowed to at least make an ap-pointment with the Arkon should I approach his interests correctly. But the cost would be high. You have seen some of that friction in the person of Bellusdeo; she is a pretext for...hostility.

Kaylin had. *The Emperor didn't bend.*

No, but Bellusdeo is literally the future of the race, if there is to be a future at all. If the Barrani declared war, he would wage it. There is no reality in which the Emperor does not protect the future of his people. I, however, am incapable of giving birth to small Dragons.

I don't think it's just because of that.

No? Perhaps not. The laws are his laws, after all. But I believe that he would command the Arkon to refuse—politely—all requests for appointment or access if they came from me.

You really haven't spent much time with the Arkon. Yes, he might ask, but command? I'd be against it. With my own money. The Arkon might consider it condescending.

The Arkon serves the Eternal Emperor.

Yes. He does. But the Emperor is younger than the Arkon, and I think less learned. The Arkon commands respect. The Emperor respects him. I don't even think he'd ask. I think he would trust the Arkon to make the correct choice.

And if the Arkon chose to meet with me?

He would assume that the Arkon's reasons were pressing and important.

And you would make this bet with your personal funds?

With my own money, yes.

Ah. We must return to this conversation at a later point in time. "Lord Bellusdeo."

The Dragon nodded, frowning. "This is where we exited the border zone." Turning so that her back faced the border, she gazed out into the streets, confirming it for herself.

Kaylin was certain she was correct. That building with the broken fence—the third slat had been snapped in half at least a decade ago, by the looks of it—had been on that corner.

It was Hope who sighed and lifted a wing, smacking the bridge of her nose with it. "I think Hope doesn't think this is the way in." The familiar didn't leave his wing across her eyes. Whatever he thought she'd see, he didn't think was relevant enough.

The gold Dragon didn't take this as a criticism. "If the Towers appear—or vanish—depending on the direction of our approach, this makes some sense."

"You don't think we'll find it?"

"I'm not sure we have much to lose." Which sounded very much like a no.

Kaylin did not make a bet—with any of her companions. But they walked down the streets she could see and Nightshade couldn't, and emerged into the fief of Tiamaris. They then turned around and came back. Bellusdeo asked them to retrace their steps, and Kaylin realized, as she turned, that the damn street was *different* seen from this side.

It looked like the border zone. It did not, however, conform to the streets they'd just passed through. And it wasn't a simple block or two, either.

But Bellusdeo insisted, and Kaylin—who wanted lunch—had developed a watchful fatalism. She wanted to get this over and done with. So they reentered the border zone from the fief of Tiamaris, the only Dragon fieflord. They walked down a different street, with different run-down buildings. From this vantage, she could see Castle Nightshade. On the way through the first time, she had seen Tara's white Tower.

"The thing I hate about magic," she said, "is that none of it makes any *sense*. It doesn't seem to follow any rules. Or logic."

Bellusdeo snorted but said nothing; it wasn't the first time she'd heard Kaylin's rants about magic, and this one was pretty clean. It was less clean when they emerged in Nightshade again, because they didn't emerge in the same place they'd left.

Nightshade's eyes had narrowed into slits of concentration. Bellusdeo's eyes were a shade of orange that implied they might drift into gold. Someday. Severn was silent.

You knew.

I suspected. This conforms to my prior experience.

Did you ever exit and enter the same location?

No. I wasn't exploring the border zone to explore. I had a goal in mind.

Did you think someone had fled into the border zone?

It struck me as a distinct possibility. It still does. But the Towers are aware of their own borders, and it's likely the fieflords are aware of breaches. I didn't necessarily want to attract their attention. They're laws unto themselves—accepted laws—and if someone flees to the fiefs, it's likely that the fieflords are aware of them.

You think whoever you were hunting had permission?

Silence.

Sometimes, he said when silence had implied a break in the former conversation, *the border zone does conform to expectations.*

But more often not?

Fifty-fifty—but I didn't spend much time experimenting. In the end, with the exception of Farlonne, it's better to take the known bridges into the fiefs than it is to trust the border. I didn't know the fiefs well enough to easily reorient myself when the displacement was several blocks.

Which appeared to be the case.

Nightshade had not yet given up. He did not attempt to enter the border zone from their first entry point; he turned immediately and reentered from the point at which they'd emerged.

He then crossed the border a half-dozen times. None of those times took him—took them, but Kaylin thought they were becoming increasingly irrelevant to the fieflord—to the large building that almost resembled a town hall.

"We will have to leave you," Bellusdeo finally said, as disgruntled as Nightshade. "But I will do one aerial sweep of the border zone."

"I do not advise that," the fieflord said.

"Oh?"

"Given the changing shape and length of the area one traverses, it is a distinct possibility that you could end up emerging in *Ravellon*'s airspace."

Even Bellusdeo was aware of the risk—of the disaster—of that possibility. She rumbled, but stalled her transformation, reversing it.

It was midafternoon by the time they returned to the Halls of Law. Food was scant in the mess hall, given the hour. Kaylin's suggestion—that they return to the Halls with a stopover at home—had apparently been inaudible.

Nightshade did not leave off his exploration of the border zone. Kaylin could feel the edge of his sharpening curiosity. *Be careful,* she told him.

This surprised them both. *I am always careful.*

She didn't argue with his use of the word "careful." *Annarion will be upset if you disappear, and I have to live with him.*

Things were calm enough between the two brothers at the moment that Nightshade could, and did, find this slightly amusing. *If I have difficulty, you are certain to be aware of it.*

I've had emergencies when the other people who knew were nowhere near. It's not as much fun as it sounds.

His amusement grew deeper.

Marcus was not impressed by Bellusdeo's natural suit of armor. His eyes were a shade of orange that would have been dangerous had they not been accompanied by an expression of resignation and disgust.

"What," he said to Kaylin without preamble, "have you done now?"

She wasn't the one wearing the armor. "Next time," she muttered. "We're going home first."

"Corporal?" he snapped in a tone that made Kaylin's promotion seem nonexistent.

"We made contact with the fieflord of Candallar."

"He attacked you?"

"No. I believe there's a possibility that we can have a meaningful discussion outside of the fief itself—but he was cautious and not forthcoming. Bellusdeo wanted to see the *Ravellon* border in Candallar. She's concerned—"

"I can speak for myself."

Kaylin shut up.

Marcus transferred his orange gaze to Bellusdeo. Frankly, if Kaylin had filled his seat, that gaze would never have left her. Although her own eyes were far more golden, she was the biggest threat the room now contained—and the room contained Barrani Hawks as well as an annoyed Leontine.

"I am unimpressed with the security measures taken by the empire with regards to *Ravellon* and its Shadows. I am unimpressed with the...fieflords, or rather, their selection. There has clearly been some difficulty with Shadows and the security and stability of the very necessary border. I wished to ascertain for myself that the border was secure."

"And?"

"And?"

"Is the border secure?"

"It is demonstrably not secure enough, but some theories have emerged; I am assessing the possible or probable dangers, but I wished to see the entirety of the border."

"The entirety."

"Yes."

"You traveled through all of the fiefs along the *Ravellon* border."

"Yes. Or is there another way to assess that I possibly failed to consider?"

"For the Records, I want it to be known that this was *not* the assignment I gave the corporals."

Bellusdeo snorted.

Kaylin said absolutely nothing. Hope, on her shoulder, yawned, which pulled a stink-eye from the sergeant.

"Are you operating under the orders of the Imperial Court?"

At this, Bellusdeo smiled. "Would that be more convenient for the Hawks?"

For the first time in a while, Kaylin saw Marcus's eyes

lighten to near gold in a Dragon's presence. "The Imperial Court trumps the Hawklord, yes."

"Very well. I have some experience with Shadow and the catastrophic nature of events when all protections fail. I am, therefore, considered the resident expert. I am capable of withstanding the attacks of even the most powerful of Shadows for a prolonged period of time, and it is very difficult for Shadow to transform or change a Dragon. I am the agent who would be sent in such investigations."

"You'll make your report to the Court?"

She glanced pointedly at the piles that comprised the surface of Marcus's desk. "I will."

"Good. The corporals have been pulled off the Elani beat while the Candallar discussion and investigation is ongoing. I expect them to be back on their beat within three days at the outside, including this one."

"Three days?" Kaylin failed to stop the words from leaving her mouth, partly because it was open.

"The fiefs are outside the remit of the Halls of Law. Your investigations might be relevant to some of the events that occur within Elantra, but we are not empowered to enforce Imperial Laws within any fief that is not Tiamaris."

"We're not empowered to enforce those laws in Tiamaris, either."

Marcus said nothing. It was a loud nothing.

CHAPTER
11

"Did I miss something?" Kaylin demanded of Tain, who had the misfortune to be at his desk. Teela was absent—probably because she'd seen Bellusdeo enter the office in armor. Marcus could be noisy when he was surprised.

"Probably."

"Did Ironjaw just say we have permission to enforce *Imperial Law* in the fief of Tiamaris?"

"You're going to have to ask him. Or look at the duty roster."

"He's a *Dragon*, Tain. He's a *fieflord*. Why in the hells would he give up his sovereignty?"

"Because he's also a member of the Imperial Court, and he owes his allegiance to the Emperor." Tain shrugged. "It's politics and diplomacy."

"Wait, back up a bit."

"To where? Mortal memory is bad, but it's not that bad."

"Duty roster?"

"I don't believe your current rounds of duty are being affected."

"In the *fiefs*?"

Tain shrugged. "Don't give me that look. I wasn't asked

for my opinion, and the meeting in which it was discussed occurred when we were all visiting the scenic High Halls."

Tiamaris had mentioned nothing. Kaylin, disgruntled, rejoined Bellusdeo.

"I don't understand what the problem is," Bellusdeo said. "Tiamaris has made clear, from the moment he took control of the Tower, that Imperial Law and its norms were to be observed—with a few exceptions—within the borders of Tiamaris. I believe it is essential if he wishes to integrate his fief with the greater city as a whole. Fill in your report, and we'll head home. I have a few things I wish to discuss with both Maggaron and Helen."

"Why Maggaron?"

Bellusdeo's smile was far too sweet. "The *Norannir* would make excellent Hawks, in my opinion."

"Helen has no say in that!"

"No, of course not. I wish to discuss other things with Helen."

"Fine. Just let me write this up and hand it to Marcus, and we can go home and eat something."

Bellusdeo had, of course, lied. She had no qualms about that. The Imperial Court had not sent her into the heart of the fiefs, and the Emperor would probably breathe fire in random directions if and when he found out she had been there on her own.

The fact that she'd been there with four other people would not mollify him. Those people were not Dragons, and when it came to brute force and dangerous combat, it was the Dragons he trusted. To be fair to the Emperor, in his position, and assuming he could choose the composition of Bellusdeo's guards, he'd go for the Dragons every time. Except Diarmat. Diarmat was likely to cause an entirely different kind of conflict, and no one wanted Dragons in combat in the middle of the city.

Kaylin was not looking forward to the Imperial discussion about Bellusdeo's current investigation. She had hopes that she could avoid it in its entirety. The conversations she wanted to be part of always seemed to occur when it was impossible for her to join them. Like, say, Hawks patrolling Tiamaris.

Helen was waiting for them when they reached the front doors—doors which were open. "Welcome home," she said. Her eyes were normal eyes, and her clothing was also vastly less militaristic than Bellusdeo's current armor.

"Have things been quiet at home?"

"For a value of quiet. I believe the cohort is currently having a debate."

"A debate or an argument?"

"Only three of them have been confined to the training room while the discussion continues."

Definitely an argument.

"I'm beginning to understand them, or at least understand how they respond to emotional duress. Mandoran and Terrano are home," she added.

"Sorry. Sedarias seemed to want to talk to Candallar, and Bellusdeo wanted to inspect the *Ravellon* border. The entire *Ravellon* border."

Helen offered a sympathetic cluck of sound. "I consider *Ravellon* to be the greater threat. I'm not certain the Emperor will be pleased."

"The Emperor is never pleased. At least not with me." Bellusdeo had headed up the stairs. Kaylin hoped she was far enough away that she hadn't heard the *E* word. "What, exactly, is the cohort debating?"

"Among other things? Candallar. Annarion, and therefore

Solanace. Mellarionne. And also the gathering of the High Court. Some of the cohort feel that Bellusdeo's presence will cause an all-out war on the premises of the High Halls."

"Not likely. The desire for all-out war? Absolutely. But... the High Halls is more like a Hallionne now, and there's no way all-out war would even be possible in a Hallionne."

Helen coughed. Kaylin grudgingly conceded the point, given their flight from the West March and their rescue of the Hallionne Alsanis.

"Mandoran is attempting to avoid the entire discussion because he feels some pressure to return to his line, as well."

"He said he was orphaned."

"He has said many things, dear. And he's Mandoran. If it allows him to avoid unpleasantness, he is likely to say anything regardless of inconvenient facts. Sedarias understands that a return to power necessitates allies and people in positions of strength.

"Serralyn has suggested that a focus on Mellarionne first would be the better plan."

"Let me guess. That's not Sedarias's intended strategy."

"As I said, there has been some heated debate."

Dinner, served slightly earlier than usual on account of Kaylin's lack of lunch, was sparsely attended. Mandoran and Terrano joined Kaylin at the table, but Annarion did not. Bellusdeo was apparently indisposed—Kaylin thought this might be because of the discussion with Maggaron, but didn't ask.

The fork was halfway to her mouth when the entire room shuddered.

Mandoran dropped his head to the tabletop.

Terrano groaned.

"Do I even want to know?" Kaylin asked.

"You really, really don't." Terrano replied. "I'm sure I

thought coming back was a good idea. Do you remember why?"

"You did miss them."

"Yes. Being in the outlands addled my brain."

"Speaking of the outlands," Kaylin said as she considered and rejected everything about Sedarias's power struggles as *not her problem*. "I've got a couple of questions for you."

"For us collectively?"

"No—that'll annoy Sedarias."

He laughed. "For me, then."

"For you. I don't know if you've ever tried to cross the borders between actual fiefs—not the *Ravellon* border, and not the city-facing perimeter—but I'd be interested to hear what you think."

"What I think of?"

"The border zone itself."

Terrano frowned. "The border zone? *Ravellon's* border?"

She shook her head. "The border between the fiefs."

"Which border?"

"Any border."

"That's where you guys went?"

"Sort of. Bellusdeo's annoyed at Candallar, and she wanted to inspect the *Ravellon* border in the fief of Candallar."

"And that led to the border zone?"

"She also wanted to check out the border zone. All of them. Since she went from Candallar into the neighboring fiefs along the *Ravellon* border, we managed this."

"There's a *but* coming."

"Not really. The border zone is…not like the fiefs. It's its own thing, and I don't understand it. It feels like it's almost, but not quite, like the outlands."

"Almost but not quite? Kaylin, you are *terrible* with words."

"Everything looks like it should, in theory, when you enter

it. I mean, the buildings and the street continue from the non-border-side view. But everything's washed out. It's almost black and white; there's a hint of color, but it's faded."

"People live there?"

"Not that I know of. I mean, we had things pretty tough and we didn't try to squat in the border."

"Why? Shadow?"

Kaylin offered him a fief shrug.

"You want me to look at the border zone?"

"I wanted to know if you wandered off track."

"We were speaking on behalf of Sedarias. What do you think?"

Kaylin grimaced. "I think I'm going to finish dinner and go to bed. I'm not sure I want you to look at the border zone, either. I was just asking if you did. You've spent more time in places like the outlands than anyone else I know. I think."

"What would you ask me if I'd gone into the border zone?"

"What you saw there. What it meant to you. When Nightshade crossed into the border zone, he couldn't see what the rest of us saw."

Terrano straightened up. "What do you mean, couldn't see?"

"He saw a lot of fog. He couldn't see the buildings the rest of us were looking at."

"Interesting. Do you think it's because he's the Lord of the Tower?"

"It crossed my mind, yes. But the only other fieflord I could reasonably ask to cross into the border zone is Tiamaris—and I won't see what he sees, or doesn't see."

"I'm done with dinner." Terrano pushed his chair back and stood.

"I do not think that's a good idea, dear," Helen said.

"It's information, right? It might be useful. At the moment we can use anything useful we can get our hands on."

"I don't think you should go alone."

"Helen, I'm never alone anymore. I've got nothing to contribute to the current discussion—mostly because I don't care—and I'm bored. Would you rather I try to alleviate my boredom here?"

"Yes, actually," Helen replied in a more severe tone.

"Don't give me that look," Kaylin told Terrano. "I'm with Helen on this one."

A wake-up call came via Helen in the middle of a night that was looking good for sleep. There were two soon-to-be mothers that Kaylin was keeping an eye on through the midwives' guild, but neither was expecting in the immediate future, and the foundling hall had been silent, the children avoiding the sometimes life-threatening injuries that required her immediate attention. Marrin's cub fascinated the kids in the foundling hall, and they variously positioned themselves as older sisters, older brothers or pseudo-parents.

Kaylin imagined that some of the kids were jealous or afraid—but Marrin was a Leontine, and her cub, Leontine as well, wasn't quite as threatening to human children as a human baby would have been. On the other hand, the foundlings tended to treat the cub as a new pet. Kaylin found this more mortifying than Marrin did.

"If a mortal infant arrives on my steps—a human infant, I mean—they tend to treat the baby the same way: as a pet."

Fair enough. Regardless, midwives and foundlings were sorted. The only thing that stood between Kaylin and sleep was the question of Hawks patrolling the fief of Tiamaris— but Marcus was in charge of the duty roster and the Hawklord was no doubt in charge of the diplomatic hassles. While it might affect her work going forward, it wasn't her problem.

Something, however, was, and it woke her in two stages.

She sat up in bed, instantly aware that something was wrong. No nightmare—and she still had plenty of those—drove her from sleep; she wasn't sweating, her hands weren't bunched in fists around the blanket, and she hadn't instinctively grabbed the dagger that rested under her pillow.

But something was wrong. "Helen, light, please?"

The effective visual equivalent of open shutters happened almost immediately.

"What's wrong, dear?"

Since Helen could more or less hear everything Kaylin was thinking, she knew Kaylin didn't have an immediate answer to that question. It was an invitation to think, to assess.

"Ah, no. The cohort is awake."

"They're always awake. The Barrani don't need to sleep."

Hope, who generally slept somewhere in the vicinity of Kaylin's face—often on the single pillow her bed possessed—was now sitting, alert, as if waiting for her to get ready.

"My apologies. It was more of an analogy than a technical description. Mandoran is on his way now."

"On his way here?"

"Yes, dear. I think Allaron is going to join him."

Kaylin attempted to figure out what had caused her to wake so suddenly and completely.

Nightshade.

Nightshade?

There was a core of silence where Nightshade habitually resided on the inside of her thoughts. She'd become accustomed to this; Helen generally kept those whose names she knew out of the house. Under Helen's roof, Kaylin could guard her thoughts because, unless Helen considered it useful, the name-bound couldn't communicate with her. Helen never kept Kaylin from initiating contact. She didn't keep a response to the attempt beyond the walls of her house, either.

But Nightshade didn't answer, damn it all.

Someone rapped at the door. Mandoran shouted Kaylin's name.

Fully dressed, Kaylin walked across the comfortingly creaky floor and opened that door. Helen had been right; Mandoran, accompanied by Allaron, stood on the other side of the frame.

"Let me guess," she said as Hope settled onto her left shoulder. "Terrano's missing."

Mandoran opened his mouth, shut it, and opened it again. "...We've lost contact with Terrano."

Kaylin looked up at Allaron, necessary because he was significantly taller, as opposed to the usual Barrani taller. "You might as well go get Annarion."

Allaron was briefly confused.

Mandoran wasn't. "You can't reach Annarion's brother, either." It wasn't a question.

"Got it in one."

"I really wish you hadn't said that."

"Why? Nightshade was exploring the border zone. So was Terrano. Did Terrano come across Nightshade?"

"No."

"Did he see what I described?"

"...Not exactly."

"Why is everything always so complicated?"

"Hey, not our fault. We didn't make the world."

"I'm thinking that Terrano is awfully good at breaking bits of it."

"Nightshade was there, too."

"I didn't say that Nightshade wasn't good at it himself." She shook her head. "Honestly, I think he'd've made a good member of your cohort if he'd been younger and sent to the green." Before she'd finished speaking the words, Annarion appeared. He didn't materialize, though—he came running full tilt down the hall of otherwise closed doors, each of which fronted one of Helen's set of individualized suites.

"Sedarias thinks you should wake the Dragon."

Kaylin didn't agree. She managed not to say this out loud because she was certain that Bellusdeo was now aware that something was—once again—happening in the house.

"Teela says you should stay put," Allaron added.

"Why are you glaring at me?" Mandoran demanded.

"I'm not."

"I didn't tell you because I know it's a waste of words, and there are already far too many words floating around." He turned to Annarion. "Kaylin's not going to stay here. What Teela wants is irrelevant."

A door down the hall opened, and the aforementioned irrelevant opinion joined Mandoran and Allaron. "We'd better move," Teela said, voice low enough it was almost a whisper.

But another door opened as the words left her mouth. Bellusdeo was already prepared. This time, she hadn't bothered with the normal clothing; she was in her full golden scale armor. Maggaron was with her.

"You weren't possibly thinking of going out without me?" The Dragon's eyes were gold.

"No, of course not," Kaylin said. She agreed with Mandoran. There wasn't much point in attempting to argue when the result was a foregone conclusion.

Kaylin was accustomed to emergency forays into the streets of Elantra in the dead of night; that was often when the midwives' guild mirrored her. But most of those emergencies involved Kaylin, and the danger was to the mother and child. It was too late to go out drinking, but this resembled—with the exception of the Dragon in gold plate—an ill-advised tavern crawl. It certainly didn't look like a rescue crew.

Kaylin asked Allaron to stay behind with Sedarias; Allaron's answer was a steady, almost unblinking stare.

"Bellusdeo is going with us," Kaylin then said for Sedarias's benefit. "Anything that can take out a Dragon could kill the rest of us with a sneeze. There's no point in risking more people."

"Remember what I said about arguing when there's no point?" Mandoran then said. "And it's not for your sake that Sedarias is sending him. It's for his." He nodded in the direction of a very grim, very blue-eyed Annarion. "The Dragon isn't going to be able to restrain him if he loses it. Allaron probably can."

"You win." Kaylin exhaled. "I think we should start with either Tiamaris or Nightshade."

Bellusdeo said, "Lead. We'll follow."

Kaylin had doubts about that, given that three of the cohort were with them. She looked at Teela.

"Where was the last place you had contact with Nightshade?" The Barrani Hawk was all business.

"He was entering the border zones between his fief and Liatt's. I wasn't following him closely, but I…" She frowned. "I think I was half listening. Like, when the cohort is talking out loud—stray words or the occasional shouting will catch my attention. It's like that."

"Did Nightshade do the equivalent of shouting?"

Kaylin shook her head. "But when you all stop talking and it's utterly silent, I notice that, as well. It's like the background noise is part of the house; I notice when it disappears."

"There was no warning?"

"I was sleeping, Teela. Did Terrano give you any warning?"

"No, but he's Terrano."

"Is this the first time you've lost him? I mean, outside of the obvious?"

"Not like this," Mandoran replied. "This is a lot more like what happened to Sedarias and the rest in the West March. There's less panic," he added.

"Not a lot less," Teela said.

"I feel less panicked." He had certainly been panicking when he'd lost contact with over half his cohort at once. "To be fair, Annarion's making up for it."

Annarion glared at Mandoran, but said nothing out loud.

Nightshade at night had Ferals. In fact, all of the fiefs did. In Tiamaris, there were patrols that hunted the Shadow dog packs before they could hunt the helpless. The *Norannir* certainly didn't fear them. But Nightshade didn't have those patrols. Kaylin highly doubted that Candallar did, either; she suspected that Farlonne might.

"Ferals are not going to be a threat tonight."

"Not to us."

Teela raised a brow at Kaylin's tone.

"I didn't know you when I was ten. I didn't know any of you. There are probably ten-year-olds squatting in silence hoping that the Ferals don't find them tonight."

The Barrani exchanged a glance. Bellusdeo and Maggaron said nothing.

Mandoran cleared his throat. "Sedarias has a question."

"Coward."

"It's not my question. I wouldn't ask it."

"Fine." They left the bridge into Nightshade and proceeded toward Liatt through streets that were empty and silent.

"The weak of any race and any species die. The strong survive."

"That's not a question."

"Yeah, I know. I'm getting to that part."

Sedarias, speaking through Mandoran, continued before Kaylin could answer. "You don't weep for dogs or animals in the wild when they die, for instance."

"They're not people."

"No. But you don't know them. You don't know the people in this fief anymore, for the most part. Why is it different? Why do you imagine that these people are somehow you, or could somehow become you?"

"Seriously?"

"We understand the grief of loss. We understand that that grief comes out of attachment. We mourn the things we no longer have. But there's no inherent pain in the loss of strangers."

"Stop," Teela said out loud. Clearly, whatever she was saying on the inside of her head wasn't reaching Sedarias.

"Why? Sedarias doesn't understand it; she wants to understand. Does Kaylin think that *all life* has an inherent value? Because there's a lot of life out there."

"Kaylin is a Hawk. It's her vocation, her hobby and her commitment. Hawks—"

"Enforce Imperial Law, yes."

"Why do you think those laws were created?" Teela continued as Kaylin opened her mouth.

"Does it matter? Sedarias doesn't understand why the laws are so complicated—"

Kaylin snorted. "That's rich, coming from a Barrani. You might not know it, but most of the complicated laws are written in High Barrani. The Emperor felt it was the perfect language for them."

This didn't slow Sedarias. Which meant Mandoran kept talking. Neither Allaron nor Annarion had anything to add. "Sedarias says the Emperor is a Dragon. He's powerful enough that he gets to make the laws. We're weak enough—for the moment—that we have to follow them when he's looking in our direction. Hawks exist to be the eyes that are looking in all directions when the Emperor can't. They're meant to enforce the more powerful person's will."

"That's not the purpose of the law," Kaylin snapped.

"Then what is?"

"We're there to enforce the law so that people *without* the Emperor's power are safe from people who have attitudes like *yours*."

Mandoran snapped his jaw shut on whatever he'd been about to say.

"Told you," Teela said quietly.

It was Annarion who caught up with Kaylin. The Barrani and the Dragon weren't far enough behind that they couldn't catch up with little effort, and even a hunting pack of Ferals was unlikely to reach Kaylin before her friends could.

"Sedarias doesn't mean to upset you. She is honestly trying to understand."

Kaylin said nothing.

"There are so many people who have no power. So many people who would be considered weak. Among our own kin. Among the mortals. Especially among the mortals. If every single person who is weaker than you somehow becomes your personal responsibility, it will kill you. You would never have a moment's peace, a moment's rest. Your needs and wants would be subsumed in their entirety by the needs of others."

"If the world were more just, more fair, they wouldn't be."

"Even with the laws you support and uphold, the world's not a just or fair place."

"But it could be."

"Possibly. But in the end, it's power that decides and power that rules. If you want to make changes, you need to have power. What you do with the power is then up to you, because you're powerful." He switched to Elantran, although he was often more comfortable speaking his native tongue. "Sedarias isn't saying that the powerful should do whatever they feel like at the moment; she is saying that they *can*.

"You can't save everyone. It's not possible. And there will always be people who need more than you and have less. Always. Even in your perfect world, unless you somehow imagine that everyone in that perfect world will all be the same. We're immortal. We have time. You don't. Would you make all mortals immortal? Attempts to do that have never worked well. Would you make all immortals mortal?"

"No."

"Sedarias wants to know what you think your ideal world would look like."

"Sedarias can drop dead."

Silence. And then, because Sedarias had not dropped dead, "If you removed the fiefs, if you reformed them as Tiamaris is attempting to do, what will you do with your warrens? They are not, she infers, any safer for their occupants than the fiefs were for you."

"They don't have Ferals."

"No; they have thugs who rule the warrens with more efficiency and more intelligence—or cunning. Your rule of law, your laws, haven't prevented the warrens from existing."

"Annarion, please stop passing on Sedarias's opinions. I don't want them, and they're not relevant to what we're trying to do here."

"She points out—"

"I mean it."

He fell silent. When he spoke again—and he did—he said, "I don't agree with Sedarias, except in one way: if you feel responsible for everything, you'll have no life of your own. If you can't do everything—and not even you believe you can— then what is the point of anger or guilt? It's like you're feeling guilty, and that makes you angry, and then you're angry at...what? The universe? The world? The people who abuse the power they do have?"

"The people who don't care."

"If we can't change things, not caring is a way of surviving. Because caring or not caring has the same effect. Yes, perhaps we could say 'but we care,' but...if it doesn't change anything, what does it even mean?"

"That part where I said stop?"

"Sorry. We find your worldview very, very confusing. Mandoran probably understands it best, but he's having trouble explaining it and he thought you'd do a better job."

"Mandoran is an idiot."

For the first time since they'd left Helen, Annarion cracked a smile. It wasn't much of a smile, but it was there.

"If it makes much difference, Teela pointed out the midwives and the foundling hall."

"In what context?"

"Well, they don't pay you. And you've saved lives."

Kaylin shrugged. "Did it make a difference to Sedarias?"

"Not really. But Sedarias's family is— Well, you've seen her sister and her brother." He hesitated. "You've been happy with the changes Lord Tiamaris is making in his fief."

Kaylin nodded.

"They make pragmatic sense to Sedarias—if your people are starving, they're going to be useless—but at heart, the world is like the fief. This one," he added, with a trace of bitterness. "If you're at the bottom, you're dependent on the largesse of the powerful. In order to stand on your own, you have to be a power. She understands ties of affection and obligation—but she doesn't understand a sense of obligation where those ties are nonexistent.

"Helen's tried to explain it. But Sedarias thinks Helen has no choice but to think what she thinks because that's the way she was built."

Kaylin was offended on Helen's behalf, and tried to squash it; Helen wouldn't be offended. She exhaled. "Can we drop it?"

Annarion nodded.

"But tell Sedarias that I go to the foundling hall because it's like seeing a bunch of little Kaylins who won't be terrified of Ferals, won't face starvation, and won't be without protection. It's like it helps me imagine a life that wasn't mine for kids who might not survive otherwise. I survived because I was lucky. And because I had Severn."

But that led to darker thoughts, and she shied away from those.

"You're not worried about my brother." The last word rose slightly.

"Not yet."

"No?"

"We bumbled our way out of trouble. I'm guessing Nightshade knows what we did and how we did it. He won't get stuck the same way we did. I'm more worried about Terrano."

"Oh?"

"He's more of a trouble magnet than anyone I've ever met."

Annarion coughed.

"What?"

"Sedarias suggests you find a mirror."

"I don't go looking for trouble. I just trip over it."

"Sedarias also says: fair enough. Is that the border?"

Kaylin glanced at Annarion; his eyes were narrowed. She hesitated, and Bellusdeo said, "Yes, that's the border. What do you see when you look at it?"

"Fog. Or smoke." Mandoran and Allaron joined him as they slowed their walk. Kaylin didn't see fog. Hope was hanging across her shoulders like a shawl, looking distinctly bored. He didn't sit up and didn't slap a wing across her eyes. Whatever she saw appeared to be good enough.

She didn't see what Hope saw.

"Teela?"

"I see streets continuing into what I assume is visually Liatt."

"Bad assumption," Bellusdeo then said. "Crossing that street doesn't take us to a street that looks similar in Liatt."

"You experimented?"

"For much of the day. I'm not sure why the Towers choose to present an illusion of streets continuing—but if we take that street and turn around the moment we enter Liatt, the street doesn't align properly."

"It's not the same street on both sides?"

"Not always, no. You see street?"

"I see what both you and Kaylin see. Allaron, Annarion and Mandoran don't. But if Kaylin had lost all contact with her name-bound, we'd know the silence was a simple effect of the border zone. Clearly, that's not the case. She could speak to the name-bound who were with her in the border zone."

"You think they found what they were looking for?"

"I think it likely."

"How do you guys want to do this? You need a rope-line?" Kaylin asked the cohort.

"Nah. We've got Teela. We'll just use her eyes."

Teela looked about as thrilled as Kaylin expected she would.

They entered the border zone from the Nightshade side, given that was the fief they were standing in. To Kaylin, the evening gave way to a twilight of gray and washed-out color, but the buildings in this light were clearer; Nightshade didn't believe in lighting all of the streets. To be fair—and this was grudging—Nightshade's streets were empty of all but the desperate and the drunken at night; the Ferals kept the streets clear.

Kaylin frowned as she studied the street they were standing on; it seemed to continue for a few blocks. She guessed that those blocks were illusory and they would exit the street to a change of environment in Liatt.

Teela didn't take the lead, and Bellusdeo, while impatient, didn't want it, either. Kaylin headed toward Liatt. "It's a proof of concept," she told her companions. "Let's see how long it takes us to get out."

The answer was three blocks. Liatt opened up to late night on the other side; the mist or fog cleared for the cohort as they reached it. Turning immediately, Kaylin looked down the street through which they'd just walked. It was different, or rather, the buildings were.

"I have an idea," she said.

"A good one?" This was Mandoran.

"Probably not. It shouldn't be dangerous—or not more dangerous than entering the border zone."

"Let's hear it."

"We're going to let you guys lead."

"We can't see much."

"Exactly. If we want to explore the border zone here, it's harder for the rest of us—we can see the street, we follow the street. I'd like to know how Nightshade or Terrano navigated when they were in that zone."

Entering the border zone from Liatt showed Kaylin a different street with different buildings. Mandoran's view was the same as it had been on the other side: a lot of fog and little visibility. This time, however, Kaylin decided to try a shortcut, passing between buildings to see if she could find another street. She used Mandoran's vision—or lack of vision—to skirt the border zone. The first time, she turned toward Elantra and emerged, eventually, at the boundary between Nightshade and the city—which would be the Ablayne.

The border zone could not be entered from the Elantra side of the fiefs. They couldn't see it; they couldn't cross into it. It appeared to exist as a function of the fiefs themselves. She wondered if the entry from *Ravellon* was just as impossible, but doubted it, and didn't ask because it was exactly the kind of question that would make Bellusdeo go red-eyed.

They entered Nightshade and started again; this time close to the Ablayne. Kaylin began to follow the border, using the cohort's lack of clear vision as a guide.

"You don't think Terrano would have been foolish enough to enter *Ravellon* by accident?" Bellusdeo asked.

Kaylin frowned. "I'm not sure Terrano would see what the others are seeing. Teela doesn't, except secondhand. They're both outliers when it comes to the cohort. Terrano is pushing the limits in one direction, and Teela is—"

"Boring," Mandoran supplied.

"Incredibly tolerant and forgiving," Teela said.

Kaylin snorted. She'd gone out drinking with Teela and Tain.

"We have lower standards for both," the Barrani Hawk

added when she caught sight of Kaylin's expression. "What are you looking for?"

"Streets."

"In backyards?"

"The visible—to the non-cohort—street follows the street from the fief. I want a street or two that goes parallel to the fief, rather than perpendicular, in the border zone. I think there has to be one—but we weren't looking when we left Killian behind; we just wanted to get out.

"Killian's building looked like a town hall, but bigger. And the exit didn't run in the same direction as the border zone streets generally run. We turned right, onto a street, and followed it out."

"And couldn't get back."

"More or less."

"Could you see it from above?" Teela asked Bellusdeo.

"No—but Kaylin wasn't keen on aerial exploration."

"That's odd—she usually loves flying."

The Dragon reached out and grabbed Mandoran by the arm. "I could see. You can't. Don't even try it."

"I could probably trace an area of the fog zone from above. I want to know what the border zone looks like from above. Is it all just fog for days or can we rise above it?"

Bellusdeo glared.

Mandoran was immune to that, as he saw it all the time.

"He's kind of tethered to the rest of them," Kaylin pointed out.

"You think it's safe?"

"Not really. But I don't think it will kill him."

"He's one of the few members of the cohort who possess a sense of humor. I'd hate to lose that."

"When you're not trying to turn me to ash?"

"*A* sense of humor doesn't imply a *good* sense of humor. It's still better than nothing."

Maggaron, who had been so silent Kaylin could forget his presence—which said a lot, given his height—cleared his throat. "I do not think I see what you see."

They all turned to stare at him.

CHAPTER 12

Bellusdeo was first to speak. "What do you see?"

"I see buildings," he finally said. "I see the street."

"Which is what we see."

"I do not think I see the same buildings."

"Why do you say that?"

"Because the buildings I see are buildings that would house my people, not the people of this city. The doors are taller. The ceilings are higher."

"How do you know that?"

"Because Kaylin said that the buildings looked the same in the border as they do in the actual fief. That is not what I see. When we enter the border zone, although the street appears to be a continuous line, the buildings themselves are… empty, deserted remnants of one of our cities, to me."

They turned to look at Maggaron; Kaylin then transferred her silent question to his Dragon.

"They look like mortal buildings to me. I see, I believe, what you see, not what Maggaron sees."

"Can you change your height?" Kaylin asked. "I mean, if Maggaron's people—"

"No. It is nowhere near as simple as that."

Mandoran spoke next, as if making a decision. "Let me go up above the clouds. I'll go straight up; I won't attempt to wander the line of fog. I have the others here; they can tell you what I see."

Bellusdeo rumbled, her wordless annoyance at odds with her appearance. She glared at Kaylin but offered the Barrani a grudging nod.

Mandoran's feet left the street. Since he couldn't see the street, it probably wasn't as unsettling to him as it was to Kaylin. She watched him rise above the two-story buildings, looking at almost nothing else, as if her gaze could somehow be an anchor.

Annarion and Allaron didn't watch, but didn't have to; Teela's gaze, like Kaylin's, was fixed to Mandoran—or the bottom of his feet. He didn't drift toward either the city or *Ravellon*. As he'd promised, he attempted to rise in a straight line.

"Something's strange," Annarion said, eyes closed.

"Is he above the fog line now?"

"Yes."

"What's strange?"

"All he can see is fog, in any direction. There's no visible fief on either side of where he's standing."

Kaylin had a very bad feeling about this. "Tell him to come down."

"He wants to look at something."

"Tell him we look with our eyes," Kaylin snapped.

"Barrani children are not raised with that phrase," Teela told her. "It won't have the same weight it does in the office."

Bellusdeo's rumble enclosed the words, "Stand back." Kaylin had seen this transformation often enough that she had a good idea of how much space "back" meant; Teela caught Annarion and Allaron and pulled them out of the way. Maggaron didn't move.

"This is a *bad idea*," Kaylin told the gold Dragon.

"Really? Why?"

"That's unkind to Kaylin," Teela said, before Kaylin could dredge up an answer that wouldn't make things worse. "You know well why."

Bellusdeo shrugged, a ripple of motion that traveled the length of her back. "You're not trying to stop me."

Teela shook her head. "I like you. I don't generally care for Dragons for obvious reasons. If the Dragon species has been whittled down to five—six, including yourself—it makes no material difference in my life. If the species remains at that number for the foreseeable future, it will not upset the balance of power.

"Some might argue that your disappearance here would be to our advantage in the long term. If you choose to be careless, if your decisions put you in the way of harm, it might prove useful."

Kaylin was outraged.

Annarion dropped a hand to her shoulder but said nothing.

"And you have no chance of personally stopping me?" Bellusdeo asked.

"None whatsoever," Teela replied, smiling. "But I would appreciate it if you did not involve Kaylin, because Kaylin stands even less of a chance and feels compelled to try."

Maggaron climbed up Bellusdeo's back. If Teela's words upset him, it didn't show—but Maggaron didn't speak much. His native tongue was not Elantran.

Bellusdeo exhaled a small plume of fire.

"Can you hurry?" Annarion surprised them all by saying. "I think something's gone wrong."

Bellusdeo was halfway to Mandoran when Mandoran disappeared. Given the grim expression on Annarion's and Allaron's faces, Kaylin guessed that they could no longer hear him. They certainly couldn't see him. She glanced at Teela, whose eyes were now on Bellusdeo. The Barrani Hawk's expression was grim, but shaded more toward frustration and disgust than actual worry.

"Tell me," she said, her throat elongated by her rising chin, "why I haven't strangled him."

"Beats me. I know why I haven't."

"You can't."

"Pretty much. You two think he's gone to wherever Terrano went?"

"Probably. It's the same—there's no fear and just a faint hint of surprise, and then silence. Nightshade?"

"I was sleeping at the time. I have no idea how or where he vanished, and no idea what he was feeling. But...if he were actively fighting for his life before he blinked out, I think I'd probably know." She cupped her hands around her mouth and shouted to catch Bellusdeo's attention. "Don't go higher!"

Bellusdeo had seen Mandoran's disappearance. Inclination aside, she wasn't stupid or reckless. And she had Maggaron with her; from what little Kaylin had seen, he was the steadying influence and possibly the only person present who could talk sense into her and have her listen.

Which, all things considered, probably wasn't saying much. But she circled the area beneath which Mandoran had been drifting when he had disappeared.

"What do you see?"

"Border zone," the Dragon replied. "It extends in all directions for as far as I can see. Which follows his comment about fog. I can't see Nightshade. I can't see Liatt. If I could go higher, I might."

"Please don't. Let's try to follow the actual zone from the ground."

"That didn't stop Nightshade from disappearing."

Fair enough. But at least they would all be together.

"What do you think the border zone is?" Teela asked as they once again resumed their march through theoretical backyards and the alleys made by the sides of buildings.

Kaylin shrugged.

"Why do you think it exists?"

"Until yesterday or the day before, I didn't think about the border zone much. It's not supposed to be safe."

"The fiefs weren't safe, given Ferals. And the buildings seem to be relatively solid."

"We didn't spend a lot of time playing in the border zone. People were rumored to have entered it and never escaped."

"Or entered it and crossed into a different fief?"

"If they never returned, no one could question them." She exhaled. "The border zone wasn't solid. It's not like you could find a place to live—an empty place—and cross back into the fiefs. If it worked that way, the border zone would be occupied. It wouldn't be empty. The Ferals didn't cross those borders; they came from *Ravellon* and returned to *Ravellon*."

"And you know this how?"

Kaylin shrugged again. Trying not to sound as defensive as she felt, she said, "We were kids. We were trying our best to survive. People we mostly trusted gave us advice; we followed it. Why didn't matter. Keep your eyes open; we're looking for a cross street that doesn't run to the fief on either side."

"What did the Arkon have to say about the border zone?"

Kaylin almost shrieked. "Nothing useful at all. But to be fair, we were asking about Killian. Mostly. Bellusdeo thinks he was hiding something."

"She didn't ask?"

"If it's something complicated, he generally says I'd die of old age before he adequately explained it."

"That's possibly true. I'd bet you pass away from aggravated boredom first, though."

"Very funny, Teela."

"Thank you."

"If you two could stop bickering," Annarion said, "I think we might have found something."

"How? You can't even see."

"Teela can. Jog to the right at the corner. I think that's like your signposts."

"They're not my signposts, and what do you mean?"

"There's a pole in the ground with a small sign sticking out of it. Well, two small signs. It looks similar to the ones you have all over the city."

Kaylin had reached the signpost that Annarion had seen; she nearly missed it because it was obscured by what appeared to be trees.

Trees in the border zone.

Even the backyards of the buildings here had been flat and gray; they implied either dead grass or dirt. But here, on this street, there were trees. Gray trees, for the most part; the leaves had a bit of color, but color in the border zone was tricky.

She reached the signpost. It was at the corner of two intersecting streets. The two signs on the post were white lettering on gray—but it was lettering that Kaylin had difficulty reading.

"You would," Teela said softly.

Kaylin didn't bridle. "What's the language?"

"It's Barrani—but the letter forms are not modern. I was taught this in my childhood; it is not used much now." She turned to Annarion. "Can you read it?"

He nodded.

"The modern forms were simplified," Teela continued. "And the road I think we want to follow is the one that continues farther down. At least this time we won't be crawling through backyards with lamentably poor fences."

Bellusdeo said, "I recognize this road."

Kaylin didn't. "You're sure?"

Dragon smoke was most of Bellusdeo's reply. "It heads down, but curves; the corner is gradual, and when the road reaches its end, it will open into a space that is blessedly free of your cramped, ground-based streets. We walked through it when we left Killian's building."

Bellusdeo had immortal memory. Kaylin's memory of streets was etched in slowly by familiarity and patrolling. She was certain the Dragon was right, and she tried to pay attention to the curve of the street and the way the buildings changed as they followed that curve. She realized that Bellusdeo was right: she could see the building in which they'd found—or been found by—Killian. That building was one of a few that were arranged in a circle around a circular road; in the center of that were more trees and what might have been a normal park, if not for the lack of color.

Would you have recognized this street if you'd found it? Kaylin asked Severn.

If I were walking it with you? Probably.

So it's not racial. It's me.

There are things you recognize that neither of us would. You're not going to be able to compete with Barrani or Dragons for recall. None of us could. But neither she nor I thought that Killian was somehow a building.

"Can any of you hear Terrano or Mandoran?"

Teela shook her head.

"My brother?" Annarion asked.

"No, sorry. On the other hand, he'd probably be disgusted at most of what I'm thinking now."

"I doubt it," Teela said.

The curve of the street widened before it ended. The buildings were now almost stately; they looked like buildings that might once have housed guilds in a bygone era. Normal people hadn't lived in them, but might have worked in them. It was hard to tell without examining the interiors.

Kaylin, studying those exteriors in an attempt to bludgeon them into memory, frowned. "Could we take a look at the inside of that building?"

"Try to stay focused, kitling."

"I am. I think I caught movement in the upper windows. And they're real windows, not shuttered gaps in the wall." She turned to Bellusdeo. "You're going to have to ditch the Dragon form if you want to go through those doors."

The Dragon's grin was all teeth. "I beg to differ."

It took all present members of the cohort some time to talk her out of simply removing the front third of the building—and it mostly came down to structural stability. The loss of great chunks of a possible load-bearing wall would make any exploration unsafe for some of the people present.

And by some, they meant Kaylin.

Maggaron remained outside with Severn. If he resented this, it didn't show. While he wasn't fond of the streets here, it appeared that his view of the buildings and their construction had moved slowly to overlap with the views of all of the people who could see them.

The fog, however, was thinning as they approached the end of the road. The cohort, with the exception of Teela, couldn't see the building Kaylin wanted to explore. They couldn't see the movement in the big windows, either.

Kaylin frowned. "Do you think the cohort itself is visible here?"

"We can see them," Bellusdeo said.

"We already know they're here. I mean—" She struggled to find words and gave up because the right words would take too long. The wrong words generally took too long as well, but for other reasons.

"I think everyone but Teela should stay outside."

Allaron nodded. Annarion's lips compressed into a tighter line, but he said nothing. Or nothing that people who weren't part of the group mind could hear. Teela was examining the doorway—a peaked arch that nonetheless contained two wide rectangular doors beneath what looked to be a stone crest of some kind.

"If the doors are locked," Bellusdeo said, "can I break them?"

"Kaylin can pick the locks if they're not magical," Teela replied, which was a no.

"There's little chance that the doors are not magically locked," the Dragon said. "I don't care if the signs are written in an ancient variant of Barrani—magic is not a modern contrivance."

They both looked at Kaylin. Kaylin's skin, as they approached the doors in question, remained normal. If there was magic here, it wasn't the type that caused her pain.

She reached the doors first and pushed against them. She was surprised when they rolled open.

The doors opened into a large hall. A desk very reminiscent of the long bar—she took care never to call it that out loud while standing anywhere near it—in the Imperial Library was the first thing they could see, but beyond that, a large hall with an open gallery that was no doubt meant for the public continued into the immediate distance. Stairs stood to the right of the desk, their width also implying a public that was nowhere in sight.

The second thing Kaylin noticed on the interior of this building was the color. Had she not come through streets of washed-out grays, this would have been a normal, if somewhat upscale, Elantran building. The woods were brown; the stone floor was gray; the emblems painted across the wall behind the bar were a bright sea of colors: reds, golds, blues. The doors had not magically slammed shut at their backs, which, given everything, was a bit of a surprise.

Do you recognize the emblem? Kaylin asked her partner.

I don't. I believe that's supposed to be a sun.

And the blue bits?

Not weapons, not any Barrani regalia I recognize. But I think it's Barrani work.

"Don't you think this kind of looks like the library? I mean, the Arkon's library?"

"But without the books and the librarians?"

"Yes. I mean—the big desk here. And the big open hall. It's like it's meant for people to visit." Kaylin headed toward the stairs. Teela caught her by the arm.

"Not you."

"I can—"

"I'll go first."

Kaylin shut her mouth. Teela was right. They had no idea who—or what—was upstairs. If Candallar was somehow involved in anything that was happening, it could very well be an unknown Barrani, and if that was the case, Teela—or Bellusdeo—was a much better choice to take point.

Kaylin did feel the tingle across her arms and legs; Teela was playing it safe.

"The large windows were probably public-facing or publicly accessible," Teela said, speaking quietly as she mounted the stairs. She examined them before she ascended, and her ascent was slow. Caution generally was, judging by the number of people who abandoned it in frustration.

The stairs seemed to continue beyond the second story, at which Teela, Bellusdeo and Kaylin stopped. A hall—a wide hall—continued straight ahead and to the left; the stairs formed part of a large corner, and doors adorned both sides of the walls in the hall itself. The hall straight ahead continued until it reached large double doors; the doors along the hall were single doors, but wide. To the left—which was the direction Teela took—the hall ended in a wall that implied another corner. There were steps there, as well.

The halls were lit. There were no lamps to provide that light, and no obvious windows. The floor itself was a dark-grain wood, with something like marble straight down a narrow width of the center, as if it were intended to be a carpet replacement. Teela took a step onto the wood, knelt and examined that stone. "Stick to the sides of the hall," she said as she rose.

Kaylin nodded. The floors, however, didn't "feel" more magical to her skin; she suspected the magic she could detect was all courtesy of Teela. And Bellusdeo.

Hope, throughout their walk in the border zone, rested across her shoulders in a limp blanket flop. He now rose to sit on her left shoulder but did so at his leisure. He didn't lift his wing, either. Whatever Kaylin could see here, he considered good enough.

That held until Teela paused in front of a door that appeared identical to every other closed door in either hall, except for the end doors. The Barrani Hawk glanced at the Dragon, and Bellusdeo, who'd been pulling up the rear, nodded and joined her.

Kaylin had to press herself into the nearest wall to allow the Dragon to pass.

Bellusdeo, however, looked at the door that Kaylin hadn't managed to approach. "I see it. Kaylin?"

Kaylin took Teela's spot as Teela moved, again using the wall. "...It's a door."

"Are there no marks or words on it, for you?"

"You mean like a nameplate?"

Bellusdeo nodded.

"No. It's a door. It's about this wide," she added, spreading her palms. "It's a reddish-brown wood with no scratches and no marks. There's a handle, not a knob, and the handle is like new brass."

"But you see no name and no marks that imply a name?"

Kaylin shook her head. "You do?"

Teela nodded. She glanced at Bellusdeo, who also nodded. "What does it say?"

It was Bellusdeo who answered. "The letterforms are old, but I believe it says Larrantin." Teela said nothing.

Kaylin's hand fell to her dagger; Hope hissed in her ear. She withdrew the hand. "Hope's alert but—I don't think he thinks we're walking into an ambush."

I don't wish you to turn an encounter into an ambush, Hope then said.

Teela accepted Hope's opinion as gracefully as she usually did; her eyes were blue, but not the shade of midnight that indicated death was probably imminent. Bellusdeo's were orange, but a darker orange.

"Hope says there's no Shadow here at all," Kaylin told the Dragon.

I did not.

The orange shaded away from the red it had been heading to.

Teela opened the door.

It was a very anticlimactic door opening. There was no magic, no visible signs of barriers being either invoked or dropped; there wasn't even a creak of hinges—and given the probable age of this building, that certainly implied magic. Or lack of solidity.

The room wasn't empty. A man—Barrani—stood by the window. The window, however, wasn't what held his attention; that was the shelves he was facing. They started at the floor and reached to the ceiling, and appeared to cover most of the wall. They were lined with books. The only other time Kaylin had seen so many books was in the Imperial Library, and she automatically stilled as they came into view. There were few crimes that would cause her as much trouble as damaging or destroying those books.

Teela walked into the room; Bellusdeo followed.

Only when her companions passed through the Barrani man did Kaylin blink. They walked directly to the window to look at the streets below. They didn't notice the occupant of the room, and the occupant didn't seem to notice them.

He did, however, look up as Kaylin followed her companions. His face was shadowed by light as he turned from the window; he mouthed a word and the walls—or ceiling—brightened. There were no obvious lights, but clearly, as in the halls, none were needed.

As the light touched him, it transformed him. He remained Barrani, but color deepened; his skin was pale, yes, and his height was the Barrani norm; his eyes were blue. It was his hair that was strange: it wasn't the pure black of Teela's, Tain's or any other Barrani with the exception of the Consort; it appeared to be gray. Streaks of white nestled within the length of the expected black and fell around his shoulders like liquid.

"Guys," Kaylin said.

Teela turned away from the window.

"Have you ever seen a Barrani with gray hair?"

"Pardon?"

"I mean, the Consort has white hair."

"*Platinum* is the word you want."

"Fine, whatever. It's white to me. All the rest of you have black hair."

"And?"

"This person has— No, I'm asking you if you've ever seen a Barrani man with gray hair before."

Teela and Bellusdeo exchanged a glance. "Yes," Teela said, as Bellusdeo shook her head. "It was not a common color, as you may imagine, and there was some concern that it implied a defect."

"And not age like it does for the rest of us?"

"The rest of us?" Bellusdeo then said.

"Well, the Arkon's gray. And also, even the Leontines get gray around the muzzle and ears. When they're older, I mean. I take it this guy was old?"

The stranger's eyes had narrowed, not in anger, but in mild confusion. "These," he said, while Teela drew breath, "are not my traditional office hours. And that is not a traditional student uniform. Are you a messenger?"

His tone indicated that her answer had better be yes, and that her message had better be delivered with minimal waste of his time.

Kaylin slid immediately into Barrani. "I am not a messenger," she told the stranger. "I am Kaylin Neya, and I've been sent here to examine what is essentially an empty building."

His brows rose. "Empty?"

She nodded. There was something about this man that was familiar. Or rather, more familiar than his similarity of appearance to every other Barrani she had ever met.

"Who are you talking to?" Teela asked.

"I'm not sure," Kaylin replied, although she didn't take her eyes off the man.

"Who are you conversing with?" the man now asked.

"Hope—can you speak to him?"

You are doing so; I see no need to interfere.

But the stranger had now seen Hope, as if the words themselves—or the squawks—had finally made him visible. The expression that he now turned on Kaylin was different.

"Who are you?" The words were sharper, the demand in them clearer.

Hope sighed. Loudly. He then squawked while the man listened. Kaylin wanted to be able to understand every word he spoke; so far she'd managed to understand the ones he aimed at her. It was better—on most days—than nothing.

"Why are you here? This is not the library; these rooms," he added, waving an arm to encompass more than the one they currently occupied, "are my personal rooms."

She offered him a Diarmat-taught bow. When she rose, his expression was calmer, although his eyes remained blue. Of course they did. "This building is currently unoccupied. You are the only person we've found in it."

"Impossible."

She was silent. He wasn't calling her a liar.

"Was an evacuation order sent? Has the day we feared come to pass?"

Kaylin had no idea what day he referred to, but she could guess. Guessing when Barrani were involved, and they were in your face, wasn't always the safest or wisest choice—not if you opened your mouth.

Bellusdeo was orange-eyed. She didn't fold her arms; she was alert. Teela, eyes a darker blue than this stranger's, was also alert. She hadn't drawn a weapon and Bellusdeo hadn't yet decided to breathe fire—for which Kaylin was grateful. She had a visceral fear of fire and books, probably instilled by the Arkon.

"Are you known as Larrantin?"

The man seemed to relax. "I am, by some. Has an acquaintance sent you to fetch me?" He tucked a book under his arm, and Kaylin looked, for the first time, at his clothing. It was oddly styled; she had never seen a Barrani dressed this way. The jacket he wore might have been at home in a painting, but not on an actual person. Also, his pants were weird.

She had some concerns about whether or not he could leave this room.

"When you refer to the day you fear," she said, as she turned and walked through his open door, "do you mean *Ravellon*?"

His steps stopped, and she turned to see if he was still following. His expression caught her; there was sorrow in it, and the color of his eyes was not the normal Barrani blue.

"Yes," he finally said as his eyes began to shade toward a color more natural for the Barrani. "We have worked and struggled here—those of us who might survive catastrophic changes in our environment—to understand what ails *Ravellon* and how it might be cured. But the sum of our knowledge is too thin, and our understanding of the Ancients and their varied knowledge, too slight.

"But you are Chosen. Do you have wisdom to impart that might have escaped us?" There was hope in the words. Hope and the usual Barrani skepticism.

"I don't even have the knowledge that you had back in the day."

"Who sent you?"

This was more complicated. "Were you here when the Towers rose?"

Silence. After a long pause, Larrantin said, "The Towers." The two words were flat. "But the selection has only barely finished, and there is some debate about the choices."

"The Towers were created, in the end, by the Ancients. I don't understand how or why, but this building—" She exhaled. "Come with me. I think you'll understand, better than I do, what's happened."

Larrantin could leave his room. He could walk through the halls and down the stairs. He could even walk past the desk. But when Teela opened the doors at a nod from Kaylin, he paused. He looked out, his eyes narrowing. "I do not believe I can leave this building," he said, the words quiet enough Kaylin could barely hear them.

She'd half expected he would vanish simply by attempting to leave his office.

"You found no trace of other people in your search?"

"No trace of the people we were looking for, no." She paused. "Do you know Killian?"

He frowned. Hope bit Kaylin's ear and whispered something longer. "Killianas."

The frown cleared slightly, and as it did, it left the mild disapproval of an annoyed teacher in its place. "Killianas, yes. It happens that I wish you to perform a small errand for me."

"And that?"

"I wish you to take this book to him. I am not certain that you will be able to do so if I cannot leave this building." He then handed Kaylin the book he had tucked under his arm.

It was *cold*. It was like accepting a brick of ice from the morgue with bare hands; had it not been for her training about the cost and value of books—which, in the eyes of many, were more than a would-be private-now-corporal was worth—she would have dropped it. She didn't. She did adjust her grip so that the bulk of the ice was pressed against her clothing and not her skin.

It helped, but not much. "I can try," she finally said. She looked at Larrantin, a suspicion forming, and held out one hand, which was almost more than she could spare, given the book.

He stared at it.

"That is not one of our customs," Teela told her.

"I know, but—I'm obviously not Barrani, and we *do* shake hands."

He continued to stare at her hand. He then grimaced and offered her his own. She took it, or attempted to take it; there was nothing there. What she could see, what she could hear, and what she could physically touch were not the same. He frowned; he could not grasp her hand.

"...I see," he finally said, and his expression made clear that he now understood something in a way that he hadn't before. "Carry the book. If Killianas has words of wisdom to impart, I ask that you return. You will find me in my office." But his eyes remained upon the open door as Kaylin, with the two companions he had not once seen or heard, left.

CHAPTER 13

"It has to be the marks of the Chosen," Annarion said, as soon as Kaylin was in hearing range. In theory, he was speaking to Teela. This was the cohort's way of inviting Kaylin into a conversation she couldn't otherwise hear.

Teela nodded. "I would like Severn to join us," she said. "It might be something as simple as mortality. Neither I nor Bellusdeo could see, hear or interact with Larrantin."

Bellusdeo, however, turned to her Ascendant. Maggaron nodded and headed up the stairs. "What?" she asked as the Barrani all turned to look at her. "While Severn is often useful, Maggaron is mortal. All of the *Norannir* are."

The door to the building was slightly ajar; Maggaron couldn't slide in the same way Kaylin, or anyone who wasn't almost eight feet tall, could. The doors themselves were tall enough, on the other hand. He opened them and passed through.

Five minutes later, he emerged. Bellusdeo looked up the stairs; Maggaron shook his head. "Let's assume it's either the marks or the familiar," the Dragon told Annarion. Kaylin had a feeling she was actually telling Sedarias. "I'm more concerned about what you're carrying."

"It's a bloody cold book."

Everyone exchanged one of those glances.

"It doesn't look like a book to you?"

"It doesn't look like a book to me," the Dragon then said. "A little more information would be helpful, here."

"It doesn't look like a book to me, either."

Since it was definitely a book and not a chunk of ice, Kaylin held it out, removing it from the layers of inadequately protective clothing and once again taking it in her hands.

She could see a spine, as books usually had or they would have been called a stack of paper. As she turned it, she could see a back cover, given orientation, and when she flipped that over while her hands began to ache, she could see a front cover. The cover contained one rune, a type of word. She couldn't read the language. That was fair; there were books in the Imperial Library that were written in gibberish, too.

They are not written in gibberish, Ynpharion snapped.

Fine. What does this say?

His silence made clear that he couldn't read the word, either.

"He asked me to take this to Killian."

"Did he say why?"

"No. Who is Larrantin? Or who was he?"

"He was a researcher of some renown, or perhaps a scholar might be the better word. I did not know him well; I barely knew him at all. His distinguishing characteristic, visually, was his hair."

"It was always like that?"

"It was always what mortals call gray, yes. He was born that way. Not much is known of him, beyond that; he disappeared almost a millennium ago."

"In the fiefs?"

"It was not clear at the time." Teela's smile was grim. "Renown, in Elantran parlance, always paints a target on the person who's earned it. If he had not been so odd, his disappearance would have been chalked down to simple assassination."

"He was political?"

"You're giving Sedarias a headache," Annarion said in a remarkably cheerful tone of voice for Annarion.

"Fine. Never mind."

"The Arkon was not considered political," Bellusdeo said. "But he fought in the wars, and he influenced the composition of the Flights. By your standards, Lannagaros was apolitical; his interests were never in the accumulation of power. But power is necessary to preserve both oneself and the things one cares about." She lifted an arm. "That," she said, pointing to a large building that occupied most of the distance, "is the building from which we emerged.

"If you are tasked with taking the book to Killian, I would suggest you do so now."

Killian—or the building in which he currently resided— had doors similar to the doors of the building which housed or contained Larrantin. They approached those doors with less caution. The doors were closed.

Kaylin had once again tucked the book between her arm and the side of her body, which was better than carrying it in her hands, but not, as the distance increased, by much. There were other reasons for wanting to reach Killian, though. Chief among them were the missing members of the cohort— Mandoran, Terrano and Nightshade. She had hope that they were somehow lost within Killian's many rooms; that opening the door and entering the building would break whatever barrier prevented them from communicating.

Helen could prevent exactly that communication between

Kaylin and any of the nameheld; if Killian was somehow a building, it made sense that he could do the same.

The doors, however, were locked. The lock wasn't mechanical, or not in a way that Kaylin understood mechanical locks.

"Is it warded?" Bellusdeo asked.

"I can't see—or feel—a ward." Given that door wards caused Kaylin's magical allergy to flare anytime she came in physical contact with one, she felt she was a reluctant expert. "But we're in the border zone."

"Try knocking?" Allaron suggested.

Annarion, however, moved to the left of the doors, to a smaller section of the wall. The stairs were wide and meant to accommodate either the very, very space-conscious or multiple people at once. "Here," he said.

"It's a wall," Kaylin offered. "Or at least it looks like a wall to me. What do you see?"

"I see a symbol. It's not a door ward," he added, "but it has a similar function. It's meant to be like your bells."

"Can you see the wall clearly?"

"I think I can see it more clearly than you can. Since we've followed this street, the fog has lifted. There's sun here," he said, glancing over his shoulder, "and the buildings themselves are not, as you put it, washed out. There are trees, and those trees are vividly green and green-blue. The only things here that seem…faded, I guess, are the birds and the squirrels."

Kaylin turned immediately to look out to the large circle transcribed by the street to which those stairs led. She could see no birds, no squirrels, could hear no insects, and see no sun. "I suppose the skies are blue?"

"They are. It's ridiculously clear here. Hold on." Annarion lifted a hand to the wall, spreading the whole of his palm against it. His fingers were long and slender.

* * *

Only Annarion and Allaron could see this brightly colored version of the building; everyone else could see what Kaylin could see. But the inside of Larrantin's building had seemed as solid, as real, as any normal building. From the inside, Kaylin couldn't tell that she wasn't in Elantra.

From the inside of Killian, the same held true, or it had on their first visit. But the inside of Killian had seemed more run-down. Larrantin's building had not. The floors hadn't been scuffed or scratched—or warped, as often happened with wooden floors. The doors had been closed but had looked remarkably pristine.

Kaylin hadn't seen nameplates—or their Barrani equivalent—on the doors, but Bellusdeo and Teela had. This whole everyone-sees-something-different paradigm was getting old.

The doors began to roll open.

Hope hissed. He leaped to his standing position, his body rigid enough it was practically vibrating.

This was not a good sign. Kaylin shouted a single word— *"Move!"*—as the doors began to open. Hope's wing rose and covered Kaylin's eyes as she followed her own advice, clearing the area at the height of the stairs and moving to stand between Bellusdeo and the open doors as she did.

She ran smack into Maggaron and staggered back. Even orange-eyed as she was, Bellusdeo snickered.

Killian stood in the midpoint of the opening doors, his Barrani face still scarred by the missing eye. His hair, unlike Larrantin's, was all black, and the remaining eye was a deep midnight blue. He didn't wear armor, and he didn't carry a sword. Whatever trouble he was expecting, it wasn't martial.

No, Kaylin thought, whatever trouble *he* was in now couldn't be countered by physical prowess.

Neither Annarion nor Allaron cursed; Kaylin was pretty certain Mandoran or Terrano would have. As the doors rolled fully open, Kaylin heard a voice.

Be careful—there is danger here.

It was Nightshade's.

Killian wasn't nearly as welcoming on this second encounter.

As the doors fully opened, she thought she saw why. Killian wasn't alone. He'd said he had no master, no lord, and she'd believed it. She still believed it. But there were people with him, one on each side, and neither looked remotely friendly.

One was Barrani by height and what she could see of his or her appearance; long robes and an unwieldy hooded cape covered most of their face. The other was human. He was taller than Kaylin, which wasn't hard; he was wearing robes similar to the robes the Barrani wore, but as was always the case, not nearly as well. His hood didn't cover his face, but draped, instead, across his shoulders and behind his neck.

Severn swore.

Of course he did.

Who is he?

Lord Baltrin. An image of said Lord formed immediately between them as if Severn were a portable Records, but better. Severn's image was not an image that matched the man standing to one side of Killian. He wore a jacket, a shirt, an ostentatious circlet; his fingers were many-ringed, and his expression was indolent, bored and slightly predatory.

You really need to study the human Caste Court, he told her. *Even if you're never sent to speak to any of them as a Hawk.*

He's an Arcanist, isn't he?

Not officially, no. It's not legally required that human Arcanists register with the Imperial Order; human Arcanists—mortal Arcanists—are rare. The bulk of the Arcanum—

—is Barrani, I know. I don't suppose you recognize the Barrani standing on the other side of Killian?

Not by chin alone, no.

Hope squawked loudly and smacked Kaylin's face with the wing that he'd lifted. He lowered it briefly, and she understood why: without his wing, she couldn't see either of Killian's companions.

Killian's companions did not expect to be seen.

Kaylin could see them, which posed a minor problem. She had no easy way of warning her companions about their presence without also alerting them.

Hope sighed. He squawked loudly. Kaylin wondered what he would look like as a translucent bird. For some reason, he smacked her face with his wing again. Killian stepped out; his companions did not. He offered Kaylin a slight nod, but his expression was so rigid it was easy to believe it might have been a trick of the light.

"Sorry for bothering you at home," Kaylin said. She fell silent. It was hard not to look at the Barrani and the human.

Nightshade, where are you?

I am in a large auditorium.

Why?

I am, apparently, attending a lecture.

A lecture.

Yes. It would, if I had any control over my presence, be of great interest to me. You have made clear that you dislike the classes forced upon you by the Hawks; I am therefore less certain that it would be of interest to you. That thought amused him. And he wasn't lying; the lecture—about theoretical magic and its practical possible applications—was of interest to him. But beneath the surface of the formed words were many tangled emotions, one of which was anger.

We can't hear you when the doors to Killian's building aren't open. The cohort can't hear their companions, either. Are Mandoran or Terrano in your lecture hall?

They are not here as students, he replied.

This did not fill Kaylin with confidence. *Do you recognize either of the two people standing behind Killian? These two are definitely not here as students.*

None of us should be here as students, was Nightshade's response. He didn't answer the question. Which meant he had no intention of doing so.

Who is the lecturer? Barrani?

He chuckled. *A Barrani man you have no reason to know.*

And you do?

I know of him. No one present knows him, in the more colloquial sense of the word. I believe, he added, his tone changing, *that Annarion's friends have found the auditorium. Quickly, then: I have attended this lecture only once. I believe the other students have heard it many times; there does not seem to be variation. I assumed, initially, that the students were illusory.*

But?

But I remember the wall you discovered. I do not believe I will be able to extricate myself from this classroom immediately.

Can we get you out?

Before Nightshade could answer, the building shuddered. The stairs shuddered. Killian, his single eye already an uncomfortable shade of blue, wheeled instantly. The two almost invisible men staggered as the building continued its ominous movement.

"This is not the place for you," Killian said, his back to

Kaylin. "You will need to discuss your placement here, should you wish to return, with the chancellor."

"But you said—"

"I cannot speak further. I must go."

"But I have something for you!"

He paused but did not turn, and the pause was so brief Kaylin wondered if she'd imagined it. The people to either side of Killian made way, moving to the left and right of the straight path his long strides demanded. But the Barrani lifted hands to his hood and drew it down.

He wore an Arcanist's tiara; set in its delicate peak was a ruby. It was not a small gem, and it appeared, to Kaylin's eye, to be pulsing.

Nightshade cursed.

The doors are closing. We'll come back a different way.

Do not return yet. I believe Annarion's friends are now causing difficulties. Ask Annarion to tell them that Illanen is present, and he is not to be trifled with. Tell them also that Illanen appears to be capable of existing slightly out of phase. He will understand what that means.

Kaylin turned to Annarion; the doors were not yet closed. "Tell Terrano that Illanen of the Arcanum is here, and he can sort of move the way you guys do. Yes, the message is from your brother."

Annarion nodded as the doors rolled shut.

Finding a way out was far easier than finding the way in had been. The streets, when followed, led naturally to streets that were more easily accessible from the fiefs. But once they were standing in the fief of Nightshade, Kaylin turned to Teela.

"Who is Illanen?"

Teela's eyes were already blue; they didn't darken. "An Arcanist and Lord of the High Court."

"What was he doing with Killian?"

"Are you attempting to give the rest of us information out of sequence?"

Kaylin flushed. "...Sorry. I could see a robed Barrani and a human standing beside Killian when the doors opened. The human is a caste lord, according to Severn. I didn't recognize the Barrani; I knew he was an Arcanist only at the end, during the earthquake. Seriously, I wish the Emperor would burn down the damn Arcanum. Arcanists are nothing but trouble."

"I am—or have been—a member of the Arcanum." The Barrani Hawk chuckled. "Even the Emperor would find it difficult to destroy the Arcanum. Have you visited the High Halls since the cohort underwent the Test of Name?"

"No, and you already know that."

"I suggest you do. It has afforded me great amusement."

"Why amusement?"

"She's a sadist," Allaron surprised Kaylin by saying. He reddened and added, "That was Sedarias."

Of course it was. "Can we get back to Illanen?"

"And the Caste Court human?"

"Severn's researching him now. Somehow."

"At this hour?"

"He doesn't sleep a lot." Kaylin shivered.

"You didn't deliver Larrantin's message."

"I did try—I just didn't expect Killian to have invisible visitors."

"Was he aware of them?"

That was a good question. "I assume he must be—but I didn't ask." Her frown deepened. "If he *is* the Avatar of the building, his eyes are metaphorical. Or something. Helen could create an Avatar with only a mouth and she'd still be

Helen and still be aware. But...I think you might be right. There are things he doesn't notice. There are probably things he can't do. I think the missing eye represents some part of that.

"And I think, in some way, the border zone is related to Killian, if not caused by him." Her teeth were chattering now. "I think," she said to Bellusdeo, "we should stop at the Imperial Library before we go home."

Bellusdeo nodded. She turned to Maggaron and said, "I'll ask you to go home with the cohort; all of the hostility we are likely to encounter in the palace will be personal and petty. And you know what I'm like." The last was said with the sweetest of smiles to grace a Dragon's face.

Maggaron, however, winced and nodded.

Kaylin cursed the Arcanum in all the languages she knew as they headed through the streets of Nightshade. Ferals howled in the distance, but the howls remained at a remove. Some part of Kaylin wanted to go out on Dragon back and turn them to ash. Some part of her wanted to give the Arkon this damn book. It was, because she was shivering, unwieldy and seemed to be gaining weight.

Bellusdeo didn't see what Kaylin saw; she could discern an object, but it was not, to her eyes, a book. Given that Larrantin was Barrani, and probably yet another Arcanist, that made sense. Whatever it was, Kaylin wanted to be done with it.

Annarion had questions about Nightshade; Kaylin answered them as truthfully as she could. She could no longer hear him, and her guess—that he had somehow been sucked into the wall—matched his. But...he wasn't dead, and if he was worried, he wasn't in pain and he wasn't unhappy. She was, by this point, very familiar with his unhappy voice.

"Mandoran and Terrano did something. Killian wasn't particularly happy about it. But the invisible visitors felt whatever it was they did, as well. I'm thinking," she added, "of strangling Terrano."

"Sedarias says: 'Stand in line.' You think they learned this from Terrano, somehow?"

"Or from someone Terrano taught, yes. He wasn't concerned about what would happen to the rest of us at the time, so he didn't exactly think through the consequences."

"He doesn't generally think through consequences even if we're going to be stuck with them," Annarion pointed out.

"I really don't think it's a great idea to have Mandoran and Terrano be your point people. Just saying."

"Terrano can still go where some of us can't. Mandoran is second best." Annarion shrugged. "And none of us can tell Terrano what to do. Or what not to do. In his defense, he's trying to be careful."

"This is not careful."

"For Terrano?" Annarion didn't wait for an answer. "We'll head home. Sedarias doesn't want us to meet the Emperor yet."

Kaylin agreed, although she wasn't going to meet the Emperor, and they'd already managed to meet the Arkon without giving or taking offense.

A palace steward was on duty though it was late in the night—or early in the morning. So were the Imperial Guards. Kaylin disliked both on principle, but let Bellusdeo do the talking for obvious reasons. And for less obvious reasons: she wasn't sure she could speak without sounding like someone in serious need of a fix.

Bellusdeo didn't have that problem. She was in Dragon armor, not the clothing most of the Dragon Court wore, which made her look—to Kaylin's eye—more regal, not less.

The palace guard were silent and invisible. If they sneered at Kaylin, as she was certain they would otherwise be doing, they did it on the inside of their heads.

The steward was clearly concerned. But…the Arkon, like most immortals, didn't require sleep. He did require a certain amount of privacy, and he disliked interruptions when he was otherwise expecting to get that privacy. Kaylin understood the steward's hesitation. Bellusdeo understood it, as well. She glanced at Kaylin. "If it is acceptable, I will not require a page to approach the library."

Silence.

"I believe the Arkon left strict instructions that he was not to be disturbed."

"I'm sure he did. You require his explicit permission?"

The poor man paled.

"Fine." Bellusdeo lifted her chin and opened her mouth. Kaylin couldn't cover both of her ears, even with this much warning, because she'd drop the book. But Bellusdeo spoke in a voice to wake either the dead or distracted Dragons, and she spoke in her native tongue.

Even the Imperial Guards cracked something that looked like an expression. Kaylin was impressed. The steward, however, looked resigned. If Bellusdeo's Draconic had been a short bark of sound, he might have managed to keep hold of the starched, stiff lines of the palace's version of helpful and welcoming—but she went on for some time. Kaylin did cover the one ear she could easily reach.

She kept her eyes on the long hall behind the obstructing desk. It didn't disgorge more guards. No, instead, two figures entered the hall, coming round a corner at almost the same time. Kaylin recognized both men. Well, Dragons.

One was Lord Sanabalis, and the other, to her surprise, was

Lord Emmerian. She was relieved to see that Lord Diarmat didn't immediately follow. The guards relaxed, although that didn't mean much; she could see it in the lines of their faces and jaws. The steward, however, looked openly relieved when the two Dragons arrived.

Dragons didn't require sleep. Kaylin wasn't certain what the long sleep of Dragonkind entailed; for some cultures "long sleep" and death were synonyms. Not so with Dragons, because Bellusdeo had been denied permission to attempt to wake some of those sleeping Dragons. But if they didn't need sleep, Sanabalis looked as if he could use a week of it.

Emmerian, however, looked exactly the way he always did. Calm, quiet.

"We will take over from here," Sanabalis told the steward. He glared balefully at Kaylin. Since various emergencies had curtailed her magic lessons with Sanabalis, she thought this unfair. He wasn't the Arkon, though; after a few seconds of orange-eyed glare, he transferred his annoyance to the person who had caused it.

"Lord Bellusdeo. While it is a pleasure to see you in the Imperial Palace, this is not the time at which visitors usually arrive."

"Not mortal visitors, no."

"Lord Kaylin is now an immortal?"

Please, Kaylin thought, *don't drag me into this*. Hope nudged her cheek and then, as if to make a point, relaxed into his draped, bored position. If he started to snore, she was going to push him off her shoulders. He snickered instead, which wasn't much better.

Sanabalis, however, had returned his glare to Kaylin. "What, exactly, are you carrying?"

"That's the question, isn't it? We're taking it to the Arkon."

Her words were broken by involuntary shudders, which she forced herself to keep at a minimum.

"The Arkon is, ah, indisposed."

"He's sick?"

"No. You appear to be ill. He is...focused. He has made clear—loudly—that he does not wish to be interrupted." Sanabalis glanced at Emmerian, as if he wished to pass the contents of this conversation to someone else. Emmerian was younger, which probably meant junior.

"Your previous visit," Lord Emmerian then said in a much less irritable tone, "caused the type of focused concentration that the Arkon seldom engages in anymore. He has not eaten and has not rested since. He has given the librarians themselves a week of paid leave because even their presence is an annoyance."

"The library is closed?"

"To the general public, yes."

Kaylin looked at the book she was carrying in the space between her clothed arm and her rib cage. "Since yesterday."

"Yes."

"And you think he'll turn us to ash—"

"You," Bellusdeo interjected.

"Fine. You think he'll turn *me* to ash if I interrupt him."

"I believe you are capable of interrupting him, but his method of displaying annoyance will be more harmful to you, yes." Lord Emmerian replied.

Which probably meant he was going to be a fire-breathing, angry old Dragon. Fire would cause financial damage to Emmerian and Sanabalis; they were wearing actual clothing. Given that Bellusdeo had left Helen in her scale armor, she probably didn't care. Dragon hair in this form didn't burn the same way Kaylin's would.

She turned to Bellusdeo. She realized that both of the Dragons had also turned toward Bellusdeo, as if the entire decision rested on her shoulders.

"I believe that he will be interested in what Lord Kaylin carries. And I believe it may be germane to his current area of study."

"What," Sanabalis said again, "is Kaylin carrying?"

"I don't suppose you have gloves? Mittens?"

His eyes remained orange, but he now looked down his nose at her as if she was sitting in the west room for one of his lessons and had failed to do the homework that lesson required.

She grimaced and pulled the book out. It was easier than trying to explain it.

Sanabalis's eyes shifted color instantly, the orange giving way to something that looked like tarnished silver. "Where did you get that?" His voice was almost a hush.

Emmerian's eyes remained the gold-orange they had been when he had accompanied Sanabalis down the hall.

Kaylin didn't answer. She wanted Bellusdeo to do it because she was pretty certain she'd bite her tongue if she tried to explain. The explanation would require a lot of talking, and she couldn't stop shivering.

Bellusdeo, being Bellusdeo, only smiled, the smile almost feline. "I don't believe we wish to have to tell the story more than once. You are *certain* Lannagaros cannot be interrupted?"

"I begin to understand," Sanabalis replied, as his eyes returned to their regularly scheduled orange, "why Lord Diarmat finds you so difficult."

CHAPTER
14

The library doors were closed. Sanabalis did not offer to take what Kaylin was carrying. Neither did Lord Emmerian. Lord Emmerian, however, produced a scarf—from where, Kaylin couldn't see—and she wrapped it gratefully around the hands that were numb, but still felt freezing cold.

"You will never," Sanabalis said as they reached the doors, "become proficient in the use of magic if you cannot make time to even learn the basics."

"Could we skip the candles and move straight to light?"

He snorted smoke. With fire in it.

"Light would be useful."

"Candles provide light."

"I don't carry candles with me."

"Poor planning."

Bellusdeo seemed to find this amusing. "She's missed your lessons," she told Sanabalis. "Given the alternative, I'm certain at this point she would happily spend a month closeted in the West Room in the Halls of Law." She then looked at the closed doors and frowned. "Shall I?"

Sanabalis didn't find anything amusing. "It depends."

"On?"

"The doors tend to raise an alarm that will wake whatever parts of the palace somehow managed to sleep through your first speech."

"And one of those people will be Lannagaros?"

Kaylin shuddered—it was the cold. "It'll certainly let him know I'm here. Unless he assumes it's someone or something dangerous."

"I see. Some warning might prove helpful."

"On the bright side, I can't feel my hand, and half of my skin feels numb."

"Then you do it—he could probably use the warning, if Sanabalis is correct." Her smile was deeper. "He was like this in my childhood. We once attempted to get his attention by causing all sorts of commotion. We certainly got everyone else's."

"Did you get his?"

"The tools at my disposal at that time were few."

That was a no. Kaylin, who hated door wards, nonetheless lifted a hand—her left hand—and placed her palm firmly against the ward.

Nothing happened.

"I see he really doesn't want to be interrupted." Bellusdeo's eyes were, of all the Dragons present, the most golden. Kaylin wondered what kind of friendship she and Terrano might have developed had they met when they were young. The world was probably a safer place as it was.

Kaylin dropped her hand to the door handles. The doors were locked. They were locked in the normal way—but these doors didn't have a keyhole of any kind on this side. Before she bent to examine the crack between those doors, she thought better of it. This was the palace.

"Oh, well," Bellusdeo said, shrugging. She then lifted her

chin and once again let loose a volley of native Dragon. Kaylin recognized two words: *border zone*. Those were in Elantran.

Silence descended—eventually—when the echoes of Draconic syllables stopped reverberating in the ceilings above. Bellusdeo was smiling broadly. "The trick," she said, "was always to understand his particular concentration if you wanted to be able to break it."

"What if he thinks you're lying?"

"He probably does." Her eyes were almost sparkling, and at the moment, pure gold. "He always did. But he couldn't ignore the possibility that we were speaking the truth."

The hair on the back of Kaylin's neck stood on end. The door wards had been reactivated.

Kaylin touched the doors, and, as predicted, the entire palace was…enlivened…by the happy sound of blaring alarms. The palace guard poured into the hall, weapons drawn; the sound of Dragon spoken at a distance joined the guards. Kaylin hoped it wasn't Diarmat. But given that the only other Dragon likely to join in was the Emperor, she squashed that quickly. Angry Diarmat, she could—and had—survived. She was certain she had never seen a truly angry Emperor. She had zero desire to do so.

The doors took forever to roll open, and by the time they had, Sanabalis and Emmerian had turned their backs on Kaylin, facing opposite ends of the halls. Kaylin wasn't certain what their rank was in relation to the guards', but clearly being a Lord of the Dragon Court meant something.

The weapons were sheathed, and the guards dispersed.

When the doors were fully open, the Arkon stood three yards away. His eyes were, at this distance, an alarming orange-red. He appeared to be breathing smoke, which probably meant fire wasn't far behind. Kaylin, being a coward, stood to one side of—and behind—Bellusdeo.

Emmerian was the first to move through the library doors; Bellusdeo had to scurry to catch up. What was almost shocking to Kaylin was that she did. Sanabalis, like Kaylin, looked as if he wanted to be someplace else. Anywhere else.

Which was fair.

It was Sanabalis who received what might have been—had it been less full of anger—a reproachful stare. Sanabalis was meant to know better. Kaylin made a mental note to visit the Arkon with Sanabalis in tow.

What interested Kaylin was Emmerian. The Arkon didn't appear to consider Emmerian to be the source of interruption, and therefore offense. Nor did Emmerian consider his presence—an interruption that was forbidden—to be a difficulty.

"Lord Sanabalis," the Arkon said, his eyes almost red, his voice chilly.

"It is not his fault," Bellusdeo then said.

The Arkon's glance flicked off her armor, his expression glacial. To Kaylin's surprise, the gold Dragon laughed. This did not improve the Arkon's expression. "Come, come," she said, approaching him. "It is nostalgic to see you so annoyed."

Nostalgic wasn't the word Kaylin would have used, if she'd dared to speak at all.

The Arkon's breath was fire, but it was contained to the air between him and the approaching Bellusdeo. "I do not know why I did not reduce you—and your sisters—to cinders centuries ago."

"Because," she said, smiling sweetly, "we were never boring." Kaylin couldn't see her expression. She did see the reluctant gentling of the Arkon's.

"Why are you here?"

"You are holed up in this library, and rumor has it that you have closed the public collection *to* the public."

"Because I did not wish to be disturbed. By anyone."

"Yes, yes. I must admit it far more challenging than it was before you became the Arkon. And I had eight helpers then. At the moment, I'm forced to make do with one."

The Arkon finally moved his glare to Kaylin. It might have stayed there except Kaylin was carrying something in her hands.

The orange of his eyes was lost not to gold but to silver. "What do you carry?" he demanded, shaking himself free of the only Dragon he seemed to adore. He crossed the room, his gaze unwavering, although he scattered words as if they were weapons.

"Sanabalis, explain yourself."

"Lannagaros."

"I was not aware that you had usurped his name," the Arkon snapped.

Sanabalis bowed his head for a moment. Kaylin could see his back, not his face. "Lord Bellusdeo," he said, the use of the title both inaccurate and respectful, "accompanied Private Neya—"

"Corporal Neya. I'm a corporal now."

"Ah. Apologies. And belated congratulations on your promotion." He cleared his throat, teacher-style, a clear indication that corporals could burn as easily as privates could. "Lord Bellusdeo accompanied Kaylin. It is, for the mortal servants and officials, either too late or too early for a visit of any sort. She wished to speak with you.

"You have left strict instructions. Bellusdeo considered the instructions irrelevant to her goals, and asked for permission to break them."

"And you gave her that permission."

"I did. I would have risked her wrath," Sanabalis continued, "had I not seen what Kaylin carried. Had I sent them both away, your wrath would have been more difficult."

"Well?" the Arkon then said, his voice testy, his eyes losing the silver sheen. "Are you waiting for an invitation? Very well. I invite you to move out of the way."

"I remind you that what Kaylin carries appears to be magical in nature, and the library and its—"

"It is mine, Sanabalis. It is my risk to take."

"But you will be in a foul mood for decades, in the most optimistic scenario," Bellusdeo added. "Honestly, Lannagaros. I have never seen you so impatient. Even in our youth, you..." Her voice trailed off, her gaze moving from the Arkon, her expression shifting from the sweet and affectionate malice with which she treated the Arkon to something almost akin to alarm.

She looked to Sanabalis, and after a brief pause, to Emmerian. Emmerian's eyes were orange now. Nothing else about his posture or attention had changed.

Sanabalis moved out of the Arkon's way. Kaylin tried to do the same. It was instinctive, and it was the wrong move, but it was survivable.

"What are you carrying?" the Arkon demanded.

Kaylin held it out to him, her arms shaking from more than just cold.

"Answer the question, Kaylin. I am at the limit of patience."

"It's a book," she told him. The Arkon was often condescending and dismissive when dealing with Kaylin. This was neither. Whatever it was, she found she preferred the condescension—something she would have bet against ever feeling.

"A book. That is what you see?"

She nodded, lifting it so that he could see the cover.

"A book." His eyes were a complicated color now. To Kaylin, they seemed to be shading from the orange-gold that was normal to something that looked almost blue. Or green. It was not a color she remembered seeing in Dragon eyes, and she was instantly tense. Green, she thought, with hints of copper. What was copper again? Sadness? Grief?

He did not lift his hands to take what she now offered.

"What does it look like to you?"

"A ghost," he said quietly, his gaze upon the object. "A dream." He exhaled. "Why did you bring this to me?"

"We didn't mean to. I mean—that's not what I was told to do."

"Told?"

Bellusdeo cleared her throat. "There was some difficulty. Kaylin was—according to Kaylin—asked to deliver this book to someone else."

"Asked by who?" Smoke thickened the air immediately around the Arkon.

"You will have to ask Kaylin. No one else could see him." Definitely stronger orange now. "If you would take the book from her hands, she might stop shivering. It is almost making me cold just looking at her."

"I am not certain I can, as you put it, take it," the Arkon replied. "I will, however, take the Corporal. Follow."

Some confusion about the presence of the rest of the Dragons ensued. The Arkon's command had been directed, without hesitation, at Kaylin—the only person in the room who actually needed sleep. Tomorrow was going to be a long day. Well, not tomorrow. *Tomorrow* was a word used to describe the day after she'd gotten sleep.

By unspoken consensus, the Dragons followed Kaylin. Bellusdeo couldn't be left behind, and Sanabalis was distinctly curious. Emmerian fell in beside Bellusdeo; he asked a question that didn't reach Kaylin's ear. After a moment, Bellusdeo glanced back at the Hawk, and then grimaced and nodded.

Emmerian then turned and left the library. Kaylin was cursing on the inside of her head. She wanted to go home.

Throughout this, Hope remained supine. The Arkon's mood didn't trouble him at all. It wouldn't, though; Hope wouldn't melt or burn to ash if the Arkon lost his temper. It was always safer to be near the heart of his collection. Here, fire would destroy more than just an unlucky corporal.

He can aim his fire quite carefully, Hope said.

She poked him, a silent version of *shut up*.

When the Arkon came to a halt, it was in front of a blank wall. Kaylin recognized this as the entrance to what was, presumably, a safe room. The Arkon barked a Draconic word, and the wall dilated. He then turned to her, his gaze traveling to her companions.

"You will not want to speak with the Emperor," Sanabalis reasonably said. "And it is possible that information will have to be conveyed." He did not suggest that Bellusdeo be that conveyance, and even in his terrible mood, the Arkon accepted that Sanabalis was the best choice. Sanabalis left to make his report.

The room contained one largish table and one mirror. It was a standing desk mirror of the type that adorned many of the Hawks' desks, and it was reflective at the moment.

There were six chairs tucked beneath the table. The Arkon gestured impatiently and Kaylin took the one farthest from where he was standing. Bellusdeo arched a brow in her direction, as if to accuse her of cowardice. Cowardice, hells. It was common sense.

"We will wait for Emmerian," the Arkon surprised them all by saying.

"Oh?"

"I can hear the corporal's stomach, and I find the sound annoying."

Emmerian brought both food and Sanabalis. He carried it himself. As he was a Lord of the Dragon Court, it probably wasn't his job—but the various servants and officials in the palace were shielded from the Arkon's temper this way. She found herself liking Emmerian better for it. Especially since she was the person for whom the food was mostly intended.

"Eat. I don't particularly care if you talk with your mouth full. Only Diarmat does, and he is not here."

Kaylin was grateful to be given an order that she could happily obey. She set the book on the table, but kept one hand on it—the left one. The right, she used to eat a sandwich. There were a lot of little ones, but it was better than nothing.

"Can you tell him what happened tonight?" she asked Bellusdeo. "I'll fill in the parts that don't overlap."

"Fine. Can you let go of the book?"

"I can, obviously; it's not attached to my hand."

"Then why don't you?"

Hope flicked her cheek with his tail.

"Never mind. Tell me," she added to the familiar, "what do *you* see when you look at this?"

Hope wasn't of a mind to answer, which was fine with Kaylin. Her hearing had recovered after the spate of native Dragon, and she didn't need more loud noises bellowed beside her ear.

Bellusdeo began. Emmerian's eyes were orange—more orange—by the time she'd finished; Sanabalis's were closer to the gold end of the spectrum, although he was frowning.

No one except the Arkon interrupted, and he peppered

her narrative with questions. Not all of them were meant for Bellusdeo.

"You could not hear Nightshade?"

Kaylin, mouth full, nodded and swallowed. "I lost him. I think I woke up because of it. But he wasn't the only person who'd gone missing by that point."

"You are certain Nightshade was in the border zone?"

"It's where he said he was going. We couldn't return to the building we'd left, or at least not quickly—as Bellusdeo said, she was doing an inspection of the *Ravellon* borders, and that ate a lot of our time. Nightshade wanted to keep exploring and searching."

"You did not."

"No—we came here."

"And Nightshade?"

"Lannagaros, if you would allow me to continue, your questions will be answered. I honestly do not know how you can, with a straight face and sense of righteous indignation, tell anyone *else* to practice patience."

He turned to her, but upon seeing her expression, exhaled. So did Kaylin.

Bellusdeo looked worried.

The Arkon closed his eyes.

Emmerian's head was slightly bowed, as if in concentration. Sanabalis, like Bellusdeo, looked worried.

"My apologies," the Arkon said before he opened his eyes. "Please, continue. I will reserve my questions until I have heard the rest of your story."

Food lost taste as Kaylin ate, because she, too, was now worried.

Bellusdeo then continued. Kaylin's eyes were practically nailed to the Arkon's face by this point. She had seen him lose his temper before; she had seen irritation result in a face full of fire—luckily, Sanabalis's face, not hers. He was irritable on interruption, and on bad days people breathing the same air was considered an interruption. She had never quite seen him like this.

Neither had Bellusdeo—but it seemed clear to Kaylin that both Sanabalis and Emmerian had. Sanabalis wasn't even looking at the book on the table. She almost asked him what he saw when he looked at it, but Bellusdeo was still talking, and she didn't like her chances of surviving unscathed if she was the one who interrupted.

But… Bellusdeo had been worried about the Arkon after their first visit to discuss the border zone. Kaylin had seen nothing out of the ordinary in the Arkon. The Dragons knew something that she didn't, which was fair.

Frustrating, but fair. The Arkon now looked attentive; he looked normal, if focused. His eyes remained a shade of orange that implied he was clinging to tolerance of interruption with main force, but—he looked like an irritable old librarian to Kaylin.

When Bellusdeo reached the part of the story with the not-Killian building, she passed the rest of the telling to Kaylin.

"Bellusdeo and Teela could see marks or words on the doors. Like—office signs."

"You could not?"

Kaylin shook her head. "But I'd seen movement in the windows facing the street, and I wanted to investigate. The doors weren't warded and they weren't locked."

"An oversight, I'm certain." His expression was pure Arkon.

"When I opened the door, I saw a room. With books in it. Maybe a personal library—but larger than any personal library

I've seen before. And a Barrani man was standing in front of a wall of bookshelves, perusing the spines."

"We couldn't see him," Bellusdeo then added.

"Was there anything unusual about this man?"

"Well, yes, now that you ask."

"And that?"

"He had gray hair. A bit like yours, but with more black and less white in it."

The silence that followed was almost suffocating in its intensity; the Arkon was frozen in place, as if even the ability to breathe had deserted him. Kaylin was uncomfortable with this type of silence, and as it grew and threatened to overwhelm all the textures of nonverbal sound, she broke it.

"He could see me. He thought—I think he thought—that I'd been sent to deliver a message. He said something." She frowned. "He said something about it being 'that time already.'"

Mortal memory was, at the moment, a curse to the Arkon, but he didn't attempt to intimidate better memory out of Kaylin. "I think he knew what had happened. He couldn't see Teela or Bellusdeo; he walked right through Teela. I thought he might be a ghost. It was Teela who told me his name. Or what he was called."

"Larrantin," the Arkon whispered.

"He could hear every word I spoke—to anyone else—even if he couldn't see them, so it was hard to discuss in his presence. But he was Larrantin. I think… I think he's living in a place where the Towers haven't risen yet. Or rather, he was. He knew that the Towers would be created. He said something about selection. But he couldn't leave the building.

"When he reached the doors we entered, he couldn't leave. So he handed me the book he'd tucked under his arm and told me to take it to Killian, and to come back if Killian had anything to tell him."

The Arkon's gaze now shifted to the book on the table beneath one layer of scarf and Kaylin's left hand. "Remove the scarf," he told her. She did.

"Open the book."

"Lannagaros, let her finish."

The Arkon exhaled slowly, as if he were counting. "Apologies, Corporal. I assume you wish to tell me why you did not do as Larrantin commanded."

"He asked, he didn't command..." pedantry was never safe when practiced on pedants "...but we'd been looking for Killian, so I took the book. I meant to hand it over to him, but when we found the building that we'd left the first time, the doors were locked. They didn't have modern door wards, but Annarion knew how to open them. When Killian appeared at the doors, his eyes were the death-variant of Barrani blue. But when those doors slid open, I could hear Nightshade.

"The cohort could hear their missing members." She poked Hope. "Nightshade, at least, seemed to be trapped in an auditorium listening to a lecture, of all things. He didn't seem upset, but he did sound frustrated; he said he couldn't leave. I mean, he couldn't leave the building.

"But that wasn't the real problem."

"I am glad to see that you are getting to it." Voice dry enough to start fires.

"The *real problem*," she said irritably, "was the two men standing to either side of Killian."

This silence was different. It was more focused and oddly less suffocating. The Arkon didn't break it.

Emmerian did. "Two men? Lord Bellusdeo?"

"We did not see them. Kaylin saw them because of her familiar's wing."

"Lord Kaylin?"

Ugh. "Kaylin is fine. Or Corporal."

He nodded. "Corporal, then. Please describe the two men."

"One was Barrani. An Arcanist; he was wearing the tiara I associate with the Arcanum."

"It is not worn only by members of the Arcanum," Sanabalis said.

"And the other was human."

"Human?"

She exhaled. "Severn says he's a member of the human Caste Court. Lord Baltrin."

"Severn did not recognize the Barrani?"

"The Barrani man was, apparently, Lord Illanen of the Arcanum."

"And the High Court." It was Emmerian who spoke. "This is not welcome news. I believe you have encountered neither before."

Kaylin nodded. "Does Bellusdeo's security detail follow us into the fiefs?"

"No. Before you ask, I am not at liberty to discuss that detail." He turned and offered Bellusdeo a shallow bow. "The Emperor does not interfere with your excursions into the greater city at your request."

"And this has caused some difficulty?"

Emmerian met her eyes, the ghost of a smile touching his lips. "We are a difficult people." Before he could continue, the Arkon roared. The table shook. One plate almost fell off it, but it contained food, so Kaylin caught it.

"I believe you may discuss—or fail to discuss—Lord Bellusdeo's safety precautions at another time. Any other time.

You may discuss the politics of your various caste courts and the breaking of the laws at another time, as well."

Kaylin's mouth fell open; Sanabalis gave her a warning stare, and she closed it again.

"...I didn't want to give the book to Killian while he was bracketed by those two. I don't know if he was aware of their presence, but I think he was aware that something was off, something was wrong.

"Nightshade's lecture hall was populated with people he thought might be part of the wall of stone people we first encountered. He's aware of himself, but... I'm not sure he can extricate himself from that wall. Neither of the cohort was part of the lectured class.

"Nightshade said they'd joined it—and then we got earthquakes. Killian didn't stay to chat after that. He immediately went back into the building, shutting the doors behind him and his two invisible friends. When the doors shut, we couldn't hear Nightshade, Mandoran or Terrano. But we know where they are." She turned her attention to the book on the table. "What do you see when you look at it?"

"Not what you see. If you have finished, I believe young Emmerian has further questions for you *which he will ask when you leave the library*. Now, I would like you to open the book."

She hesitated.

"Corporal?"

"This is the safest room you have?"

"There is a reason I chose this room. Do you believe the book is dangerous or harmful?"

"It might be meant for Killian. None of us are sentient buildings." She exhaled. "I'm not sure I can even read it. I wanted to leave it with you, but—"

"You are now thinking of Helen?"

She nodded.

"I do not believe it would be at all helpful to leave it with Helen. Open the book."

Kaylin reoriented the book on the table so that its cover faced her, or so that she faced its cover in the right orientation. In the light of the Arkon's safe room, the cover was indigo, the unreadable word that occupied most of its center, silver. Silver created a rectangular border around the edge of that cover, one that seemed to follow the height of the spine.

Hope lifted a wing to her eyes; her hand froze an inch above the edge of the book's cover.

Seen through Hope's wing, this was not a book. It was a tablet of stone or ice—if stone, it was a pale white stone, like alabaster or marble. The word written across the cover of the book were no longer visible. Had Kaylin not received it from Larrantin, she would never have called it a book.

"You couldn't have mentioned this earlier?"

There are some things that you see because you are Chosen, Hope replied. *You do not see them as we see them. You do not see them as your friends do.*

"Yes, fine— But—"

And they mentioned that they did not see a book. It is irrelevant.

"Is it dangerous to open this book?"

That, I cannot say.

She wanted to shriek, but given present company, kept it to herself. "Would you open it if you were me?"

"Given the trouble you get into," Bellusdeo said, "I wouldn't qualify the question that way."

"Can you open it?" the Arkon asked, the words shorn of the edge of command or demand.

"I haven't tried. Larrantin wanted it delivered to Killian,

and he asked that if Killian had any advice to offer, I return to him with it."

The Arkon stared at the block in front of Kaylin as Hope lifted his wing. It became a book again. "You meant to give this to me."

"You're the only person I know who collects detritus."

"Then you should get out of your house more." His fingers stroked his beard for the first time since they'd entered the library; his eyes were now a steady orange. "Very well. It is possible your familiar is correct. If this is meant to somehow waken or fortify Killianas, opening the book itself might bleed some of the magic or power from it. I am not certain that you should leave it here."

Kaylin did not stumble in shock. Sanabalis almost did.

"I thought it would be safest here."

"I am not at all certain that that is the case. I believe if you are separated from it, even the appearance it has to the rest of our eyes will fade."

"What do you mean? It'll become invisible on its own?"

The irritable snort he gave, and the look that accompanied it, were pure Arkon, or at least the Arkon she knew. "It will not be a tablet, in my collection. It will disperse. There is, of course, a way to test that—but I do not wish to lose the artifact." He then exhaled. This time without smoke and the threat of fire.

"You have given me much to consider. I ask that you remain in contact with me for the duration. I will ask to be kept apprised of the situation in Candallar—I believe it likely that you will find Candallar involved with much of the strangeness. And I would ask that you find a way to liberate Lord Nightshade. He will be absent from his Tower, and if you cannot hear him, it is very likely that his Tower will not hear him, either."

★ ★ ★

"I won't be able to *go* to work carrying this around," Kaylin said to Bellusdeo.

"I nonetheless think the Arkon correct." They had chosen to accept the offer of an Imperial carriage to return home. Probably just in time to change and head out for the day.

"I believe that the Halls of Law can do without you for a day or two; arrangements have already been made." This was Emmerian. For reasons known only to Emmerian and the Arkon, Emmerian had chosen to escort them home. Of the Dragon Court, outside of the Arkon, Emmerian caused Bellusdeo the least friction, although her eyes had darkened a shade of orange when he had first made his request.

"I would recognize both Lord Illanen and Lord Baltrin," Emmerian told Bellusdeo. "And some handful of their followers and the agents they employ and deploy. They have been under the Imperial gaze for some time; it is clear the nature of that surveillance will require some careful handling.

"I am certain that you can deal with most of the people either Lord employs, and I am certain you can provide Kaylin some of the protection required. But none of us are cognizant of the functions of the artifact she is now carrying, and where magic is used, the two might mix in an unfortunate way.

"If it displeases you, I will withdraw my request."

The gold Dragon had stood rigid and immobile for three long beats. She then nodded, the nod as stiff and regal as any nod the Emperor might have given.

Kaylin was not a very happy person when she arrived home.

Helen was waiting in the frame of the open door, her expression concerned and possibly maternal. Kaylin remembered very little of her mother, and she was past the age where she needed one.

Mostly past the age.

"What are you carrying, dear?" Helen asked, although Kaylin was pretty certain she knew at least as much as Kaylin did; the fence was the boundary of Helen, and Kaylin's walk up the drive gave her enough time to read Kaylin's thoughts.

"Yes. I see." She looked beyond Kaylin to Bellusdeo and Lord Emmerian. "Your sergeant sent you a mirror message."

"I'm on leave of absence."

"Yes, dear."

Kaylin understood that the Halls of Law could do without her for a couple of days. She understood, when push came to shove, that they could do without her indefinitely. The city was full of people, and people needed work. The Hawks who had died on the night the High Halls had come under full attack had been replaced, and some of them had been more valuable to the force than Kaylin had ever been.

But she wasn't as certain that the inverse was true. She wasn't at all certain that *she* wanted to do without the Halls of Law or the Hawks.

"I see you've brought a guest. It is early for guests," Helen added, a trace of apology in her voice. "I will ask the cohort to remove themselves to quarters that will be quieter. Wait a moment."

"I'm not sure he's staying," Kaylin began.

"He will stay if you allow it. I believe he has something he wishes to discuss with both you and Bellusdeo."

CHAPTER 15

Helen led Emmerian to the parlor, which had adjusted itself in size so that it could comfortably fit the four people who occupied it: Kaylin, Bellusdeo, Emmerian and Helen herself. Her Avatar wasn't necessary, but she liked to occupy it when guests were present. The cohort were not considered guests at this point; neither was Bellusdeo.

Emmerian declined both food and drink, and as Kaylin had already eaten, Helen didn't press it. She did offer three times, because apparently, the first refusal was somehow meant to be *good* manners. It didn't actually mean no. This made about as much sense to Kaylin as multiple forks and spoons at a dinner table.

Helen's heart, however, wasn't in it; she knew manners and she employed them, but her attention was on the book that Kaylin had set on the nearest flat surface within reach. Hope squawked at Helen, who nodded, her expression one of concentration.

Emmerian, however, did not choose to notice this yet. Then again, he didn't appear to notice more than his hands, which rested on his lap, for a long, quiet stretch. Bellusdeo was content to wait for something hot that looked like tea; Kaylin got hot chocolate.

"Is it safe for me to let this go?" she asked Helen.

"If you mean can I keep it here, then the answer is yes." She hesitated.

"But?"

"You shouldn't have it."

"We visited the Arkon in an attempt to get rid of it. He didn't want it, either. We intended to give it to Killian, but Killian was occupied."

Helen's silence was less comfortable than Emmerian's, but both felt full of unsaid things. Kaylin was tired and cold, and as Helen had given permission to let the book go, she cupped the mug in her hands, more grateful for the heat than the contents.

Oddly, it was Helen who broke the silence first. "You do not need to do this for me." It wasn't quite what Kaylin was expecting to hear.

"I'm not doing this for you."

Helen's smile was slight, but it lingered. "Killian would likely not recognize what I've become. What I've chosen to become. And we were not friends as you and Bellusdeo are friends."

"But you knew him."

"Yes. You have divined that it is, at times, lonely to be what we are."

"Everything living gets lonely sometimes." Kaylin blew on the hot chocolate, having attempted to drink it too early.

"Yes. I was not as Killian was. My function was not his function. But the level of loneliness was dependent on the lord of the manor, as it were. I was not—quite—like the Hallionne in function, if your experience with them is correct. But Killian was unique." She fell silent.

"Do you see a book?" Kaylin asked her home.

"Yes. I see what you see."

Bellusdeo and Emmerian exchanged a glance.

"But I also see what Bellusdeo and Lord Emmerian see. In neither case was this meant for you, but I believe you see a book because you saw a private library, and I believe you *can* see a book because you were meant to carry it."

"What do you think it would do to—or for—Killian?"

"I am uncertain. I am reluctant to open the book, as the Arkon suggested you do; I am even more reluctant to read it. As I said: Killian was unique. Our functions had—as most buildings must—some overlap, but he had far more flexibility. He was meant for...people."

"He vanished when the Towers rose. There was a period of perhaps twelve hours—according to the most ancient of our Records—and we have dispatched a messenger to Tiamaris in the hopes that we might discuss this matter with his Tower." Emmerian's tone was carefully neutral.

"Tara," Kaylin said, almost reflexively. "You want to talk to Tara."

Emmerian nodded. He then turned to Bellusdeo. "You have known the Arkon for longer than any of us—but you have spent far less time with him."

She nodded. "I am concerned for him now."

"As you should be. We are all concerned."

Had Kaylin's hands not been full, she would have put up her hand, as if she were in class. "Why are you guys worried?"

The glance they exchanged was clear enough that it rendered words superfluous. It was Emmerian who answered, but he was an immortal. The answer had to be couched in words before it arrived, as if it needed a carriage.

"You have been told that the library is the Arkon's hoard."

Kaylin nodded.

"You have even survived the handling of an artifact from that hoard that vanished. You are still alive."

Her nod was less patient.

"Have you never wondered at his collection? His attempt to hoard antiquities?"

"Not really. I mean, he's the Imperial Librarian."

Emmerian once again looked to Bellusdeo, but the gold Dragon was willing to leave the discussion in his hands.

"Let me then speak of Killianas. I am not Tiamaris, who is significantly younger than the rest of the Dragon Court. I did not, however, meet Killianas in my youth; my youth was a martial time." He lifted his gaze, his eyes finding a blank wall.

After a moment, that blank wall grew a painting—a large framed painting. Emmerian smiled, his glance moving briefly to Helen. "Martial prowess was highly valued by both the Barrani and the Dragons. Martial prowess," he added, "did not mean to us what it means to you; perhaps it means the handling of, the ability to handle, weapons of war—one of which would be magic. But in the absence of magic, we had the weapons to which we were born. Dragons breathe fire," he continued. "But we are not all adept at its handling; the strength of flame, the length at which we can sustain it, are elements that we must train.

"I was young enough that the training itself was considered the highest priority. It is not easy to breathe fire while one dodges the arcane arts that are cast from below." He put his hands together, and for a moment, bowed his head.

"I was not interested in war. I was interested in survival. I understood that the Barrani were far more numerous; that the Dragons—" He stopped, as if coming out of his reverie in time not to mention why Bellusdeo was so important to what remained of their race. "The war ended. Peace descended.

"Into this foreign land—this peaceful land—I walked as a

stranger. I had spent my youth and my time becoming a warrior. This was not the place, now, for us. You were impatient with the classes the Hawks required you take. You are impatient with classes, even now."

"And you weren't?"

"As I said, we were devoted to the arts of war. And then there was no war." He bowed head again. When he lifted it, he said, "To my surprise, the Arkon—who was almost a legend on the field of battle to those of us who were learning—did not take up the reins of power. He was friend to the Emperor, and friend to—" He stopped again. "But his love was given over to the fields of study that he had, in his youth, most enjoyed.

"Our war had destroyed so much, the damage incidental; Dragon breath, Barrani magic, could turn cities into broken ruins. And did. The Aeries of our birth were gone, and the stores of historical knowledge they had once contained, gone with them. He is Arkon because he preserved those relics of great historical import to our people, even when the war was at its height.

"Those he kept. He kept what he could find. He kept things once belonging to societies that had departed—whether to travel elsewhere or because the wars had left their lands unsustainable, I do not know. And he returned, at last, to his studies, many of which are still a mystery to me.

"But when I met him, he was no longer Lannagaros of the Flights; he was a legend in my mind, only. What I had wanted to be, he had been, and he had walked away from it the moment he could safely do so. It had walked away from me. I was, I admit, lost.

"He offered me a narrow path through his stacks, both literal and figurative. He woke in me a desire to turn my thought and attention to things other than the war that had defined me and defined what Dragon *meant*. I will be in his debt for that for the entirety of my life." He glanced at Kaylin, his lips turning up in a grin. "You have been remarkably patient. I am almost, you have my word, at your answer. But this is information that Bellusdeo did not know, and I believe it relevant to her, as well."

"Kaylin will not interrupt you," Bellusdeo said with the sweetest of her smiles—the one that carried the sharpest edge.

"The Arkon's store of knowledge seemed vast to my younger self. It seemed endless; the exploration of it a work of decades, of centuries. I told him this one day. He fell silent, as he often does. But then he spoke. There was an Academia, a great school, that once existed just outside of the heart of *Ravellon*. It was there, in his youth, that he learned Barrani, that he met Barrani, that he exchanged sharp words and friendly words with others of his kind.

"He did not mean Dragons. He did not mean our people, although some of those were our people. It was there," he added softly, "that he learned to read and to speak—with great difficulty—True Words. He spoke of it, spoke about it, with a longing and a passion the like of which I had never seen. His own collection, his hoard, was a pale shadow of that place, and his studies—as a singular scholar—even paler, an echo of the possibilities that once existed there.

"The Academia was destroyed."

Kaylin wouldn't have interrupted now, given the chance.

"Yes," Emmerian said, as she hadn't. "I believe that Killian, or Killianas, as Helen calls him, *was* that Academia. I believe the building you stumbled into was meant to house students—and did, in the years before the war. I believe it was the sorrow of that loss that drove him to become what he has become."

"But...his hoard."

Bellusdeo cleared her throat. "Lannagaros was always unusual. Intense and overfocused when caught in the trap of his own thoughts, his own questions. The elders in the Aerie complained constantly about it." She smiled at the memory. "His concerns were not their concerns; they were appalled by his apparent interest in things of no use or no interest to them.

"He had very little sense of humor, and what he possessed was dry; he considered his studies, as he called them, of primary import. As if to study was to survive." Her eyes closed, as if to shut out visual noise to all but the most ancient of her memories. "We were terrible to him. His studies, his ability shut out the rest of the Aerie, frustrated us."

Kaylin snorted, and Bellusdeo opened her eyes. "It wasn't the rest of the Aerie—it was you. His ability to ignore you frustrated you."

"Well, yes—but in fairness, we were children. But...we liked his odd stories. We liked his bits and pieces of history. We liked especially asking questions he *could not* answer yet. His frustration drove him inward and away—but..." She shrugged. "It also drove him to the place where he was most...himself.

"I would not have thought he would rise to the task of warrior."

"He was on the battlefield when the High Halls almost fell," Kaylin pointed out.

"As was much of Dragonkind. He watched, even then. He watched, he observed. I thought he was...not the Dragon Emmerian has described. And Kaylin, that's what he's been in my time in your Elantra, your empire. But older and far more patient."

"*More* patient."

"*Far* more patient."

Emmerian was waiting, and Kaylin realized that they'd both interrupted him. She turned toward him and saw that he was watching Bellusdeo. Wondered if that was all he'd been doing since the gold Dragon had interrupted him. But...it made sense. Bellusdeo had been smiling, was still smiling. Her smile had no edge in it. Because Kaylin looked at Bellusdeo fairly often, she'd learned most of the Dragon's expressions, the things that indicated her emotions.

"He was admired by all, but few of us had seen him in your youth; I will not say his youth, because most of us could never witness that."

"Even as a child, I was told by the fathers that Lannagaros was born old."

At that, Emmerian smiled. "I was born male; my father's advice was not...that kind of advice. We are not considered fragile, in our youth."

"Ah, no. My sisters and I were—but oddly, not by Lannagaros. Perhaps that is why we liked him so."

Silence and eddies of different memories, none of which Kaylin shared. In it, unsaid words. Worry. Kaylin exhaled loudly, for a human.

Emmerian was first to respond, to pick up the thread of his story. It was, Kaylin perceived, the reason he'd escorted them, and the reason Helen wished him to stay. "He felt the loss of knowledge keenly. He felt the loss of teachers, of people he was willing to learn from. Ah, no. Of people he felt had more information than he, and the ability to pass that information on.

"He told me of this once, in the palace, when the wars were over and peace—such as it was—a fragile, new thing. He went to the fiefs, did you know?"

Kaylin nodded. "So did the outcaste, who wasn't outcaste then."

"Yes."

"Tiamaris said the Arkon wasn't interested in the arcane.

It was Tiamaris, of the Court, who spent the most time exploring the fiefs."

"Yes. Do you not find that odd?"

Did she? She hadn't, at the time. The Arkon's hoard was his library, and Tiamaris liked to get out of the palace. If the palace were Kaylin's home, she'd've been happy to leave it. For any reason.

It was Bellusdeo who said, "It's not the library that's his hoard."

"It is, though—Sanabalis said..."

"It's what it contains. What it *represents*. Leave it to Lannagaros to declare and build such a hoard, a thing of ephemera, a thing that is not solid and does not have form or shape. At least Tiamaris was sensible." She was thoughtful; the thought was almost loud. "The public portion of the library always struck me as odd."

"That and the fact that it *is* open to the public, and the librarians the Arkon himself interviews and hires are mortal," Emmerian agreed.

The two Dragons exchanged another long look.

"You could not know," Emmerian told Bellusdeo.

Bellusdeo rose.

"Where are you going?" Kaylin asked, because Bellusdeo was raring to go; she had focus, and she had that particular look that said work had to be done and she was getting on with doing it.

"Back to the palace."

"But—"

"Now that he knows that something remains, something exists, something of what he best loved and desired in his long-ago youth, now that he knows it *can* somehow be found, nothing will keep him in the library he has built. Do you understand? He will go to the fiefs. I do not intend to let him go alone."

"Wait."

"You've had no sleep. You're almost falling over now."

"I have the book," Kaylin replied.

"It is not a book to either of us."

"No, it's not. But… I think it could be, in the end. You think he'll run off immediately?"

"I think it likely, yes. You?" Bellusdeo turned to Emmerian.

"I think you did not see the Arkon in his prime."

"You're not concerned."

"I *am* concerned." He bowed his head. When he lifted it again, he said to Kaylin, "What could you have done to stop Lord Tiamaris from claiming the Tower that is now his home?"

She looked at him as if he were trying to grow a third eye.

"Exactly. You have known the Arkon for a brief period of time. The opinions you have formed of the Arkon are accurate. He is not a man who dissembles—poisoning information is not only a waste of time; it is almost a crime in his opinion." Another smile emerged, gilded with nostalgia. "When the laws of the Empire were discussed, he was strongly insistent that lies be made illegal."

"We'd all be in jail."

"Yes. He did have suggestions on how to build a jail, or perhaps how to find one. Regardless, what you have seen is what he is. But never all of it. What we—Bellusdeo and I—now see is also part of what he is. It is part of what we all are as Dragons." He, too, rose.

"There is a danger," Bellusdeo said.

"I concur." It was the first time Helen had joined the conversation. "But I believe Kaylin is correct; the book that she sees—the book that you perceive as something amorphous—is important. If you can reason with the Arkon until Kaylin has actually managed to get some sleep, she will return to the palace."

Both of the Dragons looked highly dubious about their ability to do so.

Helen, however, shook her head. "He is driven. Perhaps he is desperate. Hope makes fools of us all from time to time—but hope is also necessary. He will, if you can intercept him, wait."

"And if we can't?"

"It is my suspicion that even if you remain at a reasonable distance, he will find his way here. He understands that Kaylin needs some sleep to function, and I believe he perceives that the book itself puts a large drain on her physical stamina.

"He is possibly—if Bellusdeo and Emmerian are correct—in a frenzy. But he would not be unkind. I believe Kaylin will find herself seconded to the Imperial Palace for the time being. Meaning that yes, you will get paid."

Kaylin would never make a bet with Helen because she hated losing bets and Helen had no actual need of money.

"Bets are not about money, if I understand them correctly," Helen said, as Kaylin got dressed the next morning. "They are about stakes."

"Fine." Kaylin pulled a tunic over her head. She'd decided not to wear the Hawk tabard in the fiefs, but it annoyed her to have to be that practical.

"You are unlikely to be troubled, given your traveling companions."

"Yes. But not less likely to be hated." She grimaced, adjusting the clothing while Hope squawked, presumably at Helen, since Kaylin couldn't understand a word. "I resented the Hawks a long time ago. I believed they were there to protect the weak." She grabbed a stick and struggled to twist her hair in the knot that would keep it out of the way. "But there were no Hawks *for us*. We were beneath them."

"And you have since discovered that that is not true."

"Not really. But I understand why now."

"You want what Tiamaris has offered."

"I do. But… I want it for *all* of the fiefs. Teela would probably kill me if she could hear me."

"I highly doubt that."

"She told me years ago that if she had to hear this *one more time*," Kaylin said, mimicking almost exactly Teela's inflection, "she would make certain she never had to hear it again. With a vengeance."

"Ah. But I'm certain she did hear it again."

"Less often. She thought I spent too much time whining about what was wrong, and not enough time figuring out how to change what could be changed. For me," she added, "I could change nothing. Or that's what I thought, back then. I think it most of the time now. But…not *all* of the time."

"And Tiamaris?"

"I didn't change that, though. Tara and Tiamaris did—or will."

"Without you, Tiamaris would not be fieflord and Tara would not be Tara."

"That wasn't why I did it. I didn't plan it. I didn't go in thinking: Hey, how about I change *one* fief by confronting its Tower? Oh, and drag Tiamaris along just because."

"No. But change is change, and you cannot entirely predict what the fruit of your actions—for good or ill—will be. You did not intend to change Tiamaris. But you went to the fief's Tower. You went with knowledge of your past, of yourself, of the things that you had done and hated—and of the things you *wanted* of yourself. You'd already begun to make those changes."

Kaylin's snort was less forceful. "I first left the fiefs to assassinate the Hawklord." She seldom said this out loud. But Helen already knew, even if she had never heard it directly.

"I do," Helen said, her voice softer. "But Kaylin, you knew you would never succeed. You didn't come to assassinate him; you came to die." Helen's Avatar appeared in her room as Kaylin turned toward the sound of her voice. There was, alongside the knowledge, an acceptance that Kaylin struggled to maintain.

Her home hugged her gently.

"What you were when you arrived in Elantra is not what you are now. The choices that you've made since then were different choices. They were not choices you could have made in the fiefs. You wanted to be a different person—but the person you are grows out of the person you were.

"You remember all of the bad things. You remember the *why* of them. You could have chosen to be far more judgmental in your work as a Hawk."

"I am." Muffled voice.

"Not to my eye," Helen replied. "And no, I don't see you at work. But I know what your day was like. I could wish you might take Margot less personally, but knocking over her sandwich board on a daily basis didn't prevent you from saving her life."

"Don't remind me."

Helen chuckled. "You have two visitors," she added.

"Two?"

"Sorry, three, but one is Severn."

The parlor—not the dining room—was where Kaylin's breakfast was served. The room had grown, but it now hosted more than four people. The Arkon was present, and with him, Lord Emmerian; Severn was, as Helen had said, here. Kaylin lifted brows in his direction.

"I was told that while you are seconded to the Imperial Palace, I am also seconded to the palace."

The Arkon said, "By whom?" His voice was chilly. His eyes were orange.

"The Lord of Hawks. Lord Grammayre."

"I see."

"The Hawks work in pairs," Kaylin pointed out.

"The Arkon," the Arkon said, "does not."

"We have a mirror, if you want to speak with someone who can rescind those orders," Kaylin told him. "But neither Severn nor I can ignore them."

Teela walked into the parlor. She was not happy. "We will be heading into the Halls of Law, and I will happily relay your discontent." Given the color of her eyes, Teela's discontent was likely to be first on the discussion list.

Kaylin decided that rank mattered for reasons of pay. But Teela and Kaylin now shared a rank, and there were things that Teela could say that Kaylin couldn't, if she wanted to *keep* her new rank.

On the other hand, Kaylin couldn't imagine the Arkon wanted *more* people as companions. He didn't seem happy to be stuck with Severn and probably accepted Kaylin under sufferance. Kaylin had the book. The Arkon did not.

Kaylin had already started a mental cringe, because if Teela wasn't coming, it meant one of the cohort was. Annarion walked into the room. He failed to meet the Arkon's glare but offered the older Dragon a perfect obeisance.

Kaylin didn't argue against his inclusion because there wasn't any point. And it made sense to her—they needed

one member of the cohort present to contact Mandoran and
Terrano.

The smart person to leave behind was Bellusdeo, and as
no one was going to win that argument, Kaylin buried it. She
had a better chance talking Annarion out of going. But she
repented when the second member of the cohort entered the
room.

It was Sedarias.

Kaylin left her chair. So did the Arkon and Emmerian.

"An'Mellarionne," the Arkon said, offering her a slight
bow.

"Arkon," she replied. Her bow was slightly shallower than
Annarion's had been but far more respectful than the Arkon's.
"If you find our company burdensome, we will proceed on
our own. It is not to cause grief or a moment's discomfort
that we have determined to return to the site at which we last
heard our lost friends." Her voice was grave, her eyes blue.
Sedarias had always had the bluest eyes in the cohort.

The Arkon resumed his seat. "It is my suspicion that you
have some familiarity with Arcanists."

"None from within the Arcanum," Sedarias replied. "And
Lord Kaylin does not appear fond of the Arcanum, so it has
not been much discussed."

"You are aware of the Arcanist Lord Kaylin could see."

"I have heard of him, yes."

"Very well. I must congratulate you."

"Oh?"

"For taking your place at Court."

Her smile was almost feline. And as Kaylin had worked
with Marcus for all of her life in the Hawks, *feline* had a distinct meaning that was not pleasant. The Arkon didn't seem to
mind Sedarias as much as he minded Severn. But he didn't ask
Helen if he could use her mirror—in the secure room—either.

★ ★ ★

Kaylin had the book bundled up in a small blanket—the kind of blanket meant for big chairs, not beds. Caitlin called them throws, for some reason. It helped, but she knew it wouldn't make as much difference an hour from now. The book radiated cold, and it ate heat and warmth.

It hadn't been nearly as bad when she'd been at home.

Helen, she thought. And Helen had said nothing; she had just gone about, as she always did, making home safe. Or as safe as it could be, all things considered.

Sedarias was armed. Annarion was armed. Bellusdeo was armored; she had given up on Imperial clothing entirely for the duration of this investigation. The Arkon and Emmerian had not. But they were comfortable with the Emperor's rules. Watching the fussy old librarian stride down the streets, Kaylin still couldn't see him as an outstanding, even legendary, warrior.

But the rest of Emmerian's words made her uneasy. If the Arkon was irritable—and he was, if your name was Kaylin—he was also steady. Solid. Predictable. He was indulgent of Bellusdeo because he understood both where she had come from, and what she had lost to return.

This version of the Arkon was a stranger to Kaylin. She wanted the old one back. And maybe if they could sort this out somehow, that would happen. But she didn't understand his hoard. She had assumed that it meant *touch this and die*, because that, at least, seemed true across all Dragons. What was his hoard, if not the things the library contained that were strictly off-limits?

If the library was his hoard, why was it open to the public at all?

"You're thinking," Bellusdeo said, falling in step beside

her. They weren't patrolling, in part because the Arkon's pace didn't allow it.

"Are my ears smoking?"

The Dragon smiled. "A bit. We will enter Tiamaris, I believe, and attempt to retrace our path to the Academia. Lannagaros believes that it will be far less of a meandering walk than it was for us."

"Because of the book?"

"Because of that, yes. He would *like* to attempt an entry from Farlonne."

"It wasn't near Farlonne."

"Yes. We did point this out, but I believe he has theories he has not shared. Today, however, he is less interested in experimentation and more in locating the building he believes existed in his youth."

Kaylin lowered her voice. "What do you think will happen?"

"Let me remind you," the Arkon said, although he hadn't paused or turned back, "that I can hear every word you say. A whisper does not, in fact, render your words private."

Bellusdeo snickered.

Kaylin rolled her eyes. His hearing was, of course, Draconic—but he didn't have eyes in the back of his head.

Hope was draped across her shoulders, looking distinctly dissatisfied with life. There was no danger in Tiamaris. There was, however, a patrol—one that consisted of the fieflord and the Avatar of his Tower, plus two guards. Kaylin recognized one of them.

That guard stepped out from behind the fieflord when the Dragons started bowing at each other.

"What," Morse said in her normal voice, which was always lower, "are you guys doing?"

"Escorting a Dragon."

Morse's eyes narrowed. "We got thrown into the streets via a large hole in the wall. The one he usually takes when he's an actual Dragon. Apparently, one of your Dragons caused him alarm."

"Concern," Kaylin said. The Dragons had finished with the bowing bits and had entered the discussion phase. Luckily, they were speaking in Barrani, not their native tongue. "The old Dragon—well, the one that looks oldest—over there? He does leave his rooms in the palace, but not bloody often, and never just to visit. Almost never," she added, to be fair. "Tiamaris was his student."

"And he's worried?"

"Well, offhand I can think of a few times that the Arkon has left the palace. The time before last it was because the High Halls were on fire, and the entire Dragon Court had taken to the skies to defend it."

"...So if he's here there's likely to be fire."

"That's probably Tiamaris's concern, yes." She hesitated. "Did you hear that Tiamaris wants to let Hawks patrol his fief?"

Morse rolled her eyes. "Yes. Don't look at me like that. I don't care about the Hawks."

"I'm a Hawk."

"Repeat my words." There was the hint of a grin on Morse's face. "Personally, I hate the idea."

Trying not to bristle, Kaylin said, "Why?"

"Because he expects me to be the liaison. And I'd just as soon punch things or kill things as talk to them."

Kaylin laughed, partly because it was true. "It'd be less work for you."

"Not punching or killing things will take all of my self-control. I won't have time to deal with Hawks. Looks like they're done."

Kaylin, looking at the Arkon, lifted one hand—the free hand—to her ear. Morse, who had been watching Kaylin, instantly lifted both of hers.

The Arkon let loose a volley of Dragon that would terrify any fiefling who could hear it—which would probably be anyone who lived in Tiamaris.

Bellusdeo rolled her eyes; Emmerian did not seem to either hear the Arkon's words or be concerned by them. Tiamaris, Lord of the fief, roared right back.

"Or not," Morse shouted—into Kaylin's uncovered ear.

CHAPTER 16

Sedarias, of the gathered company, was the only person present whose eyes had descended into a dark, dark blue as the Dragons spoke. Annarion's expression was smooth, polished, and implied the resignation, beat for beat, that Emmerian's contained. Sedarias, not so much.

Apparently, the ability to see and hear the entirety of Mandoran's and Annarion's lives from the remove of the West March didn't compensate for actual, lived experience. She was rigid as Tiamaris and the Arkon continued the thunder of what appeared to be an actual argument.

Here, Tiamaris held sway. It was his fief.

Kaylin glanced at Tara's Avatar; the Tower, like the other two Dragons, look resigned. Resigned and compassionate. As if Kaylin's glance was a question, Tara moved away from Tiamaris toward Kaylin. He didn't appear to notice. As she reached Kaylin, she offered the Hawk a hug, her clothing transforming, as she did, from the meet-with-dignitaries dress and robes into the more beloved gardening smock.

"My Lord is worried," she said. Unlike Morse, it wasn't necessary for Tara to shout. Not even here, near the border of the fief over which her Tower ruled.

"Can you tell me why?"

Before Tara could answer, Kaylin added, "Emmerian and Bellusdeo are worried, too. The only time I've really seen Bellusdeo worry, it involved Shadow. This...doesn't."

"I am not sure I understand it myself. It has something to do with Dragons and hoards. But...you've seen a Dragon stake his hoard claim. You were standing right beside him. Did he appear to be dangerously unstable to you?"

"He's a Dragon."

"Does that make a difference? I agree that the form is, for a small period, unstable and appears malleable when the Dragons choose to shift—"

Kaylin had, momentarily, forgotten the Tower's sense of humor. Or lack of one. "I don't think I had the time to notice. You might remember that there were Shadows who were attempting to rewrite your words in the heart of the Tower space."

"Ah, yes. Apologies." Tara smiled. "I remember it as the darkness before the dawn. That's figurative," she added. "Or perhaps metaphorical. My Lord feels that the Arkon is dangerously unstable at the moment, and is telling him so."

Great. They were going to be here *all day*.

"What do you think?" Kaylin asked.

"He appears, to me, to be as he was the first time he visited the fief, except in one regard."

"And that is?"

"The first time, he was happy to see Bellusdeo. It meant much to him. It was hope. It was..." Tara frowned. "Sadness. I am not certain I should be answering this question." Her hesitation was marked, and it reminded Kaylin a bit of Helen—but Helen wouldn't have answered. "I think he has been sad for as long as you've known him. Perhaps for as long as Emmerian has known him. Bellusdeo comes from a period of his life where loss had not informed him so thoroughly."

"He's not sad now?"

"It is sharper, harsher. I cannot easily describe the difference. But he is...desperate with hope, Kaylin. My Lord attempts to cushion that hope, to explain reality. The Arkon is unwilling to let it go. Hope can break people when it is dashed."

Kaylin nodded, then exhaled. "I think you should tell your Lord that there's no point. Either hope will be dashed, or it won't. Oh, unless you have information about Candallar and his visitors and their possible whereabouts. Because I think those could be a serious problem."

"My Lord reminds you," Tara said, although Tiamaris was still entangled in his discussion, "that the desire for a hoard—when the hoard is unobtainable—can drive Dragons beyond the edge of sanity. It is both purpose and obsession. He believes you have seen murders caused, by mortals, who were so obsessed, and he invites you to consider what a Dragon might be like in the same state of mind."

That was not a happy thought. "Bellusdeo and Emmerian seem resigned to it."

Tara nodded.

"And if what you're saying is true, getting in the way of that Dragon might be the thing that sets him off."

"The Arkon is important to Tiamaris."

"All of the Dragons are."

She nodded again, hugged Kaylin, and returned to Tiamaris's side. No one heard what she said to Tiamaris, but Tiamaris's flood of words banked abruptly. His eyes were a deep orange; from a distance, they might be red. But it was not the bloodred that signaled imminent death.

The Arkon's eyes were less immediately visible to Kaylin,

but while his breath was a steady stream of smoke, he seemed content to stop speaking.

"My Lord bids me tell you," Tara said to Kaylin, while standing beside said Lord, "that none of the visitors you fear entered the border zone through Tiamaris."

"I wish we could speak with the other fieflords the same way."

"So does he; he is beginning to consider it a necessity. Come back to the Tower when you are done with your exploration; there are a few things he wishes to discuss."

The border zone was the border zone; Tiamaris and Tara, with Morse in tow, accompanied them to that point, but Tara now walked beside the Arkon. Tiamaris fell in beside Kaylin, glancing at Severn as if for permission. Which was annoying.

Hope squawked.

"We cannot lose him," Tiamaris told Kaylin, the words both unexpected and abrupt. She knew where this was going. "I task you with keeping him safe."

"We've got two Barrani and two Dragons here. And you're telling *me* to keep him safe?"

He smiled. "Yes, actually. You are, I am constantly reminded, Chosen."

"Might as well tell me to worry about Teela," she replied.

"I don't require you to fuss or worry *at* him. I merely require you to bring him back."

"I thought Sanabalis was your teacher. Your former teacher."

"He was and is. But what he learned, he learned from the Arkon. The Arkon values things lost, things dead, things ancient. He believes that they have things to teach us if we can but learn. He is important to the Emperor."

"He's important to Bellusdeo, too—and she lives with me."

Tiamaris lifted his chin, frowning. "This is where we leave you."

The Arkon turned from Tara, and from what appeared to be an animated discussion, the corners of his lips heading in the wrong direction as he met Tiamaris's steady gaze. But he offered Tara a deep bow—certainly a deeper bow than any of the Dragons ever got from him.

Sedarias and Annarion had pulled up the rear—the far rear. They now closed the gap, and it was Sedarias who entered the border zone first.

"Be wary of Sedarias," Tara said quietly. "Her intentions are not bad, but her thoughts turn, always, toward the bad intentions of others. She is likely to react first, and then think."

Kaylin, however, shook her head. "Where we're going, her form of thought might save our lives."

The Arkon snorted.

The Arkon's suspicion—that the book Kaylin carried would make the finding of Killian less time-consuming— was proved right. They spent far less time crawling over fences and through backyards searching for a street that ran in the right direction.

This was good, because without Teela's vision to borrow, Annarion and Sedarias were stuck in a thick fog that made their companions almost invisible if they weren't standing practically on top of them. Annarion was willing to be grabbed by the arm and dragged along streets Kaylin could see; Sedarias was Sedarias. She strode ahead into the fog as if it couldn't disgorge anything that was a threat.

"She can hear your voices," Annarion said. "She's following those." He grimaced and added, "And cursing Teela."

"Teela would have come, but she likes her job."

"So we've been told. We've yet to ascertain why, on the

other hand. It's not so bad today. The fog. I think it's already thinning."

Annarion was the first to spot the signpost. "This is where we were," he told the gathered companions. "This is the signpost that leads into the circular road."

The Arkon could see what the other two Dragons could see, which was pretty much consistent with the two Hawks. He did, however, stop at the signpost that Annarion had picked out of the thinning fog that dogged the cohort. He looked up; he could read the words. He then looked down the street in the wrong direction, almost as if looking in the right one was something that he needed to brace himself to do.

But when he did turn, his eyes were gold, and they were lit from within by a fire that had nothing to do with combat. For just that glimpse, the Arkon seemed young to Kaylin. Young, excitable, caught in a frenzy of fear and hope. This wasn't Kaylin's youth, but she recognized it, and for the first time since she had discovered Killian, she understood why Bellusdeo and Emmerian were worried.

The two Dragons said nothing; they turned in the direction the Arkon had finally turned, and they waited while he drew breath. Kaylin, however, grabbed his arm as he opened his mouth that little bit too wide. "Remember, Killian's occupied, in both senses of that word."

Reality readjusted itself in the lines of the Arkon's face as joy ebbed. Kaylin wasn't certain she liked what replaced it. He nodded.

Sedarias did not recognize the street. But she'd heard of the building, or buildings, that comprised this place. She didn't walk with the same excitement, the same urgency, that drove the Arkon—but no one here could do that.

"Has it changed?" Kaylin asked the oldest member of the Dragon Court.

"It is...what I remember. The color is wrong—but I have been told that the border zones are like that: the buildings that remain are echoes of buildings, the streets, echoes of streets."

"That's Killian," Kaylin said, lifting her arm and pointing out the largest of the buildings, on the farthest edge of the circular road's circumference from where they were standing.

"I do not understand why you use that name."

"It's what he said his name was."

"Mortal hearing is not *that* bad."

"That's what he said, right?" Kaylin turned to Bellusdeo.

"Kaylin is correct."

The Arkon seemed disinclined to accept Bellusdeo's opinion. "Corporal?"

"It is also what I heard." As he so often did, Severn chose to speak in Barrani when speaking with the Dragons.

"He *is* in need of intervention."

Hope sat up, shifting position in one fluid motion that involved more than the usual amount of exposed claw digging into Kaylin's collarbone.

All of her companions fell instantly silent as Hope raised a wing to cover Kaylin's eyes.

"We need to get out of the street," Kaylin said, her voice low, the words urgent. "Come on. We need to move *now*."

No one argued—not even Sedarias. "Which building is likely to be real?"

"That one. The one closest to us." It was the building she thought of as Larrantin's, although when—and if—it had been a normal building, it had been occupied by far more people than a single Barrani.

They moved quickly, and only when they reached—and

opened—the doors did the Arkon speak. His words clashed with Sedarias's, but the Barrani High Lord immediately gave way.

"What did you see?"

"People," Kaylin said. "Invisible people. Until Hope lifted his wing, I saw an empty, flat circle of grass with a bunch of trees on it."

"Were any of these people the two you saw behind Killianas?"

"I didn't take the time to really look. I can go back out in a bit—but I'm fairly certain we were spotted. We're not exactly being stealthy; we didn't approach using the buildings for cover." She wanted to strangle Terrano because she was almost certain that whatever it was that allowed these people to be here in this form was directly or indirectly his fault.

Oddly, it was Ynpharion who answered what wasn't a question. *It was. But Terrano was a child. A dangerous child, yes. He did not care about the effects of his teachings on any but the cohort, as you call them—and the cohort were safe.*

They weren't so safe when Alsanis was attacked.

The Arcanists have always been ambitious. He planted a seed, and they grew it. I do not know, he added, a hint of worry in his tone, *what has grown from it, or how large it has become.*

We're probably about to find out.

I doubt you will see all of it. He paused, and then added, *Survive, Kaylin.* This was surprising enough that she almost missed a step. On flat ground.

"I need to put this down," Kaylin told the Arkon. "I can't fight while carrying it."

"Physical combat should not, at this point, be your concern," was the Arkon's reply. He turned to Bellusdeo. "Do not even think it. This hall was not meant to accommodate your Draconic form, and you cannot easily fight what you cannot see."

It was Sedarias who said, "We can."

"You did not see them, either."

"No. It's Helen's fault; she has been teaching us—somewhat unkindly, I feel—to navigate the streets of *your* city. We are allowed out into those streets now, but there are strict commands about what we can and cannot do. Terrano and Mandoran appear to be exempt from this; Helen feels that they are flexible enough to understand the effects of their power and form.

"But it is my guess that the Barrani—and humans—who have learned to be somewhat more flexible in their base state have not had Helen as a teacher. There is some danger in what they do." Her smile grew an edge. "But they have neither our experience nor our base power." That smile gentled slightly. "If you feel the need to put down the thing you are carrying, do so. It is possible that your familiar will see dangers that we cannot if we are fighting."

Kaylin turned to the long desk that fronted familiar stairs.

Coming down those stairs now was an equally familiar Barrani man. Larrantin.

She froze, her perpetual reluctant inner student coming to the fore. Beating her down, she offered Larrantin a bow. It wasn't a bow that would have pleased Diarmat, but she was cold and shivering.

Larrantin's expression was mildly peevish. "Have you failed to deliver a simple message?"

"It wasn't safe, at the time."

"Oh?"

"Killianas was otherwise occupied."

Larrantin's frown deepened, but the edges of irritation vanished. "I see."

"Can you keep this for now? We're going to try to meet with him again. It's just that there are a lot of people between him and us, and they don't want us to be anywhere near here."

Larrantin nodded and held out a hand.

Kaylin placed the book in it, unwrapping it from the small blanket she'd used to protect herself from the cold it radiated. When Larrantin took it, the runes on its cover flared blue and white; ice lit from within by a bright, steady light.

Behind her back, someone sucked in one long breath. He exhaled a word.

"Larrantin." It was, of course, the Arkon.

Larrantin frowned. He glanced past Kaylin, but her companions remained invisible to his eyes. "I will hold this for now, but I feel it essential that Killianas receive it soon."

Sedarias and Annarion headed to the right, away from the desk. Annarion stopped and looked over his shoulder.

"For the record," Bellusdeo said, "I'm against this."

The Arkon, however, said nothing.

Kaylin scurried after the two Barrani. She was joined by Severn. When she raised a brow at him, he mouthed the word *partner*. When she snorted, he said, "We were seconded by the Imperial Palace as Hawks. You don't go into a brawl—or worse—without backup."

Neither Sedarias nor Annarion appeared to be surprised by this.

"I believe you said Larrantin couldn't leave this building," Sedarias said.

Kaylin nodded. "If you two are going to melt through a wall, I can't leave that way."

"No. But I think it best not to open the doors at the moment."

"What are we doing?"

"Finding a suitable window."

Kaylin wasn't certain that the window wouldn't cause the same problem the doors would, but she deferred to Sedarias. Severn had nodded.

Hope continued to keep his wing in front of Kaylin's eyes as they moved through the wide, long hall; they reached a door that opened into a room that was much larger than Larrantin's office had been. Maybe this was where whoever had once lived in these buildings had held parties. It seemed far too fancy for lectures.

Sedarias entered this room. She had wanted windows, and windows were here in abundance, although they were above ground level, and built into four large bays. None of those windows looked likely to open without damage.

Sedarias and Annarion were silent, but it was a silence that caused a lot of shifting facial expressions; Kaylin guessed that they were discussing their next moves with the absent cohort. While they did, Kaylin approached the window from the curtain side. She glanced through it; saw grass and trees. It was interesting; through this window, the muted, washed-out colors had been replaced by the vibrancy of actual life.

The people gathered in the center of the circle had thinned in numbers. She could guess where the others had gone, but couldn't see the building's front door from this angle, and didn't try.

Eight people remained in the large grass circle. Six were Barrani, two human. Illanen and Baltrin weren't among them.

"I don't think you'll find Baltrin here at this time of day," Severn said. "His movements are more easily tracked. He's not on vacation, has not taken a leave of absence, and must therefore occupy his office and the duties to which he clings." Once again, Severn spoke Barrani, but this time for the benefit of their two companions.

"The Barrani are not so easily monitored, by either their own people or ours. It is possible—I think it likely—that Illanen will be at the front door."

"He won't be the problem."

Severn glanced at her, the tone of the flat sentence a warning.

"Killian's doors have just opened," she said. "And I think that's Candallar leaving the building."

"I see him," Severn said. His glance slid to Hope, who huffed.

"We see him, as well," Sedarias added.

They couldn't see the rest of the gathered people. Kaylin wasn't certain if Candallar's visibility was a good sign or a bad one. "Does he look normal to you?"

Sedarias exhaled. "We don't see what you see here. You've said—to your eyes—that the streets, roads and buildings are lacking color. To us, they're not. We know what you see," she added, "because it's what Teela saw. To us, then, the buildings look like Elantran buildings—but better. More impressive.

"Do the people you can see resemble the exterior of the buildings and the rest of the landscape?"

Kaylin nodded.

"Candallar?"

"He looks like the rest of us to me."

Sedarias bowed her head for three long beats. When she lifted her face, her eyes were a disturbing color; black with flecks of color. She then glanced at Annarion.

"Helen's not going to like it," he said.

The glance became a glare, and several silent beats passed before he closed his eyes. When he opened them, they were a different, disturbing color: a milky white that also possessed flecks of moving color.

Sedarias didn't tell Annarion that Helen didn't need to know, because they were the cohort. They could, with effort, hide their thoughts from Helen—but it wasn't a sustainable effort. They trusted her; she would never harm them. Helen was therefore going to know.

"We won't leave the fiefs like this," Sedarias then said—to Kaylin. "But whatever you're looking at, we can't see the normal way."

Hope squawked.

They both turned toward the nearest window, taking positions that would make them less obvious to outside observers. They were silent, which said nothing; the cohort on the insides of their heads were probably talking up a storm.

"I am going to strangle Terrano," Sedarias then said, although she didn't look away from the window.

"You missed him more than anyone," Kaylin pointed out.

"My aim is not that bad."

"Terrano seemed to think he was mostly obeying your orders."

Sedarias's head whipped around, and Kaylin saw that her eyes had shifted color: they were now the same as Annarion's. "Orders? Clearly Terrano came from a family far more lax than my own. I made *suggestions*."

Annarion snickered.

"You can see them now?" Kaylin asked quickly.

"We can."

"And this makes you want to strangle Terrano because?"

"To view them at all requires a shift in our physicality. It's a very particular shift," she added.

Kaylin frowned. "Do you think they could do this outside of the border zone?"

"Yes."

"Do you think it would be detected?"

Sedarias nodded. "Helen would notice immediately. If you're worried about the Dragons—"

"We would notice," the Arkon said from the far doors. "Or rather, the magic required would cause a significant disturbance. They are not, however, more empowered than they would otherwise be."

"Could they attempt to assassinate you without becoming visible to the rest of us?"

"We're about to find out."

"You're supposed to be with—"

"The rest of us," Bellusdeo then said, "are with him. Or we would be if he would move out of the doorway."

Sedarias said nothing; her eyes were narrowed. Annarion glanced once at her, and she nodded, but the nod was measured and deliberate. This wasn't a natural transition for Sedarias. Annarion might have had eyes like this all his life. It was Annarion who seemed to have the most difficulty maintaining the strictly Barrani biology he'd been born to.

No, she thought, that wasn't it. Terrano could shift his form at will, and Mandoran wasn't far behind. But Helen judged neither of them a threat. It had been Annarion she'd worried most about. Whatever he was doing wasn't the same thing. Regardless, he didn't seem to have trouble with his new eyes.

He lifted a palm to touch a pane of glass. "I don't think we'll have to break it."

"We will if the Dragons are going to follow us out."

"The Dragons are not going to follow you out," Bellusdeo replied, glaring at the Arkon's back. She then said to Sedarias—or Kaylin, it was hard to tell which, "I don't believe our invisible visitors can open the front doors."

"Why do you say that?"

"Candallar has just left Killian's residence. He is walking

in a straight line to the building we currently occupy. I believe Candallar will be able to do what the rest of the people here can't."

"You think that's why he's here?" Kaylin asked.

"I can't think of another reason, at the moment; I'm open to suggestions. But I don't think breaking the windows would be a good idea. To us, this room is as solid, as fully realized, as any room in the Imperial Palace would be. The exterior of the building is not. I'm not sure what happens—to this building or to its occupants—should the windows themselves be open."

"The doors—"

"Doors are meant to be opened and closed. I don't believe these windows are." She then cleared her throat, Dragon style. "Lannagaros."

It was Emmerian who entered the room; Emmerian who placed a flat palm across the Arkon's left shoulder. "Arkon."

The Arkon exhaled. Kaylin couldn't have continued to make that sound for half as long—and if she'd tried, she'd be gasping for breath at the end of it. "I concur." In tone, it sounded like an argument.

Annarion jumped up to the window ledge, his feet making no sound. He might have weighed nothing. He turned back toward Sedarias, and she grimaced, an expression very much like one that might have graced Mandoran's face. "Did I mention that I'm going to strangle Terrano?"

"Only about a hundred times this morning. I won't try to stop you if you let me strangle Mandoran."

Bellusdeo cleared her throat again. It was the same rumble of Dragon sound, but louder and shorter. She would have made a great sergeant.

"Fine. We won't stop you if you try to kill Mandoran," Annarion said.

This took the edge off the red-orange Bellusdeo's eyes had

become. Annarion smiled at her, his lips half quirked in one corner. He then turned and stepped through the windowpane. Without breaking it first.

Sedarias leaped just as lightly up to the abandoned window seat. "Go back to the front hall," she told the Dragons. "Candallar is almost at the front doors." To Kaylin, she added, "Retrieve the book from Larrantin, if that is now possible. I do not think it wise to let anything fall into Candallar's hands."

Kaylin turned immediately to leave the room. The Arkon, however, cleared his throat in much the same way Bellusdeo had.

"I have it."

The words took a moment to make sense.

"I am uncertain how you managed to contain it or carry it," the Dragon librarian continued. "It is not a book in any sense of the word; what you see as a book is...not what I see."

"Now or before you picked it up?" The Arkon was indeed carrying the blanketed bundle. "I gave it to Larrantin."

"He must have set it down, then. I picked it up from the front desk. I would have gladly taken it from his hands as you did, could I but see him."

Kaylin wheeled toward Bellusdeo; the gold Dragon shrugged. "I am not his keeper."

"It might be dangerous!"

"You cannot possibly be under the impression that Lannagaros takes orders from me. He barely takes orders from the Emperor, and when he does—"

"I understand the spirit of the Emperor's *requests*," the Arkon said.

"Oh, please. If you understood them, you wouldn't be here at all."

"I said I understood them," the oldest member of the Dragon Court said. "I didn't say I mindlessly obeyed."

Bellusdeo's snort had smoke in it. But she caught up with Kaylin and shouldered her out of the way as she returned to the abandoned front desk. Her armor gleamed in the interior light in a way that suggested a source of illumination Kaylin couldn't otherwise see. Her eyes were orange.

The Arkon, however, remained well behind Bellusdeo and the two Hawks; Emmerian stayed with him, although he'd retrieved his hand.

People were unpredictable. Kaylin had considered—and probably still did—the Arkon a source of knowledge and wisdom. If he was cantankerous, and he absolutely was, he was steady. This Arkon, she hadn't met, hadn't seen. And clearly, neither had Bellusdeo.

It was harder to read Emmerian. Of the Dragon Court, he was the quietest presence. He was the man sent to interfere with her first attempt to find herself a new apartment. She couldn't resent him for it; she had found Helen, after all. Helen was the home she had always wanted, but hadn't known enough to even daydream about. She wouldn't have found Helen without Emmerian's unwelcome interference. She'd've happily taken the room on offer.

It was Emmerian who kept an eye on Bellusdeo—but at a safe distance. She couldn't, now that she considered it, imagine that he would do so the way someone like Diarmat would. Emmerian seemed to understand what Bellusdeo required. Even here, he allowed Bellusdeo to take the lead.

Bellusdeo, who had led armies and fought until the last against the encroachment of Shadow. She had not fought in the Draco-Barrani wars, although she had been educated and trained—inasmuch as a juvenile Dragon female could be— to do so.

Kaylin had been, for the entirety of her life with the Hawks, either a mascot or a private. Until now. She couldn't imagine leading armies. If she'd daydreamed about being Empress as a child, it was because she hadn't understood the weight of the responsibility that came with that position.

Hadn't considered the guilt that followed a loss. She'd never thought to survive for as long as Bellusdeo had.

"I wish we'd kept Annarion," Kaylin said as she faced the closed front doors.

"Not Sedarias?"

"Annarion's not Mandoran, but he's used to the rest of us. Sedarias keeps her own counsel. If Annarion were here, we'd know what's happening on the other side of the door."

"Annarion's sword-work is the best of the cohort's," Bellusdeo said, her voice softer. "This is not where you want him."

Kaylin, surprised, turned to Bellusdeo—but noted that Emmerian seemed slightly surprised, as well.

"I am considered reckless," Bellusdeo said, her smile brief but genuine. "But I understand why we are here and the cohort are outside. They can see their enemies. I cannot."

Kaylin, about to tell her that a wall of fiery breath might change that, said nothing.

The Arkon snorted, as well. He didn't look over his shoulder to see Bellusdeo. "Stop that." His voice was grim.

"Stop what?" Bellusdeo's tone was so deliberately innocent, Kaylin realized that she'd missed something that the Arkon hadn't.

"Bellusdeo is willing to remain outside of the action—" Something thudded against the closed doors. The Arkon paused until it was clear that no entry was going to follow, then said, "Not because she can't theoretically see the enemy, but because it will keep *me* here.

"Because the results are the correct results—Bellusdeo remains in the safest position—I accept this. But I dislike intensely her claim to be wiser or more prudent than she actually is. I feel that my own wisdom and prudence is being used as a tool."

Bellusdeo laughed. Her eyes were almost gold. Without pause, given the second thud against the door, the gold Dragon turned and enveloped the Arkon in a hug. Emmerian glanced away. Kaylin almost did, as well; there was something intensely personal in that simple gesture. "You are the only thing that remains of my childhood," the gold Dragon said.

"I will singe your hair," the Arkon replied.

Kaylin did not understand Dragons. Emmerian, however, seemed to understand this, and so she turned once again to the doors. Her eyes stopped part of the way there, because Larrantin was present.

Larrantin was looking at the Arkon. Not through him, but at him. His expression was intent, but devoid of anger; a hint of confusion colored his eyes.

"We're going to deliver your message," Kaylin said.

He adjusted the direction of his gaze.

"Killian has guests."

"Wanted guests?" A third thud. "Perhaps that is a foolish question."

"I'm not entirely sure he realizes he *has* guests. Certainly, *we* don't want them."

"You chose to deliver my book to Lannagaros, in Killian's stead?"

Larrantin recognized the Arkon. "I promise I'll explain it all later."

The Arkon, however, turned toward Larrantin, frowning as he did. Given that they were standing in what was a magical building, and there were magical people on the other side of the door if one didn't include the cohort, it shouldn't have surprised Kaylin to feel the effects of a strong surge of magic travel across most of her skin. It was painful, not tingly.

He then looked at the book he carried. She wondered if his magic had changed what he saw, or could see, because the magic had definitely been his.

"I could almost hear Larrantin," the Arkon said. "He's here."

Kaylin nodded. "He seems to recognize you. I mean, he spoke of you by name."

The Arkon said nothing. Bellusdeo, however, cursed. The final thud against the doors had been no louder than the several that preceded it—but this time the doors burst open. They hadn't shattered, but it didn't matter.

Standing in the frame of the door was Candallar.

CHAPTER 17

Everyone in the entryway could see Candallar—except for Larrantin, whose gaze remained fixed to the Arkon, even as the Arkon stepped back. His eyes did flicker to the open doors, but Candallar seemed to be as much of a nonentity as the rest of the gathering.

Candallar had eyes for the Dragons, or specifically for the one in the gold plate armor. Bellusdeo lifted a hand, flicked a wrist, and a beam of purple fire struck the air in front of her face, rather than her face as Candallar had no doubt intended.

Clearly, the time for negotiations had passed.

The fire itself spread, the single beam aimed at Bellusdeo's head splitting into multiple strands. The strands, unlike the beam, weren't single lines of purple flame; they were much more like tentacles. Severn's chain was up and spinning; he was fine. The tentacle shattered before it could reach him.

The Arkon was, elderly or no, as fast as Bellusdeo when it came to magic or shields—and he seemed prepared for the purple fire. Prepared enough that he turned instantly to breathe in the direction of his opponent.

Candallar leaped up, and the fire passed through him.

Emmerian didn't gesture or cast; he simply breathed fire;

yellow-white flame hit purple fire, and the two sparked and exploded, one shattering and the other dissipating.

Kaylin could leap out of the way of a simple beam—and had. But tentacles were always more of a problem. Always, she thought, in Leontine. Hope managed to stay rigid on her shoulder, his wing affixed to the front of her face. He opened his small, translucent jaws; Kaylin saw a flash of crimson and then a stream of what might—at a safe distance—have been smoke. It wasn't. Hope's breath threw small flecks of sparkling color into the air.

Given that his silvered stream of smoke had struck the purple flame, she couldn't complain—but while his breath persisted, it remained a hazard for anyone else who was fighting in the foyer. The foyer had seemed large the first time she'd seen it—but it wasn't large enough to be a significant and easily traversed battlefield.

She wanted, for one visceral moment, to be a *good* student in Sanabalis's much-neglected class. Or a Dragon. She tossed away her bracer, releasing the potential for her magic. It would find its way back to her at some point, probably through Severn.

I have the weapon, Severn pointed out. *You have Hope.*

She exhaled, finding her footing. *Maybe this isn't the time to talk about this?*

It wasn't. *You have time to start beating yourself up about what you lack. This is more constructive.*

Ugh.

I think Candallar's going to try to take a window.

Larrantin could see two things: Kaylin and her familiar. He could also see the trajectory of the familiar's breath. Ah. He could see what that breath struck. For just a second, for as long as the purple flame struggled against the transformation forced on it by Hope's breath, he could see the tendril.

Larrantin's frown transformed his expression. His eyes were a midnight blue that rivaled Teela's at their worst. His hair, white and black, intensified in color, the white becoming so bright and harsh that it caused an instinctive squint; the black becoming a void, a thing that implied the absence of living color forever.

He could see the open door. He could see the encroachment of something. Kaylin had a second—less—to shout. *"Close the doors!"* She turned instantly toward Larrantin.

He froze, his midnight eyes returning to her face.

"I'm sorry," she said, holding on to the visceral fear this much anger and magic invoked in anyone sane, "but I think that's a really, *really* bad idea here."

"Where," he asked, his voice thunder, *"is here?"*

"Can these windows be broken?"

Annarion and Sedarias had passed through them. But Candallar had opened the doors anyway, and there was no sign of the two members of the cohort anywhere. Severn moved to the open doors but stayed on the right side of them as he scanned the stairs and the grounds immediately in front of the building.

"Not easily. There was some difficulty with younger students and their various games. What," he added, voice sharpening, "was that?"

"The purple fire?"

"Is *that* what you saw?"

"That's what it looks like to me. To us," she added. "I'm not alone here. I think Candallar might be trying to find another way in."

"Candallar is the source of that...fire?"

She nodded.

Larrantin exhaled. "Take the book—or see that the book is delivered—to Killianas. I will guard the building."

"You couldn't *see* him."

He was clearly not a man accustomed to argument, even if the argument made sense.

"We've lost Sedarias and Annarion," Bellusdeo said. "Can you see bodies?"

It was such a pragmatic question. Kaylin turned toward the open door. She didn't borrow Severn's vision; what she could see through Hope's wing, he couldn't see. Nor did she tell Hope to fly to Severn and allow him to look through the same wings.

Instead, she crossed a hall that suddenly seemed short and squat, it provided so little time to gather her thoughts, to center herself. Battlefields of any kind always contained corpses.

This one was no exception. She'd seen Annarion fight. She'd seen Sedarias fight—although that fight, broken as it was with fights of her own, was less fixed in her mind.

Kaylin could immediately see the injured; she could see the dead. Some had lost limbs, and the bleeding would probably kill them. Some had not. But neither Annarion nor Sedarias were among the fallen.

Did she care about the people no one else could see? Did she care about people who had intended to kill them? Was she willing to spend the power to try to heal those who might—just might—survive if she did?

No. Not now, and maybe not ever.

She exhaled and turned.

"Your color is terrible," Bellusdeo said.

"Try looking in a mirror before you tell *me* that," Kaylin snapped. "Sedarias and Annarion aren't on the field. Candallar hasn't come down, either. And if you are going to go full Dragon, inside is not the place to do it. If you break parts of the building, Larrantin is going to be upset."

"You are speaking to Lannagaros?" Larrantin asked.

"No, I'm speaking to Bellusdeo. Lannagaros is less martial." But not, Kaylin thought with a twinge, less desperate.

"I do not know this Bellusdeo. She was perhaps not a student here."

Kaylin was silent for a long beat. "No," she finally said. "Lannagaros wants to know why you're here at all."

One brow rose.

"He didn't ask, but he does want to know. I think he's hoping that he'll be able to see and speak with you soon. You can't leave this building."

At this, a slender smile graced the Barrani man's face. His eyes were blue. "No."

"Have you tried?"

"I have opened the doors," he replied after another pause. "What you see when you cross the common is not what I see. The area beyond the doors is nigh impassible."

"Can you take a look outside the doors now? Without using magic that could level a standing army?"

"There are few demands on my time at the moment." He walked to the doors and opened them. Candallar hadn't returned; Kaylin was almost certain that he didn't intend a frontal attack from the doors again.

"What do you see?" she asked.

"Corpses."

He could see the corpses. "Bellusdeo?"

The gold Dragon shook her head. She'd only heard Kaylin's half of the conversation, but understood where Kaylin was going.

"So you can see the people who were gathered here. The rest of my companions can't." Kaylin exhaled. "I think they're like you. Except for the corpse part. How much do you know about the Academia?"

This was the wrong question, given the shift in Larrantin's expression.

Kaylin.

She turned automatically in the direction of Severn's voice before she realized that he wasn't speaking out loud. Widening the arc of that turn, she realized that he wasn't anywhere close enough to speak out loud.

Candallar?

I believe he's trying to enter the building from the third story. You've lost Sedarias and Annarion?

Yes.

You might want to send Bellusdeo upstairs.

"Can these windows be breached?"

"You have already said that two of your companions left through the windows without breaking them."

Kaylin cursed.

Bellusdeo, however, said, "I am not certain that Candallar has the flexibility—yet—to do the same."

Larrantin sighed. Loudly. It reminded Kaylin of the Arkon—on a normal day. "I am unaccustomed to the building being quite so empty, but I assure you I am capable of defending it."

"I didn't notice that you were defending it from those guys."

"They had not yet had the temerity to force entry; merely the temerity to try. I will deal with intruders here. You will deliver my message to Killianas."

"I'm not sure it's safe."

"It will become less safe if what you fear is true."

"What do you mean, what *I* fear?"

"You believe that the corpses that both you and I can see are somehow part of the student population of the Academia;

you believe that I can see them because I am a teacher at the same place. We are bound here."

"Most of those people *weren't* students when you were teaching here."

"How are you so certain?"

"Lots of humans."

"You think there were no mortals here? I would find your ignorance appalling in other circumstances." His eyes began to glow, which was arresting because they were such a dark color. "But those circumstances are not these. Take my message to Killianas, Chosen."

The marks across Kaylin's arms—and probably the rest of the skin she couldn't easily see—began to glow.

Did you catch most of that?

Yes. I'm coming back down the stairs.

Good, because Larrantin is going up. I'm still not convinced that he can stave off encroachment by people he can't see—but he can see me and is likely to reduce me to ash if I bring it up a second time.

He could see the marks.

Yes. I'm not sure how. I'm not asking, either—if he has an "undress person" spell I do not want to know.

Severn's chuckle was felt, not heard.

I mean, obviously he can see them now—they're glowing. But they didn't start until he gave me my orders.

Severn didn't ask the obvious question, but Kaylin's mind was beginning to chew on it. Why? Why had the marks responded to him?

He rounded the bend in the stairs and came to stand beside her. Kaylin then turned to the Arkon.

"Larrantin feels that it is essential—utterly essential—that we deliver his message to Killianas. He could see the bodies that Sedarias and Annarion left in their wake." She spoke

Barrani. "I think they would have seen him. But I also think they would see us. Larrantin can't be seen *by* the rest of you.

"I think Sedarias should strangle Terrano," she continued, "but not before she steps off a cliff herself. This might be something Terrano taught—but I'd bet any money that he taught it at her command. Let's go find them."

"You think they're trapped the way Mandoran and Terrano are?"

"And Nightshade, yes. Which implies that Candallar can somehow trap people within the school. Or someone who is with Candallar." She glanced once at Bellusdeo. "Ready?"

The gold Dragon nodded.

Candallar was not floating above the front doors when they exited the building. There was no fiery death, no purple tentacles or streams of fire-like color, waiting for them. Kaylin tried only one experiment as she headed down the walk; she asked Hope to lift his wing.

The wing was dutifully lifted, and the bodies that Kaylin could see vanished. She could—and did—step through them. They weren't merely invisible; they weren't there at all. Hope slid the wing back into place across her eyes. The bodies were there, and her feet—the single time she tried—didn't pass through them.

So...this was some kind of shift in plane.

She wanted to pause and study the corpses. She wanted to match them to what she remembered of the wall in that first building they'd encountered in Candallar's border zone. Mindful of Larrantin, of Candallar's presence, and of the four missing members of the cohort, she didn't take that time.

They walked—or marched—across the grass, cutting between two large trees to do so. Candallar had headed out of Killian's building, closing the doors behind him. He hadn't, that she'd seen, returned—but he might have beaten a retreat after his trick with the purple fire failed. The doors had been closed, if briefly.

She doubted it, though.

Her fear, at this point, was that he intended to kill them; if not kill, then imprison them. And that he had some method to do so that didn't depend on a building in the border zone. What she didn't understand was why. If he'd stumbled across this building, this academy, what did he want from it?

How was it useful?

He was fieflord. He had a Tower at his disposal. Then again, so did Nightshade—and Castle Nightshade would probably happily murder his visitors in their sleep, or starve them to death by getting them lost in a maze of twisting passages that had no exit.

Which was not, come to think of it, that different from the odd basement space they'd encountered when they'd been transported into the wall room.

She shook herself and realigned her thoughts. She didn't know enough about sentient buildings, and would probably never know enough about them; they were people, at heart, with a lot of very complicated power that worked in a contained space. She'd learned what little she knew of each building by spending time with, or in, the building.

And Killian was damaged. This whole place was off-kilter.

Helen had damaged herself in order to be able to make choices of her own. Killian wasn't damaged in the same way that Helen had been. Why was his Avatar missing an eye? Had that eye been deliberately moved?

The wall had existed for longer than Candallar had. Kaylin was almost certain of it. And she wondered, as they strode closer and closer to Killian's doors, if one of the Barrani who had stood at the very back of that carved crowd of people was Larrantin.

There were other Barrani in that background.

Some of the people in the foreground had been caught and trapped recently. Nightshade might now exist as part of that wall. Nightshade, however, couldn't leave the building, couldn't leave the classes.

The men and women who had gathered to attack Kaylin and her party, which contained one very obvious Dragon, could and had. Ugh. She resented the lack of perfect memory a great deal right now.

Kaylin slowed as she approached the front doors and the brick that had served as a doorbell. She reached out to grab Bellusdeo's shoulder, because playing point was clearly a job for the *most important Dragon* in existence, not a lowly Hawk. Bellusdeo, to her credit, stopped instantly.

"I think we should try a different entrance."

"Why?"

"Because Candallar was trying it. There's probably some advantage to not banging the front doors. If Killian is truly a building, or still a building, he'll be aware of us—but we want to sneak past his invisible watchdogs."

There was no way to sneak into the building that anyone present could easily see. This made sense, in a way: there was no way to sneak into Helen, either. But Helen hadn't been created to host an array of students; only guests. Kaylin, whose detective work had actually taken her inside the dorms of various schools, wondered if the Academia would house Dragons the way Helen did, or Barrani, or Aerians. She doubted it, but couldn't be certain.

"There *is* a way to sneak in," she finally said. "But you're not going to like it."

★ ★ ★

They found the building fairly quickly; the houses that surrounded it—according to Bellusdeo—had changed. To Kaylin, they were empty two-story buildings. The Arkon took note of them, but was not of a mind to fully examine the subtle differences Bellusdeo's perfect memory divulged. The windowless, doorless building was unchanged.

The giant eyeball was still part of the wall hidden from street view.

This time, when they approached it, they approached as a group; Kaylin had an absurd desire for the type of rope used to keep foundlings together when they walked in the crowded streets. The eyelid flicked open at the sound of their steps and began its slow-moving sweep of the backyard.

This time, when it saw Kaylin, it seemed to widen, but without the rest of the face behind it, she couldn't tell if this was a sign of surprise.

Regardless, this odd form of portal took them into the room with the giant wall and no other distinguishing features. The Arkon was annoyed; he had been in the process of observing the eye itself, and the displacement had interrupted him.

On the other hand, they were all caught in that gaze, and they were all dumped in the same room. Kaylin considered this a win.

You weren't certain?

No. It's a broken, sentient building part.

The Arkon's irritation dissipated as he stared at the almost featureless wall. One element of that wall—the child that Hope had breathed on—could still be seen by everyone present. Kaylin's suspicion that the people contained in this wall were also contained within Killian made Hope's breath far more dangerous in retrospect.

Kaylin could see the rest of the crowd because she had Hope's wing plastered to her face. She turned to Hope and said, "Can you show the Arkon?"

Hope squawked.

"You should have done this last time," Bellusdeo said, frowning.

"Sorry—I wasn't thinking. I forget sometimes that the wing is portable." This was true. At times like this, Hope felt like a part of her, a part of her natural vision. Given that her eyes didn't usually smack the rest of her face, this was surprising.

But Hope withdrew his translucent wing, removing the sight of the gathered, sculpted crowd, and pushed off her shoulder, squawking quietly. Probably at the Arkon. The Arkon waited until Hope had arranged himself on his robed shoulder, and Kaylin tried not to resent the fact that the familiar didn't slap the Dragon's face.

It was the Dragon's face that she now studied. His eyes had widened, and he'd dropped the inner membrane so nothing about its color was muted. But the Arkon was not Kaylin, who knew almost no magic, or Bellusdeo, who knew more. "Stand back from the wall," he told his companions. He didn't bother to check that that command had been obeyed before he started to speak.

His syllables were sonorous and slow, each distinct, each flowing into the next syllable, as if this were normal speech. And as Kaylin felt the spark of familiarity, her eyes widened, although the color didn't change. This was a language she felt she *should* know every time she heard it.

Even Bellusdeo was caught in the hush the Arkon's words invoked.

True Words didn't form, as they sometimes did, in the air around the Arkon; the measure of the effect his speech had was entirely contained by the wall. The wall began to recede, as if they were standing in place and it was retreating, the movement slow but inexorable.

No, Kaylin thought, that wasn't quite right. It wasn't the wall that was receding. It was the parts of the wall that surrounded the people carved into it. Stone didn't melt; it simply faded, flat stone giving way to reliefs, until Kaylin could see them clearly. They were statues now.

She recognized one of them. He stood at the forefront of this group, and the group itself wasn't small.

"Lannagaros," Bellusdeo said. "Enough." She placed a firm hand on the Arkon's shoulder—the one that Hope was standing on. Her voice was both gentle and implacable. "We are not done here. You must conserve your power."

"I have changed very little," the Arkon said, which was demonstrably not accurate. Kaylin disagreed, but silently. She stood in front of a statue of Nightshade. "Can you see the cohort?" she asked, the question meant for Bellusdeo, who also lived with them.

"No. I do see Annarion's brother."

"So we can assume they're here, but not trapped in the same way."

"I counsel against assumptions," the Arkon replied. "But the nature of your friends might make this particular type of containment difficult."

"Particular type? What exactly does that mean?"

"Killianas was a building, and his powers were like and unlike your Helen's. Hospitality was not his concern. It was quite likely not Helen's original concern, except in a passing fashion. But security of a certain kind was."

"Of a certain kind?"

"There is a reason that the Arcanum has never been housed

in a building with the will, power and intellect to interfere with the studies of its disparate members."

"Because no one's around to make those buildings anymore?"

The Arkon did not reply. Instead, he walked through the crowd, joining Severn, who had started to walk between the statues almost the moment the Arkon had stopped speaking. He paused in front of three, as if taking mental notes, but said nothing before he continued to move.

Wolf business?

And missing persons, he replied, his tone removed, almost distant. The former was not a subject he was going to discuss.

The Arkon continued to the walk to the back of the crowd. Kaylin's suspicion that the order of visibility had something to do with the length of captivity solidified; the Arkon had stopped at the very back of this carved crowd, in front of one of the Barrani statues.

"Do you recognize this man?" he asked, although he didn't turn from it.

"It's... Larrantin. I think."

"You *think*?"

"Well, Larrantin's strongest distinguishing feature is his hair. The Consort is the only Barrani I've ever met with white hair. Larrantin is the only Barrani I've ever met with gray hair. I mean, black and white. And...this stone is all the same color."

"I have always known that mortal hearing is inferior to immortal hearing," the Arkon said, his eyes a familiar orange. "I had never realized that their vision is likewise compromised."

"The answer you want," Bellusdeo then said, far more amused than either the Arkon or Kaylin, "is yes. Yes, that is Larrantin."

"I thought he wanted an accurate answer. The accurate answer is maybe."

"You are misusing the word *accurate* in an almost unforgivable fashion," the Arkon then said. He turned away from the statue of Larrantin.

"Do you recognize the other two?"

"Yes."

Kaylin waited until it became clear that the Arkon considered it none of her business.

"You said there were doors here. Thank you," he added—to Hope. Hope squawked and pushed himself off the Arkon's shoulder to return, once again, to Kaylin's. "It is time to take those doors."

The doors stood on the left and right walls of the previously featureless room. The statues filled it now.

"What I don't understand is why we're not statues."

"Pardon?"

"We're not part of the statuary. Or whatever it is you call this place. We're ourselves."

"I will have words with your teachers when we return to the palace."

"Which teachers?"

"Sanabalis." Emmerian winced at the Arkon's distinct and chilly lack of title. "You have avoided lessons with Sanabalis for long enough. No, don't ask me any more questions; my temper is already somewhat taxed."

Bellusdeo took the lead as they descended. "The stairs," she informed the Arkon, "have not changed in shape or width."

"Pitch?"

"The descent appears to be the same."

Not only the descent but the hall itself—the endless loop of the long, rectangular hall that terminated in a door. The

damage that they'd done to the doors in their previous visit
had been repaired so well it might never have happened at all.

There was, however, one notable difference.

When they reached the end of this long hall with doors
that led into what appeared to be student rooms or offices,
they opened the door, expecting to find the same damn hall.

Perhaps it was the same hall, but standing just behind the
door was Killian.

CHAPTER 18

Hope hadn't lifted a wing to Kaylin's face upon his return to his usual perch; he didn't lift it now. Whatever Kaylin could see without his aid seemed acceptable to her familiar. Severn and Bellusdeo had seen Killian when she had first encountered him, and he was visible to both Emmerian and the Arkon now.

The Arkon drew one long, long breath. He then stepped in front of Bellusdeo without exactly shouldering her out of the way, which was impressive given the dimensions of the hall.

He bowed to Killian.

Killian's expression rippled, as if a number of different emotions were now vying for control of his face before they all fell into the deep pit of neutrality.

"Killianas."

Killian was silent. He looked past the bowed form of the Arkon, his gaze meeting—and holding—Kaylin's. "You have returned."

"We were asked to give you a message."

"A message?" His gaze flicked off the Arkon's bowed head. "Rise. If you maintain that position, it will be awkward." The Arkon rose. Kaylin wondered if he'd intended to wait until he'd been given that permission. She'd done it before, and it wasn't comfortable. But at least she'd had more of her limbs attached to the ground when she had.

"This is not a convenient time in which to receive guests."

"We weren't told to be guests," Kaylin began. She stopped when the Arkon lifted a hand in her direction.

"What has happened to you?" the oldest Dragon said.

Killian didn't hear the question. "We are experiencing difficulties," he told the mortal Hawk. "It would be best if you returned on a different day."

"We'd be happy to visit on a different day, as well," Kaylin replied. "But we need to deliver a message now. It's from Larrantin," she added, glancing at the Arkon who seemed to hold the book in the death grip of folded Dragon arms.

Killian frowned. "This is not the way messages are usually delivered."

The ground beneath Kaylin's feet began to tremble. She glanced at her companions.

I feel it, Severn told her, his expression betraying nothing.

Kaylin took a deeper breath. "We wanted to survive delivering it."

At this, Killian's single eye narrowed. "Larrantin is strict and temperamental, but he is highly unlikely to kill his students." He paused, his brow creasing. "You are his student?"

The Arkon stepped on her foot before she could answer. "She is my student," he said.

Killian's frown shifted, deepened. Kaylin nudged Hope; he smacked her cheek but didn't leave his wing extended.

Killian, however, adjusted his gaze until it fell on the Arkon. To Kaylin, it felt as if he was performing a monumentally difficult task, although the Arkon was standing right beside her.

"Your student?"

"One of few."

"She shows great potential," Killian then said. "But seems somewhat lacking in discipline and a clear understanding of our rules. Do you accept responsibility for her?"

The Arkon straightened his shoulders, lifting his chin. "I do."

"Very well. You are…" Once again, his expression rippled, his face gaining the lines of a frown that emerged from a blend of concentration and confusion. "You are Lannagaros of the Winged Fury Flight. I had not heard that you had graduated."

This did annoy the Arkon. "I graduated with distinction. I was accepted as a lecturer, and given some handful of students of my own. I had an office in this building. You may speak with Larrantin if you wish to ascertain this, but I am now very concerned. I wish to speak to the chancellor."

Killian looked at the Arkon—really looked at him, as if he were suddenly confronted with an alien, unknown species that almost defied comprehension. It would have been comical in any other circumstance.

"There is no chancellor," Killian said, his voice flat and uninflected.

This would have stopped Kaylin dead in her tracks. It almost stopped the Arkon, but not for the same reasons.

"No chancellor?"

"No."

"Who was the last chancellor?"

"Chancellor Terramonte. He ascended to the position upon the departure of Aramechtis. He did not hold it for long."

One of the two names caused the Arkon's eyes to shift color. "What befell Terramonte? He would not have surrendered the seat."

"But he did, Lannagaros. As did the council. There has been no other."

"Did you not think to exalt Larrantin?"

"Larrantin has not applied."

Kaylin thought of the book. The book the Arkon now held.

"Surely," the Arkon continued, "there are candidates under your consideration."

"I believe there are those who intend to forward themselves as chancellor, yes. They do not, however, understand the necessary forms."

"Forms?" The Arkon's exhalation was full of smoke.

To Kaylin, this was the type of plodding dream that contained details better suited to nightmares—because bureaucracy was a nightmare to Kaylin, and this sounded like an arcane version of exactly that.

The trembling at her feet grew stronger, as if the ground itself was a thin—and increasingly fragile—layer beneath which something much larger was sleeping. And waking.

"I think we have to move," Kaylin said. The words were meant for the Arkon. The Arkon wasn't listening to Kaylin.

"Forms," Killian repeated. Dragon breath might have been an everyday, mundane occurrence for all the attention he paid to the smoke. "You have some small understanding of what is required."

The Arkon nodded.

"There is a disturbance in the lecture halls," Killian said. "I cannot afford to indulge in idle conversation." He then turned his gaze—with the same apparent effort—to Kaylin. "If you are lost, I will show you the way out, but I cannot guarantee that it will be as safe for you or your companions as your last excursion." Killian turned and began his slow, deliberate walk, as if expecting to be followed.

She cleared her throat.

He paused but didn't turn back. "Do you wish to remain

here? It is safe for you and your kind, but it lacks basic amenities."

"I don't think it's going to remain safe," she told him, grim now. "Is there a reason you can't take the book from the Arkon?"

"Book?" Killian turned then, the movement far more like the movements of the Barrani she knew. Kaylin almost took a step back at the intensity of his expression; his eye had lost the appearance of natural eyes. It was, like Helen's could be when she was distracted by dangers, obsidian. But the flecks of color that added light were almost lurid.

"Larrantin gave me a book," Kaylin said, her voice steady by dint of will. She was telling the truth—but sometimes truth didn't matter to the powerful. Killian had not seemed powerful to her until the moment he turned. He'd seemed... broken, almost absent, and, although she would never say this out loud, pitiable.

She repented.

"He gave me a book to give to you."

"You do not carry a book."

"No. I—" She swallowed. "The last time you saw me, I was trying to deliver Larrantin's book. But when the door opened, you had guests."

He did not reply. When Kaylin fell silent, he said, "Continue." His voice, like the movement of floor beneath their feet, was thunder.

This had seemed like such a good idea when she'd been looking for a way into the building that bypassed the Arcanist and his crew. It didn't seem like a great idea now.

"We— I wasn't sure you were aware that you had guests. They weren't students. They weren't trapped in your wall."

Killian's eye began to glow, the black emitting a light that ate all other light. As if the remaining eye in miniature was akin to the giant eye on the wall, that dark-cast gaze traveled over all of them. Severn moved, and moved quickly, as did Emmerian, leaping into the corners formed by walls on either side of the open door.

Bellusdeo was standing too close to the Arkon to do so. Or maybe not; she didn't even make the attempt to get out of the way of a gaze that had become, in a moment, almost physical.

As the gaze of the eye in the border zone, this one swept them someplace else in an instant.

Someplace else was dark. The floor in this place was soft—which implied carpet. Or worse. It no longer trembled. Kaylin reached out with her left arm and contacted the Arkon's back. Or his robes.

"Bellusdeo?"

"I'm here."

"Could either of you do something about the lights?"

"I believe," the Arkon said, "we will leave that up to you."

"Sanabalis hasn't been teaching me anything as useful as lighting."

"I am sure he has laid down enough of the basics that you could, with effort, illuminate at least one room."

"Or you could, with no effort, do the same."

"Kitling," Bellusdeo said, voice softer than usual, "while Lannagaros was not known for the sweetness of either his temperament or his teaching, he seldom made requests of this nature without reason."

"Meaning he's not attempting to torment me or make me feel stupid?"

"Yes."

"But Sanabalis *didn't* teach me how to… Oh."

"It is a small wonder to me that you have survived Sanabalis," the Arkon then said. "I understand that Bellusdeo is with you for all of Lord Diarmat's classes."

Kaylin grimaced in the dark. The Arkon was unlikely to see her expression.

He knows you well enough to know what your expression is likely to be, Hope said. *You will want to be careful here.*

"Where is here?"

I am not entirely certain. Helen has rooms and areas in which you and your kin might not survive without her aid. This might, perhaps, be similar. The endless Hall is clearly an area for, hmmm, what does Helen call it? A time-out?

She rolled up her left sleeve. It was always the left hand, the left arm, that she exposed to danger first. As she did this, the marks on her arms began to glow. They were a dull blue, a color that indicated the possibility of magic, or magical interference, at least some of the time.

She could see the marks clearly as she rotated her arm; could see the shape of the runes, and the cohesion of each specific character.

Severn?

I can hear you. I can see what you see.

Some of the tension left her shoulders. *Nightshade?*

I am here. His voice was more distant, but it was clear, distinct. When she tried to speak to Ynpharion, however, only silence returned.

Can you see the cohort? she asked the fieflord.

No. I will say that the lecture currently being disrupted was quite interesting.

How is it being disrupted?

I am uncertain. The lecturer appears to stop and start. The words are paused, as if he is a Records replay; he continues exactly where he left off. There is no break and no repetition.

Your brother is here.

This caused mild frustration in the fieflord and beneath that a wellspring of concern.

So is Sedarias. At least, I think they're together. They went to fight their way through the small group of Barrani and humans that were going to storm Larrantin's building and then disappeared.

I think it unlikely that they will be trapped the way we are currently trapped. It is interesting, he said, worry once again receding. *Tell the Arkon that we are here as students. We are dressed as students. We are lectured as students—and at that, new students who have not yet shown the potential the various lecturers look for.*

Kaylin said, *I'll tell him in a minute.*

The marks on her arms began to glow a brighter blue, the light whiter and harsher than the light shed when they were golden. Kaylin understood neither the blue nor the gold, but in either case, the marks shed light. She concentrated now, looking at the shape of the words; divining, by sight alone, the feel of what they might mean.

Meaning was separate from language, even if words implied the existence of language. It was a language that Kaylin had never been taught, and would probably never learn to speak. Yet without speaking, she was meant to use these words.

"Can you see now?" Kaylin asked.

"I can see your marks. They're glowing," Bellusdeo said.

"What color are they to you?"

It was the Arkon who replied. "A washed-out white. Usually they shed light that is golden."

Kaylin nodded, still staring at her arm. She turned it over, exposing the inner forearm. All of the marks seemed to be evenly glowing. She chose one of the more complicated runes because she thought it would shed more light by volume, and as she did, that mark rose from her skin. It floated in the air at chin level, and it weighed a *lot*.

The marks on her skin seldom felt heavy. Hot, yes. Uncomfortably hot, even. But not as weighty as this one appeared to have become.

"Do they look different to you?" Kaylin asked the Arkon.

"Are you asking me if the composition of those marks has changed?"

"More or less."

"Since when?"

"What do you mean?"

"Since they first entered Records? Since you began your work as a Hawk and not an…adjunct?

"Mascot."

"Very well, mascot."

"Never mind." The answer was clearly yes. Aware now that people who weren't Kaylin didn't perceive the marks the way she did, she said, "Can you see the light?"

"I can. It provides decent illumination—but I don't suggest you attempt this when Sanabalis once again resumes his instruction."

"Oh?"

"It would be considered either lazy or cheating."

Kaylin did not grind her teeth. "We all have different skills and different strengths. I believe those were among his first civil words to me."

The Arkon snorted. "I believe his response would be, 'And different weaknesses.'"

The light was bright, but not harsh; she didn't have to squint or wait until her eyes had adjusted to its glow. The floating rune moved away from her, drifting forward until it was about ten feet distant. There it stopped.

"Do you think Killian was aware of his other visitors?"

"What do you think?"

"I…assumed he was unaware of them. Now I'm not as certain."

"The first time we encountered Killian he looked much the same as he looked today," Bellusdeo added. "But the assumption that he was the Avatar of a building was Kaylin's, not mine."

"What did you assume?" the Arkon asked.

"Do not take that tone with me," the gold Dragon replied. "I am not one of your students."

They appeared to be standing in either a long hall or a very narrow room. The walls were stone, and the ground beneath their feet no longer shook. "Take that tone with me," Kaylin said.

Bellusdeo's brows rose. "You hate being a student."

"No, mostly I hate condescending old men who treat me as if I'm stupid."

"I fail to see the difference in this case."

"Compared to the *Arkon*, I *am* stupid."

"Ignorant," the Arkon said, correcting her. "I have never said that I believed you to be stupid. Lazy, yes."

"Fine. You can talk to me as if I'm a student. A dim student you're saddled with because you have no other choice."

"Your magnanimity knows no bounds," was the dry reply. "Very well. What do you wish to know?"

"What's a chancellor? I mean—I get what it is in the Imperial hierarchy, but this isn't that."

"Ah. In this particular case, the chancellor is the head of the Academia. To Helen, the equivalency is tenant. You are her tenant. The rest of the occupants she houses are your guests."

"How exactly does one become chancellor?"

"When I was a student in these halls, it was irrelevant."

"Who was chancellor then?"

"Aramechtis." He exhaled without apparently inhaling first. "The Academia was lost in my youth. The rise of the Towers that guard against the spread of Shadow devoured it. There were some irregularities with its disappearance, but research into those irregularities was far more difficult, and far less accessible, given the nature of *Ravellon* and the Towers.

"Not until the two of you came to me with your suspicion—" He stopped. Cleared his throat. "I do not know. I would have said, given our experience of the border zone, that it would either be impossible for Killian to select a chancellor, or impossible for the admission of students.

"But here we are. Ah. I did not answer your question, did I?"

You noticed. She didn't say this out loud.

"I do not know. When I first arrived, I assumed it was a choice made—or suggested—by the governing council, those who taught and researched within the campus itself. That august body of intellectuals seemed the pinnacle of all knowledge; as I said, I was young."

"Larrantin?"

"He was a member of that council, yes. If you mean to imply that the message—or book—he tasked you with delivering is somehow a demand or command that Killian grant that power to you, I do not believe you to be correct."

"But you won't surrender the item, just in case?" Bellusdeo's voice was teasing. Her eyes were orange, but they had gold in them, not the red of danger or rage.

"I cannot think why I did not reduce you to ash in the Aerie."

"You would have had to leave your room."

He snorted. "I assumed—I believe we all assumed—that Killian accepted the decision of the council with regards to the position of chancellor."

"And now?"

"I am less certain. I believe a chancellor is required."

"Our location now implies he still has some flexibility, and at least the ground isn't threatening to break beneath our feet. Where do you think we are? Did your old school have dungeons?"

"Killianas was a building. My old school, as you so disrespectfully call it, had whatever rooms the chancellor deemed necessary. It is a miracle—not a small one—that anything survived at all."

Kaylin nodded.

"Why did you assume he was a building?"

She'd already answered this question in the palace, but after a pause to think about new facts, said, "Because he knew my name. Or what I'm called. I had to poke him to get out of the trap of endless halls. But…no, not just that. If he'd created a normal portal, I'd still be fighting not to throw up. When we first entered the room with the wall, it was a smooth transition. I didn't notice a difference. I mean—I noticed we weren't outside anymore, but…" She frowned.

"But?"

I believe your answer to this question is relevant, Nightshade said.

"It didn't feel different," she finally said. "It didn't feel different from the border zone itself. We see streets we expect to see when we crossed into it. The cohort didn't. They saw fog or clouds, which seemed to me more like parts of the outlands—the ones you reach by the portal paths the Hallionne create. The Hallionne have some control over the look and feel of the paths, at least up to a certain distance away. But without that, things are much more formless.

"As I said, it's not what I saw. It's not what anyone but the cohort saw."

"Are you taking our names in vain?" a familiar voice said.

It was, of course, Terrano.

Or at least it was his voice. Since she didn't know his True Name, he had always been forced to speak normally. But the light shed by her mark didn't reveal his physical presence at all.

"She is not," the Arkon said. "Can you see us?"

"I can certainly hear you. Give me a second."

"What are you attempting to do?" The Arkon's voice had sharpened, the volume rising.

"Incorporate," he replied. "I'm the only person here. Mandoran is trying to follow me, but he's not quite up to the task. Sedarias and Annarion aren't even close."

"I think he means why are you *here*," Kaylin said.

"We were having a little bit of a problem with the lecturer in portal phenomenon."

"I don't think the Arkon wants to hear that."

"It would depend entirely on who the lecturer was."

"We didn't pause to ask his name. Not that there was much of a break in the droning in which to ask a question."

"That sounds very like Caranthas," the Arkon then said, "in which case you have my blessing. I am surprised he noticed you at all."

"Not half as surprised as we were. He apparently expected us to take a seat. And have our homework done." Terrano then offered a very liberal Leontine curse. "Sorry, I can't manage it. You're going to have to put up with voice only. How did you guys get into this space?"

"This space," Kaylin replied, "seems to be a stone hall with no doors and no other distinguishing features. Oh, and no lights that we don't bring ourselves."

"Really? That's what it looks like to you?"

"I imagine you don't have much in the way of eyes at the moment, and if you do, *please* don't materialize floating eyeballs."

Terrano laughed. "You are seriously way too squeamish."

"I'll let Hope breathe on them."

He laughed again. "He wouldn't. I'm not even sure he'd see eyeballs."

Hope squawked.

"Sorry. There are a bunch of Barrani and humans scattered around what appears to be the main building. That would be the one we entered by the front door, and that you avoided."

"I didn't think we'd have much fun with the Arcanist."

"Probably not. We could avoid alerting the wandering Arcanist and his friends. We could avoid Candallar—Sedarias is seriously pissed at him right now—although that was trickier. Killianas didn't seem to notice us, and we did try to get his attention. But that didn't work out well for us."

"You got sent to jail?"

"To our rooms, or what might have been meant to be our rooms if we were students here. Nightshade was aware of us," he added. "Even when the intruding Barrani weren't. The students and teachers here exist in a different way than the intruders."

"So...you're mostly locked in your rooms?"

Terrano shrugged. "We're mostly locked in our rooms—but these are kiddie locks—I think that's the phrase?—compared to Alsanis's locked rooms. They're not meant to keep people like us in them. This room is much better constructed for it, but he didn't send us here." He paused, and then added in a softer voice, "We can't talk to him."

"He's not Alsanis."

"We can talk to Helen. We can talk to the High Halls."

She froze. "Do not tell me that you've been visiting the High Halls."

"Well, we're Lords of the High Court now, aren't we?"

"Lords of the High Court that a lot of your kin want dead, yes."

"Sedarias says that's normal. If she hadn't gone to the green, most of her kin would still want her dead. Better now than later, when she's firmly established. Where's Severn?"

"He's stuck in the maze of endless hall. So's Emmerian, if that's helpful."

"Why are you guys in this room?"

"I think he meant to send us all, but missed the other two. I told you—I think I told you—that we found our way in the first time because a giant eyeball caught us in its gaze, right? Well...this was his normal eye, and Severn and Emmerian could dodge into corners. We were kind of standing in front of it."

"Do you know why?"

Bellusdeo snorted. "We believe—and we have no more access to Killian than you—that it had something to do with our mention of the intruders here. Apparently, people who are in this building are expected to either be teachers or students. Kaylin has a message from a teacher who is demonstrably unable to reach this building, but she was unwilling to deliver it when she saw Killian's invisible companions.

"She was the only person present who could see them."

"We can see them."

"None of you saw them the last time we were here," Kaylin said. "Regardless, I'm not sure Killian can. If he could, they'd be in the same student rooms you are."

"Maybe that's why most of them are on the outside of the building." Kaylin could almost hear Terrano shrug.

The Arkon now cleared his throat very, very loudly. "It is my belief that the border zones are the frayed outer edges of Killian's territory."

Kaylin had whiplash from the change of topic. "But they're all over the place. I mean—they exist between all the fiefs. Your Records didn't—"

He cleared his voice loudly. Bellusdeo stepped on her foot at almost the same time.

Fine. "The location of the school—the Academia—was pretty fixed. I mean, it was actual geography, not theoretical geography. Larrantin implied—no, I inferred from what he said—that warning had been given to the occupants of the Academia when the Towers were to rise."

"So people who got the warnings deserted the building?" Terrano asked.

"That's probably all of the student body and all of the teachers. But... Killian's been finding new students, probably slowly, in at least the Candallar border zone. It's how we found him in the first place."

"But he didn't keep you here as a student—he showed you the way out. Doesn't that strike you as odd?"

She shrugged. "It does now. Now all we want is to deliver a message to Killian and possibly have Killian eject all of the people he doesn't seem to see."

"You don't want to know what they're trying to do?"

"I'd consider that a bonus. I'm assuming—call me a cynic—that whatever it is they're trying to do is bad. The Arkon says that there used to be a chancellor, someone who was like Helen's tenant. He either died or abandoned his post. I'm going to assume died, because—"

"If Helen wanted to preserve you in this exact situation, she'd eject you," Terrano helpfully pointed out. "It's possible that he ejected the former chancellor. Sedarias asks who that chancellor was."

The Arkon answered. "It was Terramonte, according to Killianas. Understand that the Chancellors of the Academia did not retire in the fashion to which you are accustomed. Terramonte was, I believe, an emergency choice; someone to fill that role until Aramechtis returned from the war. But

Aramechtis did not return. The last true chancellor was probably Aramechtis." His eyes were a shade of copper now. "He was chancellor in my early years in this institution. He had a terrible habit of singing in the morning."

"Why is that terrible?"

"He was a Dragon, and he liked to project his voice. To retreat from the Academia almost killed him; the war finished off what survived. He had some difficulty facing his former students and former council members on battlefields. I remember the sound of his roaring when the Towers did rise."

"He didn't know that Killian had survived."

"No. No one did. Inform us if you encounter a door or something that looks like a room." He spoke to Terrano.

"Why a room or a door?"

"It is my hope that we are here to speak with Killian."

Terrano cursed liberally. "We have a problem on our end, and it's—" The sentence came to an unnatural end.

"Terrano?"

Silence.

Nightshade?

There has been a bit of a disturbance, the fieflord replied. He sounded vaguely irritated. *If I am to be entrapped as a student possessed of no great knowledge, the only possible advantage is the knowledge provided. Most of what has been discussed by the lecturer is known material; some of his conjectures are not.*

Kaylin did not shriek in frustration. *What's the disturbance? We had Terrano—Terrano's voice—for a bit, and now it's gone, and not in a "talk to you later" sort of way.*

She felt a glimmer of amusement. *It is unclear to me what the disturbance is, but given the presence of my brother and his friends, I can guess.*

Given Terrano's reaction, I can't. If they caused trouble, they didn't do it intentionally. You've been here for a day. You've been here as a student.

I have only been here for a day. It appears—from limited exposure—that we are students who are caught in the classes and routine of the Academia's final day. Or a random day before its final day.

Some of the Barrani weren't trapped in classes.

No. But the Academia appears to have schedules that coincide with individual students. Not all of the students who occupy the class that has currently been interrupted occupy all of the classes I, in theory, am taking. I can think and speak to you, but there is a flow, and a strength to the flow, of activity. When this class is over, I will leave and head to the next class. When that class is done, there is lunch— lunch seems to be common ground for all who are students here—and then there are two more classes. I then retreat to the library to study.

You don't have a choice in this?

No. I have some choice in the perusal of titles—and I find that perusal fascinating—but I have nowhere near enough time to examine all titles of interest, and I cannot read a number of them. His tone was one of mild frustration and longing. *Dinner is also at a common time, although it is longer. I believe that all who are present on these grounds in the way I am—or the way the other Barrani are—will make their way to the dining hall.*

And after?

I return to my room. I study. I sleep.

Barrani don't need to sleep.

Killianas believes we require time in our room, perhaps to study or contemplate the lessons we have been given. I believe that most of the students here are caught in schedules of their own, but are trapped in similar fashions.

So…the people Sedarias and Annarion fought were also classed as students, but those students didn't have classes scheduled for this day?

At times, I am surprised by your perception. Yes, that is entirely possible. It is a reasonable conjecture and one that makes sense.

CHAPTER 19

"I'm guessing Terrano or Mandoran have done something up above."

"What gave it away?" Bellusdeo asked, voice dry enough it might catch fire if she breathed.

"Nightshade confirms that there's been a disturbance. And no, he doesn't know what caused it. He's here as a student. He doesn't appear to have a full range of choice over his location or his movements. He can't get up and walk out of his class, and he appears to be following a routine. Within that routine, he has choice—but not enough to break the routine itself.

"He's suggesting that some of the Barrani and humans who were headed to Larrantin's building are also classed as students—but as students who have no classes, if that makes sense?" It made no sense to Kaylin, but she'd never been sent to a big fancy school. It would have killed her. Or her teachers. Or her guardian of the time, probably from apoplexy.

"Terrano and Mandoran weren't noticed by Killian—or if they were, they weren't here as students. They had their usual control over themselves. They could see what I could see with Hope's intervention. Sedarias and Annarion don't seem to have entered the building as smoothly."

"It is possible," the Arkon said quietly, "that the damage they did to the would-be attackers was noted by Killianas. It was not his desire that students murder each other, and the student body could be...fractious. The Barrani were far more likely to carry their political affiliations with them, but they were not the only ones. I think, at the moment, if we understood how Killianas survived, we would be in a position to make plans for the future."

"I think," Kaylin said, "that if we found out why or how Candallar is even here, we'd be able to make plans."

"Agreed," Bellusdeo said.

"Were either of you under the impression that this was a democratic process? If so, I apologize." The Arkon roared. And breathed fire. When the Arkon turned and began to walk down this wide, long hall, Bellusdeo and Kaylin fell in behind. Even Hope appeared to be subdued.

Have you moved at all? Kaylin asked Severn.

If by moved you mean, are we out of the endless hall, the answer is no.

Emmerian's good?

Emmerian is remarkably calm and reasonable, given the color of his eyes.

Is the ground still shaking?

She could feel Severn's nod. *I believe the rooms might be slightly different than they were the first time we went through them——but the door at the end of the hall leads to the beginning of the hall, as it did the first time we encountered it. Killian, however, is gone.*

Terrano found us. He couldn't join us, but he could talk to us. Now he can't. I don't suppose he's found you?

Not yet. Was he expecting to lose communication?

I don't know. There was a lot of Leontine before the last sentence. We're going to look for a door. Or a room. Or something.

Do you think you're at the core?

Did she?

I...don't think so. I'm not sure if we were sent here because it's a safe "room" or not—but until and unless we find Killian, we can't ask.

You were the one who reached him in the first place. Can you reach him from where you are?

Good question. I doubt it.

Why?

Because Terrano can't.

A beat of silence, a strong feeling of hesitance. Both characterized her conversations with Severn—or at least the ones that took place in their respective heads. *Terrano doesn't have the marks of the Chosen.*

I was afraid you were going to say that. Severn knew she didn't know how to use the marks. But...the only source of light in this room came from the mark she had lifted off her skin.

"Do you have any idea why Killian is so damaged?" Before the Arkon could speak, she flushed. "No, that was badly phrased. What I meant was: he's here, and he's not. I don't think it's just the lack of a chancellor. Somehow, he managed to protect himself, his space, the region for which he was guardian. But—I'm not sure what damage was done to him that makes him barely functional, at least compared to Helen. I know what happened to Helen, and I know why.

"I can guess that something happened to Killian—in his attempt to protect himself and his function—but I don't understand the gathering of so-called students. Some people either didn't leave on time or refused to leave. Larrantin is here. Caranthas, you mentioned—I'm assuming he was one of the Barrani stuck in the wall." The wall that was not really a wall anymore.

"Yes. I recognized him."

"And to be honest, I thought the fiefs had always existed. That *Ravellon* had always existed. I mean—I knew differently, but..." She shrugged.

"You are young. All of you are young. But I was once young as well, and the world was not what it has become. I did not enter *Ravellon* before it fell. But Larrantin did, once. There is very, very little of my life lived in that world, and far more lived in this one. To me, then, this is not ancient history.

"To you, it is. To almost all who still live, it is. The children who were sent to the green—your cohort—would be considered respectably old in other circumstances, but even they did not see what this place aspired to be. I know little about buildings compared to those who once taught and re-searched here—but I know much, compared to you."

"Do you have some guess as to how Killianas survived?" Bellusdeo asked.

"No. I am grateful for the fact that he did—but I am un-certain that he will ever be what he was. If he cannot be, we will never have what we once had. And perhaps I am in-fected by nostalgia and its many traps; I am driven by senti-ment and desire."

"Which is all very well," Bellusdeo replied. "But I am somewhat tired of this drab, quiet stone. A window or a door would be appreciated." She turned to Kaylin.

"I know, I know." Kaylin knelt and placed the flat of her left palm against the ground. It felt like stone: new stone, not stone worn by the passage of many feet over many years. What had she done the first time? How had she caught Killian's at-tention when she hadn't even known his name?

She didn't know his True Name now. Even if she did, she couldn't say it; it was probably like Helen's—too many words, too many phrases, too many things. She couldn't even hold one in her head for long enough to speak it the way the Arkon and Sanabalis could.

You lack practice, Hope said. It was critical.

"Now's not the time for practice."

If it were up to you, you would lurch between crises continually—as you do now. There is never enough time. It is making time, prioritizing that time, that is essential.

"Fine. We can talk about that *later.*"

Hope snorted. He then squawked loudly beside her ear. The Arkon's eyes narrowed; his free hand fell to his beard. He didn't reply.

Kaylin closed her eyes.

She could feel the stone beneath her palm, but could no longer see it. The marks—including the one that now hovered ten feet away, shedding pale light—were visible; she was used to that. They remained flat across the skin she could see.

How had she contacted Killian the first time?

Is anyone there? I'm Kaylin. Corporal Neya of the Imperial Hawks.

"Whatever you are doing, continue until I tell you to stop," the Arkon said, his voice coming at a remove, as if he had continued to walk while she knelt.

"You could try to do it yourself," she muttered.

"I would if I knew what you were doing."

"I'm introducing myself. That's what I did the first time to get his attention."

"How are you introducing yourself, exactly?"

"Touching the floor so I'm in contact with the building, and…thinking at it." This sounded far less reasonable on the outside of her head.

"Ah. That is not what you are actually doing."

"It looks to me like that's exactly what she's doing," Bellusdeo said.

"Spoken like a warrior."

Bellusdeo's laughter implied that the Arkon's expression was sour and annoyed. Kaylin loved the sound of that laughter. There was affection in it, even if there was mockery; the mockery implied history rather than superiority or cruelty.

"What am I doing?"

"Can you not see your marks?"

"I can. They're not doing anything special; they're flat against my skin. Except for the light."

"Perhaps that was the wrong choice of words. Can you not *hear* them?"

"No. You can?"

"Not clearly enough to repeat them, but yes—I hear the echoes of words. Understand that these words are not simply spoken, although they must be spoken in some fashion if they are to be made manifest; they are felt, they are seen, they are tangible. To speak is to call them forward, to hold them in place for some small time.

"But this was not a language made for our use, except in one way."

"True Names."

"Yes."

"The thing I don't understand is how you can speak a True Name and also *be* a True Name. I mean, if I could only ever use a word once, I'd never be able to speak at all."

"Hush and listen. I will do the same. It is something that I have not attempted in the past; I have studied the configuration of your marks at the request of the Emperor, but I have seldom had the chance to do what I am now doing. You never sit still for long enough," he added. "And you are always in the middle of a crisis that necessitates movement, motion."

"I cannot hear them," Bellusdeo said.

"No. But you, too, were always in crisis, and I cannot fault the choices you did make in a past I did not experience at your side. Be our guard, then; practice what you dedicated your life to in that past."

The Arkon did not magically join her in the space she occupied behind the darkness of closed eyelids. Terrano had said that this was her way of phasing, of moving between different planes of existence. She didn't do what the cohort did, and she didn't experience it as a change in herself; she experienced it as a change in her environment.

This type of shift was not one that affected Bellusdeo's ability to see Kaylin; what Kaylin thought she was doing and what Bellusdeo witnessed were the same. She didn't become invisible or transparent to the Dragon's eye. But she was aware that communicating with buildings wasn't as simple as the Hallionne had made it out to be. She hoped that this was not like attempting to reach the embattled heart of the High Halls—because that had been terrible.

But the being at the heart of the High Halls had been aware. He had made choices. His imperatives were different than Killian's had once been. How had Killian survived? And if he had somehow managed to disperse himself between the demarcations of the fiefs, if he had somehow managed to preserve the Academia, why was he so limited?

What had she seen in the border zones that might answer these questions?

"Corporal."

She grimaced. These were all questions that she felt needed answers—but Killian wasn't here. She once again directed her thoughts toward reaching him.

She stopped searching when the Arkon began to speak.

★ ★ ★

If she couldn't see the Arkon, she could hear him. His voice surrounded her. Without opening her eyes, she couldn't tell where he was sitting or standing. She couldn't hear his breathing, but without concentrating, couldn't hear her own.

The syllables that rolled in were not in a language she knew, but he spoke a language she recognized. She almost opened her eyes.

"Are these my marks? Are you trying to read them out loud?"

He didn't answer; to answer would have been to break the flow of his speech.

Her skin warmed as he spoke. She'd intended to try to listen to the marks on her skin, but the sound she could hear with her eyes closed had been swamped and overwhelmed by the sonorous bass of the Arkon's voice.

She rolled up her right sleeve, exposing the marks on that arm. The rest were on her back or legs, and unless their lives depended on it, she had no intention of removing her shirt or her pants. The Arkon's voice didn't change, possibly because reading—or speaking—words like this took effort and time.

But as she listened, she knew which of the words he was attempting to express in sound, in syllable. She could see it clearly; it was on the inside of her left arm, which was exposed because she'd turned it up simply by opening her palm and holding her hand out.

As she'd done once before, she listened to the sound of a Dragon's voice, and she joined her voice to his, not repeating what he said, but attempting to be part of it, to overlap it, two voices speaking one word, a slow syllable at a time.

The colors of the marks on her arms began to shift, the white gaining gold, the harsher, flatter light becoming the warmer as she watched. All of the marks, not just the one that the Arkon was, slowly and laboriously, speaking.

Were they all connected? They had her skin in common, but—were they somehow connected in other ways that she couldn't see because she couldn't quite understand them?

A single word wasn't a sentence. A paragraph wasn't a page. A page wasn't a book.

Why did the marks of the Chosen exist at all?

The Arkon's voice lapsed, but hers continued for several syllables; it was softer than the Dragon's voice, and it was no longer deliberate. She realized as she caught the sound of her voice that she wasn't speaking out loud; it was a deliberation of syllables that never made it to anyone else's ears. Like thought, but without intent.

And yes, the words were, or felt, connected somehow; she slid into syllables, and then away. All of Barrani, Leontine or Aerian were ways to describe things. There were no words in Barrani for certain mortal concepts; no words in Elantran for some of the Barrani concepts. But they could be circumscribed, they could be described—it took more effort. The communication wasn't exact.

These words were like those individual words: the concepts didn't exist in the same way in any language she'd laboriously learned. But…they could almost be described.

She realized, as she thought this, that she had continued to speak, or not-speak, and as she finished, one word rose. It didn't rise from her arms; it rose from the back of her neck, almost electrifying strands of hair, because no matter how careful she was, hair always fell out of its bindings in bits and pieces.

It was glowing. She could see it, even though in theory it was behind her, behind where her eyes were. It was a deceptively simply rune, two slashes, two dots beneath them;

it was not as complicated as the one that shed light for them in this space.

She opened her eyes.

The Arkon was seated in front of where she remained crouched, palm flat against the floor. His eyes were a shade of gold that had no orange in it. And he was looking past her, above her head. She lifted her hand and turned. The rune was there; it was bright gold—a gold that was the color of the Dragon's eyes, as if it reflected him, or the parts of him that were not simple flesh or organ.

Kaylin looked away almost instantly when she realized that the Arkon's inner eye membranes had fallen, and that he was crying. Not sobbing and not in any obvious pain—but there were tears glistening on his cheeks.

"Yes," he said in Elantran. The word was quiet, almost absent force. He rose. The word that Kaylin had spoken floated until it hovered above the shoulder that didn't contain Hope. He swatted it with his tail.

She didn't feel it as a weight; she did feel the light. In theory, she'd chosen both words, but the weight of the first was physical. She could carry a torch or a lantern for a long time; it was similar—once lifted—to that. But the golden rune above her shoulder weighed nothing; it was very much like any other time the words lifted themselves from her skin—words that she could see rising, but that others, watching, couldn't. It was frustrating, this sense that they both looked at the same thing while simultaneously not seeing it the same way.

But that was witness testimony everywhere. One witness—without the intervention of the Tha'alani—could be really dodgy. So many factors went into memory. There were lies, of course—those happened a lot as well, especially in murder cases—but for the most part witnesses who disagreed with each other, sometimes vehemently, believed they were telling the truth.

And they were, but it was a different truth.

If people could speak these words, the words on her skin, the words that marked the beginning of the Leontines, the words that empowered and caged the Hallionne and other sentient buildings, there would be *one* truth.

Maybe.

But this word was a True Word, and it hovered above her shoulder and it appeared to be meant, not for Kaylin, but for the Arkon, and she had no idea what it offered him, what it meant to him or what she had meant it to say.

"Come," he said when she was slow to follow.

Bellusdeo raised brows in her direction, a silent, wordless query. Kaylin shrugged. She had no idea where the Arkon was going, but he now walked with purpose, his back straight, one arm by his side. The other held the book; he hadn't set it down once since he had picked it up. Kaylin suspected he wouldn't.

We're out of the endless hall, Severn said.

Is Killian there?

No, but the door opened to stairs, not more hall. Emmerian has picked up a few inconsistencies in the rooms in the endless hall; minor differences or distortions that weren't immediately obvious.

Why would there be distortions?

He shrugged, although in theory she couldn't see it. "Bellusdeo, question."

The gold Dragon, who had fallen in beside Kaylin, nodded.

"Severn says Emmerian found subtle differences in the rooms in the endless halls. Distortions, maybe. Do you remember anything? I mean, beside the damage we caused."

Since the stone halls appeared to be as endless as the halls that had repeating rooms, Bellusdeo was willing to put serious thought into the answer. She had almost perfect memory; the lapses were lapses of convenience—at least for Bellusdeo.

"No," she finally said, frowning.

"They're out, now—Severn said the door opened to stairs. Do you think that's good or bad?"

"I'm still thinking about distortions. This hall seems endless; there's no reason that we couldn't be in the same loop, but without a door of any kind to break the monotony. I believe it's similar to what the Hallionne do if they wish to stop intruders. They fail to reach their destination. Or any destination."

"I don't think Killian intended that for us."

"But?"

The Arkon rumbled and picked up the pace, which seemed pointless to both of the people following him, but Bellusdeo could think while she walked. "He recognized Lannagaros, but not immediately. He did see you. He saw you the first time, as well. What do you think Candallar is up to here?"

"He's Barrani."

"Not all Barrani are as fractious as some have proved to be."

"Probably because we haven't met them yet."

"That's remarkably cynical of you, Corporal."

"Clearly Sedarias hasn't been lecturing you about the evils of her people."

Bellusdeo chuckled. "No. Mandoran might, if he thought the way she did. She is both grateful to me and uncomfortable around me."

"Sometimes with the Barrani, it's the gratitude that causes the discomfort." But not this time, as Kaylin knew. Bellusdeo was a Dragon. Neither Mandoran nor Annarion cared now, although they had when they'd first taken shelter in Helen. The history of the two races, their wars and their immortal memories made peaceful coexistence difficult on a gut level.

Sedarias had a reason to fear Dragons. All of her known history was pushing her away from Bellusdeo. But Sedarias was pragmatic at heart. When she'd spent enough time with the gold Dragon, Kaylin was certain she'd arrive in roughly the same place Mandoran now occupied. Nothing Kaylin said was going to change that; nothing was going to make it happen faster.

She didn't try. "I want to know how Candallar knew to look for this place. I can't imagine that he stumbled across it by accident."

"Why not? We did."

"Because I don't think Killian gouged out his eye on his own, and I think the location of that portal eye isn't coincidental. Also: Arcanists. And human lords. And Candallar's possible involvement in the breach of *Ravellon*'s border. He said he wants to be reinstated. He wants to return to the High Halls. It's something that even Sedarias believed. The Barrani of the High Court would believe it. Those who never took the Test of Name would believe it."

"And you would not?"

"I hate the High Halls, and I hate the High Court. I could believe that someone else wouldn't hate them—but I could also believe that someone else wouldn't care. Nightshade doesn't care." Before the fieflord could interrupt her on the inside of her head, she added, "I don't think he'd say no if somehow he was reinstated, don't get me wrong.

"But I don't think he'd go out of his way to *be* reinstated. He's a fieflord. Even as an outcaste it's always been clear that the Consort likes him. The death that awaits outcastes is purely theoretical; they won't kill him while he's a fieflord because they understand that the Towers are necessary. So, hmmm, maybe we're looking at this the wrong way."

"We?" the Arkon said.

"If you have something constructive to add," Kaylin began.

"I do not fault your provisional conclusions, but neither Bellusdeo nor I are members of the High Court. I understand that motive is frequently necessary when determining murderers. But murders without motives that you would understand also exist. It is the murder, not the motive, that is of interest now. Figuratively speaking. You have asked one good question: How did he find Killian? I invite you to consider the possibilities."

"You know, you could help out here. You know more about sentient buildings than either of the two of us. Sure, Bellusdeo understands Shadow better than anyone else in the Empire, but I don't think this is about Shadow."

"He allowed someone to retrieve a Shadow from *Ravellon*," Bellusdeo pointed out.

"Yes, but I think that was about *tools*, not about Shadow domination. He let it happen because he believed that it would help his cause."

"Which we are not discussing, according to Lannagaros."

"I did not say we are not discussing it," the older Dragon replied. "Merely that it is separate from action. Our understanding of what was done, of how it was done, would suffice here."

"But we don't know what was done."

"Indeed."

"I don't think the outcomes in the High Halls were either planned or intended," Kaylin continued. "And I'm not sure they're even stable. Spike is there, along with the will and intent of the building itself—but if the Shadow it once caged decides to leave, we're all in big trouble."

"But you didn't counsel that it be destroyed?" This was not the first time Bellusdeo had asked.

"Let's focus on the fact that we're walking down an endless hall in a damaged building." She exhaled, still thinking. "Do you understand how the outlands function?"

Bellusdeo immediately punted the question toward the Arkon's back.

"No."

Not promising, not really. "When we first decided to use the portal paths, the Hallionne set us down in a forest. I believe we were meant to follow the forest path to the next Hallionne. That's not what happened—but that was what was intended. There were more dangers in that forest than we'd face in the forest above. And fewer bugs.

"The Hallionne could shape a form out of the outlands by desire or will or command or even instinct. They didn't maintain control over what was shaped. So the outlands responded to their request because no other request overrode it. The Hallionne weren't the only people who could influence the shape the outlands took." She stopped walking.

"You lost the shape of that path."

"Pretty damn quickly, yes. But there were no Hallionne fighting for control of it. There were just Arcanists and transformed Barrani."

"Which would heavily imply that in the outlands—outside of the personal boundaries inscribed by their names and functions—the will of the Hallionne is no stronger than any other will. You have assumed that the border zone is, somehow, like the outlands; you feel there is a similarity."

"I do now—but only because the cohort couldn't see what the rest of us could. The rest of us saw the streets and buildings that conformed to the fief; we saw what we expected to see. The cohort, with the exception of Teela, didn't. It was fog, and it was dense enough that they had to be led—but the fog cleared as they approached the central circle that also contained Killian. Or the building Killian is trapped in.

"If this is true—and if Candallar or one of the Arcanists somehow understood it, it wouldn't be hard to force the streets to conform to a shape that better pleased them. Say a squat building with a giant eyeball embedded in its backside."

"I don't believe that the border zone is like the outlands," the Arkon then said.

"Why?"

"Because the border zone did not exist until the Towers rose. I will, however, grant that there must be elements in common with the outlands as you perceived them. It is almost a pity that you did not retain Spike."

"Not for the High Halls."

"No—but for Killianas. What Spike saw, or could not see, would be useful, and it might better help you to solve this mystery. I will, however, grant that Candallar seems to have some element of control of his border zone. The building that we found seemed to be a fixed point—and from what's been said by those who have dared to explore the border zones, the buildings are not fixed; they are solid and traversable, but they are not reliably located.

"The squat building seemed to be of newer construction and it seemed solid; you found it easily. And the eyeball, as you call it, in the back of the building is almost certainly Killian's. Candallar, or someone with whom he has chosen to ally himself, was aware of Killian, or perhaps aware that Killian's existence was not entirely extinguished.

"If this is the case, the only question I have is: How did they remove Killian's eye? The eye is figurative. It is metaphorical. If you chose to gouge out one of your Helen's eyes, she would nonetheless still have two eyes, should she retain the ability to manifest an Avatar at all."

"Not all of the sentient buildings are awake. They can

perform their functions while sleeping—many of the Hallionne do."

"Tell me, does Killian appear to be awake to you?"

"...No."

"Hallionne exist, as you've said, regardless of their state of wakefulness. But a wakeful Hallionne is something that even the Barrani who might reside there in safety are reluctant to trust. Is this correct?"

"Yes."

"From what you have said—and your memory is a tangled, jumbled mess—the Consort woke the Hallionne as you traveled to the West March. The Hallionne had been in use before she woke them; they had served their primary function. Some of the Barrani did not choose to avail themselves of the hospitality of the Hallionne thus wakened by the Consort."

"Right."

"Killianas is not awake. But he is not the Hallionne, and he is not Helen."

"I don't think the Consort could wake Killian."

"No more do I, Corporal. But I believe if Killian could be woken, he would be in a better position to defend himself." The Arkon had also stopped, his expression troubled.

"Do you think Larrantin's book—or whatever it is—could wake him?"

"I think it highly possible."

"Then...why didn't he take the book?"

"That is the question we are attempting to answer. He sent us here, a space lacking rooms, doors, people or students, if you prefer. But if Killian believed Larrantin's message might begin the process by which he wakes, he also considered waking now to be a threat. That expression implies you are thinking."

Kaylin turned to Bellusdeo. "When we explored the bor-

der zones," she said, "we could always see the Towers. But...
we could only see one. We could see one in the direction we
were heading. If we entered Candallar's border from Candallar's fief, we could see Tiamaris or Durant. We could see the
Tower we were approaching, not the Tower that controlled
the fief we were leaving. That was true of all the Towers.
Did you look back?"

Bellusdeo's frown was as expressive as Kaylin's but was immune from criticism. Or at least the Arkon's. "Kaylin is correct. The direction in which we were moving defined what
we could see. But...we could always see the Towers."

"We could always see one Tower," Kaylin said. She
frowned. "The Towers were clear. They looked like they
normally look. The rest of the street was the same washed-out, grayish color, but the Towers were clear."

The Arkon's eyes were an orange-gold as he watched her.

"You could blink," she told him.

"He forces himself not to when he wants a student to come
up with the answer to a problem on their own. It's his method
of dealing with laziness."

The Arkon snorted. He did not, however, blink.

"I'm wondering," Kaylin said, under that unblinking not-quite-glare, "if Killian's existence—what remains of it—is
anchored by the Towers themselves."

CHAPTER 20

It was Bellusdeo who broke the long silence that followed Kaylin's comment. "That would make sense, although I confess I don't understand the mechanics involved. If the Towers somehow anchored what remained of Killian, or built anchors of some kind as they rose, their influence might be very like the influence the Hallionne exert on the outlands. The border zones," she added, "look nothing like the outlands to me. But they did to the cohort."

"It would also explain how Candallar discovered Killian at all. But if Candallar could discover Killian, I'm really surprised that Nightshade hadn't. He spent some of his early life exploring the fiefs and looking for ancient ruins before he settled into Nightshade as the fieflord."

Bellusdeo was frowning. "It's possible," she finally said, "that the discovery of Killian and the breach of the defenses within Candallar itself are interconnected somehow. I do not imagine that someone entering *Ravellon* from Farlonne could emerge carrying the entity you call Spike."

Nightshade?

I concur. She felt a hint of frustration and realized he was annoyed by Kaylin's surprise. Or rather, he was annoyed that he hadn't discovered Killian first. It was a frustration that Kaylin normally couldn't sense.

No. The word was curt. *It is not…easy…to speak with you, even as we now speak. To do so requires more reach, more intent. There is more of me present in this discussion than would generally be either wise or normal.*

This also surprised Kaylin, but Nightshade had never had problems discerning her surprise.

A function of the way you communicate when you are, as you so quaintly put it, on the inside of your own head. It is what Lord Ynpharion finds so deplorable. This, on the other hand, amused Nightshade. *It is lunch now. I am heading toward the dining hall. But your thinking in regard to Killian and Candallar seems sound to me. Judging from the Arkon's expression, he is unable to find immediate flaw with it himself.*

She felt his pang of regret as he mentioned the Arkon—but that, he had always felt. It occurred to her only now that she felt it because the regret was deep, genuine and impossible to entirely squelch.

"Do you think that Candallar set his Tower to search for Killian?"

"Yes," the Arkon said, the syllable almost Draconic in tone and texture.

"And the Tower did."

"Yes. I believe you are correct about the timing of the Candallar breach, and it would explain much."

"How did Candallar know?"

"If you will be silent for a few moments, I might be able to *think* without interruption." His eyes had grown orange, and that orange deepened. This made it pretty easy to shut up.

He closed his eyes; the orange shuttered for a moment. Kaylin could feel Nightshade leaning in, the whole of his attention upon the Arkon, as if he were present in this hall, this enclosed space.

"Karriamis," the Arkon finally said.

Bellusdeo frowned.

"Karriamis is the ancient name of the Tower that is now called Candallar."

Kaylin said, "Karriamis was a Dragon."

"Yes. Before he became the heart of, the mind of, one of the six, he was a Dragon."

She thought of the Ancestors of the Barrani; she wondered if Dragon ancestors were as terrifying. She didn't ask. Instead, she said, "You think he knew Aramechtis."

"Yes. I was young," the Arkon said. "I was young enough that even my memory is stubborn and hard to retrieve. I have not thought of Aramechtis for centuries. I have not thought of Karriamis for far, far longer. It is possible, then, that Karriamis knew—or hoped—that the Academia had been preserved in some fashion.

"You have seen the Tower of Tiamaris. You have spoken with its Avatar. Tara is what remains of the heart of that Tower. Karriamis is no longer a Dragon; I do not believe he could be retrieved and returned to us now. The changes the Ancients made were not easily unmade by any. Nor were those chosen to become our strongest defense against *Ravellon* all of one people or another. But it is possible that the Tower of Nightshade had little regard for the Academia, and little regard for its purpose.

"The same might be said of the inhabitants of the other Towers, those beings who became their core. Not all of the people who lived at the time chose to devote their time and energy toward studies such as the Academia produced. I would need to see the historical records of the student body to fully ascertain what I now suspect."

"That Karriamis was a student here?"

"Long before I was, yes. What does that expression mean?"

"I'm wondering if you know where those records would be kept."

"Yes. You've been there. They were, at one time, in the building in which you found Larrantin."

Since getting out of this long stone hall didn't seem to be an option, checking bureaucratic student records was out of the question. Kaylin, therefore, returned her attention to the word that had risen from her skin.

"Yes," the Arkon said, although she hadn't asked anything of anyone, including herself.

"Why do you think Killian sent us here?"

"Safety."

"Ours or his?"

"Both. I am, however, more concerned about Killian's safety than our own." His glance slid over Bellusdeo. Her smile was all teeth. "I believe he understands that he has intruders, but cannot yet differentiate between those and students."

"There's a child there that went missing not long ago, and he's in Nightshade's class. I'm not even sure he can read."

"That is unkind."

"Why? I could barely read until I joined the Hawks, and I was older. If reading hadn't been a necessary part of the job—reading *and* writing—I wouldn't have bothered with either."

The Arkon looked truly scandalized, an expression unfamiliar to Kaylin.

"Knowledge for its own sake is kind of pointless. I didn't have the time for it because the knowledge I *was* developing could keep me alive for another day. Staying alive for another day isn't something that worries you. You have a palace over your head. You have all the food you could want."

"Knowledge for its own sake," the Arkon replied, in a less heated and less curt tone, "can become an unexpected route to survival. The understanding gained from so-called point-less study can illuminate the life you lead now in unexpected ways."

Kaylin shrugged. "I haven't noticed that it's getting us any-where right now." She turned away from the Arkon and to-ward the rune that she had lifted from her skin. Not the one that shed light, but the other—the one that felt weightless, as if it were air.

"Do you know this word?" she asked the Arkon.

"Not well enough to explain it. I recognize it, but the words that I learned did not include this one. Speech of the kind you have heard from me, or from Lord Sanabalis, is more like a summoning than a discussion. The words on your skin are present; the words that we have learned are not. Not in a fashion we recognize.

"But there are more words on your skin," he continued, when Kaylin didn't interrupt, "and their meanings are not always clear to me. If I listen carefully, if I focus on noth-ing else, I can almost hear their echoes—but it is seldom that you and lack of interruption are present in the same space."

"But you can see it."

"Yes. As you can see the words I have spoken in your pres-ence."

"What do you think it means?"

"It is not my thought in the matter that is necessary, but yours. These words were given to you to speak, to use. These words are your acts of communication with the ancient and unknown. This single rune, this single word, is one that you chose."

But she hadn't. Not deliberately.

"I believe you chose it when you were attempting to discern how to best speak with Killian—a Killian who is not quite awake."

"I don't understand."

"You have questions, then. At times, answers beget more questions, but even the questions form a type of mental path that you can approach and walk. You understand sentient buildings; you have now met several, and you live in one of them, although it is my suspicion that you might live in any of them and the buildings themselves would be happy to have you.

"I am not certain that Killian would suit either your needs or your purposes, but had you not made the first attempt to speak with him, we might not be here now. I do not know what you were thinking; I know that this word, this true word, is part answer and part question."

Kaylin looked at the word. She reached up to touch it; it was as solid as it appeared to be to her eyes. When she closed her palm around it, she could pull it down. She didn't try to stuff it back onto her skin. Instead, she turned to her left, faced the featureless stone wall, and pushed the rune into—or onto—the stone itself.

"What are you doing?" Bellusdeo's voice was sharp.

"Experimenting?"

"In the current situation, that is *not* comforting. Honestly, I begin to see why Terrano and Mandoran like you so much."

To Kaylin's shock, the Arkon said, "We are in an entirely new situation, about which we know very little. Without some experimentation, we might be trapped here in both literal and figurative ignorance."

"I would like Kaylin not to lose her hand or her arm."

"She is right-handed, and she is cautious enough to experiment with the hand that is not dominant."

Two streams of smoke filled the hall. Even had Kaylin not been occupied, stepping between two Dragons who were annoying each other never seemed like the brightest of ideas.

The word, the rune, stuck to the rock. It flattened there slowly, as if melting, and lost dimensionality as it did. It didn't lose its essential shape or color; it remained a glowing, gold rune on the surface of the wall, as if that stone were skin.

"What do you see?" Kaylin asked the Arkon, her gaze fixed to that single word.

"A word has appeared on the wall, at the height of your shoulder. It is glowing."

"It looks like a door ward," Bellusdeo added, studying it. "Is that what you see?"

Kaylin nodded. "Yes, to all of it."

"You hate door wards."

"I know. I was just thinking that myself, but with ruder words." She grimaced and lifted her left hand. "But this one shouldn't cause actual pain to touch, if that's what it is."

"Would you like me to try it? I generally open the Imperial doors, and it cannot be as odious as the ward on the library." This was said to Kaylin but clearly meant for the Arkon.

Kaylin shrugged. "It's not a door ward. It should be fine." And if it wasn't, the last person she wanted to touch it was Bellusdeo. The Emperor would sacrifice them all in a heartbeat if it preserved the sole female Dragon in the Empire.

The Arkon said, "Move. Both of you."

Kaylin lowered her left arm.

The Arkon raised his.

"Is the book you're carrying not cold?"

The mound of the Arkon's palm made contact with the

wall, almost entirely covering the rune Kaylin had placed there. "Cold?"

"When I carry it, it's like I've brought the worst of winter with me—and I'm dressed for summer. It's *cold*."

"It is cold, yes," the Arkon then replied.

"But don't you—"

"Cold is not one of the things that will kill a Dragon."

"What we cover in racial integration classes is *not* how to kill a Dragon. For obvious reasons."

"If you wish to take umbrage at—" The Arkon stopped. His hand remained against the wall, but the rune that his palm had covered had spread somehow. The major line that formed the bulk of its shape crept out, to the left and the right of that hand; the smaller dots or strokes that formed the rest spread, as well. The whole of the word, absent only the Arkon's hand, could be seen—almost as if the wall had been built to contain it.

No, not just the wall. The upper and lower elements of the simple word continued to spread. When they reached the corners made by floor and ceiling, they didn't bend to encompass either that floor or ceiling. They seemed to vanish, but watching, Kaylin was certain that they were simply reaching for unseen heights—or depths.

The line that had been the majority of the word continued its spread to the left and right, thickening as it did. She could no longer see the beginning—or the end—of the line; it seemed to be part of the wall on which it had been placed. The Arkon's touch had enlarged it, somehow. Kaylin wasn't certain if the Arkon had done something deliberate, but if he had, it was something inaudible and invisible to her eyes.

When the whole of the wall for as far as she could see in either direction was now a golden, glowing gold, the wall itself began to shiver; the shiver built to a shudder. Kaylin took an involuntary step back; Hope bit her ear, and she stopped moving.

"You know," she told the familiar, "you *could* just speak."

His teeth hadn't caused bleeding, but he hadn't let go of her ear lobe, which implied he was keeping that option open. Since his mouth was occupied, he probably couldn't speak clearly. He didn't try.

Bellusdeo hadn't taken the same step back that she had, and the Arkon's hand still rested against what had been featureless, endless stone moments before. Kaylin should have been surprised when the wall began to crumble. She could hear the sound of stone hitting stone, but could see nothing as she watched.

"It is," the Arkon said, his hand still raised, "a door ward. Of a kind. I advise you not to move."

"Can you lower your hand?"

The question seemed to annoy him. "I advise you not to move *and* not to speak."

Bellusdeo's chuckle was low and brief. "It does my heart good to see you thus," she told the older Dragon. "It is so very, very nostalgic."

If the Arkon heard her at all, he made no reply; Kaylin suspected that he hadn't. She could see only his face in profile, but the width of his eyes, the fact that the lower membrane was open, and the hint—it was hard to see color from this vantage—of silver implied surprise. Wonder.

She understood that there was something the Arkon wanted from Killian and from this place. She thought, in the moment that the wall vanished, she understood what it was.

He held out his hand to Bellusdeo. She took it without comment. "Kaylin."

She waited for the rest of the words; she got a frustrated snort of smoke instead.

"I believe he intends that you either take my hand," Bellusdeo said, "or grab his arm or shoulder—something that you can easily reach. He is not certain that we will not be separated."

I concur, Nightshade said. *I admit I am envious. Our lunch, such as it is, is nowhere near as fascinating or compelling as what has become of your word, Chosen.*

I'd switch places, if I could. Can you see the rest of the student body?

They have not yet closed the hall's doors.

They close the doors?

I believe it is to indicate that those who are late will have to wait for the next meal.

Kaylin would never have been late. She looked as Nightshade looked, and felt both dismay and disgust.

You may see Barrani miscreants at any time. You might never see what the Arkon and Bellusdeo are seeing again.

And if I'm not looking at it, you won't see it, either?

Exactly.

We're kind of trapped in this place. So is your brother. We don't have a lot of— She raised her free arm to cover her eyes as a flash of incandescent light reminded her of old admonitions about staring at the sun: don't do it, or you'll go blind.

Blinking, she felt the Arkon move and tightened her grip on his shoulder. He didn't run; she didn't lose him. But she forgot about the dining hall; she needed to see what was in front of her eyes, when she could see again at all.

The gold-white light was slow to clear, as if the light itself had been the detritus of an active Arcane bomb, and the light that remained, the aftershock of its explosion. She felt Hope's wing bat her face and come to rest across her eyes. Since her eyes were watering, the wing didn't immediately reveal any new visual information.

"Kaylin?"

"I'm here," she said in response to Bellusdeo. "I'm attached to the Arkon's shoulder, and my eyes are watering. Yours?"

The Arkon muttered something about mortal eyes, which was brief and not complimentary. It was, on the other hand, an answer.

Kaylin had expected to be in a room—a large room, like the first of Killian's rooms had been. This was not where she was. She was now in a dimly lit room, much of the illumination provided by the rune she had deliberately lifted off her own skin.

The Arkon, however, spoke a terse word, which washed across her skin like moving sandpaper. The whole of the immediate view became instantly brighter and clearer. Kaylin tried not to resent it.

"The reason we did not attempt to cast a simple light spell," the Arkon said, although Kaylin had said nothing, "is that we could not do it."

"What?"

"I did try. Bellusdeo?"

The gold Dragon shrugged.

"Your light was necessary; it was not a test. While I have no qualms about tests, you are not my student. I was not attempting to waste your time. I believe it is safe to let go of my shoulder."

Meaning let go of his shoulder right now. Kaylin was happy to do so; grabbing his shoulder reminded her a bit too much of foundlings and rope lines. She looked past the shoulder she'd just released, and the brighter light, combined with visual acclimatization, surrendered the image of a library. She released her hold on the mark and it returned to her skin.

A large, cavernous library appeared to go on forever.

They had entered through a wall; the wall itself was gone. When Kaylin looked back, she saw shelves. The shelves were built at least three stories tall, and there were ladders that appeared to float a few inches off the ground, as if waiting to be needed.

The Arkon exhaled for a long time.

"You recognize this library," Bellusdeo said. Not a question.

The Arkon nodded, his neck craning up, and up again. "I do."

It was empty of anything except books and the three people who had entered through a wall that no longer existed. "Can you see a door?" Kaylin asked.

The Arkon said, "No. And I do not advise you to search for one."

"Meaning there's no door."

"Not in the strictly quotidian sense, no. There were portals by which we traversed the library itself. Very, very few of us were granted permission to enter this library. There were librarians," he added, "some precious few whose responsibility was to see to the safety of the collection. But all such gatherings are comprised of people who have their own desires, their own interests.

"Those who had earned Killianas's trust were allowed to remove books for personal perusal in the confines of their own offices."

Kaylin looked at the arm in which the Arkon was clutching Larrantin's book. As if that were a signal, the Arkon loosened that hold, letting Bellusdeo's hand go in order to examine the message that Larrantin had intended for Killian—a message he had not accepted the only time his Avatar had appeared before the Arkon.

To Kaylin, the unbundling of the book produced a book, which is what she'd seen the first time and every time thereafter. She watched his expression, watched the smile change the shape of his mouth.

"A book," he said quietly. "As you said, Corporal."

"Do you know where it goes?"

"I believe so. It is not immediately in front of us," he added. "Larrantin was a scourge upon the librarians and the student body. This book is not—was never—meant to be in circulation at all. He must have had permission to take it, but not even the librarians would have been able to grant that permission."

"Killian?"

"Killianas, yes."

"What is it about? I couldn't see much on the pages."

"It is about interdimensional travel."

"Really?"

"No. I am simplifying to a ridiculous degree. But to read it at all, one must be current with languages that are considered long dead."

"Meaning, not me."

"Indeed. One must be current in those languages, which is a scholarly feat in itself, and must *also* be adept at small shifts in personal placement. The words written in this particular book are on a page that is slightly displaced. I could not read it as a student. It must have been germane to Larrantin's specialization."

"What was his specialization?" Bellusdeo asked.

The Arkon laughed. It was a bold, rolling sound, one of genuine amusement. "I do not know," he said. "It was the question most asked by the newer students, who considered him a walking legend, a mystery, something almost as impossible as the Ancients themselves."

Kaylin froze.

"He was considered Barrani," the Arkon said, correctly guessing why. "He was not of the Ancestors that preceded the Barrani; there is a single word at his core, a single, complex rune. Or so we were told. But at the time, the Ancestors were still present, if few. The earliest of the wars I remember involved their presence. They were not our wars," he added. "They were not wars that required the mobilization of the flights."

"One of the Ancestors is at the heart of Castle Nightshade," Kaylin said.

"Yes. But that Ancestor's duties are not the duties of those who woke in the depths of that castle. They are gone."

"Gone?"

"Gone to *Ravellon*. Gone to death. The words that were the source of their life and thought are lost to us now." He began to walk. Bellusdeo and Kaylin joined him, and even Bellusdeo—who never seemed impressed by the Imperial Library—had a hush about her that spoke of wonder or awe.

"So... Larrantin wanted to return this."

"I doubt that. I doubt it highly. But Larrantin probably saw some necessary purpose for it."

"Do you think Killian has a core? I mean, a place where the words that govern his duties and abilities exists? He'd have to, right?"

"We oft wondered. And we did look."

"Pardon?"

"We were students here. We were away from the Aerie, some for the first time. We were surrounded, for the first time, by people who were not kin, not Dragons. The world in which we had lived until this point had cracked open, like the shell of our birth eggs, and we looked at the endless sky. In a manner of speaking.

"Of course we searched."

Kaylin's silence extended a beat as she thought. "How old was Killian when you came here?"

"Pardon?"

"Killian was here—Killian was created—before the Towers rose. He couldn't have been all that new at the time they did. I mean, you were young when you first encountered him, but…do you have any idea of how long he'd been here?"

"This might surprise you, but no. We have no historical dates for the creation of the Academia. We have no historical dates for the creation of *Ravellon*, either; I believe they were linked in some fashion."

Kaylin stared at him. "You don't know?"

"Killianas had lived through roughly three changes of calendar styling. We have some sense of his age—but it was rough, not exact. We did ask, or rather, some of us did. He was not of a mind to answer in a useful fashion. It was not his concern."

"And the chancellors didn't know? One of them was a Dragon!"

"The chancellors, if they knew, did not choose to answer lowly students. It was not always considered wise or safe for chancellors to teach classes, and it is in the teaching they would have had the most exposure to us."

"Why wasn't it considered wise?"

"Aramechtis once sat as a guest lecturer, and at the three quarters mark burned down half the classroom. There were injuries, but no fatalities."

"…Half the classroom."

"Even so. To the Dragons in the room, it was trifling; to the rest of students it could have been deadly." He shrugged.

"A face full of Dragon fire, as you put it, did not materially harm any of the Dragons; it was an indicator of the severity of the temper of the guardian, in the Aeries."

Bellusdeo winced, but after a brief pause, broke out laughing. "It is most of the reason we were segregated," she told Kaylin, amusement coloring her entire expression. "A face full of Dragon fire would most certainly have harmed us when we lived in the Aeries. I remember watching the males," she added, lost for a moment in childhood memories. "They could fly. They were not as good with speech and tasks that required manual dexterity. We wanted to join them in the air."

"In all probability, so you could injure them for their behavior," was the Arkon's clipped response.

She laughed again. "Yes. We had to learn how to be more cunning if punishment was our desired goal."

"Regardless, it was seldom that the chancellors came into contact with the lowliest of their students. And no, not all chancellors were Draconic; I am certain that the Barrani did not rain fire upon cheeky students. Is there a reason you ask? You have never struck me as one who has a particular interest in history."

Kaylin nodded. "Killian looked Barrani to me."

"He did indeed."

"But...so did the Ancestors in Castle Nightshade."

"You are making a fundamental error," the Arkon said, when Bellusdeo sucked in air in a sharp, short way. "What Killian *was* before he became the heart of this place is not what he *is*. What he is, however, is injured. He is barely functional."

"And returning a library book is going to change that?"

"Do not underestimate librarians." His brows furrowed. "Bellusdeo," he said, in an entirely different tone.

Bellusdeo had come to work, in a manner of speaking, in Dragon armor. She nodded and gestured. Kaylin's arm caught fire—or felt like it had. There was no sound in the library except for the Hawk's involuntary grunt of pain. A shield rose around them, a bubble of color that was very similar to the protections that Hope could interpose between Kaylin and, say, Arcane bombs.

Purple fire blossomed beneath their feet.

CHAPTER 21

Kaylin would have rolled to the side, but Bellusdeo caught her arm, the Dragon's hand moving so quickly Kaylin saw it as a glint of reflected light. The Arkon hadn't moved at all. Flames unfurled beneath their collective feet and rose to the height of their chests. Nothing burned except carpet—but that gave off a terrible stench as it did.

The Arkon glanced once at Kaylin and Bellusdeo. His eyes were a deep, deep red, muted only slightly by the raising of inner membranes. He was beyond angry. In a single instant, he had passed into a deep fury.

Had he been any other Dragon, Kaylin would have assumed the fury came from the possible harm done to Bellusdeo. He was the Arkon. Someone had attempted to start a *fire* in the *library*. And if the flames were purple and the heat less intense than Dragon fire, they burned carpet. They'd burn books. This was not a place in which any fight, no matter how important, was to be started. Ever. Given that the Arkon was an enraged Dragon, it was a miracle that the library wasn't *already* ash.

"Is this shield yours?" Kaylin asked the Dragon.

Bellusdeo nodded.

"Good." She drew a dagger noiselessly from its sheath. Hope's wing was still draped across her eyes. "Hope can protect me from magical attack."

"Where are you going?"

"Someplace else. If our attacker keeps this up, the Arkon is going to explode. And that's not going to do us any good."

"It's not us he's concerned with," the Bellusdeo's dry response. She hesitated for half a beat. "Go."

Kaylin left the golden half sphere. As she did, light guttered; the library became dark and cavernous. Whatever spell the Arkon had cast to improve visibility had been extinguished. Dragon eyes were more adaptable than mortal ones—neither the Arkon nor Bellusdeo required much light.

Kaylin did—but she'd spent enough of her formative years in the dark. True, that dark often included moonlight and starlight; here, the library ceiling shed nothing. But light had come from natural sources in her youth; the cost of less natural sources, even candles, had been beyond her.

And the Ferals were drawn to light, where it existed at all.

She felt Severn's wordless concern. Had she been in any other room in this building, she would have remained beside Bellusdeo and behind the Arkon. But the library meant something to the Arkon. He never left the palace, except in dire emergency—but it wasn't an emergency that had driven him here. He'd practically left on his own, determined to find Killian.

Determined, she thought, to find this place: the library. Kaylin wasn't certain that the library itself wasn't magical, wasn't the product of Killian. The library in the Imperial Palace was normal architecture, if impressive. But she thought the palace library was an echo of this one.

This was what he wanted. Perhaps this was what he had

always wanted. The Imperial Library seemed now like a substitute, an attempt to rebuild.

Fighting here was not an option. She had rarely seen the Arkon's eyes take that color; had never seen that expression distort his features. She'd been told that there were certain things that could drive Dragons to madness. She believed it now in an entirely visceral way.

Yes. The voice wasn't Severn's; it was Nightshade's. Shorn of amusement, she could feel the weight of his focus and almost turned her head to look back at the two Dragons. She didn't; the impulse lessened. *You are correct. There is a danger here.*

Do you have any idea who could be attacking? That's Arcanist fire.

It is Shadow fire. Not all Arcanists would be capable of casting that spell; I do not believe An'Teela would be.

"Terrano?" Kaylin whispered. Silence. Disembodied Terrano didn't reply. On days like this, she sincerely wished Mandoran had been allowed to give her his True Name.

The fire hadn't been directional; it had sprouted beneath them. The Arkon had had enough warning to give Bellusdeo a single command. Kaylin had seen nothing—and felt nothing magical—until Bellusdeo had summoned her protections. The fire had come from beneath their feet.

She wilted.

An interesting idea.

Can you ditch lunch?

I have tried. I have found at least three men I recognize in the halls.

Have they found you?

If they have, they have not chosen to acknowledge me. It is my belief that they have not yet differentiated me from the general student body.

They're not part of that student body?

They are, but they appear to have more freedom of movement—as

I said, the day seems to follow the same loop, and it is clearly a day on which they do not have classes.

Kaylin frowned. The frown deepened. The fire that had come from beneath their feet could have been a trap, much like an Arcane bomb—but she doubted it.

Oh?

No one who wanted to take control of this building would want to start a literal fire fight here.

No one who wanted what the Arkon wants would, no. But knowledge, if it is power, is also a weapon. It is quite likely that if the depths of this knowledge could be plumbed, those who sought it would desire exclusivity.

There's no way they could have learned everything this library contains.

You are not goal-oriented, Kaylin. They might very well feel that they have learned everything of value contained herein. Ah. Lunch is over. I believe we are to head to our classes now.

Kaylin frowned. She remembered the rough layout of the library she had glimpsed in the Arkon's light and reached out. Her hand touched shelving. She'd reached a wall. Her fingers passed over something that felt like a collection of book spines, and she exhaled.

Did you get to choose your classes?

No. I was deposited in them as if I had been a student for longer than I have. There are children—literal children—who are in the classes with me. One at least does not appear to find the material confusing.

Which one? She attempted to dredge up the features of the boy from missing persons.

Yes. That would be the one.

And you said that this was a class about spatial dimensions?

Yes.

What is the class you're heading to now?

There was a beat of silence before Nightshade answered, and the answer contained some confusion. *I am now uncertain.*

Uncertain?

This is not the same hall, or the same floor, as it was yesterday. The students, however, appear to the same students. I will let you know if we also have a different lecturer when I arrive in the lecture hall.

He'd said that the day was repeated. The class schedule was repeated. *Can the students who aren't on the class schedule actually enter the class in question?* As she spoke, she moved. The one good thing about the consistency of these floors was the fact that they didn't creak. If she could breathe silently, she wouldn't be heard. She might be seen—but she doubted it. Humans were never considered the most dangerous thing in a room that also contained Dragons.

The cohort could, but I believe their presence caused...difficulties. They are not, or were not, in the dining hall. I believe they have a freedom of movement that is not implied by differing schedules.

Meaning they're considered intruders.

Yes.

In a sentient building that doesn't approve of intruders.

...Yes.

The Arkon didn't speak. Bellusdeo didn't, either. Whoever had attacked them was silent, taking advantage of a lack of visibility. If Kaylin could attack from anywhere, and she was facing Dragons, she wouldn't attack from the heights—the ceilings here were easily tall enough to accommodate Aerian flight, and she had a suspicion that full-body Dragons could manage, as well.

No, if she were going to attack, she'd do it from a vantage of stealth. She'd attack using the books as cover, where the shelving allowed for it. And even if it didn't, she'd still use the books as cover. The Arkon would be hesitant to attack if the contents of the library might be damaged.

Would the attacker know that? Would they be aware of that weakness?

This is interesting, Nightshade said, interrupting the thought. *You're in the classroom?*

Yes. And we have, as you must have suspected, a different lecturer. Do you recognize him?

Yes, but not because I have personally seen him before. You, however, have.

Larrantin?

No. It is Killian. And it appears that today's lecture is about linguistics.

Pardon?

I believe he intends to speak about the nature of True Words.

She continued to move, but moved slowly, her hand anchoring her with a light touch across rows of shelved books. The shape of the library—from the little she'd seen—seemed to be honeycombed multistory sections of nothing but books. There had been no cabinets, no display cases. Just…ladders, and rounded walls of books rising from the floor.

Can you ask him a question?

Pardon?

Can you interrupt his lecture—if it's even started—to ask him a question?

In the previous lectures, questions have been taken at the end of the lecture; some have been allowed during the lecture if the student in question feels the lecturer was unclear. This does not always result in better explanations. Even among my kind, there persists the belief that shouting the same words—or humiliating the questioner—will somehow result in better absorption.

Is that a yes or a no?

What do you wish me to ask before he starts his lecture?

It was a fair question. The curve of book spines—a gentle curve given the shelves were so large—ended. Kaylin pressed her back into the shelves before she headed out into the next section of the library.

Does he give any indication—beyond the subject itself—of what this lecture is about?

Today's class is apparently about the intersection between dimensional space in confined quarters and True Words.

Confined quarters. Is that building-sized confinement? Or a closet? I assume the former.

Could that apply to library-sized quarters?

I am not of a mind to interrupt him to ask that question. If, however, you come up with one that is more immediately relevant, I shall make the attempt.

Kaylin considered it relevant. She wanted to return to the Arkon's side, to ask if Killian himself had ever taught classes, but she was pretty certain the answer would be no. In which case, this was deliberate on Killian's part.

Killian who had said that there was no master here, no lord. No chancellor. She assumed that Candallar or one of his allies wanted to become that chancellor, somehow. Or wanted the power that came with control of the building—if that power now existed.

Killian was spread, in a fashion she couldn't see, across the fiefs; squeezed between the boundaries transcribed by the Towers. He had not been aware of her until she had tried to communicate with him—by introducing herself.

Ask him, she said, *if a sentient building can fully exist in the outlands, and only the outlands.*

Pardon?

The Hallionne border the outlands, but they exist—they were created—in lands people like us can occupy. They aren't part of the out-

lands, but they can use the…the…miasma to effect temporary change. We know that living buildings are the sum of the words at their core, whatever those words are. But those words exist here.

They demonstrably continue to exist when we enter the outlands. If you wish to exempt the cohort from this rule, I will allow it, but Bellusdeo was also with you in the outlands, and the outlands did not strip her of the power of her essential nature.

But it's a nature that's defined by *the world we normally live in. It's why Terrano couldn't continue to be* Terrano as he was. *To take the name back, to take the word back, to acknowledge it again, he had to accept confinement or containment. Yes, the cohort isn't what it once was, and yes, they stretch the boundaries of what Barrani are—but there are limits, I think. They can't both be here and be completely other.*

Nightshade cleared his throat; she could feel the sound as if it came from her. She could see Killian clearly, the ruin of his eye larger and darker in Nightshade's vision than it had been when she had first encountered the Avatar.

Killian looked across the room to meet Nightshade's gaze.

Or to meet Kaylin's. She asked the question through Nightshade.

"A perceptive question," Killian replied in that stiff and annoying way that reminded her of Imperial Mages. "No. A sentient building, as you put it, cannot exist only within the outlands. Buildings are defined by their function, and their function is rooted here."

"But what's to stop a building from fulfilling those functions in the outlands?"

"There are no words, in the outlands, except those they carry within them. The buildings cannot be created—or birthed—in the outlands."

"But that wasn't the question I asked," Kaylin said. Nightshade almost stopped her. "My question was: Can a building that was created the normal way fully exist in the outlands?"

"Hypothetically?"

"This *is* the Academia," Nightshade said, voice dry.

Killian's smile was stiff but in spite of that felt natural.

"Hypothetically, yes."

"What conditions would be required to allow that?"

"I cannot answer that question. A building such as you describe has not been created in the outlands since—but no, that is a topic for another day. Robin, you did not bring your book."

Nightshade turned slightly to see one of the students. A child.

"No, sir."

"I believe we've had this discussion before."

"No, sir."

"Ah. I would like you to remain after class. You as well, Calarnenne. Honestly, students these days are of a lesser caliber when it comes to dedication."

Kaylin didn't snicker, but it took effort—and given her actual, physical surroundings, it shouldn't have. Hope's wing glowed faintly as her vision and attention returned to the darkness. She assumed that the glow couldn't be seen by whoever their adversary, or adversaries, were. But she concentrated, and as she did, she could make out the shadow-shrouded contours of the library, or the section of the library in which she now lurked in silence.

She turned to look back at the Dragons, but the wing remained fixed in the forward direction. She didn't ask Hope why; her voice would carry, even if his reply wouldn't. Instead, she looked, her brows creasing as she squinted. It was dark, yes; she couldn't see individual books, but could feel the nubs of spines as she continued to use the wall as a guide.

I think Candallar's people are looking for Killian's core.

Nightshade's thoughts did not divulge frustration, but she felt it regardless. *Yes. It is possible that they felt that the library would be the most likely place for it.*

You don't think so.

No. They are remarkably unimaginative for a group of learned people. Were it not for Terrano's intervention—before you met the cohort—I do not believe they would be here at all.

And Candallar?

I am less certain about Candallar. I do not believe his position here is that of a student; nor is he a lecturer. He appears to have, and retain, a freedom of movement that those who live here do not.

The Lord of the Human Caste Court—whatever his name is— doesn't live here. I highly doubt the Arcanist who accompanied him lives here, either.

I concur. But I believe, if they found their way to this place, they were led here by Candallar. You believed that he wished to be reinstated in the High Court. Do you understand why he was made outcaste?

No.

It was after my time by a few centuries, and information is not always accurate. I would suggest you bespeak Ynpharion, if and when a window opens in which you might effectively do so. In the meantime, be cautious. If we are dealing with Arcanists of any renown, they would hesitate to engage a Dragon—or two—in a terrain that is not under their control. As they are attacking, they must believe they have that control.

Given the way said Dragon had arrived in the library, Kaylin agreed.

Find it and break it, if that is possible.

Kaylin nodded. *I know he won't answer, but—if not a library, where do you think the core that defined Killian might be hidden?*

None of the other cores, as you call them, were in physical areas. Tara's was closest; Helen's was not. There was no way to approach Helen's core without her permission.

I'm not sure Killian is in a condition that would allow that permission to be granted. She frowned. *Or he wasn't, the first time I met him. There's something about him—as a lecturer—that seems more...present? More personal, somehow.*

I believe the Arcanists have searched this building—but again, they are not your cohort. Their ability to move requires a flexibility that they may only barely possess. They have had the knowledge Terrano imparted for a handful of years, at best.

Have you seen the others at all today?

I have seen none of the cohort today, as you call it.

I've found Mandoran, a new voice said. It was Severn. He had been listening closely to Kaylin, and to Kaylin's part of the conversation with Nightshade and Killian. *Or rather, Mandoran has found us.*

Is it just Mandoran, or does he have the other three with him?

At the moment, only Mandoran. We are still, he added, *in the trap of the endless hallway.*

How's Emmerian doing?

He seems remarkably relaxed. Mandoran found his way here and he's offering to release us. Ah, I hear Sedarias. She doesn't think it's a good idea.

Because you're safe there.

Because we're safe here. She has reconsidered this because you, Bellusdeo and the Arkon are no longer in the same trap. Severn was amused. Kaylin was annoyed. The difference in these reactions described much of their relationship.

Can Mandoran get you out without alerting the wrong people?

He believes he can. Severn spoke to Mandoran, but Kaylin

couldn't hear his words. Nor could she see Mandoran through Severn's eyes. The cohort made everything difficult, without even trying.

Mandoran asks me to pass on a message from Terrano. Wherever you are now, Terrano can't find you.

You told him we were in the library?

I did. Terrano says he hasn't seen a library. He's managed to penetrate active classrooms or lecture halls; he can enter the dining hall at any of the mealtimes. The offices are hit or miss—and apparently there are offices here. There are six people Sedarias considers dangerous. One is the Arcanist that you first identified.

And the other five are Barrani.

Severn winced. *Yes, of course. There are no Dragons, if that helps.*

Has Terrano managed to penetrate other occupied classrooms?

No, Severn replied, after a brief pause. *Mandoran clarifies: there are no other occupied classrooms. The occupation, such as it is, seems to involve one thread of students—the group of which Nightshade is part. No harm has come to the students; I don't believe Killian would allow harm to befall them, even in his damaged state. Annarion is calmer now; he understands that while the cohort—and the rest of us—might be in actual danger, the students, and therefore his brother, are not.*

Yet.

Not yet, yes. His tone changed. *You said you've found people in the library.*

Kaylin nodded. *I think I've found our intruders.*

Given the uniformity of their heights and the robes they wore, Kaylin assumed the three were Barrani. One of the three wore a tiara consistent with the tiaras members of the Arcanum sometimes wore. At this distance, she couldn't be certain that the crowned individual was the Arcanist Sedarias had recognized. With her luck, it was an entirely new Arcanist.

Some conversation—quiet and tense—appeared to be taking place among the three Barrani; it was hushed enough that Kaylin could guess at its existence by the small movements of mouths and the shifting lines of shoulders or arms.

She couldn't close with three Barrani. Even had one not been an Arcanist, that was just suicide. She had a chance to injure—or possibly kill—one if she was fast enough and quiet enough, but the odds were not in her favor.

What had Killian's enemies achieved so far? Was Killian more present because of something they had done? Was Killian missing an eye because they had somehow removed it? Had they removed it to create a back door that made the Academia much easier to find?

All reasonable questions, none answerable now. Even if she had answers, they were likely to lead to more questions, not fewer.

I've explained how you gained entry to the library to Mandoran, Severn said. *Terrano has a suggestion.*

Is his suggestion physically possible for anyone other than him or Mandoran?

According to Terrano, yes.

Fine. I have three Barrani here. I'll attack them if it becomes necessary to interrupt their spells, but I'd rather not throw my life away pointlessly. What's his suggestion?

He wants you to find the doors.

Pardon?

The doors to the library. He thinks there had to be a legitimate way in. It wouldn't be useful as a library otherwise. Killian might house the entirety of the collection—but you said yourself that Larrantin's book was likely once part of that collection. The library, in Terrano's opinion, wasn't Killian's; the books it contains were real.

Kaylin was dubious. *The book Larrantin gave me only looked like a book to me. No one else saw it that way. If that's your idea of a physical book, I don't know what to tell you.*

Terrano says that the book itself was likely protected in some fashion against the fall of the Academia and the rise of the Towers. That's his guess. He thinks it is a book...but displaced. You could see it as a book because you yourself were partially displaced. He believes you still are.

But the Arkon and Bellusdeo are both here.

Yes. That's why Terrano thinks you can open the actual doors. Oh—he also says he thinks the Barrani are displaced in the same way you are. You could see them, the day Annarion knocked on the door. The rest of us couldn't. He's telling you that if you try to attack the three Barrani here, the Dragons are unlikely to be able to help.

How can they attack us when they're displaced?

I am not asking him that question now.

He's busy?

He'll answer. Meaning it would take an hour or two, if sense could be found in the answer at all. *But Mandoran says the cohort is currently displaced in a different way. He believes that Killian is aware of both of you; he doesn't seem to be aware of the Barrani.*

You don't agree.

Not entirely, no. The Barrani can interact to some extent with the movement of the daily lessons—they can enter the dining hall. Nightshade can see them. I'm not certain I would. I'm not certain they see Nightshade, either.

Kaylin asked.

Nightshade was irritated by the interruption; he was now absorbed in the lesson that Killian was attempting to teach. Kaylin fell silent as the reason for the irritation made itself clear. Nightshade felt this lesson was relevant to the situation in which they were all trapped.

I'm going to try to find a door, she told Severn.

Terrano says: About time.

Kaylin was almost certain she'd been seen by the Arcanist, Illanen, and the Caste Court Lord Baltrin when she first attempted to deliver Larrantin's message. She wasn't willing to bet a lot of money on it. It was possible that their concern had been Killian's movements. The people that had gathered to attack Larrantin—or Larrantin's building—had clearly seen, and been seen by, Annarion and Sedarias. She was certain that Candallar could see them all.

If she was right, Candallar had somehow led the others here. Candallar had somehow found the Academia in his tenure as fieflord. If it had value to Candallar, she thought it the value of a cage: it was a great way to do away with inconvenient people. No bodies would be found, and therefore no messy investigations would occur.

Not that investigations would occur in the streets of his fief, either. He was fieflord. He could just as easily rid himself of inconvenient people within his Tower. On the other hand, he couldn't have gotten rid of Kaylin that way because she'd never have willingly set foot in his Tower, and the Barrani weren't famously trusting. Not even of their allies. Or perhaps not especially of their allies; their enemies weren't close enough to stick knives into their rib cages.

Regardless, someone had to find Killian first.

How? If it weren't for the fact that she'd been deposited in a trap, she would never have found him—would never have thought to look. Severn had explored border zones before he'd joined the Hawks and hadn't stumbled across this place, either.

She held her breath as her path brought her closer to the Barrani; their voices grew no louder, although it was clear that their discussion had developed some heat. Hope hadn't dropped his wing once, an indication that they would have remained invisible to her had she not had a familiar perched on her shoulder.

She moved quickly, steps as silent as she could make them; they were standing in the space between the honeycombed shelving, which made bypassing them more of a challenge. She kept her dagger in her hand, but it was more for comfort than use now.

It was not the Arcanist who turned in her direction; he was involved in the heated discussion Kaylin couldn't hear. She moved quickly, as the Barrani man glanced around the room; she could see his features clearly. His eyes were narrowed. She didn't wonder what had drawn his attention; no one could move completely silently if they were larger than a cat. Even with the noise he could hear—the argument in progress—he was watchful. In this situation, she would have been, as well.

Unless she was the one doing the arguing.

Hope was stiff on his perch, his legs tensing as his claws dug in. He seemed to be deciding against pushing himself off her shoulder, which was probably for the best. She doubted the Barrani could hurt Hope, but the attempt to do so would cause damage. Probably.

She headed away from the Barrani, and farther away from the two Dragons who had stepped into an area of floor from which purple fire had sprung.

CHAPTER
22

The library was gigantic. Kaylin had known the collection itself wasn't small, given the height of the shelves, but this was far larger than the intimidating Imperial Library; it was larger than any single room that Helen had ever created for any of her guests—or her tenants. To be fair, she could no longer tell how tall the shelves she was touching were; she knew that they still housed books because those were her anchor as she moved. Her fingers continued to brush across the spines.

Only when one bit her—literally—did she stop. She sucked in air, but let it out in a silent exhalation, lifting her hand to examine it. She could see no blood, but her middle finger was numb.

She was grateful that this library had no Dragon as its hoarder. She paused in her search for a door, a more traditional point of entry, and moved her hand back toward the book that had caused the reaction.

With as much care as she could manage given the poor visibility and her instinctive desire to avoid something that caused pain by simple light touch, she attempted to pull the book off the shelf. She was half expecting alarms to start; the ceilings here would create a resonance that was certain to cause them to carry.

The book came free from the shelf cleanly, easily; touching it caused no further pain, although she felt it as a warmth against her palm. It was the type of warmth living skin shed. The thought took root and would not be dislodged.

Many of the books you have seen in your life are bound in the hide of dead creatures, Hope said.

The operative word there was *dead*.

She examined the front cover of the book. It didn't surprise her to note that there was a rune emblazoned across what she assumed was the cover. It was from the rune itself that the warmth radiated. She opened the book—and nearly dropped it.

As the book itself lay flat, a cover across each of her palms, light rose from its pages, denying the lack of illumination that darkened the whole of the library. That light gathered into a pillar and the pillar itself into something that resembled a man. A Barrani man.

No, she thought. Not Barrani. She almost dropped the book; she certainly closed it, tucking it under her left arm as she retrieved her dagger. Closing the book didn't immediately banish the man. But if he was emerging from these pages, his solidification stopped at the ghostly. He lacked the color of a living person.

His eyes were the only thing about him that weren't pale and translucent; they were black. He reminded Kaylin of Hope.

Those dark eyes rounded before narrowing; surprise before inspection. When he opened his mouth, words Kaylin could understand emerged. "Chosen." There was a slight lift in the last syllable, as if he doubted the evidence of his eyes.

Kaylin nodded.

"It has been long indeed since I have been wakened. I will not ask you the date—that produces frustration on both my part and the part of the reader, since dating systems so seldom overlap." Both of his brows rose as his gaze moved from Kaylin to Hope.

Hope was silent, but his gaze was anchored to the face of the stranger this book had produced.

"It's been a long time since the library has been open to—to students," Kaylin said, her voice as low as she could make it.

"I understand the infernal rules about noise within the library," the stranger said, obviously irritated. "But surely anyone who gains access here can shroud the noise they make enough that it is not of concern to other students or masters."

She assumed that his irritation wasn't her whisper, but what that whisper represented; she was more afraid of those theoretical masters than she was of the man she now faced. Respect in this case being a loose translation of fear.

Or an exact translation, Nightshade said. *There is little room for subtlety when the power differential is great.*

What is he?

I believe you recognize the form he has chosen to take. He is, or was, an Ancestor. You might ask him what he prefers to be called— but not now. I will not ask how you found the book you now carry, but would ask that you not set it down for the moment.

You think he's trapped in a book.

Trapped *lacks nuance,* Nightshade replied. *Words can exist within the primal ether—that is, for want of better words, what Killian calls the outlands.* Kaylin suffered from momentary mental whiplash. *But they cannot be spoken there. When words of power, when words of life—I believe this is what he considers True Names to be—are...summoned? Chosen? Invoked? Regardless, they cannot be invoked within that ether.*

She felt Nightshade's focus and frustration, and was almost surprised that he had noticed the occupant of the book at all.

I could not fail to notice your sudden alarm. I believe, however, this lecture is relevant, and would appreciate no further interruptions. Once the names have been uttered or bound, they can continue to exist in the outlands—but they will lose form and power, the bindings unraveling, if they have no anchor to the reality in which they were first... created. Someone has just asked what the source of those words are.

She thought of the Lake of Life. This did not impress him.

The question itself did not impress Killian, but the student—the boy—received a nod from Killian, derailing the thrust of his lecture for the moment.

Kaylin returned to the ghost in front of her eyes. "I am not able to summon a circle of silence, or whatever the spell might be called." She spoke in High Barrani.

"If I might be allowed to provide?"

"Please."

She felt a wave of pain across her skin. It was instant and jarring but was more like a full-body slap than fire. She hesitated. He marked it.

"Why have you wakened me?"

Her hesitance grew. *I don't know* wasn't going to be an any more acceptable here than it had been in the nefarious classes taught by Imperial Mages—and this man was far more dangerous, even half-dead, than those mages had been in the Halls of Law. She'd been certain that if she survived the lessons—and passed them, as the Hawks' training required—she would be free of arrogant, condescending teachers for the rest of her life. She'd done both, and then been saddled with literal Dragons as teachers.

And now this.

"My apologies if I disturbed you," she said, knowing that awkward silence was worse than most of the words she could offer in her defense. "The library isn't open to the residents of the Academia, and I've been tasked with discovering how to open it."

"You?"

Ugh. "Yes."

"Let me be certain I understand what you are saying. You have entered a library that is not currently available to any member of the Academia."

She wilted. "Yes."

"And you have been tasked with opening this library."

"Yes."

"How, then, did you enter it at all?"

This was one of two questions she'd been afraid he was going to ask, the other being *by who*. She exhaled. "I used the marks of the Chosen on a flat, unadorned stone wall."

Unlike any other teacher who knew her, he accepted her words at face value. He had no idea that she didn't know how to use those marks, after all. His nod was brief, and his gaze drifted away from her face, past the shoulder that didn't contain a familiar.

"There appear to be occupants, regardless."

"Yes, I'm sorry. Two of those occupants came with me."

"Those would be?"

"The Dragons."

"And the other three?"

"I have no idea how they arrived here. Wait, you can see them?" This was the wrong question, but it fell out of her mouth before she could shut it.

"Of course I can see them." The answer was superbly waspish.

"It's just—no one else can."

"I beg your pardon?"

"No one else can see them except me." Before he could

speak again, she said, "Killian couldn't see them. I think he knows something's wrong," she added, to be fair.

"I dislike translations," he finally said. "They are cumbersome and frequently inaccurate. You are now telling me that Killianas cannot see these intruders?"

"Killian—Killianas—is perhaps not what he was the last time someone wakened you." She desperately wanted to leave the rest of this conversation in someone else's hands—but the Arkon was nowhere near where she now stood, and going back to him with the book required that she walk through three Barrani.

"What do you mean?"

Exhaling, she said, "When you entered the book, for want of better words—"

"For *severe* want of *much more intelligent* words. Continue."

"—was *Ravellon* the center of the world?"

"It was not the center of mine, but if you speak of my tenure in this position, yes. *Ravellon* was considered by many to the center of the world. Of all worlds." He lifted a ghostly chin in silence; Kaylin thought he'd finished. "So—it came to pass, then. *Ravellon*'s fall, and its entrapment. We heard of it; we spoke with the last chancellor, Terramonte. He came to offer us warning, having evacuated all that he could find. Some were not willing to leave. Some of lesser power had no choice."

"You chose not to leave."

"We cannot leave. While we exist, sleeping or waking, the library exists. Tell me, how large an area did the Towers encompass?"

Kaylin swallowed. She wondered if this man had *wanted* to be a librarian. "The Academia was between two of the areas assigned to the Towers.

"Larrantin is still here. I think a couple of others, as well.

Having spoken only to Larrantin, I believe he was distracted and missed the timing."

"That would be young Larrantin, indeed. Very well. How do the Towers function? What is the theory behind their abilities?" His frown deepened. "Shadow."

"I'm not certain how they function. But they exist in any state of reality I've experienced."

His expression made clear just how little he thought she'd experienced. It raised hackles—but it always did—and she forced herself to swallow the knee-jerk reaction. Later, she'd complain to Helen about it. Now, she needed to give him the information he'd asked for—or as much of it as she could manage.

"They exist in the outlands."

"...Outlands?"

What had Nightshade said? "Primal ether?"

This made more sense to him; his gaze turned toward the floor, or rather, drifted there, while his thoughts went elsewhere. "I require more information," he finally said. Kaylin waited for questions that she knew she couldn't answer to his satisfaction—she couldn't answer them to her own, either.

Clearly, waiting was not the right choice.

"You will pardon my frustration," he told her. "Anyone who has permission to enter the library the usual way would understand what I require."

She had told him that she'd entered via a stone wall—a wall that didn't happen to sport a door.

"Follow me. No, do *not* put the book back on the shelf. Among other difficulties it would cause is your inability to shelve it in the correct place."

To Kaylin's surprise, the nameless man was not anchored to the book in any way she could see. He had freedom of movement and used it, forcing Kaylin to walk quickly if she wanted to keep him in sight. His feet, on the other hand, made no sound against the floors, and hers did.

"Do they teach you nothing about the library?" he asked. "Not even the rudiments of basic navigation?" If he'd been carrying a large sign that said Get Off My Lawn, it would have fit right in with the rest of his tone.

You will find this interesting, Nightshade said.

Which part? Get Off My Lawn *has nothing new to offer.*

Words cannot be invoked or spoken in the primal ether.

Yes, you said that.

Buildings such as the Hallionne cannot be rooted there. The rooting of the words to a specific plane of existence—ours—is considered immutable fact, or it was. In theory.

She wanted to ditch her boots; they made much more noise than the bare feet did. She didn't. She lengthened her stride. *In practice?*

If one required True Words or True Names—I believe the latter, but he seems to use the terms interchangeably—to be invoked, they had to be carried.

How in the Hells—oh. She looked down at her skin.

I do not believe that was his intent, but it's intriguing, no? His smile was slight; she could feel it in the curve of his mouth. *The other way to carry words is the more obvious one.*

Meaning True Names.

Yes.

How exactly does one access those words without killing the person they're inside of?

I have allowed Robin to ask that question, he replied.

You made a human child ask that question?

I did not instruct him to do so. He is remarkably curious.

Fine—what was the answer?

Killian has not answered it yet.

Interrupt me if the answer is important. I'm about to lose the nameless ghost in front of me.

"He is not nameless," Killian said, looking up to meet Nightshade's eyes. "Were he, he could not be where he is."

"What do I call him?"

"Arbiter Androsse. Arbiter will do, given your relative difference in status." His single eye seemed to spark as he spoke. "He will do what must be done."

"Can you allow my friends greater freedom of movement?"

"They have freedom of movement as it is," was the not very encouraging reply. "Feel free to interrupt my lecture again if the Arbiters have information they wish to convey."

Arbiters. Plural.

The plural was enough of a warning that Kaylin wasn't particularly surprised when Arbiter Androsse came to a stop in front of a bookshelf. The book itself was placed on a higher shelf than his had been; Kaylin could reach it—with effort—if she stood on her toes. Or climbed the shelves, but she didn't consider that smart.

This book, just as the first, bit her fingertips when she touched it. It also came easily to hand; she'd tucked the first book under her right arm to use the left, and was grateful that the book didn't fall on her head as a result of her tenuous reach.

Hope's squawk was soft, and as it didn't contain words, wasn't meant for her. If she'd had a free hand, she would have clamped his mouth shut; as it was, she froze, waiting for some sign that she'd been discovered.

In the distance, she heard a Dragon roar. Book in hand, she wheeled, breath held.

Arbiter Androsse smiled. "That is a very nostalgic sound," he said—and appeared to mean it. The smile vanished into a much more pinched expression of frustration. "Well, what are you waiting for? You have said time is of the essence."

Kaylin looked at the word that was emblazoned across the cover of this second book. She opened it. The figure that emerged was, as the first Arbiter, a thing of light. Of light and shadow—but not the type of shadow that meant imminent death. As the first Arbiter, the second started as a pillar, but the light here twined around darkness, like a braid. Like Larrantin's hair.

The person that emerged had nothing else in common with Larrantin. Or with Arbiter Androsse. It was a thing of ghostly scales and ebon claws, and its eyes were the size of Kaylin's head. She'd made as much room as she could while still carrying the book.

"Arbiter Kavallac," Arbiter Androsse said—whether for Kaylin's benefit or as a greeting, she wasn't certain.

Arbiter Kavallac appeared to be a Dragon.

"I was sleeping," the ghost said, its voice a Draconic rumble. "Is there a *reason* I have been disturbed?" Her gaze swept across Kaylin, pausing briefly to narrow in Hope's direction before it settled firmly on Arbiter Androsse.

"Yes, actually. It appears that we have not been considered necessary for the functioning of the Academia in some long while."

"Oh? The library does not appear to be on fire."

"Not on fire, not precisely. But we are needed now. If we perform our duties well, it is possible the chancellor will allow you to eat a recalcitrant student or two."

"The last one was not to my liking," Kavallac replied. "Very well. This one does look more promising." The Dragon's pale head stopped directly in front of Kaylin. "She is Chosen?"

"Apparently so. Nor is that the strangest of the things I have heard since she chose to retrieve me."

"I am uncertain that I wish to hear stranger."

"It might be best if you choose a more compact form," Arbiter Androsse replied. "There are apparently intruders in the library itself."

"Impossible."

"So I would have said—but what Starrante feared has come to pass."

Silence then. *"Ravellon?"* It was a whisper of a word, a hollow, quiet sound that Kaylin would have sworn a Draconic throat wasn't capable of uttering.

Androsse nodded, and the Dragon began to dwindle in shape, light and dark coalescing into the ghost of the form Kaylin considered mostly human.

"I suppose we are going to wake Starrante?"

"We are. The young Chosen has been tasked with the opening of the library."

"Pardon? If this is one of your ill-considered attempts at humor—"

"It is not. The library is not, apparently, open."

"How did you get in, then?" the Dragon ghost demanded of Kaylin.

"Through the wall."

The Dragon then lifted her chin. "You were not the only one to enter."

"No. I had two Dragons as companions."

"Either your ability with numbers is deplorable, or you did not bring the other three with you."

"I'm trying hard to avoid catching the attention of the other three," Kaylin whispered. "They've already set a fire trap—" She slammed her jaws shut before more words could escape.

Neither of the Arbiters said a word for one long, unfortunate beat. "You are concerned about the presence of the other three?" the Dragon finally asked.

"We sure as hells didn't set any traps. We don't want to have any fight here."

"You said you entered through a stone wall."

Kaylin nodded.

"And your friends—the Dragons—entered with your permission."

Breaking a hole into a wall—however it was done—wasn't exactly permission, but Kaylin nodded anyway.

"Androsse," Kavallac said, although her gaze remained on Kaylin, "perhaps you had better tell me the rest."

"I would prefer to wake Starrante first to avoid pointless repetition."

"I had not noticed that you had any disinclination to repeat yourself."

Hope snickered.

Arbiter Androsse did not. He did a pretty good imitation of an ice sculpture. To Kaylin he said, "Lead the way."

Since Kaylin had no idea where Starrante was, this caused a few seconds of confusion for everyone, and annoyance for Androsse. He resumed the lead; the ghostly form of Kavallac drifted to Kaylin's left—the arm in which she carried both books.

Hope was rigid, his wing plastered to Kaylin's eyes. She wondered if she would see the two Arbiters at all if he lowered it. She didn't ask him to experiment.

Kavallac said, "This is not good."

Androsse, however, had stopped. Kaylin didn't run into his back because the Dragon had spoken. The first Arbiter turned to face the second.

"His book is missing?" Kaylin asked.

"His book," Androsse confirmed, "is missing."

★ ★ ★

Kaylin had no hope of finding the missing book; Kavallac and Androsse moved ahead and began to search—which mostly involved standing in place and lifting and lowering their gaze.

"If someone else was holding this book," she said, "would I be able to see the Arbiter it contained?"

One ghostly stream of irritated smoke accompanied the curt answer. "No."

"So you're not really here?"

"We are not, as you put it, really here. Unless and until you have the three Arbiters gathered, our ability to interact with the rest of you is limited. Some flexibility exists for the Arbiters if they are wakened individually."

"Can you tell if Starrante has been wakened?"

"No. But in general, it was Starrante who was wakened first. It was," she added, "Androsse who was generally last to arrive."

"Would that have something to do with positioning in the library itself?"

"Yes. I am uncertain why the library is not accessible to the student body; perhaps the chancellor felt that there was enough of an emergency that it had to be secured."

Arbiter Androsse sighed. Loudly. "Perhaps I will consign myself to repetition," he said. He told the Dragon Arbiter what had happened.

Being a Dragon, if a ghostly one, Arbiter Kavallac was severely unimpressed with the lack of detail. "You are telling me that there is no chancellor." Her tone indicated disbelief and a rock-solid lack of any sense of humor whatsoever.

"I'm telling you what Killian told me. And he didn't use

the word *chancellor*, either. I'm not sure he intended to survive the rise of the Towers."

"It was not the rise of the Towers," Androsse said quietly. "But the fall of *Ravellon*. For Killian—for most of those assembled here in one fashion or another—the loss of *Ravellon* would be like the loss of a beating heart for one of your nature. You have never seen it."

"No. The loss happened long before my time. Whatever once dwelled within *Ravellon* is gone..." she frowned "...or enslaved. That's not our problem here. Killian is still alive. The Academia still, in some form, exists. But the place we're in now—it's like your primal ether. We call it the outlands."

"That should not be possible," Kavallac said. "But demonstrably you are here, and we, for the moment, are here, as well. More discussion is required."

"If the intruders found Starrante—"

"It would be almost impossible for the intruders to find Starrante if they were not already aware of his existence."

Kaylin cleared her throat. "I found Arbiter Androsse without being aware of his existence." The Dragon clearly felt that this should be impossible; Androsse's presence, however, belied that. "Arbiter Androsse found you. If Starrante's book isn't where either of you expect it should be, could you find it?"

The two Arbiters exchanged a glance. "It is possible, but by no means guaranteed," the Dragon finally said. "Our abilities at this stage are, as I said, limited. If the intruders have Starrante, it is possible we lack the power to liberate him."

"If they hold your books, do they effectively hold you?"

"Before the books are opened, yes." The Dragon's smile was deeply unpleasant. "What do you think? You hold both books; are you up to controlling or commanding us?"

Kaylin shook her head.

It was Androsse who said, "You have not tried, Chosen. It

is my belief that you could, in fact, control our actions should you make that attempt."

"Because I'm Chosen?"

"Indeed."

"Well, they're not. That I know of," she added. "Do you know the word on his book?"

They both stared at her.

"...On the cover of each of yours, there's a word. A rune."

"Different runes?" Androsse asked.

She nodded.

"I invite you to examine the books now."

Kaylin did.

"Do you still see a rune?"

She nodded. The runes were part of the front covers of each book; they hadn't vanished when she'd opened them. Nor had they risen or deserted the books in question when the Arbiters had appeared. Their looks and shapes hadn't changed; the color of the golden light had dimmed—but that could be a trick of the light, which remained poor.

Turning the covers toward the Arbiters, she said, "Can you see it?"

The glance they exchanged implied no.

She returned the books to their temporary resting place. "Let me ask a different question, then. I've been tasked with opening the library, right?"

"So you've said."

"How, if the library is closed, is anyone supposed to open it? I'm assuming they don't walk through walls the way I did."

"The library is never closed to the chancellor."

"I've been told that no chancellor exists. Look—I was never a student here."

"Demonstrably," Kavallac said.

"I live in a sentient building. I've visited the Hallionne. I understand a bit about how they work—but at least my home doesn't have rooms that have to be opened using magical books that are *inside* the room."

"No, but your building does not exist in the primal ether."

"It can, but that's not where it's rooted—and it's irrelevant for the purposes of the library. If there's no chancellor..." She frowned. "If Killian is sleeping, and there is no chancellor, how might he be awakened? The Arkon said—"

"The Arkon?" Kavallac said, voice sharp.

Right. Dragon. The Arkon wasn't a person, but a title. "He's the oldest of the Dragons who are currently awake. He was a student here, before—"

"When?"

"Toward the end. His name—or the name it's safe to call him—is Lannagaros."

"And young Lannagaros is now the Arkon?"

"That's mostly what he's called now, yes. He was a student—"

"I am aware of that. Even Androsse must remember him. Continue."

Since it was Kavallac who had interrupted, her irritation struck Kaylin as unfair. Then again, so did life on some days. "The Arkon said that there was an emergency chancellor, a fill-in, when the chancellor of the time was drawn into the Draco-Barrani wars."

"And it was under Terramonte's stewardship that *Ravellon* fell?"

"I...think so?" Kaylin forced herself not to wilt, but her tone implied a wealth of ignorance, which was fair: she was ignorant. Her sense of history was so compressed and so vague that she had no clear idea of how that war had even started. She'd seen some of the cost of it in Teela and the cohort; she'd seen the fall of the High Halls.

But she had also seen their rise, their renewal. She had seen the cohort home.

If given time, she would sit down beside the Arkon—or at his feet—and try to separate the strands of that ancient history into something more closely resembling an actual timeline. She had known that the Arkon was old; she had never imagined that his distant youth would have encompassed the fall of *Ravellon*.

Her ignorance didn't change facts. The facts remained, hidden and out of reach. It was her job to find facts, to sift through them to find those that were relevant or meaningful.

She lifted her chin, met Kavallac's gaze, and said, "The Arkon is here. I told you that two Dragons accompanied me into the library. He was one of them."

"Did he come prepared for combat?"

"I'm not sure what that means," Kaylin replied. "He's a Dragon. In the city as it exists outside of the Academia, being a Dragon *is* all that's required for combat. Most combat."

"Very well. That is not a promising reply, but it is acceptable." She began to walk.

"Wait, where are you going?"

"I am going to speak with the Arkon," Kavallac replied.

"To speak with the Arkon, we have to pass through the other three intruders."

"No," the Dragon replied. "We do not. Androsse?"

Arbiter Androsse grimaced. "I had forgotten how much I enjoy solitude."

Kavallac began to transform.

CHAPTER 23

This transformation was unlike the transformation most Dragons underwent, to Kaylin's eye. The uncomfortable transitional moments where skin became scale and limbs both elongated and bent in directions that would have caused severe injuries in any other race were missing in their entirety. One moment, Kavallac was a woman about seven or eight inches taller than Kaylin, and the next, she was an amorphous cloud. The spread of cloud or fog continued—at speed—until the entire area in immediate view was covered in it.

The fog then solidified, all of it drawn into the hardening lines of a ghostly Dragon.

"Climb," the Dragon said.

"I will walk," Arbiter Androsse replied. "Chosen?"

Kaylin looked up—pointedly—at a ceiling she couldn't quite see.

"It is best that you accept Kavallac's kind offer. Hold the books, Chosen. And if it is possible, while you are airborne, read the words."

"The runes?"

"The runes that adorn the covers of these books."

"It's not possible while I'm in flight. If you want me to try, I'll need to stand here for a bit."

"I will not drop you if your attention is momentarily elsewhere."

It wouldn't be momentary. Kaylin, books clutched in one arm, attempted to climb the Dragon's back. To her surprise, the ghostly and translucent body was also rock-solid. Kavallac's Draconic form was as real as Bellusdeo's would have been.

Kaylin doubted that Bellusdeo would attempt to fly in this room, though. The ceilings that she had seen in the glow of the Arkon's summoned light were high—but not, in Kaylin's opinion, high enough. She wasn't about to argue with Kavallac's certainty that they were, though.

The thing I don't understand, Kaylin said to Nightshade as she seated herself, *is Killian. We're in the outlands, or the primal ether—whatever it's called. You—and a couple of other Barrani—are here, and you still have your names.*

The names are anchored to us; we are inseparable.

She nodded. *But... Killian is here. There are words here. The... Arbiters are here. Larrantin, in some form, is here. Let's ignore the question of True Names. If Killian is, like Helen, composed of and driven by the words at his core, those words shouldn't lose their power. Killian is alive.*

Yes.

So the prohibition—or the inability—is based on the speaking of words, or the speaking of words that grant life, in the outlands.

I believe that is what has been said. I also believe that the roots that you speak of are bound by form. My True Name is mine. It is rooted in me. I am of our plane of existence, even here. To shift that, to change it, requires time—time that the cohort had in their slow transformation over the centuries. Time and will.

The Arkon's True Name is likewise rooted and preserved. But Killian's is not. The physical body he possesses requires external an-

chors, external roots. He cannot move those roots; no more can the Hallionne. Killian was cast into the outlands by the very nature of the Towers that rose.

But if he's a building—

He was not built to withstand the Shadows, Nightshade replied. *I believe he wishes to speak with you.*

He's becoming more...more awake, isn't he?

I believe so.

"The words themselves both provide power and sustenance, and require it. They were, for the Ancients, the very source of life, and even in smaller fragments, they are potent. You are not wed to those fragments—you and your kin. We are. But we are wrought from the story of the world itself; we are not added to it. What is the question you wish to ask?"

Kaylin drew breath; Nightshade did not. "Was it the Towers? When they rose, did the Towers anchor you somehow, so that you might survive their creation?"

"That is my belief."

"If you're anchored to the Towers, can you speak with them?"

One eye narrowed, as he only had the one. "That is not a question that occurred me to ask," he finally said.

Robin's hand shot up. "I need to use the bathroom," he said. This was not what Kaylin expected.

"Very well. You have permission." August permission, indeed.

Robin left his seat and headed out of Nightshade's line of sight, but Nightshade marked this, as well.

Does he do this often?

I would say it depends on how bored he is. Since the classes themselves repeat, and by your own estimation he has been here for some time, I would imagine that boredom has become a pressing issue for him.

I need you to ask another question. She looked down past her feet to see the crowning heights of shelves pass beneath them. She could not believe that she could be here—on a Dragon's back—and bypass unwelcome intruders unseen. But apparently, this was a different version of reality; she tensed and held breath—as if her breath would be the most notable thing in the library—as the three Barrani intruders passed beneath her.

What question? Ask.

"Can you make that attempt? Can you try to speak with the Towers?"

He stared at her. Not at Nightshade, who had theoretically voiced the question, but at Kaylin, who was behind his eyes.

"What material benefit would that have?" he finally asked.

"It would—" Nightshade then took over, it being his mouth and his voice. "It would establish parameters—physical parameters. If the Academia survived the fall of *Ravellon* and the ascendance of the last and greatest of our defenses against what now dwells there, it is possible that the presence of the Academia itself can be strengthened."

"To what end, Chosen?"

Since those words had been Nightshade's, she grimaced. The fieflord's face bore no trace of that grimace. "I think you need to be in control of yourself. You're outside of the Tower's duties and responsibilities. They aren't set to watch against you or guard against you. And I think at least one of the six was aware of you, and valued you highly. At least one." She shook her head; Nightshade again remained still.

Yes, he said with some amusement. *I have some dignity and wish to retain it.*

"There's a border zone between each of the territories protected by the Towers. It's shifting; it's not static. I think—or smarter people than I think—that it's part of the outlands. Part of," she corrected herself, "the primal ether.

"I think you were valued highly by one of the Towers, but

on ascension, all of the Towers agreed to somehow help anchor you, to maintain some element of your presence or life. They might have thought you couldn't do it on your own, if the words—"

"They would be correct," he said quietly. "You are...in the library."

"I am. I have Arbiter Androsse and Arbiter Kavallac with me; we are searching for Arbiter Starrante."

He closed his eyes, one luminous, one a void. She could see his hair begin to move in the windless room; could see a faint glow as it outlined the whole of his body. His mouth moved, but silently, or quietly enough that she couldn't hear his words. Given that the ears she was currently borrowing were Barrani, she assumed the former.

"Arbiter Starrante is not situated within the library at this current time."

"Do you know where he *is* situated?"

"He has not been removed from the Academia, although it is possible that such removal has been tried. Keep the Arbiters with you, if that is at all possible. I can hear them, and through them, Chosen, you. There is more life in the Academia than there has been in far too long." His smile changed the contours of his face. "Ah, I believe I hear Lannagaros. It has been long, indeed, for Lannagaros.

"Too long, I think." The smile fled his face as he opened his eyes and stared through the window Nightshade had become. "If you intend to attempt to repair me, as you once repaired others, you will be frustrated beyond endurance. I do not have, as the Towers or your...Helen...do, a central core, a central heart. When I was built—and that is a crude word that will only barely suffice because time is scant—I was not built the same way.

"But if you have been tasked with opening the library—

and I will not ask by whom—I feel that you will come to understand this, in time. If you survive. I…do not see the intruders to whom Kavallac refers." He smiled again, but this smile was softer and more careworn. "I do not believe you will accomplish what you hope to accomplish."

"You don't think we can get the library open?"

"That was not the goal to which I referred. Now go. You are interrupting my lecture."

Kaylin. It was Severn. His voice reached her the moment Killian dismissed her—and it was a dismissal.

She nodded.

We have a…guest.

What do you mean?

A young man. An older child. He looked—was looking—in the direction of that child. It was Robin.

I thought you were in the endless hall?

Terrano felt it best to move. Mandoran agreed. I believe it was Annarion who opened the actual door that led to ascending stairs, but if so, he didn't remain. Emmerian agreed with Terrano; I think he's beginning to worry about Bellusdeo and the Arkon, although he's voiced no obvious concern. The halls were designed to be a pleasant trap—something that would confine those who required confinement without, in theory, causing harm or offense. Apparently, at random intervals, food will appear in the side rooms.

There'd been no food in the side rooms when Kaylin had been trapped there. *Did you catch the gist of the conversation Killian and I had?*

I did. I've passed it on to Mandoran. They are now looking for either a book or a ghost. He said this last with a hint of humor. *What do you think their chances are?*

Higher than ours, to be honest.

Ours or yours?

*Both. I also think there's some possible danger in it for them.
They're not students here.*

And Killian is becoming more active.

*Yes. I'm not sure why, but…yes. He can hear me pretty clearly, but
he attributes that to the books I'm carrying. Well, no, to the people
the books appear to contain. But Killian's suggestion that we open
the library meshes with Terrano's. I wish he could find a way in.*

"He will not find a way in until and unless the library is
opened," Killian said.

Kaylin blinked; she was no longer seeing through Nightshade's eyes.

Have a care, Kaylin, Nightshade said. *He was not, I think, fully
aware of the cohort—but he will be now. They have not been granted
permission to be here; they are as much intruders as the Barrani Arcanists and their friends. If Killian wakes fully—and I am uncertain,
given the nature of this lecture, that that is even possible—they might
well suffer the same consequences as those you care far less about.*

She had never had much luck hiding her thoughts from
sentient buildings. Nightshade could, and did. Teela could.

"If Terrano won't find a way in, how did *they*?" she demanded. Nightshade allowed it, as Killian appeared to able
to distinguish between them, even if they were sharing the
same body.

"I believe you already have the necessary answers."

"I don't. If the missing Arbiter is anything like the two
I've already met, he was *in* the library. How could someone
enter the library if my friends can't? They could enter—and
leave—sentient buildings by the time we met."

"I am, I admit, uncertain. There is a possibility, a remote
one, that the interim chancellor might have had methods of
doing so that were emergency contingencies. I believe you
made the attempt to return a book to my library; I was occupied and could not accept it at the time."

"And you can't open the library yourself?"

"No, Chosen. Not yet."

"You believe," Kavallac said, as if the entire conversation had been audible, "that Killian is like other buildings of your acquaintance."

"I did."

"The Academia was not like other such buildings. Killian is not the entirety of it, although he is its most certain steward. His ascension was not determined the way other such ascensions once were, and while all such ascensions were voluntary, the restrictions and responsibilities accepted at the outset defined them.

"The nature of the Academia, the purpose with which it was built, the optimism on which it was founded—these were not what your Towers were built for, nor your Hallionne, nor even your Helen."

"What was the nature of the Academia?"

"Ah, I believe I see your Dragons now."

Given the distance Kaylin had covered by foot—albeit slowly and carefully—she was surprised that it had taken so long to fly back. Which was probably a clue: this wasn't actual flight in any fashion. She landed behind Bellusdeo—Bellusdeo turned instantly, her eyes a shade of orange that was almost red.

Kaylin slid off Kavallac's back; Bellusdeo's eyes lost some of their orange as they met Kaylin's gaze. "What," the gold Dragon said, "have you done this time?"

Arbiter Androsse appeared from behind Kavallac's landing spot; it was easier to see him because Kavallac chose to transform into the more compact form. She was slightly taller than Bellusdeo, but had not adopted the natural armor that

Bellusdeo had. Usually, in Kaylin's reality, this would mean she was naked.

She wasn't. She wore loose robes, the same pale color as the rest of her; only her eyes now resembled the eyes of the two Dragons. The Arkon turned more slowly than Bellusdeo had.

"Arkon," Kaylin said quickly. "This is Arbiter Androsse. And this is Arbiter Kavallac."

Kavallac surprised her. She bowed, and the bow wasn't a superficial display of good manners; there was genuine respect in it.

Nor did the Arkon demand that she rise or put aside the frivolity of the manners Kaylin often thought were a waste of time. He waited, straightening his shoulders; his eyes were a complicated color, hard to see clearly in the dim light.

"Arbiter Androsse," he said. "Arbiter Kavallac." When he spoke her name, she rose.

"You have aged," Kavallac then said. Kaylin was never going to understand manners.

"I have," he replied with the shadow of a smile. "You met me in a youth that is so distant even I can barely recall it."

"You did not remain here."

"No. Very, very few did. We were called away to war, and war was joined on many fronts. I am almost surprised to be recognized."

"The Chosen mentioned you by the name you once used. As she is not Draconic, I beg that you overlook this."

Kaylin flicked a glance in Bellusdeo's direction. Bellusdeo, however, was a warrior queen in this place. Ice would not melt in her mouth.

"I am familiar with Lord Kaylin and her antics," the Arkon replied. "She has been of aid many times to my Flight, but she came late to etiquette; hers is predicated on survival."

"How comes she to know that name?"

He then turned to Bellusdeo. "This is Bellusdeo; we were Aerie kin before her disappearance. She has only recently returned, and when we shared that Aerie I was not—and would never have dreamed of becoming—Arkon. Her early greetings were therefore far less formal."

"How come you to be in this space?" She already knew how; Kaylin had told her.

"The Chosen opened a door for us. We are therefore intruders."

"Yes," Kavallac replied. "But the chancellor has given no instructions and made no requests of us."

Kaylin was certain she'd said there was no chancellor, as well.

"No. The chancellorship has not been decided. Someone, however, appears to be acting as interim chancellor—without the blessing of Killianas."

"Who?"

The Arkon shook his head. "We do not know, Arbiter. It is, perhaps, to discover that that we have come. Has the Chosen spoken to you of the current condition of the Academia?"

"Not at great length, or perhaps not in useful detail." Kavallac's smile was mostly teeth. "But there are less welcome intruders than you, and also, we appear to be missing Starrante."

Silence.

Robin and Terrano have been talking, Severn said.

About anything that might be useful?

Sedarias is, at a distance, attempting to keep them on topic. I'm not certain where she is.

How's that working out?

It's Terrano. Robin's excited about the new class.

Oh?

Because it is *a new class, a different lecture. He's been experi-*

menting. The day is otherwise, as Nightshade suggested, on repeat. Robin, however, finds the Academia interesting.

He's from the warrens.

Yes.

The warrens could have been the fiefs if the Hawks and the Swords were entirely removed from the area. Here, Robin had a bed of his own, a room of his own, and three meals. He was learning—somehow—to read and write. He'd been here for much longer than Nightshade, but was otherwise a recent arrival.

At meals, Severn continued, *the students have more freedom. Robin can finish lunch quickly or can linger until the dining hall is closed. If he finishes quickly, he can interact in a nonscripted way with other students. I believe one or two of those students have taken it upon themselves to teach him to read and write.*

How did he get here?

Interestingly enough, he was escorted here by Candallar. Or rather, escorted to the building in the border zone by Candallar.

You're certain it was Candallar?

Robin is certain it was Candallar. It is possible that someone else chose to use the fieflord's name. Robin, like either of us at his age, would have obeyed an adult Barrani.

And for the same reasons. *How long does he have before he has to return to the classroom?*

Uncertain. In general, he cannot leave the classroom while there's a lecture in session. But Killian has never lectured before. Why?

The Arkon is glaring at me. "Sorry," she said to the Arkon, and indirectly to Kavallac. "There's a lot going on outside of here, and I'm trying to make sense of it."

"Meaning?"

"Killian's teaching a class, for one. I can speak with one of the students, and Killian can speak to me through that student. Terrano is talking to a different student, who asked permission for a bathroom break and was granted it. Terrano wants to know how flexible this repeating schedule is.

"The important information: Candallar was the person responsible for the boy's disappearance from the streets of Elantra. Candallar led him to the building in the border zone—the one with the eyeball in the back wall."

"You can speak with Killianas?" Androsse said.

"Through an intermediary, yes."

"Does he know the location of Starrante?"

"Not the exact location. Starrante doesn't appear to be in the library, or if he is, he's invisible to Killianas."

"That should not be possible. But...the Academia in this condition should not be possible, either. Tell me, what was the name of Candallar's Tower?"

Kaylin cringed, but inwardly. The naming conventions of the fiefs would not be useful information to the Arbiter, and the Arbiter expected useful information.

"The name I believe you desire is the first name; much has changed in the time since the Towers themselves ascended. The Tower was, at its dawn, Karriamis."

Kavallac's eyes began to glow. "He chose, then," she said, so softly it was almost a whisper.

"I was not present when the Towers rose," the Arkon replied with genuine regret. "I had, by that point, been seconded to the war flights."

"You?" Kavallac said. Clearly, respect for his position only carried one so far.

The Arkon took this in stride. "Without those duties—and the necessity of them—I would have been here to watch history unfold. The Ancients walked in concert, or so I was told. The Towers rose in a single day." He shook his head, regret fading from his expression. "Karriamis is Candallar's Tower; it is Candallar who commands the Tower."

"It was almost certainly Karriamis," Androsse said, "who set his captain in search of Killianas."

"Karriamis has been a Tower for a long time—why now?"

"I do not know the constraints by which the Towers were constructed; I did not personally know all of those who were chosen to become the heart of those buildings."

She turned to Kavallac. "You knew Karriamis."

"I did. We were kin, if distant."

Kaylin made a mental note never to visit Candallar with the cohort in tow. Or ever, really.

"What would make Karriamis relay this information now? Instead of earlier or with a different fieflord?"

"I am not a building, Chosen. I do not know. What we can assume—and it is an unverified assumption—is that he did communicate this, and Candallar chose to act on that communication. Perhaps he made the attempt centuries ago—who can say?"

"Candallar."

Nightshade. As he gave wordless, motionless permission, Kaylin said—through his mouth, "You haven't taught a class here since the rise of the Towers."

"That is true. I feel that I had little incentive if things were going smoothly."

"You're teaching one now."

"Also demonstrably true."

"You're more aware of your surroundings, of the Academia."

He nodded, his single eye almost flashing. She had the attention—well, Nightshade did—of the entire class, but in Kaylin's admittedly limited experience, that was the norm when one asked questions.

"Why?"

"I have more engaged students," he replied. "I have students who might learn something. They have questions, and some of those questions might lead them to answers that other students in our history have not achieved."

She frowned.

"So...students are important?"

"Students are the heart of the Academia." Something about that answer stuck and echoed. "Students, scholars, sages. You are searching, perhaps, for something I lack. You will not find it."

"Were the students in the classes introduced to you recently?"

"Some of the students in these classes have been introduced to the Academia over a period of decades, in your time. Some, however, never chose to leave; they are not all contained in this classroom."

"And some are here as students on an off-day?"

"They have not been admitted into the current academic stream."

"By their choice or by yours?"

He frowned; the frown had texture. It had a physical force that Kaylin should not have been able to feel—but did.

"Admittance was not, in general, my responsibility," he finally said. "I could, however, insist if I felt a student that had not shown promise in an obvious way, nonetheless had promise."

"And the current crop of students?"

He frowned again.

Before he could answer, Kaylin said, "Can you tell us where Candallar is?"

"I am uncertain. Lord Candallar," he continued with emphasis on the title Kaylin felt no need to respect, "has freedom of entry."

"How?"

"It is a request received by…"

This was the answer Kaylin wanted, but he stalled out, his eye narrowing, his forehead taking on lines of intense concentration. He failed to speak.

Kaylin said, "Karriamis?"

He lifted his face, his neck extending as his gaze sought the admittedly impressive ceiling. His face ran parallel to the ceiling; his neck bent in an angle that no one else in the room could achieve without breaking their spine. Without lowering his face, he said, "I cannot confirm that. I cannot find an answer. You will excuse me," he added. "I have lost the thread of this lecture, and must continue it or the students will miss their next class."

She blinked. The three intruders had not approached the Dragons. The Arbiters stood to either side of Kaylin, possibly because she carried the books. Turning to Kavallac, she said, "Can I give these books to the Arkon?"

"You may give custody of these books to the Arkon," Kavallac replied. "Where do you intend to go?"

"I don't intend to leave—but the Arkon has a far better chance of protecting the books if it comes to a fight."

The Arkon was already carrying the book that Larrantin had ordered Kaylin to convey to Killian. He accepted the weight of the two she added to that pile. As he did, both Kavallac and Androsse said, "Wait."

He stopped instantly, the books still in Kaylin's hands.

"What are you carrying?" It was Androsse, voice sharper, who spoke first. He wasn't a Dragon, and the respect necessary for the Arkon wasn't his concern.

"A book," Kaylin said before the Arkon could answer.

"Yes, we can *see* that," Androsse snapped, never taking his eyes from the Arkon.

"Can you?" the Arkon asked. "The only person present who sees a book when they look at this is the Chosen."

Androsse turned immediately to Kaylin, who stopped herself from shrugging. "I see a book. I saw a book when Larrantin handed it to me. The book has a rune on its cover. It's similar to yours."

Both of the Arbiters exchanged a glance. This time, when the silence was broken, it was broken by Arbiter Kavallac. "Tell me, Arkon, do you see what the Chosen carries *as* books?"

"The two, yes."

"You said Larrantin had what you currently carry in his possession?"

Kaylin nodded.

"...And it does not look like a book to anyone but you."

She nodded again.

"That is very unfortunate. If we are not mistaken—" and her voice allowed no probability that they were "—that is Starrante's summons."

CHAPTER 24

"I don't understand," Kaylin said.

"Chosen, this book was in Larrantin's possession?"

She nodded.

"How did he come by it?"

"It didn't occur to me to ask him," she replied, which was the truth. In her experience with people like Androsse, truth was irrelevant when what he wanted was specific information. He proved true to type.

"It did not occur to you to ask him why this book was in his possession and not within the library that is its natural environment?"

"I knew nothing of Arbiters or summons. It was a book, to my eye, with a single word emblazoned on its cover. I thought if I delivered it—as requested—to Killian, it would have some effect on him. A positive effect," she added, in case this wasn't clear.

"Larrantin should not have been able to remove it."

"It's possible that he didn't. He might have recognized it for what it was—but I think it's now clear that Starrante is not in the library."

"We have no simple way of opening the library without his presence."

"Is there a complicated way?"

"Demonstrably." Androsse's eyes were midnight blue, which added color to his otherwise ghostly countenance. Kaylin wasn't particularly surprised to see that Kavallac's eyes were dark crimson, either.

"Could Killian find Starrante?"

"I believe you made clear he could not. If something has changed in the interim, it would be to our benefit." She heard echoes of other words as he spoke. They were worried for Starrante.

Kaylin exhaled. "Can you let us out of the library without fully opening it? And can you do so without injuring yourselves?"

"We are not certain, Chosen."

Hope sighed. He then began to squawk loudly in her ear. Since she couldn't understand a word he spoke, she assumed this was meant for the Arkon or the Arbiters.

"Yes," Kavallac finally said, clearly in response to Hope. "If there were a chancellor, the chancellor could open the library. But if a chancellor existed, Killian would not now be in the state he is in."

"Killian could open the library?"

"That is not how Killian was built," Androsse said.

I think, Severn then broke in, *that we know where the chancellor's office is. Does he have more than one?*

Kaylin conveyed the question.

"No, Chosen. There is one office of the chancellor. It has multiple rooms, some meant for public interaction, some for private, but it is the chancellor's home within the Academia."

Robin?

He's apparently skipped a lot of meals before getting dragged back into his classes.

I thought he was learning to read.

He's a bright kid; he's done that. And he's not bad with High Barrani, either. It's Terrano's conjecture, Severn added, *that the students—the missing people—were brought for the purpose of making Killian minimally functional. Apparently, the Academia requires students.*

Kaylin nodded. *That was my thought, as well. But…*

The Arkon?

She nodded. *I don't think it's a coincidence that Killian's become sharper and more focused in his interactions since the Arkon set foot in the Academia. I think the presence of the Arbiters also helps.*

Can you get to us?

I'm not sure. We still have intruders in the library, but they haven't advanced to where— Never mind.

In the darkness of shelves, made brighter by the presence of the Arkon's magic, Kaylin could see movement in the shallows of the light.

"We have company," she said, voice barely audible.

"I cannot see the intruders. Bellusdeo?"

"No."

Kaylin turned to the Arbiters then.

"Yes, Chosen," Androsse said, his voice less quiet. "We can see the intruders. We could sense them when they were not immediately visible. Were they wise, this is not the place at which they would choose to mount an attack."

Kavallac smiled. The smile had teeth in it, and those teeth grew larger and longer. So did the mouth that contained them, elongating as she once again chose to adopt the Draconic form. There was a glow to her scales; she was silver—

silver and white—except for the inside of her mouth and the deep, deep red of her eyes.

Kaylin turned to Hope. "Protect the Arkon and Bellusdeo."

Do not engage them.

"I'm not trying to engage them."

There is a risk to the library. There is a risk to the structure it currently maintains. Killian is not Helen, but there are rules that govern the sentient buildings, and Killian's rules are complex. The library is meant to house not books, but knowledge. The accrued knowledge of the ages. Theories that have been disproved. Theories that have not. Stories and legends that bear no resemblance to their progeny, the stories you heard on the streets.

There is art here that only certain eyes can see; poetry that once moved the people of races that have vanished. And there is history that has long been lost to your people. All of your peoples.

"We're not going to destroy that."

You cannot control the flow of the battle.

"No," Kavallac said, making clear that she could understand the words that Hope now spoke to Kaylin. "She cannot. But we are Arbiters, and this is the ground upon which we are at our most powerful if we are not a triad. We will control the flow of battle; it is the reason for our existence." Her grin was a baring of teeth. "It is us that they are likely searching for, and we are grateful that you found us first. You will not fall here."

"We *don't know* how they found Starrante—but they clearly did, and they've somehow—"

"We will find out."

"The library—"

"Stay with the Arkon," Kavallac said, her voice a rumble of thunder.

"If she means," the Arkon said quietly, as Androsse and Kavallac advanced toward the intruders the two normal Dragons couldn't see, "protect the Arkon, I am inclined to take offense."

Bellusdeo chuckled.

"Maybe she means protect the books," Kaylin offered.

The Arkon turned a baleful glare in her direction.

Robin is now leading us to the chancellor's office while he still has the flexibility in his schedule.

How long will that last?

As long as the professor is not inclined to be annoyed by his bathroom break.

Good. If we can figure out how to get out of here before you reach the chancellor's office, we'll try to join you.

Severn didn't like the odds. The good thing about communication via True Names? Volume wasn't necessary to be heard. Or to hear. Kavallac's roar would have drowned out normal speech. *The chancellor's office seems to hold a specific weight and meaning within the greater Academia. If there is a ringleader to be found, they are likely to be found there—and they have demonstrated a much clearer understanding of the Academia than we currently possess.*

You have a Dragon with you.

You have two—or three, if you include the Arbiter. On any other field, the three Barrani would refuse to engage. They are not refusing now; they must believe they have the power or the knowledge to survive three Dragons.

The floor shook beneath Kaylin's feet. Hope squawked, but she ignored it because squawks weren't meant for her, and she was juggling too many conversations as it was.

Light washed over the library in a wave. The heights of darkened shelves, made invisible by heavy shadow, appeared to go on for as far as the eye could see, or the feet could walk. Above their heads, behind their backs, and ahead of where they stood, the breadth and depth of a singular collection were instantly made manifest.

The Arkon spit out three sharp words; Kaylin felt a full-body slap as he adjusted what she presumed were his protections. It was clear that what Kaylin could see with Hope's wing, the two Dragons by her side could now also see.

"Well met," Kavallac said as the three intruders froze in place. "Welcome to the library over which we are custodial guardians."

Two of the intruders remained frozen, words deserting them. One, however, did not. At this distance, Kaylin couldn't see the color of his eyes, but assumed they were blue; his lips, however, turned up in what might be misclassified as a smile.

"You must be Arbiters Kavallac and Androsse," he said, tendering them a brief bow. "We have been searching for you."

"I'm sure," Kavallac replied, "you have."

"We have the requisite permissions required to traverse this domain."

"Granted by whom?"

"By Arbiter Starrante. He was concerned for your welfare; this building is not what it once was, and he could not be certain that you were not injured or damaged. He will be pleased to note that you are well."

This was not entirely what Kavallac expected—but that was fair. It wasn't what Kaylin had expected, either.

"If you would accompany us, you might speak with him yourselves."

"Perhaps," Androsse said, entering the conversation, "you might bring him here. It is neither our place nor our desire to leave the library; the library is the heart of the Academia."

"I'm afraid that will not be possible."

"Oh?"

"I see that you are both materially whole. Starrante is not, and he cannot be easily moved."

The silence took a turn for the chilly. Kaylin turned to the Arkon. "Give me Starrante's book." To his credit, he didn't hesitate.

It was, as it had been every other time she had touched it, cold. She wondered if the Arkon himself felt the ice of it. She turned it in her hands until she could see the rune emblazoned on its cover. The rune that the Arkon couldn't see.

Killian had not taken the book. The Arkon had carried it; Killian had implied that the message might be delivered at a better, or different, time. But Larrantin could touch it; Larrantin could carry it. Larrantin had meant for Kaylin to deliver it to Killian.

Killian, however, had not seemed interested in receiving it, perhaps because he didn't recognize it? It had been Kaylin's belief that Larrantin had given her the book because she was the only person present he could see—and the only person present who could see him.

She revised that now. He had given it to her because she was Chosen. And because he understood what the book represented. Starrante had been removed from the library.

She turned her thoughts to Nightshade as she looked at the book in her hands. *Ask Killian,* she began.

Ask him yourself.

Fine. "Can the interim chancellor grant access to the library?"

"Indeed. The interim chancellor has most of the powers granted to the chancellor himself, when someone is willing to take on the burden of that role."

"Most?"

"Most. There are some permissions that cannot be granted to someone who does not serve fully."

"Are there qualifications to be interim chancellor?"

"Yes. They are the *regalia* of the office; the external trappings."

"And they'd be found in the office itself?"

"Yes."

"Can they be removed?"

"Not easily. But if the Arbiter has been removed, it is possible the *regalia* has likewise been relocated. Location is not of relevance, but the *regalia* is required for rudimentary control of the Academia."

"And that rudimentary control includes control of you?"

"Some elements, yes. But I am, as you guess, far more awake than I was when Karriamis's Lord first contacted me. The interim chancellor has provided a very modest student body. The Arbiters Kavallac and Androsse have been awakened, and they are whole: I can hear their voices.

"They are not...pleased," he added softly. "Regardless, Starrante is not visible to me. I would suggest that he is not within the remit of my current existence."

"You think he's outside the Academia?"

"I believe he is in what you would call the border zone."

"But..."

"Yes?" This was a sharper word; it implied annoyance at the continued interruption.

"You're in the border zone."

"I would suggest, instead of plaguing the class with questions that do not pertain to the subject I am attempting to teach, that self-study might be of value."

Her attention was caught by a plume of white-gold, which also happened to be fire. The Arkon stiffened, his eyes red;

his arms tightened around the two books over which he'd kept stewardship. But he didn't—although this took visible effort—shout commands of any kind at the Arbiters. He had chosen to trust them. They were guardians of this library. Their fire would not harm it.

Belief, however, was a struggle.

Only when the fire splashed to either side of the spokesman did he relax; the fire didn't harm the books at all.

"I think they pulled us into whatever phase the intruders are in," Kaylin helpfully offered. "And I'm not sure they can harm the library itself in that phase."

Clearly condescension of any kind was only acceptable when it was coming from the Arkon, given his expression— and Kaylin had intended no condescension whatsoever. "You asked for that book for a reason. I suggest you see to it."

The rune was bright; it looked like the words on Kaylin's arms—and probably the rest of her body, as well. But its color was not quite the same gold, and it seemed, as she looked at it, to be carved into the cover, rather than engraved or painted on it.

She frowned. The marks on her arms had shifted color until they were the same as the word she now thought of as Starrante's. Not his name—never that—but the word that might wake him, invoke him, summon him. She touched the surface of the rune on the book's cover.

As she did, the marks on her arms began to lift themselves off her skin. She was now aware that this was a visual signal that only she could see; she'd never worried about it because the lifting didn't shred her shirts or tunics. Or pants, if it came to that.

The surface of the word wasn't flush with the cover; it was

farther down or in. She had to reach to contact the word, and her fingers dipped below the surface. Her hand did, as well.

The Arkon's silence was loud. His attention was torn between the literal fight that was now occurring between three Barrani and the two Arbiters, one a very loud Dragon, one a silent...something else, and Kaylin's handling of the object he had never seen as a book.

Had he, he might never have surrendered it.

When her hand dipped beneath the outer surface of the cover, he cleared his throat. Given Kavallac's roars, she shouldn't have heard it.

"I'm *trying* to reach the word on the cover. It's there, visually—but it's not there physically. And it seems to have taken the actual physical dimensions of the book cover with it wherever it is. I promise I'm not damaging a book."

"You had better not be," he growled.

"Lannagaros, honestly."

"I mean it."

Kaylin grimaced but didn't respond; there was nothing she could say. The word—Starrante's word—seemed to be attempting to evade her.

I'm not sure what the Arbiters have done, Severn said, *but Terrano believes he can locate you now.*

Tell him to stay where he is.

Severn didn't bother with a verbal reply, but Kaylin understood. Telling Terrano to stay where he was was a waste of breath. Helen could manage to both say it and enforce it. Maybe. No one else stood a chance.

I mean it—if Robin manages to get you to the chancellor's office, Terrano's the one most likely to be able to ignore inconvenient things—like, say, doors or walls. If he needs to go on a seek-and-find mission, he should be looking for Candallar. I'm willing to bet Candallar is the interim chancellor, and it's Candallar who holds whatever di-minished keys are necessary to open Killian's figurative locked doors.

Terrano doesn't like it; Sedarias agrees with you. She also points out that she's not sure how long we'll have Robin, so the office comes first.

Kaylin nodded. Sedarias was the person she'd send to find Candallar—Sedarias or Bellusdeo. The latter, however, was here and likely to remain here in the immediate future.

A geyser of purple flame interrupted that thought, given its location: beneath Kaylin's feet. The Arkon's protections buckled for a moment, but didn't break. Bellusdeo headed toward the visible fight.

The Arkon didn't stop her; he didn't even try. "Corporal?"

She shook her head. The book itself obviously occupied dimensions quite different from its physical shape. She thought she could climb into Starrante's rune—if she was conveniently sized and shaped in a way that would fit through the window made of lines—and still be no closer to actually touching it.

A thought came to her then, and she turned—as she had done before and would no doubt do in the future—to the Arkon, the ancient Dragon whose life had been given to the gaining of knowledge.

He seemed to be waiting, as irritable as he often was when interrupted. His eyes were a deep orange, the inner membrane raised to slightly mute the color.

"I can't touch the word on this book."

He nodded; he'd seen the attempt.

"I can see the shape of it—but the shape is now a series of holes or windows. I can't pull the word from it. And I'm pretty sure I don't have that word just hanging around the rest of the marks on my skin."

"I cannot see a word," the Arkon replied. "I could not see a book. I can make assumptions on what I should see based on the two books belonging to the Arbiters, but those assumptions will not grant you the insight you desire."

"Should I try to…speak this word?"

"In some fashion, I believe that is what you were trying to do."

"No—I was only trying to touch it."

His eyes narrowed; his face shifted into a familiar expression. She'd just seen it on Killian's face. "You have had little experience with the speaking of these words, but if your assumptions are correct, you have had more experience than most of the Barrani—and mortals—assembled here. What they did did not invoke that word."

"That's not what I'm afraid of."

"You are afraid that they have somehow managed to siphon the power of that word?"

She nodded. "Killian can now locate the other two Arbiters. He still can't locate Starrante, but…he's aware of his presence. Peripherally. Not in a way that would be useful to us. If he were truly awake, I don't think we'd have any problem finding Starrante."

"Then speak the word, Chosen."

"Could I just—I don't know, give it a different word?"

Orange tilted toward red.

"Or not."

"It is not a name as you perceive True Names," the Arkon then said, relenting. "It is a word. Starrante did not require a True Name to become an Arbiter. He came with the True Names he required, as did Kavallac and Androsse."

"But the words on their books aren't the same."

"As each other's?"

Kaylin nodded.

"No. The words are doors, if I understand their use—and, frustratingly, my knowledge in this regard is scant. If I could see the word, I could attempt to speak it; I am not guaranteed to succeed. The words you have heard me speak—the words you have heard Sanabalis speak—are words that were taught to me in the distant past.

"But you are aware of the effect those words might have on the Leontines, a race that does not require True Names in order to live. Words have power, Kaylin."

"Yes—but those words had specific power."

"So, too, these. And they are simple words; they are not an entire tale. The power that those who attacked the High Halls wished to access was those True Names. This is not that. You will not, speaking the name, bind Starrante in the fashion you clearly fear."

"Will I bind him in some other fashion?"

"I believe you will build a connection, yes. But it is a connection that has, in some fashion, already been built by someone else. You have the advantage of holding that book." His tone implied that she had better make use of the minor advantages she had—and quickly.

But words weren't spoken quickly, if they were spoken at all. She wished strongly that she could use the magic the Arkon possessed to create a visual, visible illusion; she trusted the Arkon to speak what must be spoken.

Fire erupted in the distance; it was a white-gold fire, and it was accompanied by a very familiar voice: Bellusdeo's. The Arkon tensed, but said nothing.

Above Kaylin's arms and around her legs she could see the marks of the Chosen. They were golden now, their light a glow that implied warmth, not the chill of ice. Starrante's book was before her, and she could now see that it, too, was golden. It just wasn't solid.

Her own marks, her own words, were. She could reach out and touch them—and did, to ascertain their solidity. She hesitated for one moment, and then turned, again, to the Arkon. He understood, and reluctantly held out one book for her inspection: Androsse's. Kaylin was certain this was mostly by chance.

Androsse's word was solid; it was part of the cover of the book. It didn't rise or float; it didn't spin. But it was present. She assumed the same of Kavallac's, but the Arkon didn't offer the second book; having confirmed that Kaylin's fingers didn't dip below the surface of Androsse's, he was done with the experiment.

Kaylin's familiar had dropped his wing at about the time Kavallac had chosen to engage the intruders. He'd folded it, and further, had collapsed on her shoulder like a bulky shawl. He said nothing, and offered no advice or criticism.

The Arkon didn't, either. She could hear the sounds of battle, all of it magical; there didn't seem to be one drawn sword in the fracas. But she could also hear syllables, words—as if catching the mood and tone of an entire crowd. A crowd that was not, or had not yet become, a problem for the Swords.

These syllables, much like the random sentences spoken by people in a gathered crowd, overlapped and clashed; none were terribly loud, and none demanded instant attention. But none would; none of the syllables conformed to a language she knew. None implied intent or danger. They were a simple gathering of sounds with nothing to collect or catch her attention.

No, she thought, that wasn't true. She understood as she listened—closing her eyes as she often did to aid concentration—that those syllables emanated from the marks themselves, as if they, rotating in place, were desperately attempting to be heard. She listened now.

As she listened, she began to search for words that seemed to be written with a similar foundation to the one on Starrante's book—bold double horizontal lines as the central composition, with a slender, slightly curved line to the left of the whole figure that seemed to anchor the rest of it. There were very few of the squiggles, but three dots had been added beneath the second horizontal line.

She knew that the pronunciation of true words wasn't dependent on the composition, or not precisely dependent on it. The rough alphabet that comprised true words had never appeared to be phonetic. This language wasn't like Elantran or Barrani, where at least ninety percent of the words could be sounded out by someone just learning to match speech to the written equivalent.

But this was what she had, at the moment. She chose to touch the marks of the Chosen that most closely corresponded in general shape and composition to the rune on Starrante's book.

As she touched them, she could hear them. She could hear how they might be pronounced—or perhaps how they might be pronounced by Kaylin. It hadn't occurred to her until this moment that they might contain sounds that her human throat couldn't, or didn't, naturally make. When Sanabalis spoke these words, or when the Arkon did, they spoke with normal voices—but louder, deeper, richer in intonation. They didn't wrap the sounds in the Dragon thunder that passed for conversation in their native tongues.

She would have to remember to ask the Arkon whether or not he could speak True Words in Dragon.

She couldn't. But she could hear syllables now. She could hear the similarities in pronunciation as she moved from one word to the next. She had, with the help of Tara and Tiamaris, repeated words and sounds, struggling to force them into coherence. But she understood now that it wasn't just sound; intent was required.

She had learned to look at carved words, to see their shape, and to understand when that shape had begun to shift or change in ways that were wrong. But she didn't read them out loud; she didn't speak them. There was nothing wrong with the shape of the word that graced Starrante's book. There was no disfiguration.

Her eyes were closed, or she would have closed them again. The syllables that she heard were different enough that she couldn't quite match components to sounds—and she was aware that there might be no actual match.

Speak, Hope said.

She didn't argue with him; she wanted to, but there was nothing to be gained by it. If writing words, if holding them in the correct shape, was a matter of instinct, of recognizing the harmony in disparate shapes...was speaking like that, as well?

Yes.

"Not with normal language." Damn.

You think of the words as language. This is both right and wrong.

"Fine. Tell me how it's wrong. Wrong is what I need to fix." She raised her voice as the sound of cracking, breaking rock swamped Hope's possible answer.

They are words. They are language. They are life. Think of true words as the blood of the Ancients. You have seen this before in glimpses of ancient Records.

"Our blood doesn't work that way. We bleed when we're injured, but the blood's not alive."

Hope didn't reply.

"Hope?"

Silence.

"Look—you don't actually expect me to *heal an injured word*, do you? Words aren't singular. Even true words. It's not like it's said once and that's done forever and ever. If I could only use each word once, I'd never be able to talk!"

Her familiar glared at her.

"Even if I wanted to heal this particular word, I can't touch it. I've been trying."

"Corporal," the Arkon cut in. "I believe you are looking at this the wrong way." She didn't open her eyes, so she couldn't see his expression, but she could pretty much hear it. "In this case, you do not need to touch the word. You need to *speak* it."

"I was trying that—"

"Yes, you were. But in all of the times you've possessed the marks of the Chosen, you've shown competence in utilizing their innate power in only one way: you heal. Speaking the words as I've spoken them will not, I think, resolve the issue we face."

Kaylin was almost frustrated enough to open her eyes.

"You must speak them, Corporal, with the power you have always used to heal. The only power you trust enough to use willingly and deliberately."

"I lit the room," she said. Hope bit her ear. But if he wanted her to use that power, she had to touch the rune. So that wasn't what he was saying at all. He was asking her to speak a word she didn't know—which she'd been trying to do— while using the power of the marks of the Chosen to heal a word in a completely unnatural way.

What was healing? What did she do in order to heal?

Touch the body. Touch the injured person. She didn't trust her powers; she trusted each body's knowledge of itself. Regardless, touch was essential and there was nothing to touch here.

Sorry to interrupt, Severn said, *but we may have a problem.*

More of a problem than three Barrani Arcanists attempting to kill us in a library no one else can reach?

Terrano says he's found a way into the library.

And that's bad?

Not for Terrano. The rest of us have found the chancellor's office. We didn't have to pick the lock; the door was open.

…Someone was in the office.

Something was in the office, yes.

Without another word, Kaylin pushed her awareness behind Severn's eyes. In theory, the connection between them was built on her name—a name she had picked for herself from the Barrani lake of life—which meant Severn had power over Kaylin if he wanted to wield it. In practice, that had never been an issue.

She swore, apparently with her own mouth. The Arkon said, "What is wrong?"

"Starrante's a Barrani name, right?"

Silence. The pause held the crackle of lightning and the roar of Dragons.

"Ah. It is indeed a Barrani name—but it is a name that was adopted for ease of use by the students and the academic committee overseen by the chancellor."

"Starrante's not Barrani."

"No."

"Did you ever actually meet him when you were a student here?"

"Yes."

"Did he happen to, I don't know, eat the students when he was in a bad mood?"

"In his time, he was considered the most gentle of the Arbiters; I believe it was Androsse who caused occasional structural damage when disappointed."

"Fine. Was he a giant, hairy, eight-legged spider-like... creature?"

"Ah. I believe Corporal Handred has found some part of Starrante."

CHAPTER 25

Robin had led them to the chancellor's office, and was peering through the door; Kaylin was aware of his presence because Severn was. The child kept Severn and Emmerian between him and the open door. Annarion had taken up position by the side of Severn that wasn't occupied by a Dragon.

You should tell Robin to go back to class, Kaylin said.

Severn, however, lifted an arm. Given the proximity of Annarion's sword, this took courage. "The Arkon says that this is one of the people we're looking for."

Given that the creature had not yet attacked, although what might have been a head had swiveled in their direction, Annarion said nothing rude. He didn't sheathe his weapon but did lower it—without removing Severn's arm. Emmerian was, in theory, unarmed. Dragons considered swords of nonmagical origin inferior to the gifts granted them by nature. This was because they were.

The creature that looked like a giant spider opened a mouth that was distinctly fleshy. Its voice was a screech of sound, like large chunks of rock rubbing against each other in the middle of an earthquake, but quieter.

No one spoke in response, and the mouth opened again.

The creature appeared to be sitting on an impressive desk, and it flexed four of its legs to sidle off the flat surface.

"Arbiter Starrante," Severn said. "We apologize for interrupting you at your work." He spoke in High Barrani but spoke slowly. Annarion was willing to allow Severn to speak for them, which probably meant Sedarias was occupied.

The spider creature's mouth closed slowly. Yes, he did have a head that was separate from the rest of his body. That head rose on something that resembled a leg rather than a neck. The head itself appeared to be mostly mouth, but the round, dark things that might be eyes sat at the four corners of a mouth that seemed rectangular in shape.

The creature spoke again, but this time, Kaylin could understand the words. They were Barrani. "You are not in class."

"We have permission to leave the classroom."

"Impossible."

Robin said, "Killian gave me permission." He spoke from behind Severn's back. "You can ask him."

"Ah." It was hard to tell if Arbiter Starrante was frowning. His eyes, however, seemed to be shifting in color—or at least the two lower eyes. They had gone from black to a pale blue. The upper eyes remained dark, but Kaylin could see—through Severn's eyes—a flicker of something that might be gold. "I am afraid Killianas is not responding."

"Killianas requested that the library be opened."

"That is not Killianas's decision to make," Starrante said, more edge in the words.

"Is it yours, Arbiter Starrante?"

Careful, Kaylin said.

The head lowered, retracting into the body.

"Are you the chancellor?" Severn asked.

"Of course not."

"Who is the chancellor?"

"There is no chancellor," Starrante replied, his head now so flush with his body he once again looked like a spider. A spider that was making its way to the door.

"Who is the interim chancellor?"

"There is…no…chancellor." The words were louder, and not just because he was closer.

Severn—

He moved, grabbing Robin and vacating the open door. But even moving, he could see—and therefore Kaylin could see—the color of Starrante's upper eyes; they were a livid, ugly purple. She had no idea what race Starrante was; had he been less solid, she would have thought him a one-off Shadow, straight from *Ravellon.*

Giant spider legs with terminal claws crashed into the door frame. Annarion, like Severn, had leaped out of the way. Starrante's movements were jerky, unnatural and punishingly swift. The door frame cracked under the weight of the sudden blow; it cracked again when the second leg joined the first.

Severn retreated down the hall, shoving Robin in Annarion's direction.

"Don't attack him!" he shouted. "Avoid closing."

"Easier said than done," Annarion replied. "He doesn't seem to be under the same restrictions."

"I don't think he's doing this of his own volition!"

Nightshade—we're having a bit of trouble with Starrante. We've found him, she added. *Can you tell Killian—or ask Killian—if he can interfere?*

Interfere in what?

I think Starrante is trying to kill Severn and Annarion.

"I doubt that. I doubt it highly," Killian said. Nightshade had not spoken. "If Arbiter Starrante truly intended to kill your friends, they would almost certainly be dead." He frowned. "I do not include Lannagaros in that number."

"He's not the only Dragon that came with me—but they're trapped in the library. I've found Starrante—he was in the chancellor's office."

Killian frowned. His expression was more fluid, more dynamic, than it had been the first time she'd met him. "I see."

"Can you do anything to interfere in the—the conflict? I don't think the Arbiters are supposed to damage—"

"There are no students present. No people with requisite permissions— Ah, no. I am incorrect." His smile was slender. "Robin has apparently lost his way in an attempt to reach the…bathroom. Yes, I believe I have the authority to intervene in this case."

He lifted his head. "Arabella, self-study does not mean doodling. And give Taran his book back, please. He will be in some trouble if he loses another one." He lifted his voice. "We have discussed the nature of True Words in the insubstantial ether. We have discussed the possibilities inherent in the primal ether. If one has the ability to reform that ether into a shape and a solidity of one's choice, why can the words find no anchor?"

Severn?

Starrante has…vanished.

When?

Just now. Killian's still lecturing?

He is. He was waking. Helen could have continued the lecture while also separating combatants.

"Killian, we need to speak with Starrante."

"I am afraid that that is not possible at the moment. The Arbiter seems to be engaged in an internal conflict of his own." This last was said with some concern. "He could not hear me, and he was damaging himself in an attempt to disobey the compulsion laid against him. I have removed him to a place that will be safer, for the moment."

"Can you send him to the library?"

"No, Chosen."

Kaylin exhaled. "Can you speak the word that will summon him?"

He stared at her. Or stared at Nightshade, whose voice spoke the words she wanted to say so naturally she almost felt as if she were in the lecture hall.

"Yes," Killian said, "it is almost as if you are here. But this takes a toll on Calarnenne, and it would be a pity to exhaust him so completely he retains nothing of this lecture."

"The word to summon Starrante?"

Killian closed his eye. When he spoke—when his voice formed the first of many syllables—Kaylin could hear it so clearly he might have been standing beside her.

I cannot hear it, Nightshade said.

Neither could Severn.

"Calarnenne, please. You have allowed yourself to be distracted enough—and I would like your input. This is a question that is not often asked of students as junior as yourself, but it is a pressing matter that might well define your future."

"I'm sorry," Kaylin said in her own voice, in a library that was vibrating with sound. "Please, repeat the word."

What did Hope mean? What was healing? How did it relate to the sound of this single word? She sat cross-legged on the shuddering ground and placed Starrante's book in her lap because she could no longer hold it in her hands; the cold had numbed them so completely she couldn't be sure she wouldn't drop the book.

She looked at the word as Killian spoke it. She tried to retain the sound of the syllables, the way they flowed into each other. He spoke slowly, but the speaking of these particular words always seemed slow, as if each part of the word had intimidating depth and one couldn't speak them without intent. The choosing of words, the placement of words, the sense of their weight, were not things that she considered often in her normal life.

If every word had to be spoken and chosen with so much care, would the meanings of those words—far fewer in number—somehow be clearer?

She shook her head. No. Listen. Listen to the sound. Find a way to voice it. Will. Intent. Meaning.

Meaning. In the end, she didn't know the meaning of this word. She knew how it was used. No, she didn't even know that. She hadn't needed to speak the words on the outer bindings of the other Arbiter's books. She'd merely had to open them.

This book hadn't been in the library; it had been in Larrantin's possession. And Larrantin seemed to understand that it had to be returned. She couldn't imagine that he had taken the volume out of the library—but he'd found it, somehow.

She began to speak, repeating the syllables she could hear, her voice just behind Killian's, like a stutter. The frustration of attempting to match her voice, her pronunciation, her enunciation to his absorbed most of her thought.

The Arkon's voice overlapped hers, but his contained words she recognized *as* words—none of them happy words. She lost the flow of syllables as she spoke a single word: *Hope.*

Her familiar said, *I will aid him—but be wary; I will not be here. No—do not stop. What you do now, you must do. If the Arkon were capable of it, he would do it himself. He is not.*

She didn't even feel him leave her shoulder, and once again closed her eyes.

That is not wary.

When she closed her eyes, she caught the thread of the word; understood that this was not the whole of it, and waited until Killian began again. This time, the sound was clearer, perhaps because she had struggled to match it. But she understood what she was doing wrong and cringed.

This time, when she opened her mouth, she began to sing.

Kaylin's singing was…not good. It had never been good. Out of kindness to her friends, she kept it to herself. Her lousy voice was so low on the list of things those friends had time to care about at the moment, she forced herself to work past the bitter self-consciousness. Now was *not* the time for it.

Singing was better. The extension of syllables suited song more than it suited speech; it felt more natural. There was, about the joining of voices—even when one of them was hers—something harmonious. The background of roaring and thunder could almost be percussion, if the percussionist was bad. It was easier to sing a note than it was to speak a long, extended syllable.

Notes had tone. The only reason Kaylin tried to sing— when she was relatively certain it wouldn't offend anyone— was that songs contained emotions; she could return to a song in different frames of mind and be drawn almost instantly into the immediacy of the feelings it invoked. Even if she didn't know all the words by heart.

She could hum. She did hum. As she did, as she felt the melding of Killian's voice and her own, she was enmeshed in a wash of emotion for which she had no words.

Starrante's word was a song.

It was a song of welcome and grief, of loss and unexpected joy, of things broken and things mended and made whole. Her own words couldn't have conveyed half of what she now felt, but they would have been irrelevant. She found she was crying as she sang; she lifted hands, turning them palm up, as if to catch something—or to offer it.

She shifted her voice, shifted her volume; breath came naturally in the small pauses between syllables. She let the melody carry her and surround her. She had heard words from this language spoken before; they had never sounded like this. But maybe those words had been echoes of words like this one; shadows of the story that had brought the Leontines to life as a people.

This was not the story of a people; it wasn't as grand and extended as that. It was not an act of creation—and yet, on some level, it was. This was a song she had never heard before, and would now never forget.

She put her own emotions into the syllables as it progressed; put the weight of those feelings—lightness and joy, heaviness and rage—into her enunciation of the syllables, as people did when singing. She made of it something personal. She hadn't created it, wasn't certain how someone else would sing it, and at the moment didn't care. She could hold on to this.

She could hold it, beginning to end, in her head.

When Killian's voice fell silent, she noticed the lack of his guidance. But she no longer needed it. She didn't think, didn't panic, didn't heal in any way that she understood—but she could see her own marks gently glowing as she focused on what she'd learned.

This time, on her own, she sang.

The rune on the cover of a book made of ice began to rise. It rose as the marks of the Chosen did. She reached out to touch it; it was now solid between her palms, and they'd recovered enough that she could feel its surfaces against her skin.

She wasn't expecting the rune to pull away. She wasn't expecting the book to fly off her lap. She opened her eyes without thought, her voice dying into stillness as she met the midnight-blue eyes of Candallar.

★ ★ ★

She moved, throwing herself out of the range of the spell that her skin told her was coming. But she moved in the direction of the book. Candallar had, she thought, kicked it or sent it flying in some purely physical way. She didn't reach the book first; the Arkon did.

The Arkon had not moved.

Purple fire scorched the floor where Kaylin had been seated. The Arkon snapped a single Draconic word that reverberated down Kaylin's spine. The specific meaning was lost, but the tone made clear that he intended Kaylin to get behind him.

Fire followed her steps; purple lapped at her legs. It didn't burn; it numbed. She stumbled into the Arkon's left arm, and he caught her before she could hit the ground. All around him, she could see a luminous, faint sphere.

So could Candallar.

"Leave them!" he shouted, although he didn't take his eyes off the Arkon—and Kaylin. "What we want is *here!*"

The Arkon exhaled a narrow plume of fire; it blossomed across Candallar's chest without apparently burning anything. Candallar, however, shouted no further instructions to his distant companions.

No, he focused on the two people in front of him, and on the three books one of them now carried.

"You do not have permission to be here," he said, his voice a curious blend of ice and fire. His eyes widened slightly as his words died into a silence battered by distant roars and combat. Those eyes narrowed as he spoke the words again: *you do not have permission to be here.* The words echoed and repeated as if Kaylin were hearing them spoken by more than one voice.

"Neither do you!" Kaylin shouted back.

This time, his eyes narrowed until they were almost closed.

He lifted a hand, and in it, Kaylin could see something that looked like a rod—small, compact, not terribly useful for fighting. It seemed ceremonial.

He pointed the rod at Kaylin. *"Leave."*

"I'd suggest you consider it," a familiar voice said. Terrano stepped out of the shadows.

Terrano was unarmed. Sedarias, however, was not. She joined Terrano, her hair a flyaway mess, something seldom seen on a Barrani when they weren't in motion.

"Lord Candallar," Sedarias said, her eyes a shade of blue that made clear her displeasure.

"Do not interfere here," Candallar said, struggling to keep his voice as smooth—and cold—as Sedarias's had been. "You are intruders, and as intruders, you have no hope of survival. This is not Mellarionne, An'Mellarionne. You will find that you have no power here, except the power I choose to grant."

The Arkon roared.

Candallar appeared unmoved.

"You are in the library," the Arkon said. "And your people are intent on causing damage to it."

"The library is part of the Academia, and I am its Lord."

The floor shook beneath Kaylin's feet.

The Arkon looked singularly unimpressed. Sedarias and Terrano joined Kaylin; Sedarias did not put up her sword. But it was Sedarias who spoke.

"What claim have you over the Academia?"

"I told you—"

"And what use is it to you?"

"Do you not understand what is gathered here in the detritus of ancient history?" Candallar's voice was soft.

"You have intrigued with the Lords of the High Court who are discontent with things as they now stand," Sedarias continued, as if she had not been interrupted. "None of us do so without goals. You will not and cannot claim the High Seat, and given your role in the recent difficulties, your reinstatement to that Court is nigh impossible."

He said nothing.

"I have offered alliance, and you have failed to respond to that offer."

"And you will offer it again?" There was no trace of sneer in his voice or his words, but it was clear that he didn't believe it.

"There are things that I can, and cannot, accept," Sedarias said. "I am An'Mellarionne, as you have clearly ascertained. I speak with the voice of Mellarionne."

"You yourself were not obedient to your brother when he ruled your family."

"We are never obedient when the goal is our destruction, no. But your destruction was both ordained and escaped; you are fieflord, and your Tower is Candallar. Do you wish to be relieved of the burden that preserved your life?"

Silence.

"I cannot see what you hope to gain in your intrigues at Court. You cannot be both fieflord and a Lord of the High Court; in the history of the Court that has happened only once. You rule your domain, and what you make of it reflects your concerns, but the power of the fieflord is almost absolute in the fief that bears his name."

"Is that what you believe?" An edge of anger inserted itself into the words.

"That is what we have been taught, yes. And we have seen the truth of it in the fief of Tiamaris." This wasn't strictly speaking true—but Sedarias was Barrani, and it was pretty close to facts as Kaylin understood them.

"Perhaps Tiamaris's Tower is different. The Tower of Candallar is not obedient; it conveys power, yes, but it is more of a cage than a shelter. I cannot leave it."

"You are demonstrably not within your Tower now."

"No? I can hear the Tower's voice while I stand in this place. It is aware of everything I do while I am here. I can escape that voice if I enter the city—and I have entered Elantra—but I cannot dwell within that city if I am still labeled outcaste."

"Nightshade does not consider his Tower to be a cage."

"Lord Nightshade wields one of the three," was the edged reply. "And he was skilled in arts Arcane before I was birthed. He is outcaste, yes—as am I—but for different reasons. The Lady favors him, regardless." This last was said with a bitterness he could not hide.

"He could survive those who curried the High Lord's favor. No one who hunted him returned to the Court. None of his kin, and none of his enemies. I had hoped that the taking of the Tower would elevate my power; I had hoped that I might become like Nightshade. I have not.

"I have gained power, yes—but it is equal to power that has been gained by those who are not outcaste, though in greater measure. I want to leave the Tower—and I cannot, unless I am reinstated."

"And who will captain the Tower, if not you?"

Candallar's shrug was a fief shrug. "That will not be my concern. The Tower can hold its own for some time while it searches. But I have nothing to offer you," he continued. "If I understand what your brother feared, you have nothing to gain. Should you wish to take the Tower, it would be yours; I would step aside."

That is not how the Towers work, Nightshade said.

Weren't you supposed to be paying attention to the lecture?

It is over—but I am fully capable of doing two simple things simultaneously.

Kaylin didn't interrupt the conversation, because it was clear to her that Sedarias didn't believe they worked that way, either.

"Break off your negotiations with your former allies, and we will consider the difficulty the Tower presents," Sedarias finally said. "I cannot offer you the reinstatement you desire; it is possible that I might offer protection from those who would otherwise see you dead."

"What is offered me now—by the allies I have gained—is of far more worth; you will spend your life protecting yourself, and it will not be enough. The enemies you have made at Court are powerful and established; they will not falter in the face of junior Lords such as yourself."

Sedarias smiled. It was a lazy, slow smile. Terrano took a step back, which brought him in line with Kaylin. "This might get messy," he said in very quiet Elantran.

"Ask them," Sedarias said, "whether or not their voices— voices of established, old lineages—are heard by the High Halls. Because, Candallar, mine *is*."

He fell silent. He could not ascertain the truth or lie in her claim. To be fair, neither could Kaylin.

"Regardless," Sedarias continued, when Candallar failed to speak, "you have something of value that is not yours to claim."

His brows rose. "And you seek to claim it for yourself? You?"

"No," Sedarias said. "Not for myself. If I understand this place—what this place once was—it is not for me. But it is not for you, either."

"I have spent decades building it," he replied, voice sharper again, the nod given to Sedarias and her iron self-control. "I searched for it. I found it. I have attempted, where possible, to repair it—"

"Repair?" The Arkon's voice was a rumble. "Is that what you call *this*?" He lifted the arm that did not hold the three books, tracing an arc that involved the combat in the distance.

"This? It is a library, no more, no less; a collection of books, some of which might have useful information, most of which is fanciful conjecture or history. We have attempted to ascertain where books of use might be found, but it has been cumbersome.

"Think you the library essential? It is not. Killian has coped quite well without access to its dusty, dead contents."

"You are a fool," the Arkon said.

"There were three things of value here; we found one, but its retrieval was tricky and it has not been fully repurposed to our needs. You have, apparently, found the other two— but you have no idea how to utilize their potential power. At best, they will remain sentinels in this place—they will have no wider or greater purpose.

"But perhaps, just perhaps, they might form the basis of a true negotiation."

"Pardon?" Sedarias shifted in place.

"You do not know how to use what you have. We do. We would be willing to teach you what you must do to take control of the books in your possession, and would ask only that you return the book that was in ours."

"How did you get it out of the library?" This was Terrano. He winced, no doubt from Sedarias's internal and private rebuke.

"That would be one of the things we might demonstrate. There is no need to fight as you are currently fighting."

"We are not doing the bulk of the fighting," Sedarias then said. "If you will take the risk of letting me out of your sight, you might see for yourself who is. If you are wise, you will not, but let me explain. The Dragon and the man who might be one of our progenitors from long ago are fighting three Arcanists who I assume are your allies. They are residents of this library."

The implication was that they now did Sedarias's bidding.

"Regardless, you have made a fatal error. You recognize Dragons, surely."

Candallar had stiffened. This wasn't a surprise; Barrani reacted poorly to condescension aimed at themselves. He didn't dignify her question with an answer.

"You do not recognize them individually, or perhaps you do not understand the significance of one of our visitors."

He did turn then; when he turned back, his eyes were almost black. "You brought the female Dragon *here*?"

Sedarias, however, said, "You are a fool. Perhaps my brother and his subordinates found you useful—but in my experience fools are a double-edged weapon that cannot be relied upon in a battle."

"Get ready to move," Terrano said.

"Why?"

"Because as far as I can tell, he *is* interim chancellor. It's the only possible way he could be here at all."

"Can you stay here?" Kaylin said.

"I can—but it won't be safe if he decides we don't have permission."

"Why?"

"Enough." Candallar lifted the arm that held the rod; for a moment, Kaylin could see a flash of something that looked very like green fire flare in a circle in the center of the fieflord's chest.

Terrano didn't answer.

Or perhaps she couldn't hear the answer; she blinked once and found herself in an entirely familiar room.

She wasn't alone.

Bellusdeo and Sedarias were with her. The Arkon, however, was not. The room itself was large enough to house an angry Bellusdeo in full Draconic form; it was the room in which they had first entered Killian's domain. The statues that had once been carved reliefs took up more of the room than they once had, but Bellusdeo's presence did not destroy any of them.

Candallar is the interim chancellor, Kaylin said—to both Severn and Nightshade. Neither seemed surprised.

You expected that, surely? Nightshade asked.

She nodded, although he couldn't see it. *We're in the statuary that we first encountered when it wasn't a statuary. It reminds me of your throne room. We need to get back to the library.*

That will be challenging, Nightshade said.

The Arkon wasn't ejected with the rest of us.

You suffer from two misapprehensions, the fieflord said. *You feel that because the Arkon is so old, he is weaker than Bellusdeo. And you believe that because he is a scholar, he is less familiar with combat. You know his history. You know that he fought in the wars. You have heard—briefly—that he was honored for his skill as a warrior.*

But he's alone—

No, Kaylin, he is not. I believe the reason he was not removed instantly from the library is that he could not be: he was carrying and protecting the tomes that serve as portals for the Arbiters. The Arbiters cannot leave the library.

Starrante is—

Yes. But according to Killianas, he is struggling against the imperatives the chancellor has laid upon him, and he is not nearly so

*much of a power as he would otherwise be should he join his two
comrades in combat.*

Do you know where Starrante is now?

*I believe you will find him soon. Tell Lord Bellusdeo that it is
best—for you—if she takes the lead.* She could feel the frown
settle in the corner of his lips. *Where is your familiar?*

*He's...probably in the library—with Terrano and the Arkon. Terrano is kind of slippery when it comes to buildings, and the Arkon is
holding the Arbiters' books.*

She turned to her companions, but Bellusdeo had shifted
into her armored human form, and she had headed immediately for the nearest door. That door led to the endless maze
of hallway. Sedarias glanced at Kaylin.

"Your familiar?"

"Probably in the library with Terrano and the Arkon."

"Then I will take the rear."

"I don't need—"

Bellusdeo roared. Kaylin shut up and let Sedarias take the
rear.

CHAPTER 26

The stairs led to the hall. The hall was unchanged. There were closed doors on either side of the narrow stone hallway. Bellusdeo marched down the hall toward the closed door at its end.

"If you can somehow bespeak Killian," she began.

The door she had just passed on the right burst open. Or rather, it burst outward, sending large chunks of heavy wood and small splinters flying. The bulk of the heavy wood slammed into the wall inches behind Bellusdeo, who was already on the move.

They passed almost a foot in front of Kaylin. Splinters scraped her face and lodged in her hair. Neither the splinters nor the hair was of much concern right now. The creature in what remained of the doorway was.

She had seen it through Severn's eyes, sitting on the large desk in the chancellor's office. Seeing it in person was a new—and unwelcome—experience. Its head was high upon the hairy, leg-like neck, swiveling in a full circle to take in its surroundings; its eyes—all four eyes—were crimson.

Without taking a breath for thought, Kaylin jumped forward, not back. Legs rose on the creature's left. Kaylin didn't attempt to count how many; she leaped past them before two implanted themselves firmly in the stone of the floor. Reaching out, she placed one palm safely against the bulk of its body—its hairy, disturbing body. Eyes opened on either side of her hand.

This creature really did remind Kaylin of the most dangerous of the Shadows that *Ravellon* produced: it had too many eyes, too many legs and a mouth the size of a Dragon's sitting sideways in what passed for a face.

Behind her, she could hear Sedarias shout a warning, and she shouted back, "No, wait, both of you!"

Fire did not consume the spider creature. Which was good, because while it probably wouldn't have killed the spider, it certainly wouldn't have done Kaylin any good. The spider's flesh was much warmer than she'd expected.

Warmer, fleshier, the feel belying its appearance—then again, she'd never tried to touch a spider, and certainly had never tried to heal one. If this could be called healing at all.

She couldn't see a True Name centered within it, but she didn't have time to look. What she wanted now was to understand the shape and the constitution of Arbiter Starrante. To heal him, in fact.

Hope's suggestion—that she somehow heal the word—had met with uneven success. Maybe because words weren't alive without people behind them. Maybe because what Hope perceived in the shape of True Words wasn't what Kaylin herself perceived. Or maybe because life—as she understood it—existed only in True Names. Power existed in True Words, in True Language—she'd seen the truth of that herself. But life?

Starrante was alive.

If she had never seen someone from his race before, it didn't change that fact. He was alive; he had once lived in the same reality Kaylin occupied most of the time. He'd lived, breathed, eaten—no, wait, *do not* think about that—and probably slept. Something about the book that Larrantin had passed, without warning, into her hands had been damaged or broken in a way that allowed Candallar to command Starrante.

"No," Starrante said, his voice the same grating screech of sound that it had been when she'd heard it through Severn's ears. Its neck had curved in a half circle, which allowed the very large mouth to move much closer to Kaylin's face than anyone without a death wish would have liked.

"It is the chancellor's *regalia* that gives him rudimentary control. The chancellor has the right—in an emergency—to engage the services of the Arbiters. It is that contingency that has controlled my actions. My apologies if I have harmed you. You have an odd taste about you—are you Chosen, perhaps?"

"How did your book get out of the library?"

"Ah. That is a perplexing question."

"Do you still feel like killing us?"

"At the moment? No. I feel remarkably clearheaded, given the terrible confusion and disorder of recent days." His head tilted, but it was hard to tell by features other than the placement of neck whether or not it was upside down. "The young these days are impatient and foolish; they do not understand that rituals came into being for a reason. I apologize; I was perhaps annoyed at the state of my captivity, and the door was locked.

"Are you well?" he added, his head leaving the vicinity of Kaylin's face and turning toward Bellusdeo.

"I am uninjured," Bellusdeo replied. "You are not."

"Ah, no. But the injuries were largely self-sustained, and I believe the Chosen is repairing them as we speak."

Kaylin winced. If healing was what she was doing, it was almost accidental. The shape of Starrante's body was surprisingly normal, if one didn't consider the configuration—it certainly felt more natural than a Dragon's duality and the threads that bound both forms into a single whole.

The legs were legs, the arms—which looked a lot like legs except for the odd digits at the end—were arms. There was muscle beneath what had appeared chitinous, and that muscle was connected to a circular spine within which the major organs were housed and protected. The neck that had been so disturbing was very similar to the legs, but the head could actually retract into the body almost entirely.

She couldn't see anything broken, but she could see the damage done to muscles, the slow decay of some element of the spine itself. Age? She wasn't certain. Barrani and Dragons didn't age into weakness the way mortals did. They didn't really age at all beyond a certain point. If this creature were as old as they were—or older—it was likely that it, too, was immortal.

But injured, as immortals could be.

"Yes, but the injuries were self-inflicted, I'm afraid. It is what happens when we are at war with our own impulses. Killianas is not pleased." He said this with what she assumed was a smile, given the shift in tone. "I have attempted to converse with him, but the conversation was not productive."

"Not productive or impossible?"

"Beyond the initial displacement, unproductive. I thought perhaps my inability to fully control myself was causing interference—but the compulsion seems to have lifted somewhat. Ah, that one is an older injury, and I feel it would be counterproductive to waste power attempting to correct it."

She froze.

"You can feel what I'm doing?"

"Yes?"

"No, I mean—you can feel exactly what I'm doing?"

"Yes? Is this uncommon?"

"I've never healed someone like you before."

Starrante stilled. He had not attempted to move away from Kaylin's hands for the duration of their conversation—but even the movement of breath paused. He might have been made of warm stone.

It has happened, then, he said. She knew it was Starrante she heard, but his voice was free of the verbal tics that made listening to it difficult. *You have not seen my...kind...before?*

She didn't answer. He was able to hear her thoughts because the healing magic was a bridge. It was why the Barrani refused healing when given the option. A brief image of Shadows, of shadow, of creatures very like Starrante, flipped open in the filing cabinet of her mind.

We were not a numerous people, he said. *Ravellon was our home. I had some interest in the world beyond our nesting grounds, beyond our duties, and after some study, I came here.*

She didn't ask him how—or why—he'd become an Arbiter. She asked nothing. Not with words.

I have, or had, kin in the heart of Ravellon. I do not know if they now exist as they once were—but we were useful; we could spin webs that existed in many states simultaneously, as you yourself are doing.

"I'm not."

Perhaps you are unaware of it. It matters little. I can feel someone familiar, but I cannot yet see him. I believe I can hear Kavallac. She is...hmmm. Furious? I would suggest you avoid the library for the time being.

"We'd like to get back to the library, if it's all the same to you. Do you think you can move?"

"Yes."

"Do you think you have enough control of your actions that you won't try to kill us?"

"Yes. Yes," he rumbled as he began to move the bulk of his body through the hole he'd created by destroying the door.

"My return to the Academia was…imperfect. But I heard you, Chosen, and I am awake now. I would like to know the name of the interim chancellor."

"You don't know?"

"No." Given the weight of the single syllable, Kaylin thought his ignorance was good for the continued health of that interim chancellor. Probably a pity for the rest of them, though.

"How were you awakened?" she asked. Bellusdeo's eyes were now an orange that looked almost mellow; Sedarias's eyes remained a martial blue. Starrante cleared what Kaylin assumed was his throat, and Bellusdeo stepped aside—or as far aside as the opposing wall would allow. He then took the lead.

"*Awakened* is an interesting word," he replied. By unspoken consent, Kaylin now walked by his side, her hand resting against his body as if it were a guide rail. "It is not entirely accurate, although you could be forgiven for using it. I was not awake. Not as I am now."

"You were dreaming?"

"That is a good analogy, although it is not entirely accurate, either. But let us use it. I was dreaming. Dreams are somewhat unpredictable."

"I'm surprised you need to sleep."

"Oh?"

"The Barrani and the Dragons don't."

"And you are one of the multitude of mortal races?"

She nodded. "I need sleep."

Starrante's head once again mostly separated from his body as he turned to look back at the Dragon and the Barrani. "Now I remember. But…if you do not sleep, how do you dream?"

Sedarias said, "Our dreams are more focused, more tangible."

"And less dangerous?"

"Perhaps. But danger is oft in the eye of the beholder."

"Well said. Are you perhaps a student here?"

"No. My classroom is less structured."

"A pity. It is seldom," he added, "that we converse with those who are not students. I cannot think of another time—"

"The interim chancellor is not a student."

"No. I believe," he continued, after a distinct pause, "that I was sleeping."

"Yes, but you weren't in the library."

"No."

"How did the interim chancellor even find you?"

"That is a very good question, but not one I can answer at the moment. How did you find me?" he asked of Kaylin.

"I was—until very recently—in the library. I found Arbiters Kavallac and Androsse; they're still there. We're...not. When you were last seen, you occupied the chancellor's office."

"Ah. I believe the intent was protection of that office from intruders; it is not clear to me why such protection was felt necessary."

"Whose intent?"

"The interim chancellor. In an emergency, the chancellor's office has authority to make and request changes."

"He could order you to guard his office without your conscious intent?"

"Demonstrably." The tone conveyed annoyance—that and the color of the eyes. "I believe I dreamed of the Chosen," he added as he ambled down the hall. "And possibly others. There was a student—quite young, by appearance—who appeared to have been skipping class. That is frowned upon here, unless one is given permission."

"He had permission."

"That could not be verified."

"Where are we going?" Sedarias asked.

"We cannot stay here to any great effect," Starrante replied. "We are therefore returning to the Academia. If you could, Chosen, I would ask you to wake Killianas—but Killianas is a subtle creation, and the waking is not entirely in your hands. As it is, I believe we will find answers of a kind in the chancellor's office itself."

"You're certain that you're in control of your actions now?"

"At this moment, yes."

"Will you remain in control if you enter that office again?"

"That is a very good question. There is only one way to find out, yes?"

Kaylin didn't appreciate that.

"You are clearly not a scientist."

"I like my head to remain more or less where it is in relation to the rest of my body, yes."

The door at the end of the hall opened to stairs; the stairs, familiar to Kaylin, led up into the body of the building in which Killian resided. She didn't ask Starrante how he'd bypassed the trap. By this point, she was pretty certain that Killian was awake enough that he'd let them out.

"How did the interim chancellor come into possession of that title?"

"It is not a title," Starrante said.

Are you still anywhere near the chancellor's office? Kaylin asked Severn as they walked. Starrante didn't seem to be in a great hurry, and given the speed at which he walked, this was all that allowed Kaylin to keep up once they'd crested the top of the stairs.

I believe so.

Robin?

He's still with me. Annarion is here, and Mandoran has joined us, as well.

Kaylin nodded. This meant Terrano remained in the library. *We're going to head to where you are.*

"We need to find an alternate route to the chancellor's office," Sedarias said.

Bellusdeo glanced at her.

"Mandoran says the halls are occupied with people who appear to be more martial in nature; they didn't catch him, but they're not letting anyone pass. Terrano believes they have the ability to interfere—no classes in this repetitive day take place on the route to the chancellor's office, and it is not yet mealtime."

"The day repeats?" Starrante asked Kaylin.

"Yes. Apparently it's been the same day of classes for... actually, I don't know how long it's been. But the day itself repeats. Today, for the first time, there's been a break in the pattern. Killian decided to give a lecture on the nature of True Words in the primal ether."

"An interesting choice of lecture, given the situation in which we find ourselves."

"I thought so." She hesitated, which didn't annoy Starrante—but did annoy Bellusdeo. "Do you know how to get to the chancellor's office from here?" She might as well have asked him if he knew how to breathe. "There are people in the halls who don't want anyone to approach that office—but my companions are waiting for us there."

"I believe I can deal with fractious students."

"Some of those fractious students started a firefight in the library."

Given the color of his eyes—a different color than the ones they'd taken so far, Starrante was outraged and offended. "In the *library*?" His voice was a very, very loud screech.

"Yes, sorry. I believe they want the Arbiters' books."

His eyes became larger and far more luminous—a shade of gold that was almost white. "That must not be allowed to happen."

"Kavallac and Androsse are certainly fighting to make sure it doesn't."

Starrante began to *move*. He could cover half a hall by the time Kaylin had taken two steps—two wide steps, given the length of her stride. Neither Bellusdeo nor Sedarias chose to run to keep pace with him; they fell in on either side of Kaylin.

"I think he's heading straight for the roadblock," Kaylin told them.

"We'll soon find out if all of Candallar's associates were aware of Starrante, then."

They followed in Starrante's wake. It became clear that Starrante had chosen to use the same halls that Robin had; Severn marked the turns as they progressed.

Mandoran says Sedarias is in a mood.

Yes. A bad one.

She could feel his brief chuckle. Before she could reply, she could hear the panicked shouts of people in the distance.

"I guess that answers that question: no, they weren't."

The distant language was mostly Barrani, but she recognized the word for Shadow: they made the same assumption that Kaylin would have made were it not for the Arkon. Starrante was, physically, a walking nightmare. She picked up her pace, breaking from a fast walk into a jog. All of the attention would be focused on Starrante.

"Dragon?" Bellusdeo asked as she caught up.

"Up to you. I think Starrante has—" The sound of steel against steel could be heard in the distance. Jog became run.

Starrante hadn't been carrying swords, and Kaylin was pretty sure swords were being used.

The main hall that had been cut off was a mass of bodies in motion. One of those bodies was Starrante. He was neither Dragon nor Barrani, with their immediate history of war; he was the thing that had forced pockets of peace upon both peoples at the height of their conflict.

Shadow.

Ravellon.

He was also apparently proof against the swords wielded by the mostly Barrani intruders; some of the humans had them, but most were standing back. Kaylin could feel the hair on her arms begin to rise as a precursor to cast magic; none of it caused by her companions.

Starrante didn't appear to be casting spells. He had lifted four of his eight legs and was using them to parry the swords wielded by his attackers—people who had formed a line across the width of the hall. It was a wide hall. The width allowed three people to stand and fight, but not safely, and not well.

She wondered what was happening in the library now that she was no longer in it; she couldn't speak to anyone she'd left behind. Sedarias could—unless Terrano had been blown out of the library by Candallar's command, but in an entirely different direction. Or dimension.

Stay there, Kaylin said when she felt Severn's decision to come down the hall from the other side, which would leave the effective equivalent of Barrani thugs trapped and fighting on two fronts.

Should I send Emmerian?

No—if Candallar retreats to that office, we want Emmerian with you. Can Robin get out a different way?

He's more than willing to try—we've been practically sitting on him. He wants to be helpful, he added.

Tell him helpful is staying where he is. No, wait. Don't. She hadn't been Robin, but she'd been his age—and he'd been pretty damn helpful already.

Can you contact Killian? He had Starrante removed from the chancellor's doorway because conflict—deadly conflict—involving members of the Academia is strictly forbidden.

I would—but I don't think he'll distinguish between Starrante as he was and Starrante as he is, and I think we want to get Starrante to the office somehow.

Severn, possessed of the same facts as Kaylin, nodded in the distance.

Sedarias and Bellusdeo had caught up with Starrante by this point, but Starrante had taken most of the hall's width as his personal fighting position, and it left little room for Sedarias unless she wanted to leap over the heads of the people who had been ordered to secure the hallway and keep visitors from going any farther.

The halls were tall enough that Sedarias could—with some magical aid—clear the heads of Candallar's gathered guards; she was less certain to clear their swords if they noticed, and she'd land as a force of one on the other side. Unless she had no intention of fighting, in which case she might be able to run toward Annarion, Severn and Emmerian.

Bellusdeo didn't consider the height of the halls suitable for flight but seemed content to observe the third Arbiter as he muscled his way through the roadblock. She took position behind his left side, and Sedarias stepped in line with the Dragon to cover his right. Kaylin saw why.

The Barrani to the left and right of Starrante, pressed into the walls and parrying the Arbiter's blows, would be left behind; they might be able to attack Starrante from the flanks more successfully than they had from the front. This didn't seem to concern the Arbiter.

It should have concerned the Barrani more than it had, because annoyed Dragon—Bellusdeo—or annoyed Sedarias was probably more deadly than Starrante; they just weren't as instantly viscerally terrifying.

Nightshade.

He was both annoyed and amused.

You said Killian had finished his lecture. Is he still there?

He is quizzing us.

What, without any time for study? Shut up, Kaylin. *Sorry—whatever he did to Starrante, I need him to do to Candallar's thugs.*

Why? I do not see any cause for concern in the current interaction.

No, he wouldn't. *They'll die. All of them will die. I think Starrante would leave them behind but*—she was interrupted by a scream of pain as fire enwrapped a sword arm—*Bellusdeo and Sedarias won't. If he can send them to their figurative rooms*—

Killian glared at her. "I begin to understand why so many of your companions find you so trying. I do not believe this fracas involves any of my students, and the Arbiter's role is a more independent one. I fail to understand why you are concerned with these intruders—they would not be at all concerned were you or your companions to die in these halls."

"Because I could have been one of them, years ago and in a slightly different life."

"I fail to see the significance."

"I learned things I didn't know between then and now. I believed that I could live a different life—but I had to be *alive* to do that."

Nightshade's amusement deepened, probably because Kaylin's frustration had. But the frustration was irrelevant to Killian, and the attackers weren't irrelevant enough to Bellusdeo and Sedarias. Both of the Barrani that Starrante had already shunted to the sides were bleeding on the floor; one might survive, but the other wouldn't make it.

The Barrani at the back of this ten-person group—now eight people—took stock of the situation in front of their eyes, and began to back up or to look for side routes down which they might escape. Solidarity of purpose vanished as the immediate desire to survive took over.

Starrante didn't seem concerned with those who fled; Bellusdeo and Sedarias appeared to consider pursuit. But Starrante's movement through the hall was, attackers notwithstanding, a rush of motion, and in the end, they chose to abandon pursuit of enemies in favor of the Arbiter.

The combat had slowed him enough that they were starting from the same place again, and this time, when the blockage cleared, they moved far more quickly to keep up. So did Kaylin. The odd, awkward gait that had characterized Starrante in Severn's eyes was gone; he moved gracefully and swiftly— very like the spider that he appeared to be. He knew exactly where he was going.

Severn knew it, too—Severn had always had a much better eye for geography, and a much better memory for it.

Starrante climbed a wall, skipping two squares of the hall; Sedarias leaped above them. Bellusdeo grabbed Kaylin and did the same. No one asked why; they attempted, with two normal legs, to follow a path that eight made far easier. Kaylin felt a painful slap across her skin as Bellusdeo cleared those squares. Starrante had clearly seen whatever lay across the floor.

Bellusdeo—and probably Sedarias—could; Kaylin could. But detecting magical traps and dangers took time. It was time Starrante didn't have to expend.

Regardless, that corner was the last corner; she could see, if not the chancellor's office, her companions. Emmerian stepped up, passing Annarion, as Starrante approached. Kaylin didn't blame him; Starrante was definitely in the lead, even if both Bellusdeo and Sedarias were running to catch up. It probably wasn't clear whether or not they were in pursuit because he was a danger or an enemy was escaping.

But no, that wasn't true. Emmerian's gaze hit Bellusdeo, and he immediately stood down—figuratively speaking. He could see the gold Dragon's eyes. They had been orange, but it wasn't the orange that could threaten red at any time. She was not afraid of Starrante.

Bellusdeo set Kaylin on two feet. Kaylin scurried past Starrante, who had stopped in the hall, his front two legs weaving in the air as if they were weapons. Which, practically speaking, they were. Annarion's sword was raised, but he didn't step in to attack. Of course not. He'd be aware of anything Sedarias was aware of. His take, on the other hand, was always his own—it was amazing, on some days, that the cohort could get anything done, they spent so much time arguing among themselves.

Kaylin pushed herself to stand in front of Starrante, and as she did he lowered his limbs. "Arbiter Starrante, you might have encountered these people earlier—they're our friends and allies. This is Corporal Severn Handred. This is Lord Emmerian—"

"Lord?"

"Emmerian is one of five Dragon Lords. The Imperial Court—the Empire of the country in which the Towers stand—is composed of Dragons."

"And not Barrani?"

"It's complicated. But the wars between the two—Barrani and Dragon—are over. They are in the past, and we intend to keep it that way."

"In my day," Starrante said, "Dragons were introduced by the name of their flights."

"Yes, well. It's been a long time since your day, and none of the rest of us were around for it. Well, almost none of the rest of us."

"Very well." Starrante opened his mouth and roared.

Bellusdeo startled, and then looked to the side—Starrante's body was, given the position of his hind legs, almost even with her head. She then grinned at Kaylin, her eyes as light as they had been since they'd set foot in the Academia, and responded in kind.

Emmerian's manners had always been flawless; he did so, as well. The stone hall proved to be acoustically perfect—if one *wanted* to amplify the sound of native Dragon. Apparently, Draconian greetings were long-winded affairs, and Kaylin's ears were ringing by the time everyone was satisfied that they'd done a good enough job.

She did manage not to cover her ears.

"…This is Annarion An'Solanace. And behind them is Robin, one of Killian's most promising students."

"I see. I would dearly love the opportunity to spend time with someone Killianas considered promising, but that will have to wait. Gentlemen, if you would step aside from the doorway, I believe we need to enter the chancellor's office."

"Kaylin," Annarion said, "I think we might have a problem."

"What's happened in the library?"

"It's hard to pick it out—Terrano's still there, but…there's interference."

Starrante said, "Come to me *right now.*" Emmerian turned, picked up a terrified Robin and made haste to obey; Severn and Annarion were on the move before the last syllable had stopped resonating in the ceiling above.

Something like mist crept out of the chancellor's open doors—mist with glittering shards enfolded in its gray, cloudy form.

CHAPTER
27

The mist encircled Starrante. It didn't touch him—and it didn't touch anyone who had made their way to the umbrella of his direct surroundings. The Arbiter cursed in a language that seemed to be composed of rapid clicks instead of the usual syllables. Kaylin wasn't certain she could repeat it, but she recognized useful street language when she heard it.

The Arbiter heaved a rattling, terrible sigh. Kaylin would have worried about the state of his lungs if he were any of the races with which she was familiar—and she dropped a hand to the side of his body instinctively. There was, however, nothing wrong with his body if one accepted its base state.

"This reminds me of my distant youth, before I was out of the web," Starrante said.

"Did all of your siblings get out of the web?"

"No, of course not. We were little, unlearned savages; things like self-control were won only if we survived."

Please don't tell me you ate your siblings. She kept this to herself, largely because Robin was already glassy-eyed and terrified of a giant talking spider.

"But this is very carefully wrought, this work. I would

suggest those of you who have little experience with arcane displacement avoid it."

"Arcane displacement? You mean like portals?"

"Ah, yes. The problem with this particular variant of a much more benign spell is that different parts of you will end up in different places. This does not generally work out well for those of us who were born to this plane. Ah, apologies, to the plane from which you came."

"Can you get rid of it?"

"With some effort—effort attained by lack of interruption."

"Then the answer," Sedarias said, "is no—because an interruption is incoming." She remained in the invisible circle Starrante had drawn, but stood at the part of its circumference that was closest to the open office doors, her sword ready.

The incoming interruption was Candallar—Candallar, an Arcanist, and the human Caste Court lord. Lord Baltrin. Kaylin wondered when he'd returned to the Academia, and wondered whether or not he was a mage.

The Arcanist's tiara was bathed in a livid red; the gem was pulsing steadily, as if it were a living, exposed heart. The light of it was almost hypnotic, and Kaylin looked away, remembering Nightshade's warning. Avoid Lord Illanen, of both the High Court and the Arcanum, the latter blindingly obvious at the moment.

"He's dangerous," Kaylin told Starrante softly.

"They are *all* dangerous."

"One is mortal," Sedarias then said.

"So, too, is this Chosen. Mortality does not preclude power; it precludes the gaining of wisdom and knowledge— but even then, mortal minds move quickly because they have no choice. And magic, like fashion, changes; knowledge that I have not personally accrued can alter all arcane landscapes and combats." Starrante's smile—and he was smiling as he turned, briefly, to look at Kaylin—was terrifying. It looked like a gaping void, with frills like teeth around its edge.

It took effort to remember that he was an ally, but she made the effort, because in the near distance, Illanen had withdrawn something from the folds of his voluminous Arcanist robes. It was a book. Kaylin couldn't see the cover, and even if she had, the entirety of the book was colored by the light of the gem in his tiara.

She thought red was fire affinity, but had never asked. Fire, on the other hand, would not harm at least two of the people now facing the Arcanist. Severn had his weapon chain unwound, but there was no room to rotate the chain at full length—not when he was surrounded by spider body, legs, and the rest of his companions.

Kaylin caught Robin by the shoulder and pulled him close. "The spider," she whispered in his ear, "is on our side."

His nod went on for too long, and she wondered what his odds of leaving safely now were. Kaylin could feel the Arcanist's magic across the entirety of her body—even defended, as she was, by Starrante's invisible barrier.

She wanted her familiar or her familiar's wings.

Nightshade!

I am here. Killian's test is in progress.

Good. Tell Killian that Robin is—is lost in the halls.

Silence.

Tell him he's missing the test!

She felt the wall of his refusal without the need for words. Words did follow. *Think. There is* one *student with you. Only* one. *Some of Killian's ability to interfere relies on the student body. If—as you suspect—Killian can somehow remove Robin and return him to the class, you will have no legitimate students by your side. I have not been granted permission to leave the room, and it is highly unlikely I would be granted that permission should I ask during a test. It is,* he added, *only partly written; the rest is oral, and Killian is making his way through the classroom as we speak.*

But Robin—

I understand your fear. And he didn't share it. *But if your safety, the safety of Bellusdeo, and the safety of my brother depend on one mortal boy, the possibility of his death is a necessary risk.*

Had she expected a different answer?

"What is that book?" someone demanded. Kaylin turned toward Sedarias, because only Sedarias would demand answers from Starrante in the current situation.

"Very good," the spider said. "I believe I understand some of the difficulties the would-be interim chancellor now faces."

Lord Baltrin did not carry a book, and he did not wear a tiara; he did, however, carry a staff. It was Kaylin's height, but slender and straight—a thing of wood and gold. Sanabalis would have heaped ridicule on the necessity of it, had he been here.

The interim chancellor in question stood between the Barrani Arcanist and the human Caste Court lord. His eyes, at this distance, were black. The medallion on his chest was gold, if gold were somehow lurid; the rod he carried in his left hand was now the same color.

"Any problem he faces would help us," Sedarias said.

"Yes, perhaps. But he carries only two of the three significant objects he requires to assert better control over the Academia."

"And the third?"

"The young man with the ugly crown."

"The book?"

"The book. Killian is not fully awake, and because he is not, the interim chancellor's power is muted. We would be facing a much harder fight were he more aware."

"Us? Why us?"

"Because the interim chancellor's authority would carry far more weight. Even were he to be more awake now, the authority is split in a fashion that it is seldom split. We have had interim chancellors in our history, but they are an emergency measure. They are not chosen with care—care is seldom exercised in an emergency—and they make their presence known by the three insignias. Without them, Killian is unlikely to hear either their requests or their commands."

"And Candallar only has two."

"Yes. It would appear so."

"They can hear you, you know," Sedarias then said.

"Ah, no, they cannot, unless their ears are a reconfigured version of the ones they were born with. And in my opinion," the Arbiter continued, "if they could hear it would be to our advantage. It is not possible that your Candallar did not understand that the three separate items were necessary—which implies heavily that there is a lack of trust or cohesion among his council."

The ground beneath their feet shook—but it wasn't the ground that was the problem; Kaylin saw this perhaps seconds before the Arcanist gestured at the ceiling. The ceiling came down in large stone chunks.

Starrante turned a clicking motion into a roar of sound and the chunks of rock dissipated, as if they were illusion or fog.

"If we close with them, they'd be more careful about what they drop." This was Bellusdeo. Chunks of falling ceiling were unlikely to kill her in either of her two forms. Before Starrante could answer, she exhaled a plume of fire in a much wider cone than the size of her current mouth should have made possible.

It melted rock.

It didn't touch the chancellor or his companions, although

Lord Baltrin blinked rapidly as it passed them by. In spite of himself, Robin's fear diminished. "She's a Dragon!"

"She is. Her name is Bellusdeo. When she transforms, she's the color of the armor she's wearing now."

Purple fire raced down the hall in response to Dragon fire, but with as much effect. No, Kaylin thought, that wasn't true. It left a pale, opalescent wash across the stone floor, colors glittering there like shards of glass. This time, Starrante cursed in his clicking, toothy tongue.

He lifted his face toward what remained of the ceiling, and when he exhaled, a stream of sticky white took root; he caught it with his front legs—four of them—and began to tease it into threads. While he did, Bellusdeo once again took aim at the chancellor's party, and this time, Emmerian did the same; the former aimed directly at the floor beneath their feet, and the latter, at the ceiling above their heads.

The flames obscured normal vision—in both directions. Starrante, however, didn't appear to notice. He was, as his form suggested he might, building a web. This web was like a spider's web to begin with—but the strands and their configuration seemed somehow more mathematical, more precise. Robin, in Kaylin's shadow, drew his fascinated gaze from the fire to the web itself, as if compelled.

His eyes narrowed as his chin rose; the whole of his neck was revealed as Starrante's web began to spread.

"I've—I've seen this," Robin whispered.

"You've seen this web?"

He shook his head as if the web itself were irrelevant. "That." He pointed at one section of the web—the section almost directly in front of Starrante, rather than overhead. "That pattern. That one there. I've seen it before. Look—it's repeating."

"What is he doing?" Kaylin asked, bending as the fire

cleared and the fire resumed. "What are the patterns meant to do?"

But Robin barely heard her. His gaze drifted from the webbing being constructed, up the limbs that were constructing it, and to the eyes of Starrante himself, because Starrante was looking at Robin, not the pattern he was creating. "What do you see?"

"You're walking a pattern," Robin replied with vastly less fear than he had shown moments before. "You're walking a pattern with your limbs. Are you *Wevaren*?"

"Yes. That is not what we call ourselves, but yes, that is what I am."

The Dragon fire was answered by purple flame—but this flame glistened, and it moved like a wave, not a cone. It was darker in color than the purple fire Kaylin had seen used before, and something about it set her teeth on edge.

"Don't let it touch you!" Kaylin shouted, mostly at Bellusdeo, who stood at the outer rim of Starrante's protections.

"You think?" the Dragon replied in annoyed Elantran.

Robin's gaze moved, briefly, to this new wall of ugly flame, this new wave. Kaylin could see that the opalescence was stronger here. She had always considered this type of glittering, ugly color to be a thing of Shadow, a property of the Shadows—but she knew that was wrong; Hope's eyes sometimes glittered in the same way.

"No," Robin said, looking at what now approached them like a wall of death, all sight of the three behind it obscured. "I think—I don't think that's the pattern you want."

Starrante's eyes didn't seem possessed of lids, but they widened at the effrontery of Robin.

"Master Larrantin said that that was the way it was done a long time ago—but he said there were other, more efficient patterns that had been developed since." His Barrani was astonishingly good, given his age and the area he'd called home before his disappearance.

"Larrantin?" Starrante did not spit but might have had he a normal mouth and the usual saliva. "And what, exactly, would you suggest?"

"Can I touch it?"

"Boy—"

"No!" The two words collided.

Robin nodded. He was frustrated; there was no way to draw what he wanted to draw, and he clearly did, because his hands were moving almost as if he held a quill. Those hands, she now saw, were ink-stained, the nails chipped. "That line," he said, shouting to be heard over the roar of two Dragons. Their breath could keep the purple fire at bay, but it was a losing battle; they slowed its advance but did not destroy it.

"This one."

"It's—you've created five diamonds, repeating—but you don't need five."

"You have no idea what path is being traced."

"I *do*. I know what path you're tracing—Larrantin said it's an important pathway."

"Larrantin thinks his *hair* is important on a bad day."

"Move that line and that one. Shorten them. In the center, the shape should be different."

"Different?"

Robin nodded. He could speak High Barrani, but communicating what he could see on the inside of his head was almost beyond him. Starrante, however, studied the pattern for a long beat while fire approached. He did not call a retreat; he didn't appear to notice the fire itself.

"I understand," he finally said, "why Killian considered you promising. Very well. Let us walk a different pattern.

You wish the center to be more curved, then—the diamonds less exact?"

"Not less exact, just less diamond-shaped. Master Larrantin said if the structure is looser it flows as one would expect."

"I will have a word with Larrantin later. You seem young to be so advanced in your studies." His limbs moved as his mouth did.

Robin said, "The shiny bits in the purple stuff match the patterns better. You're trying to collect them, right?"

Kaylin was almost dumbfounded.

"I am. Now hush; this takes concentration."

And spinning the complicated web didn't. Kaylin had never heard of Starrante's race, but clearly Robin had—and he had done so in the Academia. For one moment, while Starrante's entire body tensed, she wondered what else she might learn if she were a student here. Whatever it was, it seemed vastly more valuable than etiquette.

The fire hit the web directly in front of Starrante—and everyone else, for that matter. Both of the Dragons took a measured, deliberate step back, retreating into the space between two of Starrante's legs.

As the wall of flame hit the web, it stuck there, struggling to push forward. Kaylin flinched, half expecting the fire to break through the holes circumscribed by strands of web. It didn't. It seemed to travel along those strands, lighting the web, and darkening it, as well.

But if the fire that contained opalescence spread, the glittering bits didn't. And as Kaylin looked at them—really looked at them, studying them as if she were Robin—she could see them not as scintillating, ugly colors, but as windows.

Small windows, opening to landscapes of blue, dark blue, green; of red and orange, of the white of terrible blizzard and the white-gray of fog.

Starrante had said that these were like small shards of portals, and she understood now. None of these shards, none of these spinning splinters of moving color, were large enough to fit through. But they were large enough individually to take her body apart if she stood in one place while they advanced.

"If Terrano taught them this, I'm going to kill him," she heard herself saying.

"Terrano did not teach them this." Sedarias, eyes midnight blue, watched the web, her glance flitting to the Dragons and back.

The pieces of color were caught between strands and held fast there. She could almost feel them click into place, as if the web itself were the frame into which colored glass might be fit. But all of those pieces still opened into disparate spaces—spaces she could see much more clearly now that they weren't in motion.

Robin was practically vibrating in place, excitement and fear mingling. He counted as pieces were caught by the web and locked in place; the whole of the slowly growing window shuddered violently each time it happened.

"Be ready," Starrante told them.

Clink. Clink. Clink. The sounds grew louder as the web retained the pieces; the pieces themselves began to shimmer with a gray, almost reflected light—probably Starrante's body. The lower corners of the web and the upper corners on both sides caught pieces, as well—smaller shards that did not fit precisely, but were being kept at bay. Kaylin's skin felt normal now; whatever magic was being done was not the magic that caused agony when it was cast.

But it was magic, and when the last of the pieces—or the last of the useful pieces—fell into place in the center of the web, there was a loud, shattering sound—a sound that was the exact opposite of what she would have expected, given what her eyes could see. The strands of webbing between the disparate pieces shivered in place, the motion itself like the refrain of a familiar, wordless song. Starrante's clicking seemed to keep a beat, a rhythm, as those strands vanished and left, in their place, a single plate of what might have been glass.

"Now!" Starrante barked, his voice as loud as a Dragon's. And speaking thus, he swept Robin and Kaylin into that glass plate.

It wasn't glass.

They passed through it, as Starrante had no doubt intended. So, too, did the rest of their companions, their feet hitting stone, their eyes bouncing off darkness. It was dark here.

It wasn't quiet.

"Do not touch *anything*," Starrante said, his voice a rumble of thunder as he made his way through a pane that was almost too small to contain him.

"Where are we?" Bellusdeo demanded—just before Sedarias could.

It was Kaylin who answered. "We're in the library."

On the other side of a portal that had not closed was a hallway. It was familiar, and the gaping hole left by falling roof framed the top edge of the portal.

"Can you close the portal?" Emmerian asked. Kaylin was surprised by this because he seldom spoke in larger gatherings.

"With effort that I do not choose to expend, yes."

"They can follow us."

Starrante's grin was, again, disturbing. The portal shed light—probably the light of the hallway—which caused his fangs to glint in the darkness. And he did have fangs. "One can only hope. Ah, this is much, much better." His head rose on the stick-like neck he could contract to invisibility. His eyes were red.

"What are they *doing*?" His feet shifted direction, even if the rest of his body remained fixed in place.

Kaylin was viscerally relieved not to be part of that *they*. His neck seemed to extend forever as he lifted his head; outrage seemed to cause this buoyancy. The library wasn't silent, but the sounds that she could hear were muddied, almost unidentifiable—as if there were crowds of people in every direction, engaged in...something.

"You're certain this is the library?"

Starrante failed to answer.

Bellusdeo, however, did. Sort of. She spoke a word—a sharp word that caused Kaylin to flinch—and light flooded the area. Starrante had been right: this was the library. But it was the library in pieces. Not collapsed and not damaged—but disjointed, as if seen through a broken mirror.

No one moved; Sedarias seemed to be examining the floor. As it was the floor across which they'd otherwise be moving, Kaylin did the same. But even the floor, like the shelving and the hint of distant wall, was cracked and disconnected. It wasn't like the bits of portals that were certain death; it was different. This *was* the library—but Kaylin didn't like their odds of surviving should they attempt to move across it.

Starrante didn't like those odds either, because the only thing that moved now was his head. And his mouth.

"What have they done?" he finally asked, apparently of no one.

"I believe they attempted—or Candallar attempted—to break the power of the Arbiters within this space." It was Sedarias who answered.

Kaylin swallowed. "Where is the Arkon?" she asked.

"He is with Terrano," Sedarias replied. "I can't say he's

happy to be there, but they are both alive. Terrano advises us to move very, very carefully if we're going to move at all."

"Speak in a language I understand," Starrante then said—in Barrani.

"My apologies, Arbiter. We have been advised not to attempt to traverse the library floor—by which I assume he means that we are not to move. The Arkon and Terrano are currently standing on a patch of floor very like the one we occupy now."

"And the other Arbiters?" Kaylin asked—also in Barrani.

"Terrano is uncertain. Mandoran attempted to keep them in one location but believes that Kavallac might have been injured in the fracturing. There is one bit of welcome news, however. Candallar's erstwhile allies in the library did not survive the attempt to disempower the Arbiters, and the Arkon has not once set the three books he carried aside."

"That's two bits," Robin said.

"The library," Starrante said, "is the heart of the Academia."

"I thought it was the students. The people," Kaylin amended, when Starrante's head swiveled in her direction.

"If you insist on being pedantic, call them the brains of the Academia. But the library is its heart. It has been damaged," he added, although this was unnecessary. "But the space is not yet broken."

"I am not at all certain that Illanen will be pleased by this turn of events." It was Sedarias who spoke, her voice laced with grim humor.

He will certainly not be, Nightshade said.

Kaylin caught—and held—the threads of his internal voice; they were muted and almost distant. *How is Killian?*

He has dismissed the class, Nightshade replied.

Did he finish his test?

No. The dismissal was not, in my opinion, planned. He is no longer in the classroom. Robin is with you?

Yes. Robin, Sedarias, your brother, Severn and the Dragons. Can Starrante fix what was broken?

I am not the person of whom you should ask that question, Nightshade replied. It sounded a lot like no. *But the day's schedule appears to have resumed; we are expected at our next class.*

"Arbiter," Kaylin said, remembering at the last moment to inject respect into her urgency. "Can you repair the damage to this space?"

"I am attempting to do so—I cannot assess the full extent of the damage unless we move. And we will move—but you will all have to be mindful of where you step, and how. I will repair the space beneath and around us as we move—but you will lose limbs—or worse—if you do not observe carefully where you place those limbs.

"This was not well done, on the part of the chancellor. It is clear to me that he does not understand what the library is; clear, as well, that his understanding of Killianas is flawed in the extreme. If his companions have a better understanding, they were not willing to share it."

Kaylin doubted they did—but regardless, neither had been present when Candallar had attempted to divest the Arbiters of power.

"I don't understand," she admitted.

"A good first step in the gaining of knowledge," Starrante replied. He coughed up a large blob of glistening white; it hung suspended in the air in front of his space. "Robin," he said.

Kaylin blinked.

"Larrantin clearly had much to say about paths that could be woven and walked."

"Yes, sir."

"Did he speak about cohesion?"

Robin's yes was slightly more hesitant.

"Very well. If you could stand here—between the front legs, beneath my head—I would have you watch what I am about to do. You may interrupt at will, until I am finished.

"I apologize," Starrante added. "But it is the safest place for you to stand. You have a value to Killianas that the rest of the people present lack, and it is important, now, that you be preserved, even if they cannot be."

Robin glanced over his shoulder at the Dragons, at the Barrani, and at the Hawks. He was both worried for them and pleased for himself; in such company as this, he'd probably never thought to considered valuable at all.

"My apologies, Chosen. Unless Robin interrupts you, you may tell me what it is, exactly, you do not understand."

"I was in the library before the chancellor tossed us out. He threw us into the halls in which we first met you."

"Yes?"

"Before he did, I saw the Arbiters in action."

"I imagine so, given everything done here. What is it that you fail to understand?"

"They were using skills and weapons that…we would use. Dragon breath, claws, teeth; magic." Before Starrante could tell her to get to the point, she said, "There was nothing about their power that seemed to come from the outside. Kavallac was no match for Bellusdeo, in my assessment."

"Your assessment is in error." He spit out more white goo. Robin tensed, but didn't move. Starrante then began to weave with it—but the weave was not a web that crossed the space in front of him, at least not yet; it was web that he stretched along the obvious cracks in the floor. "Forgive the incomplete reply. Your assessment, were you all to be situated outside of the library itself, might be factually correct.

"The power of the Arbiters in this space, however, is two-fold. The Arbiters may use the full force of their powers and abilities without causing harm to anything that belongs within the library, and the Arbiters are capable of closing the space to all, save the chancellor."

"The interim chancellor counts?"

"Apparently so, although I would have argued against it. Understand that none of the three of us have seen the Academia in its riven state; what we know—and know well—is the Academia when it is fully functional. Things have broken; they are woefully chaotic. I am almost surprised that an interim chancellor could even be acknowledged."

"Killian said—when we first met him—that the building had no master, no lord."

"He was inexact, in my opinion."

Robin lifted a hand. "I think you missed a bit."

Starrante broke off, extended his neck in the direction to which Robin now pointed out. "My eyes," he said to the young man, "are not what they used to be. You are correct."

"It's only a small bit," Robin offered, almost apologetic.

"And a single eye is only a small bit as well, when measured against the rest. Is there anything else you have noticed?"

"Larrantin said that dimensional spaces have weight and gravity—but not like our classroom did."

Starrante's nod was impatient.

"But he said that in our school, that weight and gravity were far more important, because, hmmm, we lack the regular kind. So maybe you can fix this, but it's not..." He trailed off.

"It is not anchored, as it once was, in the reality of the Academia—because the Academia is, itself, unanchored now."

"That's not quite what he said," Robin replied. "I—

Larrantin was a bit weird. I mean, *all* of the teachers were a bit weird, but Larrantin was the worst."

"How so? Not that I disagree with you; he could be remarkably lazy and irresponsible on the best of days."

"He sometimes faded. I mean, in the middle of a lecture or the middle of a sentence, he'd turn into a ghost. But…it was the ghost bits that seemed to make the most sense. When he was ghostly, his lessons were different. When he wasn't, they were the same. Things don't change a lot from day to day in the classes—it's only today that we got an entirely new one. And I missed some of it," he added with what sounded to Kaylin like genuine regret.

"But Larrantin taught different things, some of the time. I listened to the new stuff because…it was new."

How long had he been here now? Bellusdeo had recognized him from a missing persons report in Records, but Kaylin couldn't recall the length of time for which he'd been missing. And even if she had, she wasn't at all certain that the days here matched the days outside, in the world from which Robin had come.

"I think we might progress," Starrante said. In the distance, reverberating, he could hear the roar of a Dragon; he lifted his head, opened his mouth and responded in kind.

The silence that followed was full of echoes and rumbles. Robin nodded.

"I hate to interrupt a necessary discussion," Sedarias then said, "but could you possibly close the portal behind us?"

"Not with ease. They will find it difficult to pass through it," Starrante added.

"Not difficult enough."

Kaylin turned toward the portal through which they'd arrived. She could see Candallar, flanked by Barrani Arcanist and human lord; his hands were turned, palm out, toward them, and something was writhing its way from the mounds of those palms through the portal itself.

CHAPTER 28

Severn stepped back; Bellusdeo caught him by the shoulder. "Not here," she said.

He nodded and allowed the Dragon to breathe. Emmerian stood between the Hawk and the former queen, watching; Kaylin could see his back, but not the color of his eyes.

"That is an interesting weapon," Starrante said as he worked. "I will ask you to use it with care here until we are more firmly established. Kavallac understands what has happened; the current stability of the library is due in large part to Androsse's efforts. Kavallac was flexible in some ways, but...she disliked shifts in dimensions unless it was absolutely necessary."

While he spoke, tendrils of purple and gray pierced the portal at his back. Kaylin realized that Candallar's palms were pushing against it; Starrante had been right. They couldn't gain access easily. Not the normal way.

Fire did not burn those tendrils, although both Dragons made a serious effort; Kaylin could have cooked food from where she was standing if the heat of those flames continued. It was Sedarias who grimaced and headed toward the portal.

Annarion said, "Not you." He grabbed her by the arm;

given her expression, Kaylin wouldn't have dared. She doubted Terrano would have either, if he'd been present.

"What are you going to do?" Kaylin, caught at the side of Starrante, couldn't easily navigate through the cage he'd made of his legs. She tried, and they tightened.

"It is not for you, Chosen," he said softly. "The two who are arguing now might succeed."

"Succeed?"

"You cannot see the shadows they cast," he said without turning his head to face her. "I can. They remind me of my infant kin in the days at the dawn of time: they have their feet in many places at once, and with care, they might survive in all of them."

"And me?"

"You are not what they are." He raised his head. "But if I am allowed a vote, I would suggest that you allow Annarion An'Solanace to attempt to displace that magic."

"And not Sedarias An'Mellarionne?" Sedarias demanded.

"No. Remain as anchor to the young man. It is my belief that you are more tenacious; what you claim, you will not let go of while you breathe. And if I do not understand them precisely, I see the webs and strands that bind you, each to the other."

Kaylin didn't know—would probably never know—what Starrante perceived. She didn't see webs and strands; she knew that they shared True Names, but that wasn't visible, either. But she thought he was right: Sedarias would be the best anchor anyone in the cohort had if they were tossed at sea.

Annarion didn't draw his sword; he sheathed it. He displaced Bellusdeo, not Emmerian, and Bellusdeo gave him her spot at this small front, with a whisper that didn't reach Kaylin's ears. It did, apparently, reach Emmerian's and Sedarias's, judging by their reactions.

They didn't respond. Before they could, Annarion reached out and grabbed the tendrils.

Caught between Starrante's iron legs, Kaylin watched as Annarion dissolved. She felt Nightshade's fear, but it vanished as he severed most of their already tenuous link; there were some things Barrani Lords did not share with anyone, and fear was probably at the head of the long list. He had not argued, had not attempted to make an argument through Kaylin; he had, as Kaylin had, remained silent.

Had Annarion been her baby brother, she wasn't sure she could have done the same.

"Arbiter," Sedarias said, the force of her voice denying the inherent politeness in using the title, "speed is now of the essence."

Starrante understood. His chatter, such as it was, vanished as Annarion did. The only time he spoke, he spoke to Robin, and Robin's replies were brief and muted.

They began to move.

Candallar's palms were pressed flat against the portal, his mouth open, his eyes slits. Kaylin could see the upper edge of the portal waver, as if it were liquid; it didn't break, but the undulations expanded. She had no idea if this would grant Candallar access to the library or not.

She turned to look ahead, rather than behind at the portal, squinting into the darkness with its flashes of moving light. Around Starrante, the library could be clearly seen. The ceiling above their heads was cracked, as the floor beneath their feet was; Starrante made no effort to change what lay above. Instead, his forelegs moved at almost blinding speed, interrupted only by the coughing spit of globs of web. Some of those hung in the air, as if they'd hit invisible walls; some traveled ahead and landed on floor. It was in the direction of the floored webbing that he appeared to be working.

There was a method to his madness, a reason for his rush. It came into view as illumination followed his path, clinging to it rather than moving with him and leaving darkness in his wake. Ahead of Starrante and to the left, she could make out the form of a Dragon. It crossed three broken panes, its wings across them bent at odd angles, its central body preserved.

"She is Arbiter," Starrante said before Kaylin could speak. "Even broken, this is her space. She is injured, and there is a danger—but Androsse was not caught in the same way."

"And he's helping."

"We are a trinity, Chosen. If one falls, we will dwindle, and what we protect will be lost. We are not, perhaps, friends or kin; we are comrades, and our duties are the common ground that binds us." He roared.

Kavallac roared back—and Bellusdeo snickered; Emmerian winced.

"Clearly she is still healthy," Starrante said in Barrani.

Kaylin couldn't hear the Arkon in the distance. Sedarias had said Terrano was with him; she hoped Hope was with him as well, but didn't ask. She looked back for any sign of the reappearance of Annarion.

Someone else stepped onto the path, but not through the portal. He was pale; the whole of his body seemed haloed in a gentle light.

It was Androsse. "If you could hurry," he said, "we might preserve *some* of our hearing." His eyes were Barrani blue, but lacking whites, and his hair had lost all color; it was a thing of light, a cape that moved in a breeze that, as usual, touched nothing else. "I will aid the child; this is more than he can accomplish on his own. Had he more time, I might be content to watch his progress."

"Be wary—the interstices here are more fragile; they are wild, almost primal."

"Ah. I would not have noticed that myself," Androsse replied, demonstrating that Ancestors, with all their supposed power and gravitas, still understood the weight of sarcasm. He walked, tracing Starrante's path, toward the portal and the threats contained on the other side.

"I would appreciate it," he said without looking back, "if you could mend the difficulties soon. I have some desire to have words with the children who have dared to invade my space." As he spoke, he began to fade, just as Annarion had done; the shadow left in his wake was light in Barrani shape and form.

Starrante's repairs, such as they were, continued. Kaylin peered into the distance that Kavallac's shards implied. No Arkon there, and no Terrano. No familiar, either.

"There is a danger," Starrante said as he reached Kavallac's feet. "The repairs that are done here are a boon to any who enter the library—and with the *regalia* of interim chancellor, your enemies will be able to do so in some fashion. They made their way in the first time."

"Where did you wake?" Kaylin asked.

"I am not like the other Arbiters; some essential part of my nature allows an existence that spans many spaces. They could not do the same for the others, or to the others." For a moment, his voice rumbled, the Barrani syllables oddly draconian in nature.

"Be ready."

"Androsse—"

"Yes. But Androsse is not chancellor. None of us can be now. Were it not for the presence of the children, I do not think I would have allowed it." By children, Kaylin thought he meant Annarion, as Robin remained with him. He spat a gob of thread, and this one had a faint tinge of pink to it. Kaylin immediately placed a palm against the bulk of his continually moving body.

"Yes," he said, although she hadn't asked, "there is a cost and a danger. But if we do not have Kavallac, we cannot repair the damage."

They didn't have Androsse at the moment, either, but Kaylin said nothing. Instead, she let her power hum through the Arbiter as if it were a song. It hadn't occurred to her—to any of them—to question his ability to do what he was now doing. He could clearly achieve it. But the cost? They hadn't questioned that, either.

Her power did now.

His legs stretched and stretched again, becoming oddly diffuse as they did. Robin's head followed the movement of those legs, his eyes darting between the strands that were now laid out. Even between the cracked pieces that contained or entrapped Kavallac, Kaylin could see the minutiae of pattern, of small geometries, the things he had identified as paths.

They shuddered in place as smoke and fire crept up from behind them.

Severn glanced once at the ceiling above his head and then unwound his chain. He'd shortened it by changing the center point he gripped—but Starrante had already said it was risky.

It wasn't likely to kill Severn; it could quite possibly destroy the weapon. But the chain, when spun, served as a magic-breaker. None of their enemies had condescended to draw actual swords. All of their attacks would be spells, and at least so far, those spells involved range. Starrante had proved very competent at shielding himself—and those in his immediate vicinity—from arcane attacks, but he was facing in the wrong direction.

They needed Kavallac. Kaylin focused on that. Severn was her partner; he'd heard everything she'd heard and if he had his own spin on it, he also understood what needed to be done.

Mostly, survive.

"Where's Annarion?" she shouted, as Sedarias readied herself, bending slightly at the knees.

"He's behind us and in front of the portal. They've breeched it, but they can't cross it yet. Androsse is doing something—" Sedarias broke off. Wordless, she leaped toward the portal, landing on a floor that, lit, was easily distinguished from places that weren't guaranteed to be safe.

She didn't disperse.

Bellusdeo moved, as well; Emmerian lifted a hand to touch her, and lowered it before he made contact.

"Warrior Queen," he said, his voice soft but audible.

Bellusdeo did not hear him, or if she did, didn't acknowledge the simple words.

Her hands shot forward, as if in a blindingly fast prayer; when her palms touched, she spread her hands wide and lightning flashed, with the Dragon as its center point. The lightning spread to the floor, surrounding Bellusdeo as she crackled.

Emmerian's hand was on Kaylin's shoulder before she could move. "You have your duties," he said. "And the lightning was Bellusdeo's. It was not an enemy's attack."

"I've never seen—"

"No—nor have I. The Arkon would have recognized it. Help the Arbiter. If it becomes necessary, I will stand beside Bellusdeo."

"But she—"

"She is precious to our kind, yes. But on fields of Shadow

and imminent loss, she has no equal. There is a reason she was queen."

Lightning-robed, Bellusdeo then walked toward Sedarias, and toward the portal that was no longer a flat pane of something glass-like. It was bulging now; from cracks that had not yet widened enough to allow passage, fog and smoke poured, the former falling to the ground, the latter rising to the ceiling.

Kaylin understood why Starrante had forbidden flight or shifts in shape when she saw that smoke—glittering smoke, of course—hit the first of the odd breaks that characterized every part of the library; half of it was lost in an instant. It did not leak across a crack to fill the ceiling in other pieces of the heights—it simply vanished.

She returned her attention to Kavallac, to Starrante; Kavallac's wings existed in two separate slices of library. They had not vanished into the ether—or the primal ether which was where Kaylin now suspected bits and pieces of people would go if they moved carelessly. She thought again of the attack from which Starrante had built his escape, his return to the library.

What she didn't understand was what Candallar had *intended* for the library. She wasn't like the Arkon; she wanted to be *doing* instead of learning about what long-dead people *had done*. She didn't want to be surrounded by dusty, silent books for whom her entire existence was irrelevant. But...

She would never, ever have tried to break or destroy the library—even without the Arkon standing behind her like enraged death waiting to happen.

"He was not trying to break it," Starrante said, a reminder that she was connected to him through a bridge of healing. "He was trying to break *our* power over it. He did not understand that the two are utterly entwined. I believe he stopped his destruction when he did. He is young and foolish."

He wasn't young. Kaylin had no desire to argue with the "foolish," though.

"Were he to know our names, he would control this library completely. It is the only way such control would be possible. Robin?"

The boy hesitated. But Dragons—even silver and slightly translucent—were clearly nowhere near as terrifying as giant hairy spiders, and as he was now comfortable with the latter, he stared at Kavallac. Starrante bopped the back of his head—but gently. "You may speak with her when we are done, but we must be done soon—this is far too taxing."

Robin then looked at the strands that led to the space that most of Kavallac occupied. He frowned. "I think," he finally said, "that it has to be done all at once. This part," he added, pointing to something that was invisible to Kaylin's eyes from this distance, "and this part—there has to be a third repetition."

"I will cheerfully strangle Larrantin the next time he dares to set foot in my library," Starrante then said. "The third is echo or reflection."

"I think so—I think that's what Larrantin meant—but she's not trapped in an echo, right? I think you'll hurt her if all of the parts don't come together at the same time."

"Be patient, mortal child. This is new to me, as well. I have never seen the library in this state; had you asked me, my theory would have posited an entirely different outcome. What your eyes see is not what my eyes see—and perhaps situations such as these are the reason two very physically different sets of eyes exist at all."

Kaylin turned back to the portal.

It had now expanded, its shape uneven and splotchy—like a very badly blown piece of glass.

"Be ready!" Sedarias shouted.

"Corporal," Emmerian said, "stand back."

"Don't!" Kaylin shouted. "It's not safe! You'll be too tall as a Dragon!"

"I understand that," Emmerian said without looking back.

Kavallac roared, her red eyes very much centered on Starrante. Kaylin didn't understand native Dragon, but she knew a *shut the hell up and get moving* when she heard it.

They were almost out of time. Starrante had not yet finished. He was pushing his body—and spitting up even pinker webbing—as fast as he safely could, where safety in this case relied on having a healer attached like a barnacle to his hairy, heaving sides.

Kaylin turned, once again, to look at the blobby, misshapen portal. Bellusdeo was standing directly beneath a growing outcrop, and at her back, his hands deformed into the longer claws of his people, stood Emmerian. To Kaylin's eye, it looked as if he had attempted to transform, and had been stuck at a midpoint; it wasn't comfortable. His skin was a gray-blue shade, his claws the blue of his Dragon form.

The misshapen portal didn't shatter. It melted. Bellusdeo moved—quickly—to avoid the possible splash, but there was no splash; it dripped its way to the floor, and as it did, Candallar finally emerged.

He was robed in light and shadow; his eyes at this distance were black, and seemed too large for his otherwise regular features. His hair was a nimbus of moving color.

Bellusdeo's breath struck him full in the chest as he placed his feet firmly on the ground that Starrante had cobbled together. He took a step back at the force of the flame, but it might have been hot air for all the effect it had otherwise;

his cape seemed to undulate in a way that put the flames out, reached around either side of his rib cage to do so.

In his left hand, he carried the rod; across his chest, a medallion shone harshly white. He also now carried a sword, as if he meant to close with his enemies. Kaylin shouted a single word as Bellusdeo tensed to leap; it was Emmerian who pulled her back.

The sword struck the path that Starrante had built, and as it did, the path cracked. The crack traveled slowly toward the Arbiter. There was nothing that any of the three—Sedarias, Emmerian, Bellusdeo—could do to stop it. Nothing Kaylin herself could do, either.

But Annarion became visible. He stood astride the path, watching as the singular crack approached them all; he knelt. Kaylin couldn't see his eyes, but she was certain they weren't his normal eyes. He carried something in his hands—a dark strand, something that did not look at all like rope.

It was the magic that Candallar had used to attempt to break through Starrante's webbed pane, but Annarion held it in both hands. It moved as if it were a snake. Annarion drove it into the ground, into the crack that had started to form.

To either side of Candallar, in the lee of his cape, stepped two men: Illanen and Baltrin. Illanen carried the book in his left hand; his right was free. Baltrin continued to hold his staff. In the odd light cast by Candallar's magic, both men looked different to her eye.

She was watching them as they lifted their right arms; watching as those arms fell. In Baltrin's case, that was a literal description. His right arm fell away from just above his elbow as something cut or pierced it. She thought it was because of the cracks and breaks that Candallar had reintroduced to the library by his arrival.

No.

Mandoran had arrived. She saw him flicker in place; saw the glint of his sword; saw him disperse. He had not spoken a word, and his expression was…not an expression that normally adorned his face.

Baltrin cried out, the spell that he intended to cast forgotten; Candallar turned toward Mandoran, and purple fire exploded in exactly the place he'd dispersed from. But this wasn't simple invisibility. Had it been, Mandoran would likely be dead.

He reappeared behind Annarion, and Kaylin saw that he'd lost hair. The black drape of Barrani locks was now a jagged, diagonal line that started somewhere below his shoulder and reached to his waist.

Annarion said nothing; Mandoran, sword readied, back to Kaylin, stood his ground. Sedarias's sword cut the wave of purple flame meant to keep them all at bay, and it traveled to either side of her—and to either side of Annarion.

Androsse stepped out of thin air, placed a palm on Annarion's bent head, and whispered a series of words that tickled Kaylin's hearing. The syllables were faint; she couldn't resolve them into language—but they set up a buzzing on the inside of her ears that she could feel travel along her spine.

She pushed the healing, surprised at how much damage Starrante's body was sustaining. All she could see was the webbing, and the speed at which he arranged it—and nothing in that was obviously damaging.

Starrante pulled the webs tight, a sudden motion that strained every muscle in his body. She was half-afraid his limbs would break or snap; the webbing was heavy, and it resisted. "Androsse!"

Kavallac snapped into place. Kaylin could feel it because Starrante could feel it; the weight of the webs abated, and the Dragon Arbiter dwindled into her human form. "About time," she said, her words and voice clear. She was in front of Starrante, but they now existed in the same slice of library space. "Androsse!"

"I am somewhat occupied," the Arbiter replied.

"The occupation would be unnecessary if you could join us."

"A moment, please." He placed both hands on Annarion's head, and once again spoke. "Speed will be of the essence unless you wish to sacrifice our allies," he said without looking up.

"We will sacrifice everything if you do not hurry. Your eyes in this space are not what they should be!"

Androsse then turned to close the gap between Starrante and him, leaving Annarion, Mandoran and Sedarias to hold the ground steady for as long as it took. Bellusdeo, lightning sparking, was deflecting the incoming magical attacks, but those attacks had a momentum, a force, that drove her back. Emmerian was her wall. Kaylin saw the moment his legs—or his feet—transformed; his boots tore, as did the legs of his pants. He dug claws into the stone as Bellusdeo found her footing.

Androsse had reached a midpoint between Starrante and Kavallac; he reached out with both hands. Starrante reached out for his right hand; Kavallac reached out for his left. She could see Kavallac clearly, Androsse in profile; Starrante she could sense because she hadn't lifted her hand. To her surprise, Starrante bent a limb in a way that implied it was broken; he wrapped it carefully around Robin.

All three of the Arbiters began to glow. Kaylin didn't have a word to describe the color of that light. It *felt* golden to her. It felt very like the light her marks sometimes shed. Those marks were silent and still; the Arbiters were likewise silent and still.

But in that stillness made of odd light and silence, she heard the sound of stone cracking—but backward. They were asserting control over the library, and it was a delicate, perfect control. She wondered if books had been lost to the breaking of the space the Arbiters called home, but didn't ask. The only lives that had been lost were the lives of Arcanists who had come in search of Kavallac and Androsse, and no part of Kaylin could regret that.

Annarion rose as the stone pathway seemed to melt and absorb the breakage he had been desperately trying to slow. Mandoran remained by his side.

Lord Baltrin had dropped to his knees, but he was not dead; the flow of blood from a severed limb had been staunched by flame. The scent of burned flesh lingered as he pushed himself—with the aid of his staff—to his feet. Human eyes didn't change color by dint of emotion, but their expressions did.

She let her hand fall away from Starrante.

"Gentlemen," Kavallac said, "You are not welcome here." Her eyes were a glittering red.

To Kaylin's dismay, Illanen handed Candallar the book that he had clutched so tightly, bringing the tally of symbols the fieflord now possessed to three. In this space, he had finally claimed the full power of an interim chancellor—or of a chancellor.

"You are mistaken," Candallar said. His cape fluttered before it joined the still fall of his hair. "The library is the heart of the Academia, and I am now its lord." Illanen was uninjured, but his perfect skin was dark with what appeared to be ash. Baltrin, robes bloodied, was likewise whole. "It is your companions who are not welcome here."

Kaylin grimaced. Candallar—without the book—had thrown most of them out of the library once.

"They are welcome here," Androsse said. "They have our

permission to enter the library. The student body has that permission now."

"Denied," Candallar said. "The library might be your province, Arbiters—but the Academia is mine." Kaylin heard his voice as if it were a storm.

"What is the Academia without its heart?" It was Starrante who spoke; he had turned to face Candallar. "You have almost destroyed its heart; we preserve it. You understand the chancellorship only in terms of power, but your definition of power is far too narrow. Seek you to destroy us or master us for your own purpose? When we were sleeping, that was a possibility—but a distant possibility."

"Oh?" Illanen said softly. "We found you." His smile was chilly but pleasant. "Your time is past—long past. In the world now, only the Dragons remain, and they, too, are in their twilight."

"Knowledge remains," Starrante said. "You are chancellor, Candallar, but interim. Killianas would not accept you as you are now."

"Where I have power, he will. I found this place. I worked to bring it what it needed. I woke him." He lifted his hands, and Kaylin could see, circling his wrists, light: blue, red, purple, glints of opal and obsidian between them as if they were chains. "I say again: the library is *closed*. Return to your resting places, Arbiters—you are not yet required here!"

Kaylin watched, mouth half-open, as the Arbiters began to fade. She reached out to grab Starrante again, but her hand fell through his side—and his leg passed through Robin.

The Arbiters were being dismissed, and when they were gone, Kaylin thought nothing would prevent Candallar from trapping them—and killing them at his leisure.

As if they could hear that thought, the Dragons moved in concert. Bellusdeo tensed. Emmerian sprouted the wings

that could not safely be spread before the Arbiters had solidified the library space. But he did not fully transform; Bellusdeo didn't try.

The two Dragons roared, the sound almost deafening.

Across Candallar's brow, lights sprang into being—lights
similar in motion and color to the bands around his wrist.
He lifted both hands as the Arcanist by his side began to cast.

"Leave the female Dragon," he told Candallar.

Kaylin wasn't certain that Candallar had heard him. His
eyes reflected moving light, the surfaces dark enough they
implied the shadow that distorted and transformed. He didn't
call purple flame; he didn't call anything. It seemed to Kaylin that he was absorbing light and color as Bellusdeo leaped.
She didn't hit him.

She didn't move at all. Some invisible gravity held her fast.

Something was moving, though. From the heights of the
library, wings spread, jaws open in a roar of sound, came a
gold Dragon. His breath was silver fire—but no, it wasn't the
Dragon's breath at all.

It was Hope's breath. Hope was with the Arkon.

Silver fire—silver mist—blanketed the air and the ground
directly in front of Candallar and his two companions; Illanen's eyes widened until Kaylin could see the whites from
where she stood. The Arcanist stepped back, breaking the determined formation of the three; Lord Baltrin's eyes narrowed
and widened as he, too, realized the source of that breath.

Only Candallar stood firm; the silver mist stopped a yard
from his face and shoulders, and hung there like a limp
cloud, falling slowly to the ground. The ground and its shape
changed, bubbling and melting as stone came into contact

with the familiar's breath; steam—or something like it—rose, an opaque wall.

Into the mist, the great golden Dragon landed.

The Arkon had arrived.

CHAPTER 29

"How dare you!"

Whether the floor shook from the Arkon's voice or his landing wasn't clear. Kaylin had heard the Arkon speak his native tongue before—but even his native tongue's natural thunder was no match for this.

She had interrupted him countless times at his work, or what passed for work within the bowels of the Imperial Library; she had seen him irritated. She had thought she'd seen him angry. She'd been wrong.

This was the Arkon's anger. It was impressive. She reached out for Robin, wrapping both of her arms around him as if to shield him from Draconic rage. The Arkon's tail was less than a yard away from where Robin stood.

Pale mist rose to the ceiling, shuddering at the echo of the Arkon's words. The ceiling contained and magnified them. Kaylin thought the magnification unnatural—but the dim forms of the Arbiters could still be seen out of the corners of the eye.

"I tried to calm him," a familiar voice said. Terrano appeared, as if stepping sideways out of thin air. "Did you know he used to babysit?"

Kaylin couldn't easily see past the bulk of the Arkon's body, given his wings and his placement in front of both her and Robin. "Babysit?"

"In his Aerie, when he was younger. Before all the wars. He was considered patient enough."

A roar dimmed the rest of Terrano's words, although the Barrani's mouth was still moving. "...patient to me. I'm probably the only Barrani to see Dragon eyes go that color and survive."

"I? How dare *I*?" Candallar's voice, muted but audible, pushed past silver mist and fog. Kaylin had no doubt that the fieflord would soon join them. "You have entered *my* domain, and you are *not welcome* here."

The Arkon's roar was less deafening, possibly because it made no attempt to contain words. But words followed that roar. "This is not your domain."

"I am lord, here. I am chancellor."

"You are interim chancellor—a position created at need, for need's sake. You would never, and will never, *be* chancellor. Your stupidity in this space has destroyed some of the books—"

"Some books? Look around you—there are so many books in this place, eternity might be required to fully read them all! Almost nothing has been lost—"

The Arkon roared again. "You have *no idea* what has been lost. You have no idea what knowledge, what thought, what lore graced the pages of books destroyed by your juvenile need to shout *mine, mine, mine*. You are a disgrace to the word *chancellor!*

"Even your antics—" Kaylin quibbled deeply with the word *antics* here, but did so utterly silently "—in the Academia almost endangered the life of a student."

"A student that would not be *in* these classes or this place had I not delivered him."

The Arkon fell silent. After a moment, in a far more normal tone, he said, "Students are not your possessions. They are not currency."

"You show your ignorance. They are the currency Killianas requires to live and breathe." His voice was clearer now.

The Arkon's, however, had not wavered. He raised it. "Come, Starrante, Androsse, Kavallac. Return to your duties and do not leave them while danger remains." Kaylin couldn't see what he'd done—but knew, regardless.

Kaylin was closest to Starrante in position, and was therefore aware of the moment the Arkon's words—and the books he held—had their desired effect: the Arbiters began to brighten in color, to solidify in shape. She pulled Robin to the side, but let Terrano make his own way clear.

Starrante didn't seem to notice either of them. Kavallac and Androsse were also turned toward the Arkon's back—and perhaps to what lay beyond it: Candallar, Illanen and Baltrin.

"I think," Starrante said softly, "it is time you returned to your classes." He spoke to Robin, because no one else in the library was part of those classes.

"I'm not sure I can," Robin replied. "I don't know how to get there from here."

"You found the chancellor's office. I trust that you can, with some effort, find a door."

When Robin failed to move, he sighed. "I will never do this again," he told the boy. "I am too old for it, and students are not meant to harry and make demands of librarians—beyond the permissions they seek to study the books the library contains. Remember this."

"I'm *never* going to forget any of this," Robin said.

Starrante spit out a gob of webbing—this time, without the

pink residue that strongly implied internal injury. He worked that into a web, just as he'd done any other time. But this web closely resembled a door, and when it was done and Starrante breathed on it, it became a door. With a handle.

"Your classes, Robin. Do not neglect them." He straightened. "I believe you will find them much changed in the near future. Go now."

Robin clearly wanted to stay. But he recognized the authority inherent in a giant spider, and he understood that the library itself was a hazard zone. He reached for the doorknob, opened the door and stopped.

A familiar man stood in the doorway.

Killian.

It was a Killian that Kaylin had never seen before, although she did recognize him. He had both of his eyes. Those eyes were narrowed, glinting and completely black. The Arkon was angry, yes.

So was Killian. He glanced at Robin. "You took a detour while attempting to find a bathroom, yes?"

Robin cringed.

"This is not the place for you, and you missed the oral portion of your test. I'm afraid it will be reflected in your overall evaluations."

"Yes, sir."

"Good. I believe you are already late for your next class. Do not let us keep you." He stepped into the library but held the door open. Robin glanced once at Starrante, nodded and stepped out, leaving the door ajar.

Killian closed it.

"Killianas, you are late," Androsse said.

"I believe I requested, through an intermediary, that you open the library."

"Ah. There were some impediments to your request."

"Yes, I see that." He lifted his face, and his hair, a pale sweep of color that now matched the pallor of the Arbiters, hung down his back like a cape—a cape of office. "You could not deal with them?"

"We were not given permission to remove chancellors. I believe you argued against it, at the dawn of things. My memory, however, is not what it was," Starrante said.

"He did," Androsse said. "I believe it took some decades to come to an agreement."

"A compromise," Killian pointed out.

"There is a reason that 'compromised' is not considered a good thing."

To Kaylin's surprise, Killian laughed. "Come," he said. The Arbiters nodded as one. Killian made his way to the Arkon's side.

Candallar was, for a moment, at a loss for words. He did not find them quickly enough.

"Killianas," the Arkon said.

"You might consider the number of people in this area, Lannagaros."

The Arkon's eyes had gone from red to orange in an instant, and—as if he were as much a student as Robin—he made haste to return to his human form. He was forced, by lack of clothing his transformation into Dragon form had caused, to wear golden scales as plate armor, just as Bellusdeo did, but he was now recognizably the Arkon with whom Kaylin was most familiar.

He carried three books as he turned to face Candallar.

"Do you know me?" Killian asked of Candallar—or his companions.

Candallar nodded, the nod stiff. "You are Killian."

"I am, at last, Killianas of old." To Kaylin's dismay, he tendered Candallar a very low bow; it practically seethed respect.

"Respect is due, Chosen, and it will be offered. It was Karriamis who set you upon this path; Karriamis who guided you to what remained of the Academia of old. Did he tell you of our history?"

Candallar was almost at a loss for words. Given the words he did speak, that would have been a boon to him. "Karriamis is mine; I am Lord of the Tower that once bore his name. It bears mine now."

The Arkon said something that didn't reach Kaylin's ears; it did reach Killian's.

"And I bear the symbols of the highest office in the Academia. I am chancellor here. I am *lord*."

"I do not believe Karriamis intentionally misled you," Killian said. "But what he is, and what I am, are not the same. We were not built for the same purpose, and we were not built in the same environment. Chancellor is the word for one who rules the Academia—but it is a word that implies responsibility, not power.

"You are, I perceive, young. Young and afraid, as the young oft are."

Candallar's eyes were indigo. Beside him, Illanen took a step back.

"I owe you a great debt. If you failed to understand what the Academia represents, you nonetheless offered me a new beginning. The reasons for it matter little to the boon itself. I am loath to reward your service with death." As he spoke, a breeze caught the drape of his hair.

His hair, now the same color as the Consort's.

Kaylin had never asked the Consort why her hair, alone of all the Barrani, was white—but she would, the next time they met.

"I am not Barrani," Killian said, and Kaylin remembered

that Killian was a building. "Nor was I, before the Academia at last came into being."

Ancestor, she thought. Just as Androsse had once been.

Illanen stepped to the side, to increase the distance between him and Candallar; his gaze briefly touched the book he had surrendered into Candallar's keeping. Baltrin, noting the Arcanist's subtle retreat, retreated, as well. Neither ran nor gave voice to their growing discomfort.

Candallar was alone. He was not afraid. Not yet.

"The items you possess are keys," Killian continued. "They are keys to a home that are left should disaster strike; you have used those keys, and you have entered the Academia. I hear Karriamis now, although his voice is distant; I hear Durandel, as well.

"If you ever desire it, you are welcome to study here—but those keys must now be left behind, waiting upon another emergency, another great cataclysm." He stepped forward and held out his left hand.

Candallar retreated, the movement slow. The indigo of his eyes developed flecks of livid color.

"That," Killian said in a sterner voice, "is forbidden here. You play at magics you do not understand, seeking power; in your ignorance, you—and your foolish allies—will doom yourselves.

"It is not your doom that is my concern. You are free to play at power—but you *will not do it here*."

His voice was soft; the room shook anyway. The light went out of Candallar's eyes.

"You have heard that knowledge is power."

Candallar said nothing.

"And in some fashion, it is. But incomplete knowledge is not power; it is death and destruction. In some things, you cannot merely retrieve knowledge at your convenience and disregard the rest. I say again: I owe you a boon. But a boon is not, in the end, a form of mindless slavery. What the Academia was, and what it will be, is not a simple game of power and control.

"In the meantime, I will ask you—and your followers—to leave. You may leave by the front doors, or you may be ejected in a harsher fashion; the choice is up to you."

He then turned to Illanen. "Yes," he said, although the Arcanist had not spoken a word. "There is knowledge here—and should you desire it, you are free to apply to join the student body. Your application will be considered by the masters on the committee—and by me."

The three Arbiters turned toward each other, their backs forming a triangle as Killian continued to speak. Their voices were muted; barely audible.

"You will, however, leave the keys; the keeper is now awake and aware, and they will no longer be necessary." Once again, he extended his hand.

To Kaylin's surprise, Illanen said, "Give him the...keys."

Candallar did not move.

"Can you not sense it? The building is alive, just as the Hallionne are alive. There is no unguarded thought you might have that the building does not immediately hear. If he will allow us to walk through the front doors on our way out, accept that offer."

Candallar shook his head, at a loss for words. Kaylin, under different circumstances, might have pitied him.

"Open the library, Arbiters."

Kavallac cleared her throat. "It is not," she said gently, "your command to give."

"It was a request."

"Very well. And it is not a request to which we can accede at the current time." She walked toward Killian and stopped as she approached the Arkon. Although she was pale and ghostly—as she had been the first time Kaylin had seen her cohere from the pages of a book—her eyes were a luminous gold.

"Lannagaros," she said, voice gentle. "You are Arkon. You are Arkon in a time of peace. Will you relinquish that responsibility?"

The Arkon turned toward Kavallac then. His eyes were a color that Kaylin had never seen Dragon eyes take. No—that was wrong. She had—but the Arkon's refused to remain in any of the many color states; they were a flickering of colors, a constant shift, as if no single emotion could anchor them for long enough.

He was the Arkon.

Kaylin understood, at this moment, that Kavallac was asking him to walk away from that. While he considered her words, Kaylin approached Emmerian. Bellusdeo had eyes only for the Arkon.

"I don't understand," Kaylin said quietly.

"I think you do. He has been the Arkon since the end of the last of the wars between the Barrani and our kind. He has held the medallions of the flights, gifted us in times long lost to ancient history. Kavallac now asks if he can relinquish the one responsibility that has defined him to the Dragons."

"Okay, yes, I got that part—but why?"

Emmerian's smile was slight and informed in every motion of lip and eye by melancholy. "Do you think that he could command the Arbiters to remain without reason? Do you think that he could do so only because he carries those books?"

"...Yes?"

"Yes, perhaps. Perhaps that might be true of you, had you continued to carry them. Understand what this place is."

"It's a library."

"It is *the* library, Lord Kaylin. Corporal Neya, if you prefer. It is the library of his youth; it is the library that existed before war all but devoured us all over the passage of centuries. This, then, is the place that he was forced to leave to go to war. This is the place that was lost—forever, he thought—when the Towers rose.

"And he stands here, now, in a place that was not destroyed. Lost, yes—but it has been found. He has returned." Emmerian hesitated. "You understand—you understood—that the Arkon's hoard was the library and the things it contained."

She nodded.

"He built it in both sorrow and rage, in regret and, yes, desire. What could be saved, he would save. What could be learned, he would learn. What could be taught, he would teach—or failing that, allow others to teach. He could not build this place—none but the Ancients could, and when the Towers rose, the Ancients faded. Had he been offered the chance to become what Killianas was—and perhaps will be—he would have taken it in an instant.

"No such offer was made. No such campus was built. He understood—as all must—why the Towers were created; what use was knowledge if there are none to learn it, none to question it?"

"And he can't be both Arkon and chancellor?"

"No. He cannot be Arkon and chancellor both—and yes, I believe that is what he has been offered."

"So...who would be Arkon?"

"That is a question that I cannot answer. So few of my kin survive, and of those, half sleep the long sleep, while the ages pass around them. You do not ask who might be chancellor in his stead."

She shook her head. "I think... I think I've seen this before."

"Ah—you were present when Barren became Tiamaris."

She swallowed and nodded. "But—it's different. I don't..." The words faded. Tiamaris had found the heart of Tara, and Tiamaris had—at that moment—desired to possess it, to protect it, to know it.

This was not the same.

"He was always, of all of us, the most quietly responsible. Irascible, yes, and opinionated. But in his fashion, indulgent and even, for a Dragon, gentle. But this is what he wants. This. It is the thing that he will willingly devote the entirety of his remaining life to, the thing he would die to protect."

"The thing," Bellusdeo said, speaking for the first time, "that he would kill to protect." Her eyes were copper and gold. "And they know it. All of them understand—the Arbiters, Killianas. Us."

None so well as the Arkon. Kaylin saw him and thought he had never looked young to her. She'd never been able to conceive of an Arkon in youth. But he hadn't been the Arkon in his youth. Hadn't been a soldier, a warrior. There had been no Empire, the Aeries of the Dragons still existed in the heights, and the wars themselves were a distant, distant storm on a horizon that had already been darkened by Shadow.

It was Emmerian who shook his head. "This is his hoard," he said softly. "I think it always has been. If the city were under attack, the Emperor would call up every man and woman at his disposal to defend it, yes?"

Kaylin nodded.

"Where the attack was surgical, he would send in the ground forces; Dragons in flight do much damage, and only in cases where necessity dictates the risk of that damage be taken will we fly."

She thought of the attack on the High Halls.

"But were he to lose half the city, and yet emerge triumphant, the city would survive. It would be no less his, no less the heart of his hoard. He would rebuild. His hoard is larger, grander, and less physical than it first appears.

"So, too, the Arkon. How does one own knowledge? How does one own the thoughts of others? What does such knowledge become if it is not shared, if like minds are not invited to discover it, and to add knowledge of their own?"

"Lord Candallar," Killian said for a third time. "The keys you carry have no value now. Set them down and leave."

Illanen and Baltrin—the latter silent—had already begun to fade. Candallar wheeled in Illanen's direction, but the Arcanist's head was bowed; his expression could no longer be seen.

"If you desire it now," Killian said, "Karriamis will free you. He will free you without devouring you, without destroying you. He has long been the most intense, the most focused; it is difficult to command him, and difficult to ignore him. You have said—you have thought—Karriamis a cage.

"But Candallar, you have made of me a cage for others, and that cage, too, is open. Those who do not wish to remain are free now to enter the stream of the lives they once had. I do not understand what you desired of the Academia. Freedom? Power? These things might exist here. But your cage is of your making; Karriamis did not cage you.

"Go. The Arbiters are restless, and none of the three are inclined to accept my judgment in this regard. Should you choose to remain, I cannot guarantee that I can continue to protect you from the consequences of your actions in this space."

Candallar faded. He did not, however, release the objects that in theory governed the Academia.

"That," Starrante said, "was unwise in the extreme."

"It was Karriamis's only request of me."

"Candallar is a small man; it is not in him to allow others to enjoy what he himself does not control or possess. If he cannot have you, Killianas, he desires that no one does. Can you not feel it? I could feel it from here."

"He cannot harm me now."

"It is not for you that we fear, you fool. Think: Candallar understood—in a rudimentary, solipsistic fashion—how he might set about waking you. He understood you required a student body to function; he did not understand what a student *is*. But in his slipshod way, he has provided you with one: one significant student. There might be others—but they are not his equal.

"That student is no longer in the library. And if the insignia of office, of control, is no longer absolute, it is not a mere trifle."

Kaylin understood. She understood at least as well as Starrante, and she turned to the Arbiter. "Send me," she said, voice low. "Send me to Robin."

Starrante built a door; the entire process seemed agonizingly slow. Hope sat on her shoulder, silent, as that door solidified and emerged; Starrante opened it.

"I cannot leave the library," he said, "and remain as I am now. You retrieved me the first time, Chosen."

Killian vanished as the door opened, and Kaylin stepped—or jumped—into an empty hall. Severn was beside her; he cleared the door first, both of his feet hitting solid stone on the other side before hers did. He ran, and she followed.

Nightshade!

Here, he said.

Where is Robin? Is he with you?

He is. He has taken his seat.

She couldn't risk running and looking through Nightshade's eyes at the same time; she didn't. She trusted Severn to know where he was going.

Nightshade said nothing more. But she heard the breaking—the shattering—of a door long before she could see that door. And she heard distant shouts and screams.

Candallar didn't understand that Robin was the heart of this tiny student body. He understood that students were necessary—and he intended to kill them all before he retreated—if he retreated.

She hated Arcanists, the instinctive emotion fueled by years of experience with the Hawks—but she was grateful that Illanen had chosen to retreat. Candallar was on his own here.

...Candallar was enough. Robin was bright, yes—and better fed, in the end, than Kaylin had been at his age. But he was as much a match for Candallar as Kaylin had been for Nightshade at the same age. She didn't assume that the older students were in any better situation—they were here, after all, and they hadn't chosen to be here.

Severn rounded the last corner, and the hall in which the classroom was situated came into view. Kaylin could see Candallar. His hair and his cloak were a mass of swirling darkness, lifted by arcane winds that touched nothing else. No, not nothing. She could see the advance of mist, of fog, lit on all sides by sparkling, moving color. She'd seen this before.

Candallar's hands were on fire, the fire white and purple; she couldn't see his eyes in the shadow of his profile.

But she could hear a familiar voice bark orders, and those orders seemed to dim the screaming and the shouting.

Who's teaching this class? she demanded.

Larrantin.

She could briefly breathe again. She turned to her shoulder ornament, and he squawked, pushing himself off her shoulders as they approached Candallar at a dead run. Severn was armed, a blade in each hand.

Kaylin had a dagger.

Candallar turned as Severn covered distance, his obsidian eyes widening. There was no fear in his expression; his right arm shot out, and purple fire left the heart of his palm, heading toward Severn—and Kaylin, who ran behind him. Severn's blades came up, bisecting the fire as if it were a living limb. It passed to either side as he cut a path through it. There were benches and chairs in this hall, and the fire devoured them instantly, leaving not ash but an oily residue in their wake.

Candallar was forced back by Severn's weapons; he raised hands, and swords of purple flame came to them. He parried the strike that would have removed half his throat, but the solidity of the flaming swords buckled as they met Severn's blades. Around Severn's waist, the weapon chain was glowing faintly.

Two steps, three, and then the edge of those twisted blades caught Severn's arm—it was a glancing strike, but purple fire took root instantly in the fibers of the cloth.

Kaylin shouted a warning as Severn retreated; she came in from his side, using the retreat to cut Candallar's wrist. It was the wrist of the hand that held the book; her blade made contact with skin. But the skin had the consistency of a grinding stone; she felt the resistance and saw the lack of a wound in its wake.

An invisible wave threw her back; she hit Severn in retreat. They had Candallar's attention now.

The person who didn't—the person who leaped through the door and above the fog that now covered the floor in front of it—was Nightshade. He was armed, and his sword—his sword did not strike invisible stone.

Candallar's left blade rose to parry. Kaylin heard the crackle and hiss of fire as Nightshade's blade hit Candallar's—but Candallar's sword was a thing of magic, an emergency measure. It had buckled under Severn's attack. It was bisected by Nightshade's. The parry was enough to save Candallar's life—but the sword was gone, and he did not have the time or concentration to reform it in the wake of Nightshade's attack.

If you can, Nightshade said, *enter the classroom.*

Kaylin looked at the floor.

Enter the classroom, he repeated, attempting to force Candallar farther from the door.

She passed the message on to Severn. Severn's initial attack had driven Candallar out of the frame of that door; he stood maybe two yards from where he'd chosen to make his attack. Nightshade's attacks drove him toward the wall, between two long wooden benches that were otherwise unadorned.

Kaylin grimaced as Severn asked her wordless permission. She nodded. Facing the open door at an angle, she tensed into a running leap that would, with luck, carry her over the mist on the ground. If it was the same as the one Candallar had used in the chancellor's office, missing her mark by a few feet would be deadly.

She landed, pushed herself immediately off her feet, and entered the heart of the classroom.

"No—she's one of us!" Robin shouted, as the hair on her arms and neck stood instantly on end. "So is he! Don't hurt him!"

"I can hear you, Robin, there is no need to shout." Standing in the group of assembled students—away from what looked like the blood and the limbs of those who had been closest to the door, and the back of the class—was Larrantin.

CHAPTER 30

Larrantin's hair was salt-and-pepper gray. Age didn't have that effect on Barrani. His skin was flawless, almost luminescent, as Kaylin met eyes that were a familiar shade of indigo.

"Do *not* just stand there. It is very taxing to protect a larger area than I am already protecting. Honestly—this is the first class in which we have fully advanced our subject in what feels like centuries. You felt a need to interrupt it *today*? No, do *not* step there. Come to the right. Immediately."

Robin was grimacing behind Larrantin's back, his eyes a bit too wide. Kaylin and Severn obeyed Larrantin; the moment she saw that Robin was uninjured—blood-spattered, but uninjured—she sagged. Severn had torn the arm off his shirt; his skin was reddened and puckered in a ring where the purple fire had taken root.

"You took your time delivering my message," Larrantin said.

Robin's glance bounced between them.

"But the message was delivered, in the end, to the right person. I apologize for my inability to be more precise at the time. But the air is changing. Can you sense it?"

She could smell it; things were on fire. She looked at the

classroom closest to the door. Not all of the students had survived. And Robin had likely been close to that door when Candallar had destroyed it, given his late arrival to Larrantin's class.

Hope squawked. Larrantin frowned. "You are *certain*?" he finally asked the familiar.

Hope squawked again.

Kaylin, standing beside Robin, dared a look through Nightshade's eyes. The hall in his immediate vicinity was a sparkling darkness, a silent shade of death. Candallar had moved all of his attention to Nightshade. Nightshade who was, demonstrably, a student of the Academia for a little while longer.

Yes, he said. Nightshade spoke a word—more felt than heard—and light brightened the unnatural darkness. In its glow, she could see the dim outline of Candallar, his right arm raised, fingers pointed toward her. No, toward Nightshade.

"That will not do," Larrantin said softly. He gestured. "Killianas, if you would be so kind, I find the walls here an impediment to the continued health of the students who survived." He didn't gesture, he merely glared.

As if the walls that contained what was left of the door were part of the student body, they shifted, pulling out of the way of Larrantin's line of sight as if they were eager to avoid it.

Kaylin could now see the darkness that surrounded Candallar. In his hand was a book of flame, pages alight not with purple but with a deep red. Around his neck, the medallion burned a pale white-blue; she couldn't see the rod.

The darkness had devoured the hall where Nightshade fought. Kaylin couldn't see the floor—which was fair, given what covered it—but she could no longer feel the floor beneath Nightshade's feet, either. That the darkness had not yet destroyed him was a miracle.

Nightshade didn't like the thought.

"Killianas," Larrantin said. "We seem to be having a difficulty that should be resolved. My class—"

A roar filled the hall. It wasn't Candallar's, and it wasn't the roar of Starrante—she would have recognized that. He had said he couldn't leave the library without damaging himself, and she believed it—but she had seen him spit webs with blood mixed in, and knew that damage to himself wasn't his primary concern.

"Ah," Larrantin said softly. "My apologies, Killianas. It has been long, indeed, and I forget myself. Robin, please remain where you are standing."

"She's leaving—"

"She is not a student here; she is not my responsibility."

Kaylin approached what was no longer technically speaking hallway, and she saw, at the far end, a glint of gold: gold scale, gold neck, gold claws. The Arkon had left the library.

The Arkon faced Candallar. "Lord Calarnenne," he said, his voice a rumble of thunder, "Return to your class."

To Kaylin's surprise, Nightshade did exactly as commanded. She felt a flicker of grim amusement as he leaped to where Larrantin now stood. *I am a student*, he said. *I have less freedom of movement than you have been granted. Now hush.*

The Arkon walked to where Candallar stood. Candallar was not idle; he retrieved the rod from the folds of a roiling robe; he held it in his right hand, as if it were a sword, while his left held the open book. He turned to face the Arkon as if all other concerns were irrelevant here, and perhaps they were. Stone halls and short ceilings—short relative to the full height of a Dragon—were not the Arkon's preferred battlefield. Not in the full Draconic form.

He didn't choose to adopt the human form in response to his surroundings. That should have told Kaylin something. What, she wasn't certain.

Bellusdeo and Emmerian didn't join him. Killian remained absent—although the fading walls showed that he was fully awake.

Only the Arkon and Candallar stood in this hall. Killian could repair the damage done to the furniture and the floor—but he couldn't repair the damage done to the students; Helen couldn't bring the dead back to life beneath her roof, either.

"Enough, Candallar," the Arkon said. "If you will not relinquish the insignia while you live, you will die here."

"I *built* this place," Candallar replied, voice low. "I took the risk of *finding* it. I claimed it—it is *mine*."

"It was never fully yours," the Arkon replied. "As it will never fully be mine. No more is the Empire fully the Emperor's, although he rules it. The chancellor is not ruler here—that is what you have failed to understand. He is steward. I am loath to destroy you; you are fieflord, and the Towers bear the weight of the world's safety in their vigilance. But you are not chancellor here, and you will never be chancellor."

"I was—until you arrived. I was, until the Arbiters were fully wakened. I will be—"

"No. No matter what you do, no matter what you destroy, you will never be chancellor. You will never again be interim chancellor. The Academia has a chancellor now."

Kaylin couldn't see Candallar's expression; it was turned toward the Arkon. She could see the stiffening of his back.

"You do not understand why. It is not a position of power and endless self-indulgence; it is a gift and a responsibility. A gift must be given. A responsibility must be shouldered. Your shoulders have never been broad enough."

Light filled the hall, or rather, an absence of darkness as the magic cast by Candallar was lifted. It wouldn't return.

The Arkon was chancellor now, and Kaylin knew he would remain chancellor while he lived; he had asked for time to think, and Candallar had rejected that time, as not even Killian and the Arbiters had dared to do.

Candallar's wordless cry was a thing of fury, edged in fear and defiance.

The Arkon's mouth opened again, but this time he offered Candallar no words; instead, he breathed the fire of his people, and Kaylin understood why he had been feared above most others in the skies in which the Dragon Flights had once reigned. She could feel the heat of that fire as it traveled the length of the Academia's halls, heading toward Candallar, the man who had almost destroyed the library, and had threatened the heart of what the Academia represented in his rage.

She thought, as the fire engulfed the fieflord, that Candallar's destruction was what awaited the Dragons who desired a hoard and could not control the emotions that were born of that desire: what they could not own, they would destroy so that no others might claim it.

The heat of the flame was so intense that it moved the air around it; not even the scent of burning flesh remained in Candallar's wake. Only in the passing of that flame, the dying of that heat, did the Arkon dwindle in size and shape, until he once again wore the plate armor of the Dragons: gold, as Bellusdeo was gold.

He walked down the hall and paused in the spot that Candallar had occupied. Bending, he retrieved the symbols of the office that he had accepted. The fire that had instantly destroyed Candallar hadn't even marked them. He didn't require their authority, but he understood that they served a purpose.

Turning to the class, or rather, the lecturer, he bowed. "I have interrupted your lessons, Master Larrantin. You have my apologies; things should never have reached this point."

"No, they should not. I assume they will not reach this point again in the future."

Killian appeared by the Arkon's side. "They will not, but we will have to convene a meeting of those who remain; you are not the only one—but you were certainly the most independent."

Larrantin nodded. "Shall we dismiss class for the day? It has been long since I have entered the library."

"Starrante wishes to know how you obtained a book that should never have been removed from it."

"I recovered it, but was not the person who removed it."

"Very well. We will require students, of course—but I believe they will come, given our chancellor and our library." His eyes, both of his eyes, were an odd color—but if he looked like a Barrani, or perhaps an Ancestor, he was a building, and the eye colors of buildings were often unusual.

"Chosen." He bowed. "Lord Calarnenne."

Kaylin blinked and turned toward Nightshade.

"Robin was not the only student to engage with the material here," Nightshade said, with a small smile. "Had the situation been what it will become, I might have been grateful for the opportunity."

"You are welcome here," Killian said, his voice gentle.

Larrantin cleared his throat.

"...There are formalities to be observed, of course—but you have been a student, and your status is unlikely to be withdrawn without cause."

"I see you really are awake," Larrantin said. "Given the unprecedented disaster to face my class today, I will allow you to clean up. There are, no doubt, authorities of some sort to inform."

"And you?"

"I have words for Starrante, and would like to deliver them in person—with your permission, of course."

"You have my permission," Killian said, the gravity of the

words belied by the breadth of his grin. "You will, however, require his. He holds a long grudge when books are removed from the library without permission."

Larrantin then turned to Robin. "You did well. My attempts to teach you matters of modern import were fractured; it is a wonder you managed to retain any of it."

Robin was clearly pleased by the praise—but Kaylin would have been beaming at his age. Oh, who was she kidding? She'd be beaming at the age she was now.

"Can I go with you?" Robin asked, before Larrantin had reached what remained of the door.

"As class has been dismissed, you have the remainder of a free period. I see no reason why not."

Nightshade looked very much as if he wished to join them; he did not ask. "My Tower's name was Durandel, of old," he said to Killian. "And if he was not aware of your existence—"

"He was."

"Or not as invested as Karriamis, I feel he will value it now. I must repair to the Tower. We have much to discuss."

"I hesitate to advise discussion," Killian said, surprising Kaylin slightly. The advice did not appear to surprise Nightshade; it did appear to amuse him, if darkly.

"Durandel and I have reached an armistice of sorts. I am fieflord; I am captain of the Tower. He has accepted that, and has even gone so far as to save my life. The method of salvation, on the other hand, left something to be desired—what little I clearly remember of it.

"I will speak with Durandel; if I understand what has happened here, Karriamis was instrumental in preserving what he could of the Academia. There are six Towers. It is not a burden I would see him bear alone."

Killian bowed again. "I believe you will find all of the Towers are peripherally aware of my existence; they have accepted it in some fashion, if not consciously. I have never quite understood the nature of the dreams of such buildings."

"Karriamis will need a new Lord, a new captain."

"Ah. Yes."

"And the Dragons," Nightshade added softly, "a new Arkon."

"I hope they do not resent him for his decision. He meant to confer with his Emperor and his Dragon Council—but he did not have time. It is typical of Kavallac's machinations."

"Oh?"

"Starrante might have built a door such as the one that delivered Robin and the rest of your friends. I note that your mark is upon the Chosen," he added, voice neutral.

"What caused Starrante to hesitate?" Nightshade asked, avoiding the topic of that mark entirely.

"Kavallac. She pointed out that Starrante was already well past the limits of his endurance—a half truth, given the intervention of the Chosen—but Starrante did not argue; he was becoming frantic."

"And you were not?"

"No, although it is difficult to move with ease between the library and the rest of the grounds. I understood what Kavallac wished to test."

"And you were willing to risk the students?"

"You were here. Larrantin was here."

"You were willing to let Kavallac play this game."

"I wanted what Kavallac wanted," he said, which sounded like a multisyllabic yes. "Lannagaros understood that if he accepted what was offered by our very minimal council, he might come immediately to Robin's aid. To the aid," he added, "of the rest of the students. He understood Kavallac's game and Kavallac's calculus; he understood the damage that might be done to me should that gambit fail.

"It is not as grim a manipulation as you seem to be afraid it is, Chosen."

"Because the Arkon wants this."

"Because he wants it so clearly. I am slightly surprised you cannot hear the echoes of his internal roaring. He is old, and he was always responsible; he was responsible enough to walk away from the Academia when he was called to war. So, too, did Aramechtis, the last of the great chancellors. But that war is done; one war hovers on the horizon, now, and it does not require the gathering of the flights—or the sole flight that now wakes and rides the wind. He wants this—and we want him no less intensely.

"He took office to save the students—you among them. And now Lannagaros is chancellor. You will have to stop calling him the Arkon, however; it is not a name, but a title, and he has renounced it as of today."

"He can't stay here."

"He most certainly can."

"He can't stay here without somehow relocating the contents of his personal library."

"Ah." Killian paused, blinked and nodded. "You are correct. He also feels he owes at least the duty of apology and proper transfer of responsibility to the one who will carry the duties of Arkon in his stead."

"Can you make it less difficult for us to *find you*?"

"I believe that can be done, yes. Return at your leisure. I do not think you have the makings of a diligent student in you—not yet; you are given to the practical, or to what you see as practical; you want an immediate use for the knowledge you gain, and you want to study only those things that will have that immediate use.

"Perhaps this will change with time; perhaps not. I believe there are those among your houseguests who might be at home in the Academia, but Candallar's method of inducting students was never ours." He bowed again. "You will always be welcome as a visitor."

Bellusdeo, Emmerian and the Arkon left together; they were followed at a discreet distance by Annarion, Sedarias, Mandoran and Terrano, although Annarion fell back to walk beside his brother. There was no hostility between the two brothers, which was almost a first.

Kaylin and Severn walked together. She glanced pointedly at his singed arm, and he just as pointedly refused to notice the direction of her glance.

The Academia looked normal: the grass, the trees, the buildings all had the color one would expect had they been situated in any other part of Elantra. The grounds weren't empty; the cohort, the Dragons and the Hawks were not the only people leaving. Not all of the people Candallar—she assumed it was Candallar—had inducted into the student body had enjoyed their endless and repetitive captivity.

One or two looked back, as if they were afraid that freedom was the dream and the Academia the only reality—but they continued to walk toward the streets that would lead them, eventually, to Elantra.

Those streets, however, like the Academia, were solid. The cohort could see them as clearly as anyone else; they no longer saw the fog that obscured the buildings everyone else had seen.

Killian was, as Kaylin had half suspected, the border zone.

She wondered if the streets that led to the fiefs—but no, there were no streets now. The border zone, with its changing width, length and unpredictable buildings, was gone; what remained was a pleasant single street that led directly into the fief of Nightshade.

The fieflings and the Barrani who served Nightshade directly wouldn't have dared to stop the large party that now entered the fief; they might seek Nightshade's command, but as he was walking with them, they failed to emerge. He walked them to the bridge that led across the Ablayne.

"I would invite you to visit," he said to his brother, "but Durandel is difficult and willful, and I do not think he has forgiven you for the last visit."

Annarion was in no hurry to return—not to Castle Nightshade. The whole of the cohort, however, seemed eager to return to Helen. To Helen or the rest of their number, who were waiting.

Kaylin understood; she wanted to go home, too.

But Lord Emmerian invited her to accompany them to the palace. Her expression must have been honest because he winced. Bellusdeo, however, put her foot down.

"We will accompany Lannagaros to the palace. He will need to speak to the Dragon Court about what occurred— and you are one of our primary witnesses."

Hope squawked.

"Yes, I'm aware of that—but there will be questions, and we thought it best to allow Kaylin to answer them. I am not certain the cohort is prepared for the Imperial Court at the moment, and even were the cohort prepared, I'm not certain the same could be said for the Court. You are their spokesperson, as well."

"Sedarias wouldn't agree to that."

"No, of course not. But Sedarias is with Helen, and her reaction is your problem."

"Can I remind you that you also live under the same roof?"

Bellusdeo grinned. With teeth.

Kaylin wanted Severn as company; she wanted Severn to clean and tend his arm.

He shook his head. "I've had worse injuries. This is almost nothing."

"It's a burn. Burns are—"

"It's not a burn. It's fine. I highly doubt the Emperor—or the rest of the Court—will look twice at my lack of a sleeve given the news the former Arkon is about to impart."

Sleeves might or might not be an issue, but sleeves—attached to a shirt—were brought by pages when Severn arrived at the palace. He and Kaylin, following Emmerian, had been escorted to Sanabalis's offices. Sanabalis was in those rooms at the time. He didn't look exactly pleased to see Kaylin, but his eyes retained their predominantly golden hue, and he did offer drinks and refreshments. For once, Kaylin declined.

Emmerian spoke briefly with Sanabalis, whose eyes did shift to a more martial orange. He nodded, and Emmerian left—no doubt to speak with Lord Diarmat and the Emperor, the two Dragons not yet in the loop.

"I hesitate to ask what you've done this time," Sanabalis said when Emmerian had left them. "I note the Arkon and Bellusdeo did not join you here. What is the current emergency?"

"The Arkon," Kaylin replied.

"He was injured?"

"Not precisely. Look—I'm tired. No, I'm exhausted. I want to go home and put my feet up someplace where they won't get bitten off. But Lord Emmerian and Bellusdeo insisted I accompany them to the palace, where people could question me endlessly if they needed answers." Answers that were never going to be complete enough for the purposes of annoyed Dragons.

Sanabalis transferred his gaze to Severn, who offered a polite version of a fief shrug. Kaylin noted that Sanabalis didn't pressure Severn for more information.

The meeting of the Dragon Council was two hours in the making, largely because the Emperor had appointments that could not be broken with ease. Had the city been on literal fire, he might have been justified in canceling—and to be fair, he was Emperor, and he could damn well do what he liked. But he was aware, as Kaylin had become aware, that there would be a future cost for that, and he chose which costs he was willing to pay.

The Dragon Court, with Bellusdeo and the two Hawks in attendance, met in a throne room that was empty of all save a handful of select Imperial Guard. Tiamaris, as a member of that Court, was also present. Kaylin was surprised, and it showed; the youngest member of the Court grimaced, the expression smoothing into a genuine, if chagrined, smile.

Kaylin cringed just before the discussion started because it hadn't occurred to her until that point that it would be held in their native tongue; the ceilings here were acoustically unforgiving. But aware of the eyes of the Imperial Guard, she made no attempt to cover her ears or otherwise preserve her hearing.

The discussion reverted to Barrani when the Emperor had questions; he asked those of Severn and Kaylin. But for the most part, the discussion was for, and by, Dragons. Hope joined in on one or two occasions, and the Dragon Court accepted his input without comment or resentment.

The Arkon then withdrew a box from the folds of his robes—a box that shouldn't have fit there. It was familiar to Kaylin; she'd seen it before. He didn't open it this time; he approached Sanabalis and, to Kaylin's surprise, knelt.

She understood, then: Sanabalis was to become the Arkon.

Sanabalis, Imperial mage, Dragon who had not yet found his hoard. She wondered why the Arkon hadn't chosen Diarmat, a man whose sense of duty and responsibility defined him and sucked all the humor out of his life—but perhaps that was answer enough.

Sanabalis didn't bow. "You are certain?"

"I am certain." The Arkon rose to his feet. "As in all decisions of note, there are lingering shadows, lingering desires. I have been Arkon for most of my life, and I am aware of the burden it places upon your shoulders. I am not caged or confined as chancellor; indeed, it will be my responsibility to find students who will benefit from the Academia and what it has to offer; if I do not, we will continue to remain trapped in a history so ancient the Empire has never even heard of its ending, never mind its beginning."

His eyes were gold as he turned to face the Emperor. "I remain, as young Tiamaris does, a member of your Court and a member of your Flight; in times of danger and war, the chancellors were not exempt from the demands of their kin."

The Emperor's nod was regal, but not remote. "I am… happy for you, old friend. In all of the futures I imagined we might face together, this is not one I had ever considered a possibility. It brings me peace to know that in the heart of my Empire, you have found your way back to the heart of yours. Take what you have gathered with my blessing.

"You will, however, be tasked with personally overseeing the transport of your collection. I expect all of the people you choose to aid in this endeavor to survive more or less unscathed."

Which was a pity, because given how touchy the Arkon was about his personal collection, Kaylin didn't.

As if the Emperor could hear the thought even Kaylin knew better than to put into words anywhere within the palace grounds, he chuckled. "I have oft been accused of unreasonable expectations by Lannagaros; I am certain this will not be an exception."

He then turned to Sanabalis. "Arkon," he said.

"Your majesty." Sanabalis bowed, box in hand. "I believe the empty interior of the palace currently occupied by the Arkon would be a suitable haven for the symbols of the office I have accepted." He glanced once at the former Arkon—Kaylin was going to have a hard time with the names going forward—and tendered him a bow.

His eyes were gold, as were Emmerian's.

Diarmat's were gold, which was far more of a surprise. Kaylin could not recall Diarmat's eyes ever lacking a tint of orange.

Bellusdeo's were luminous and shining. She eschewed Court decorum in its entirety, and not, this time, to annoy Diarmat. She threw both arms around the older Dragon's neck and caught him a bruising hug that would have cracked bones had she done it to Kaylin.

Wordless, he returned the hug. "You will visit."

"I will continue to bother you, yes."

"Good."

"I shall remind you that you said that."

EPILOGUE

Kaylin felt she hadn't been home for days. Weeks, maybe. She was stiff and sore, but Helen had made certain she was no longer hungry. Her room was dark, and the halls beyond it almost unnaturally silent.

"You are worried." Helen's voice was gentle.

Kaylin said nothing.

"If you don't wish to speak about it, I will leave."

"You never leave."

She could almost feel her house smile. Like the voice, it was gentle.

"Candallar's dead," she finally said, pulling the counterpane up and tucking it beneath her chin. Hope was curled up on the pillow—the second pillow—and appeared to be asleep.

"Yes."

"His Tower is empty."

"Yes." Kaylin's silence extended, but it was wakeful. "You are worried about Bellusdeo."

Kaylin nodded. Unlike Helen, she didn't need to actually say words to be heard.

"You are worried about yourself."

There was no point in lying or denying it; there was no one but Helen to hear her.

"She will not leave yet, Kaylin. But she is not a child. This is not her final home."

"She could have babies here."

"Not yet. You are to help Lannagaros in the morning. Sleep."

Bellusdeo was commandeered by the Arkon to be one of his moving aides. Bellusdeo, in turn, commandeered Maggaron, who was built for it, and Kaylin, who was not.

The cohort, however, was teeming with almost indecent amounts of curiosity; they had never visited the Imperial Palace and had therefore never come close to any of the Arkon's personal hoard. Sedarias offered to help Bellusdeo in her assigned task—where, by offered, one meant commanded, no matter how it was phrased.

Bellusdeo chose to find it amusing rather than annoying and agreed instantly. Kaylin almost pitied the Arkon, who was likely to be frazzled and aggravated even if everything went perfectly. Where the cohort was involved, perfect was a distant, never-visited country.

But Valliant and Serralyn were practically quivering with excitement. Helen was less sanguine than Bellusdeo.

"I am not at all certain they are ready to enter the city streets," she confessed. "Annarion still has difficulty in certain circumstances. I am not worried about Sedarias, Mandoran or Terrano, and Allaron and Fallessian have never caused any detectable problems."

"We're going by way of Tiamaris, and Tara should be able to dampen any noise they make."

"Dampen, yes. I think you will find that you lose some of the cohort to the Academia."

"I'd be surprised. Sedarias—"

"Sedarias is not the cohort, as you well know."

"No, just the boss of it."

Helen chuckled, but once again lapsed into her worried expression. "If they weren't so interested in the Academia, I think I would counsel heavily against their help."

Kaylin felt the same. "Terrano will be with us, and he seems to be able to hear when things are off. I think he can keep them in line—or enough in line—until we reach Killian. They'll be safe there; they won't have to worry about being heard by things we'd prefer didn't hear them."

Helen nodded.

All eleven of the cohort in residence piled out of Helen's front door in Bellusdeo's wake. Mandoran was underfoot—Bellusdeo's feet—the entire way to the palace. Only Teela was absent, but she would be aware of everything the cohort experienced.

The Arkon's expression upon sighting the cohort was instantly pinched and weary. And no, Kaylin thought, although she hadn't spoken the title out loud, he was no longer the Arkon. He was, as Bellusdeo had always called him, Lannagaros.

Kaylin's arms were numb by the time the Arkon decreed the wagons—four in total—ready to go; he had clearly taken magical precautions to protect the contents of these wagons, and it was the type of magic that gave her figurative hives.

"These aren't the only wagons," Bellusdeo said. "But these are the ones that contain cargo he feels is delicate or priceless."

"I'm surprised there's only four."

"The interior space of the wagons—you will note they're all covered—is somewhat larger than the exterior suggests. I highly doubt, given the tenor of the escort, we will encounter difficulties. I believe the Arcanum is preoccupied, and the human Caste Court likewise in flux."

And those were the two most likely to cause problems.

★ ★ ★

If the procession of wagons headed toward the bridge to Tiamaris drew stares, people remained at a distance. This wasn't only because the Barrani were out in force; Maggaron was here, and at nearly eight feet in height, he was the most visible guard present. The irony, of course, was that he was probably the person least inclined to violence in the caravan; size told a story to the people who stood back, near the walls of the buildings that lined the street, but it was the wrong story.

Still, it meant there would be very little in the way of interference. The Arkon—no, the former Arkon—had received Imperial writs and permissions to temporarily close down traffic from cross streets, never a popular move, to get from the palace through the rest of the city to the fief of Tiamaris.

Tiamaris was waiting on the other side of the bridge. His eyes were golden as he met the former Arkon. "Lannagaros," he said, offering the oldest member of the Dragon Court a perfect bow.

"Tiamaris." No word of thanks passed the older Dragon's lips, but his eyes, like Tiamaris's, were gold.

"I would offer you refreshments, but I see that you are anxious to reach your destination. Might I accompany you?"

"Yes, in fact. I have a need to speak with your Tara shortly, although your permission will, of course, be required."

"You are always welcome in my fief."

"Ye-es. It is not entirely a matter of the fief."

"I suspected it might not be, given your destination. But where it is possible to do so without compromising our own responsibilities, you will have our utmost aid."

"Good. One of the most promising of the students Candallar happened to haphazardly locate came from the warrens."

"I see."

"There are citizens within your fiefs that might benefit from some study—although that will have to be discussed with Killian."

Kaylin, listening, considered this. Robin had been a prisoner in the Academia, but even so, had not appeared to be unhappy there. And why would he? If the lessons were repetitive—and that wouldn't be the case going forward— the day started with breakfast, was broken by lunch, and finished with dinner.

If he learned nothing from his time in the Academia, he was fed and he was safe. But he'd clearly learned something.

Tiamaris was as good as his word; he accompanied the caravan from the fief over which he ruled to Lannagaros's new home. In the streets of Tiamaris, the sight of the *Norannir* was far more common; it was the Barrani cohort who kept the curious at bay. Kaylin considered this a more reasonable reaction, given Sedarias.

Tara didn't join Tiamaris, probably because she couldn't cross the border—a border that had become fixed, solid. The fief of Nightshade clearly existed in the distance, and Kaylin had only to cross a street to enter Nightshade's domain. But a road now existed at a T junction, and that was the road down which the Arkon's possessions—and all his various attendants—now traveled. The cohort had no issues with visibility this time. They could see the same street as anyone else; the street was narrow, which made travel more cumbersome.

But aside from an orange-eyed Dragon, the travel went smoothly, and the larger campus, with its circular road, came naturally into view.

As if that were a signal, the cohort took off at a swift run, spreading out across the grass as they angled their way to the main building; the doors were already open, and a stone ramp now existed in the center of the long, flat steps that led to the interior.

At the head of those steps was Killian, watching the progress of the new chancellor's caravan almost impatiently. If he wasn't a building the way Helen was, he resembled her strongly. There was a gravity to Killian at the moment that Helen lacked, probably deliberately.

Gravity, however, was vanquished by the impatience of the Academy's youngest student; Robin kept peering around the open door, his head moving back and forth as if everything caught his attention but failed to hold it for long.

Only when he caught sight of Kaylin did he leap through the door and bound down the stairs, Kaylin being the least intimidating of the assembled group. Even this didn't last; his eyes were drawn to the chancellor, or rather, his wagons. Maggaron was first in line. Killian descended the steps to offer to immediately relocate the more delicate items in the collection.

And of course he could.

Lannagaros—Kaylin was never going to get used to this, because "the Arkon" had practically been his name—stood at the foot of the stairs, and looked up, and up again, his gaze taking in the whole of the central building.

He turned once to look at the park, and once to look at the building in which Larrantin had been found, and then once again faced forward.

Robin said, "I'm staying!" as if that had been in doubt. But...for Robin, it probably had. Candallar's people had been ejected, one way or another. Candallar's other prisoners—Kaylin couldn't bring herself to call them students—had departed with as much haste as they could muster.

Robin remained.

"I'm not alone," he said, smiling. "I think Calarnenne will be here, too. He's pretty smart."

Kaylin didn't choke, but it took effort.

"Are they going to be students?" he asked, lowering his voice as he glanced at the cohort.

"I think some of them will—but I'm told there's an admission process."

"Huh. Like…permission?"

"Worse, probably. Bureaucracy."

"I heard that, Corporal." Lannagaros spoke without turning to them.

"You're not denying it, I note."

"Organizations require some oversight."

"But… I'm in, right?" Robin asked.

"You are a student, and unless you do something that threatens the Academia or another student, you are, as you put it, in." The chancellor drew a deep breath, which was just enough of a warning that Kaylin could cover ears that had barely recovered from yesterday's council meeting.

Hope, on her shoulder, crooned softly.

Kaylin couldn't understand native Dragon, but she knew, without needing to, what the former Arkon had said.

Bellusdeo wandered across the grass until she could sling an arm over the chancellor's shoulder. "Yes," she said. "You are home."

He said nothing in reply. With Bellusdeo's gentle urging, he mounted the stairs and entered the Academia.

* * * * *

ACKNOWLEDGMENTS

I am an author whose lifelong favorite Sesame Street character is Oscar the Grouch. And not only because I'm certain the interior of his trash can is as messy as my house. If writing a novel is a solitary activity, family isn't, and mine have, as usual, had to deal with my frenetic attempts to shut the metaphorical lid and sink into my trash can, loudly.

Thanks to my mother and her deep love for her (adult!) grandchildren, no one starved. Thomas and the rest of my home team (John, Kristen, Gary) accepted, as always, that there were days when I was fretting in a corner. Terry Pearson provided both writing-retreat space and first-read everything.

Margot Mallinson is my MIRA editor and has to deal with me. Kathleen Oudit has been responsible for all of the covers to date, including this one. But the MIRA team I've met, and some of the team I haven't met, are also working hard to get the book from the inside of my head to you, the readers. Special shout-out to Lauren Nisbet!